INTERCEPT

OTHER BOOKS BY PATRICK ROBINSON

Novels

Ghost Force
Hunter Killer
Scimitar SL2
Barracuda 945
Slider
The Shark Mutiny
U.S.S. Seawolf
H.M.S. Unseen
Kilo Class
Nimitz Class
Diamondhead
To the Death

Nonfiction

Lone Survivor (written with Marcus Luttrell)

*Horsetrader: Robert Sangster and the
Rise and Fall of the Sport of Kings*

*One Hundred Days: The Memoirs of the Falklands Battle Group
Commander* (written with Admiral Sir John Woodward)

True Blue (written with Daniel Topolski)

Born to Win (written with John Bertrand)

The Golden Post

*Decade of Champions: The Greatest Years in theHistory of
Thoroughbred Racing, 1970–1980*

Classic Lines: A Gallery of the Great Thoroughbreds

*A Collosal Failure of Common Sense: The Inside Story of the
Collapse of Lehman Brothers* (written with Lawrence G. McDonald)

INTERCEPT

A NOVEL OF SUSPENSE

PATRICK
ROBINSON

Vanguard Press
A Member of the Perseus Books Group

Books published by Vanguard Press are available at special discounts for bulk
purchases in the United States by corporations, institutions, and other
organizations. For more information, please contact the Special Markets
Department at the Perseus Books Group, 2300 Chestnut Street, Suite 200,
Philadelphia, PA 19103, or call (800) 810-4145, extension 5000, or e-mail
special.markets@perseusbooks.com.

Editorial production by the Book Factory.
Text design by Cynthia Young in Minion Pro.

Cataloging-in-Publication Data is available at the Library of Congress.
HC ISBN: 978-1-59315-584-1
Mass market ISBN: 978-1-59315-634-3
E-book ISBN: 978-1-59315-612-1

10 9 8 7 6 5 4 3 2 1

Prologue

S UNRISE TAKES ITS sweet time up here among the high peaks. To the east stand the awesome ramparts of the Himalayas, 1,550 miles of towering summits that block out the early morning light from the western escarpments, all the way from southern China to Afghanistan.

There are tiny mountain villages clinging to the slopes of the Hindu Kush range where the sun does not peer over the pinnacles until long after the herdsmen have led the goats to the damp pastures above the mud-built dwellings.

The light is soft and suffused, the brightness in the sky being perhaps ten thousand feet higher, like God's fluorescence, and the valleys seem gloomy, painted only with the colors of the earth.

It was into this half-lit melancholy that SEAL Team 10, representing an infuriated United States of America, came bursting through on a cool autumn morning in 2004. The time was 6:30 a.m., and there were twelve of them from Foxtrot Platoon, fanning out, pounding across the rough ground, taking this apparently peaceful and defenseless township by the throat, terrifying women and children.

The U.S. troops unleashed the occasional burst of machine-gun fire, in staccato volleys designed to intimidate, to display this frontline U.S. muscle, as if anyone could possibly have doubted the deadly nature of their purpose.

All twelve of them were heavily bearded. Ten of them stood more than six-foot-three in height. Any two of these giant warriors would have made a massive presence anywhere. The dozen, working as a trained fighting force, would have frightened the bejesus out of Genghis Khan.

Each man was dressed in combat "cammies," and eight of them wore their "drive-on rags," camouflaged bandanas. Eleven of them carried the SEAL's preferred personal weapon, the M4 light machine gun. The group commander was armed with a Mark 12 .556-caliber rifle. In their wide leather belts they each carried a combat knife and a SIG-Sauer 9mm pistol. Four of them had a half-dozen grenades strapped into their battle-harnesses. The rest had a minimum of two grenades, instantly reachable.

The SEALs moved door to door in pairs, shouting harsh, controlled commands, ordering everyone out into the main open area between the two streets. It was like a cattle roundup, except the young bulls in this coral were all bearded, wearing turbans and light sandals. The women and children were herded into a separate area. From afar, oxen, tethered to homemade carts, stared balefully at the shattering interruption being conducted in a village devoid of upheaval for centuries.

The SEAL leader, a powerful-looking officer aged around twenty-eight, stood in the central area, barking short commands: *"Door to door, guys. No houses unsearched. Keep it moving. Don't turn your backs. Get against that wall. Hands high. Anyone breaks, shoot."*

From time to time, he murmured into his comms transmitter, *"Moon men on station, sir. No casualties. Village under tight arrest. Roger that, sir. Over."*

Within ten minutes of this astonishing uproar among tribal lives unaltered since biblical times, the whole population had submitted to U.S. interrogation, except for two early herders up on the high pastures. And one by one the SEALs singled out men from the crowd, taking them aside, searching them for hidden weapons and cell phones, examining their beards, hair, fingernails, toes—always rough, always with methods designed to frighten.

These were the most dangerous lands in the world, the lawless high peaks of the Hindu Kush, home to the outlawed Taliban, to the regrouping tribal warriors of al-Qaeda, the men who hate the United States as no other nation has ever been hated, not since Nazi Germany crushed the European mainland sixty years previously.

The village men were generally of far smaller stature than the giant U.S. Navy SEALs. The Americans had little difficulty in manhandling them, slamming them against the wall, roughing them up, demanding answers from men who claimed to speak no English. The watchwords were truculence, sullen obdurate defiance, and, of course, the burning, seething hatred.

There was yelling, and the occasional scuffle. One youngish man spat in the face of a SEAL and received a thunderous right hook to the jaw, which snapped it clean in half and dumped him half-conscious on the rough, sandy gravel. A hundred yards away his mother wept uncontrollably, his father, had he carried his tribal dagger, would have gladly plunged it into the heart of the American. Generally speaking, the SEALs were carrying out their ruthless mission to the letter. There was, perhaps, some weakness in the hearts-and-minds department.

It was impossible to ignore the rough edges and dark anger of the U.S. Special Forces. Just as it was impossible to ignore the inner loathing the tribesmen and women displayed toward them. It was an emotional stand-off beyond redemption. The big men from the West had traveled far and suffered greatly to reach this wild and inaccessible place, where there were no roads, no electricity, no radios, no transportation. For their part the Afghanis knew only that these armed, bearded monsters were their most implacable enemy.

And what did the Americans want? They wanted two men, two highly qualified al-Qaeda field operatives (one of which had been educated at Harvard), who had created a bomb—a regular IED—that had blasted to pieces a truckload of Marines in the outskirts of Kabul. The bomb killed everyone, fifteen United States Marines and two SEAL Team 5 guys from San Diego. The highway had run red with their blood. Two of the SEALs rampaging in the village had helped clear the remains of their comrades from the scene.

U.S. military intelligence had moved into high gear. Every mole, spy, agent, and informant had been alerted, and, in the end, someone came through. The two men were holed up in the high peaks, some fifty miles northeast of the U.S. military base at Bagram. There was only one village inside the GPS numbers U.S. INTEL had issued. And it had taken three days trekking, in shocking weather, across the mountain, for the SEALs to get here.

They came in off a night insertion by helicopter. Twenty of them. The other eight were hunkered down on the face of the mountain high above, their powerful binoculars trained on the uproar their colleagues were causing in the village. Up here, ten thousand feet above sea-level, the treeline shuts down suddenly. The green does not taper off, it just ends.

This particular mountain, which was often lush from the rains and tumbling streams fed by melting snows, was a stark and overwhelming study in two parts: the green and verdant lower half, and the moonscape from the upper treeline to the snowcapped summit. There is no cover up there. It's a near vertical landscape of dust, sand, rocks, and shale, inhabited by no one. Which was why the eight-man SEAL back-up team was camped in the highest vegetation, concealed, staring down, ready to move to the village at the first sign of Afghan resistance. So far there was none, at least nothing worse than a foolish act of messy bravado by the kid with the now-shattered jawbone.

Five times during the night, on the way into the ops area, they had checked the validity of the INTEL. And five times they had been told the two men were in there, tracked by the United States, all the way up through the passes, by careless use of their cell phones.

And now they were cornered, desperate to lie and cheat their way out of trouble, determined to pass themselves off as innocent goatherders. Unhappily for them, SEAL Team 10 knew precisely what they were looking for.

Ibrahim Sharif and his childhood friend Yousaf Mohammed, both twenty-four, were the men who made the bomb that killed the Americans. Devoted followers of Osama bin Laden, each of them was being groomed for al-Qaeda's highest command. They were mountain men by birth but had been selected in their early teens to be educated in the west, backed by family money from bin Laden, or, The Sheikh, as his followers preferred.

Ibrahim had found his way into Harvard by way of the University of Cairo. Yousaf had taken a degree in chemical engineering at the Aga Khan University in Karachi, followed by a post-graduate course at the University of London. Both men had enjoyed the freedoms of the West, but at the conclusion of their studies were once again drawn back to the fanatics of al-Qaeda, the mountain warriors whose trade was murder and mayhem, and whose creed was to spill blood in the name of Allah. American blood.

And now they stood among the tribesmen, herded into a group, watching these massive U.S. troops haul out their countrymen from the pack, ram them back against the wall, searching and shouting. Four houses down the rough, unmade street was the house of Ibrahim's father, the house in which they were staying, a crude place of standard Afghan construction (three rooms on three levels, with a cooking stove in the center, goats in the lower floor) built into the side of the mountain. And five tons of crated TNT hidden in a stone cave hollowed out of the mountain, right below the goat hooves.

Two SEALs had been staring hard at the two men, and one of them was the platoon commander. And now he snapped out an order, instantly obeyed, "HIM! The guy with the red vest. Get him over here."

Ibrahim swiveled half-left to see who had shouted the command, and in that moment, the SEAL commander knew the Afghani understood English. Two of his team moved forward and dragged Ibrahim out from the crowd. Futilely he resisted, pulling back, trying to escape. It was like trying to break out of a sealed bank vault.

The iron men from Coronado hauled him into the open and pinned him against the wall. The commander stepped forward and demanded, "What's your name?"

Ibrahim, a red mist of anger, resentment, and flaming hatred for the infidel, this intruder, this disgusting American, kicked out at the SEAL leader, who, in one movement struck back. He grabbed Ibrahim's ankle and pulled it three feet above the ground. Then he grabbed the man by the balls and tipped him backward to the ground.

The Afghan never uttered a sound, crashed back onto the mud-dried road, shaken and slightly unhinged. When he refocused he found the SEAL leader's boot on his throat. And then he was dragged up, right next to an overflowing rain barrel, and asked his name yet again. He made no reply and then the big SEAL asked him where he kept the explosive. Again there was no response, just a hard-eyed stare of pure hatred.

Ibrahim, silently enraged, pulled up his head and spat at his captor. He missed and too late recognized his mistake. The SEAL grabbed him by the beard and plunged him facedown into the rain barrel.

Ibrahim kicked and struggled, and almost resigned himself to a one-way trip into the arms of Allah when the American pulled him out and demanded to know the whereabouts of the explosive.

The half-drowned Afghani said nothing, and by now every eye was turned onto this one-sided confrontation. Again the SEAL leader plunged Ibrahim's head into the water, ramming his head back to the bottom of the barrel. This time he kept him there for twice as long, finally dragging him into the air when the desperate struggles had ceased.

For a split second, it seemed that Ibrahim was dead, but two SEALs grabbed his feet, turned him upside down, and pummeled his back. Water gushed from his mouth. And Ibrahim breathed again.

"Listen, pal," said the SEAL commander. "Right now, I'm going to kill you, right there in that goddamned barrel. I know you understand me, and you got just one last chance to save your own life. Where is the explosive? You got exactly five seconds to live. . . ."

Ibrahim was only mildly afraid of death. He had been brought up to understand the glory of the martyr in the eyes of the Prophet. He had no doubt whatsoever this brutal enemy would carry out his threat, and no doubt Allah would await him when he crossed the bridge. But there was terror in his heart at the thought of drowning in that deep rainwater. He could not tolerate that, and he trembled with fear, justifying his own cowardice by reasoning that these Americans were going to find the dynamite anyway.

He raised his right arm and said quietly, "Third house down there. Under the basement."

The SEAL leader detailed four of his team to tie Ibrahim's wrists and then march him to the house. Then he turned again to the crowd and shouted, "Guy in the orange vest. Over here, pal. And look real quick about it."

And Yousaf Mohammed, the ex-London University chemical engineering student, the only other "tribesman" but Ibrahim, who had clean hair and fingernails, soft hands, and a groomed beard, stepped forward, betrayed by his personal hygiene, and, unknowingly, by his obvious comprehension of the English language. No goatherder, this guy.

The four SEALs who had tied up Ibrahim now lashed the wrists of Yousaf together, and the six of them marched off down the street, directly to the third house, the one in which the half-drowned member of the village had been born. His cohort, the fanatical jihadist Yousaf, from across the border in Pakistan, was already wanted by the Americans for multiple acts of terrorism, including gunning down a U.S. diplomat and blowing up a hotel in central Baghdad.

The two men tethered together, walking in company with the warriors from SEAL Team 10, were among the most dangerous terrorists in the free world. But even if the explosive was discovered, there would be almost no evidence against them, no proof, no documents.

They were just a couple of unknown killers, without passports or identity, known perhaps only to Allah and their earthly families. The American military did not even know their true names, but they had tracked them for many months, and assessed that these were a couple of utterly ruthless characters from whom the public must surely be protected. The military had risked the lives of twenty SEALs and a gunship crew to make this insertion to either capture or kill the two men. And the U.S. military does not make such decisions without cast-iron reasons.

Now the six men reached the third house down the street, and the SEALs began the most dangerous part of their mission. For all they knew the place was booby-trapped. Somewhere inside there could be a concealed detonator. The touch of a button could blow them to pieces. Like the Marines. Like the two SEALs in Kabul.

Both captives were now murmuring lines from the Koran, repeating constantly a mantra in Arabic that the SEAL 2I/C understood: *Allah is great. There is no other God but Allah. Guide us on the straight path. Light upon light. Allah be praised, for you are great.*

One of the SEALs told them both to zip it. Ibrahim shut up, but Yousaf kept right on murmuring in praise of Allah, and the SEAL commander kicked him straight in the ass, sent him sprawling into the doorway. He climbed to his feet and there was hatred in his dark eyes and murder in his heart. One day he'd get his revenge. And silently he swore that to himself. Nonetheless, he held back on the prayers.

The stench in the house was overwhelming, which was not all that surprising since a half-dozen goats lived on the floor below. The pall of smoke hung in the air, for there was no chimney, and the stove in the middle of the room was alight and ready to bake the morning flatbread.

Ibrahim led the way through the suffocating air, down the steps, past the goats, and onto the mountainside. He moved carefully down a pathway to a rocky area and pointed at the boulder in the center.

Two of the SEALs grabbed it and heaved. It rolled forward revealing a stack of crates, low flat wooden boxes, more like gun cases than crates for high explosive. The hiding place was sensational. Anyone could have searched these mountains for a thousand years and never found them—unless they had the assistance of the still-waterlogged Ibrahim Sharif, bombmaker.

And so concluded the mission to capture the two terrorists and dispose of the explosive. The SEALs detonated it high on the mountain about a mile away. The Commander held the villagers under arrest, while he opened up the comms to Bagram and called in a big MH-47 army helicopter for the evacuation of his troops and their two prisoners.

The copter touched down on the edge of the village shortly before 0930. The SEALs' commanding officer made the forty-five-minute ride up into the mountains to familiarize himself with this village, which was plainly so important to the remnants of bin Laden's murderous secret army. He walked down the ramp to congratulate his mission commander. He shook his hand and said firmly, "Great job, Mack."

FIVE YEARS LATER

FOR FIVE LONG YEARS, Ibrahim Sharif and Yousaf Mohammed had never stepped beyond the razor-wire of the Guantanamo Bay Prison. They were separated immediately upon arrival, and spent the remainder of their captivity meeting only in the exercise area.

Both men were subjected to rigorous interrogation, but neither of them ever cracked again—not since the SEAL commander had held Ibrahim's head under the water in the rain barrel and forced him to reveal the whereabouts of the local dynamite supply.

Routine waterboarding deep in the interior of the Guantanamo Bay complex did not have the same effect. It scared both Ibrahim and Yousaf, but not to death. They both understood that even the dreaded splashing of water on the back of their hooded heads was a whole lot better than having their necks severed in the time-honored traditions of al-Qaeda or the Taliban.

Neither man ever revealed his full name or identity, nor indeed his nationality and certainly not his link to Osama bin Laden. Inside the camp, with its rigid security and dozens of very defiant men, Ibrahim and Yousaf were standouts—revered hard men, of whom even the guards were extremely wary. The cage-like cells of both men were searched every few hours. No visitors were ever allowed.

There was no communication whatsoever with the outside world. And there was little doubt in any of the guards' minds that, were the opportunity to present itself, either one of these two former al-Qaeda hitmen would have coldly murdered their captors.

No one had ever seen either of them smile. They were just there, two glowering permanent residents, brimming with hatred, waiting for their chance to get out and resume their timeless battle with the Western world, prepared with each passing hour to carry the fight to the Infidel, to murder and maim citizens of the West, whenever and wherever the winds of revenge took them.

They were both twenty-nine now and had taken enormous care of their physical strength, exercising in the soccer area, using the makeshift gym, and trying to retain their mountain-men fitness. They made few friends and spoke to the guards only in Arabic, with sentences so clipped and threatening they were rarely released from their ankle manacles. They were readily identifiable, by anyone, as two of the most dangerous men in the whole of Cuba, never mind Guantanamo Bay. And their chances of release hovered somewhere between zero and minus six.

It was plainly beyond the comprehension of either Ibrahim or Yousaf that their lives would have improved if anyone in authority had the slightest idea who they were. But they had been extricated from that almost inaccessible Afghani village with absolutely nothing in their possession. Not one single document. Thus, devoid of passports, cell phones, credit cards, driving licences, or even a letter from a loved one, they were utterly bereft of identity or nationality.

And in the great scheme of things, this made them ineligible to face a U.S. military tribunal, where experienced officers could decide what to do with them. The mind-blowing five-year silence of Ibrahim and Yousaf had rendered them outcasts even in one of the strangest communities on earth—making them no-hope prisoners too defiant to take advantage of the normal course of justice.

There was nothing to do with them, save to lock them up indefinitely, in the certain knowledge that if either of them received even half a chance, they would probably commit some diabolical crime against humanity. No one was prepared to take that kind of chance.

The years had rolled by. In the swamp-green, hard-wired corridors of the camp, hundreds of prisoners lived out some kind of twilight existence. In each cell, copies of the Koran were slung from the wire in surgical masks, mostly to prevent the Christian guards from touching the holy book.

Every few weeks, Ibrahim and Yousaf were subjected to interrogation of the most rigorous type. They were deprived of sleep, kept out in eighty-degree heat, marched in and out of cells specifically designed for questioning, always wearing both leg and hand shackles. They were zipped into orange jumpsuits, seated in chairs, and robbed of any form of sensory sensation, blindfolded and masked, with ear-muffs and mittens—the classic methods of the U.S. and UK military, designed to break down totally any man's resistance.

There were hundreds of al-Qaeda and Taliban terrorists in Guantanamo, and the U.S. interrogation techniques mostly worked—in the end, detainees would answer truthfully the questions fired at them by seasoned military personnel.

This did not, however, apply to men like Yousaf and Ibrahim, who seemed to accept their fate that they would live and die in this hell-hole, unloved, unknown, except unto Allah and to their surviving relatives and colleagues in the faraway Hindu Kush. For them there was no calendar, no time frame, sometimes there was no night and no day. There had long ceased to be any normal frame of reference whatsoever.

The best life offered them was a living space eight feet by six feet eight inches, and eight feet high. There were twenty-four of these cells to each "detention block"—and there were several blocks in each of Guantanamo's six camps. Yousaf and Ibrahim both lived in solitary confinement in Camp Five, a place most often described as "utterly inhuman" by various world human rights agencies.

But, as one U.S. Army general succinctly phrased it, "Well, where the hell do you want us to put guys who for two cents would blow up the Empire State Building with everyone in it? The fucking Waldorf Astoria?"

There were no windows in these cells. The front wall on the block corridor was built on a solid, reinforced steel frame with heavy wire mesh through which prisoners could stare at the empty throughway. They slept on mattresses and were issued a blue blanket, pillow, and prayer mat. Yousaf and Ibrahim usually fell asleep dreaming of the verdant green slopes and fast-flowing rivers of their mountainous homes, half a world away from this baking hot United States internment center at the rough eastern tip of Castro's Cuba.

The U.S. Navy Base at Guantanamo Bay is the oldest overseas base ever occupied by U.S. forces. Its position on this rugged deepwater coastline creates a perfect set-up for a supply-line directly into the only U.S. base in the world located on Communist soil. The camp is peppered with stark and sinister-looking watchtowers, equipped with laser-strength searchlights and staffed by heavily armed guards.

Anyone trying to make a break for freedom would be lucky to survive for thirty seconds. This place is high-security to a degree worthy of Stalin's archipelago, with perhaps an even more ruthless edge. The U.S. military considers the inmates of Guantanamo to be a potential menace to the health and well-being of all its citizens. For years, the accepted creed was: *No one gets out of here. No one.*

And it was a creed that pervaded the quiet, lonely corridors of the camp since first the prison was constructed back in the winter of 2002. Since then, they closed down the most primitive sections of the original facility, the dreaded and feared Camp X-ray, where the most disturbing images of Guantanamo had been photographed.

The lines of hooded, blindfolded prisoners pictured kneeling in their shackles under a pitiless sun shocked most of the humanitarian agencies for the humanities who tried, without much success, to demand an instant relaxing of this apparently brutal U.S. regime of capture and interrogation.

It looked, of course, rather different to military personnel, men who'd had friends, colleagues, and sometimes relatives, blown to smithereens by terrorist bombs and booby traps while on active duty on behalf of the United States—men from whom the sorrow would never pass, but who were now faced on a daily basis with these killers, these jihadists, with their sneering hatred and loathing of the western world.

Today the old camp is an overgrown jungle. In its place has emerged a smoothly efficient modern prison—no longer a throwback to the Dark Ages, but the very epitome of an iron-clad, high-security jail. The hatreds are still there, and the determination, by some, to stand tall against their American captors, remains undiminished. But no one has ever escaped.

Yousaf and Ibrahim both understood their predicament, particularly the no-escape clause. So far as they could tell there was not a chance of release. Of course they both knew they had committed heinous crimes against the U.S. military, but the light of battle had not entirely dimmed in their minds. Theirs was a Holy War, and they had fought it with similar heroism to that of the mighty Kurdish warrior, Saladin.

And deep in their most private dreams they each heard again the words of the immortal Sheikh Osama Bin-Mohammed bin Laden—the words that were spoken only to the glory of Allah—and the Prophet Mohammed-stated: "I have been sent with the sword between my hands to ensure that no one but God is worshipped. God who put my livelihood under the shadow of the spear and who inflicts humiliation and scorn on those who disobey my orders."

Yousaf and Ibraham understood those orders. Because they were not temporary orders. They were lifelong commands to wage war against the Infidel. Prison could shackle them, but it could never wash away the commands of Allah through his Servant Osama. *"We will avenge the American wars on the Muslim world. We will attack them, strike at them at random in Europe and then America. We have bled, and now they will bleed. Never say that those slain in battle in the cause of God are dead. Because they will never die. They are alive, but you are not aware of them. Again I beseech you, in the name of God, you will fight the Infidel!"*

And not all the influence of the University of London nor Harvard could remove these truths from the minds of Yousaf and Ibrahim. They did not need it to be set down on parchment. It was branded into their hearts. But even so, each man had written down the resounding words in Arabic, on the first blank page at the front of his American-supplied copy of the Koran.

Yousaf had added the phrase, again in Arabic: "What can you possibly know about our pain?" He could not recall why, and indeed when, he had written it, because the years of deprivation had left him mentally numb in any number of ways. He did not even know which year it was, forget days and times. But his phrase stood out in the holy pages of the Koran, and he stared at it often, linking his own personal pain with that of his people. And in these quiet times he swore vengeance upon the Great Satan, even in the certain knowledge that he could never get out of this place.

And his dreams were sometimes illuminated by the vision of the Great Osama, sword drawn and mounted on a battle camel thundering across this hot, dusty coastal wilderness at the head of a marauding jihadist army, which would blast away all of the Americans and spirit him, Yousaf, back to the place where he belonged, in the unending service of Allah.

Inside the camp, there were only a few like Yousaf, men for whom the Dream would never die, men whom those in the west could neither recognize nor understand. So many in the United States believed that *everyone* was sick to death of the War on Terrorism; that the American people just wanted it over, and that their enemy was as tired of it as they were. He's not. His perception of time is different. Beyond the razor wire of Guantanamo there were thousands who believed what Yousaf believed. Men who seethed against poverty, and burned with frustration, anger, and passion.

In Guantanamo their thoughts were sometimes expressed in murmured defiance, in the strange mutterings of the permanently incarcerated, spoken softly as if to another self, the person they once were, and which now gave the impression of encroaching madness.

It was these slender indications of continued rebelliousness that kept an ever-watchful force of guards on the very edge of vigilance. Occasionally personnel fluent in Arabic were inserted into the exercise areas to listen and try to comprehend the current mindset of the prisoners. And they would hear the suppressed jihadist phrases of the camp's toughest inmates. *"We will not negotiate, neither will we rest, nor put down the sword until every infidel across the face of the earth is either converted to the true faith, or lies dead at our feet. Allah is great."*

These swarthy captives had been taken prisoner on the battlefield. They were illegal combatants, guilty as all hell, and ought rightfully to have been executed by military firing squad. But right now U.S. law did not permit that, and here they must stay, in Guantanamo, until, if necessary, the end of time.

Which left Ibrahim and Yousaf somehow stranded with their dreams and beliefs. Of the two, the dark, powerfully built Ibrahim was more the warrior. For him, much like the SEAL team that had captured him, there were very few of the world's major problems that could not be solved with high explosive, a science upon which he was an expert. Yousaf was the more thoughtful, the planner, the strategist, always ready to assist Ibrahim in the manufacture of an Improvised Explosive Device to attack the enemy. But he was more at home at the feet of bin Laden, or Ayman al-Zawahiri, sipping coffee, studying data, and scheming.

Now, however, he did not know whether The Sheikh was even alive. And his innermost thoughts remained rooted in the mountains, in the high caves and hollows, where al-Qaeda and the Taliban came together, in secret, unseen councils of war.

Yousaf never allowed himself to consider that all might be lost, and that The Sheikh had been killed by the Americans. He was forbidden to tune in to any form of news program on the radio, and he was not allowed to read newspapers or to watch television. He was a man in a vacuum, out of the loop, alone with his memories, with the minimum of human contact.

For him this terrible place was a daily nightmare. Cuba has rock-steady temperatures of above 80 degrees F, give or take a half-dozen degrees to distinguish summer from winter. Guantanamo lies just a fraction north of the twentieth parallel, while Yousaf's home village above the Chitral Valley on the Pakistan side of the frontier high in the mountains, was almost sixteen degrees further north, and subject to very different seasonal changes.

The mountains there, spectacular among the awesome peaks of the Hindu Kush, lie well beyond the clutches of the monsoon, and the lower valleys are just deserts. High up however, the villages are irrigated by wide mountain streams that come rushing out of the heart of the range, fed by melting snows.

This cool temperate zone was home to the lean, hook-nosed Yousaf, and the constant high temperatures of the eastern Cuban prison camp almost drove him mad. He longed for a respite from the heat, but the only time he got it was in the rainy season when the occasional hurricane swept in on the veering northeastern trades and almost blasted the place to hell and back. But it was mercifully cooler and Yousaf lay on his back in his cell, listened to the wild wind and contemplated his far-lost homeland.

And always in his mind were the words of the Great Osama, and Yousaf tried his best to remember them, and when eventually he had arranged these innermost thoughts into the order that The

Great One had recounted them, he spoke softly in his cell, more a murmur than a mantra.

And he knelt down and clasped his hands together as if seeking comfort from the Prophet. And he said the words solemnly, and he begged Allah to hear his cry, that he was not finished, and within him there still beat the heart of a loyal jihadist warrior:

> *The Arabian Peninsula has never—since God made it flat, created its desert, and encircled it with seas—been stormed by any forces like the U.S. Crusader Armies now spreading across it like locusts—consuming its riches and destroying its plantations.*
>
> *The United States has been occupying the lands of Islam in the holiest of places, humiliating its people, terrorizing its neighbors. It has been forming a spearhead with which to fight under the banner of the Crusader-Zionist Alliance. So far they have killed more than a million people in the northern section of the peninsula—and now they come to annihilate what is left of us.*
>
> *The United States' aims are both religious and economic, designed to serve the Jews' petty State and divert attention from its occupation of Jerusalem and the murder of Muslims there. Their aim is to weaken us all, and, through this weakness and disunion, to guarantee Israel's survival, at any cost, in Muslim blood.*

These sentiments, which probably would not stand up under serious historical scrutiny, were originally part of the Fatwa "Urging Jihad Against Americans," and published on bin Laden's orders on February 23, 1998. Since then the Saudi-born terrorist godfather had rewritten them in many forms, and Yousaf Mohammed had read them many times.

And now, in a soft monotone, he repeated them over and over. And despite the religious overtones with which he invested the text, he never once gave a thought to those he had personally blown up and killed.

If he ever got out of Guantanamo, Yousaf was destined for high command in al-Qaeda, whether or not bin Laden still lived. His name was remembered with immense respect in the high caves of the Hindu Kush. Not as a fanatic, but as a highly educated battle commander, of the quality required for the jihad. In the minds of the al-Qaeda elders, Yousaf Mohammed was temporarily *hors de combat*. But one day he would return.

Ibrahim Sharif, too, was in the thoughts of the senior jihadists who formed the leadership of al-Qaeda. Since the 2003 attacks on Baghdad, there had been a tightening of the alliance between bin Laden's councils and the leadership of the Taliban, but they had drafted top commanders into Iraq and they had died by the dozen in the face of the U.S. onslaught on the terrorist enclaves.

Men like Ibrahim were still valued, and the memory of them was still vivid, if only because so many had died. At least Ibrahim and Yousaf had lived, although where and how was unclear. According to the intelligence network of al-Qaeda, they were both held captive in Guantanamo, but maybe not forever.

Forces were gathering worldwide to have the place closed. And this was despite the granite resolve of the Pentagon that it could not, must not, ever be shut down, because there was nowhere else to hold the world's most dangerous illegal forces, without trial.

And the situation in the mountain villages of Afghanistan was becoming more and more complex. The regular Pashtun communities, with their two-thousand-year-old tribal customs, did not approve of the unrelentingly harsh doctrines of the Taliban, nor did they see much point in staging some kind of nutcase war against the most powerful nation in the world—one that had already proven it could smash them to pieces any time it felt so inclined, like in Tora Bora, 2001.

Which left both the Taliban and al-Qaeda in a never-ending quandary. They had little success in recruiting senior men from the villages, and could only find new followers among the very young, impressionable kids, thrilled by the prospect of one day becoming warriors for the jihad.

By that method al-Qaeda had recruited Ibrahim, but in the law-abiding communities it was not approved, and as the years had passed there was much disquiet among the village elders about both al-Qaeda and the Taliban, and the manner in which they located potential freedom fighters.

Indeed it was a Pashtun village, way up there in the Hindu Kush, which in 2005 decided to save the badly wounded Navy SEAL Marcus Luttrell, in the face of stringent opposition from the Taliban and al-Qaeda. The villagers remained defiant to the end, saved Marcus, and flatly refused to surrender him.

The problem with the jihadists in the ensuing years was they were becoming tougher and more aggressive all the time, with an unmistakably threatening swagger to their approaches to the villages. They stopped short of announcing they would burn the place down if families were not prepared to hand over their young males to undergo an indoctrination process.

But there was an unseen line, across which both sets of armed fighters were unprepared to venture: the fact was they needed these tribal villages for food, water, and shelter during their long months in the mountains, avoiding U.S. troops. They could afford to threaten, but not to declare war, since one such incident might easily cause dozens of Pashtun communities to shun them permanently.

The Pashtuns were by nature a peace-loving group, but, when roused, were apt to declare blood-pacts to stand shoulder-to-shoulder and fight their enemy until no one was left alive. This held no appeal whatsoever to the tired and dispirited Taliban and al-Qaeda fighters who sought only allies, not enemies, on the high slopes of northeastern Afghanistan.

Across the border, in the northern provinces of Pakistan, the Pashtuns were known as the Pathans, the world's largest tribal society. The ancient beliefs and folklore of this group was not far removed from the rigorous codes of behavior of the Taliban—in many ways just as harsh and similar in doctrine.

Yousaf Mohammed was a Pathan, with deep Pashtun roots stretching back through centuries in Afghanistan. His family had crossed the border into Pakistan in 1973, and twenty-five years later, the young Yousaf had re-crossed, back into Afghanistan, recruited into bin Laden's mountain strongholds at seventeen. Both he and Ibrahim were devout, lifelong Muslims and trusted above all else the words of both the six-foot-five modern-day Sheikh and the ancient Prophet Mohammed. The bonds of Islam have always held together both of these adjoining countries.

Each day in Guantanamo, the prisoners were lined up and permitted to pray before dawn. At this ritual, conducted outside under usually cloudless skies, the two men were kept deliberately apart.

However at the daily gathering for exercise, they were permitted to work out close to each other on the rowing machines, and at soccer games were allowed on the same teams. By running across to the far touchlines, away from the camp guards, they were able to exchange what meager information they possessed.

And right here, in the hot and still Cuban air, they each encountered a new ally—the regular goalkeeper, Ben al-Turabi, a twenty-five-year-old Gaza-born Palestinian bomber, disciple of bin Laden, colleague of Sheikh al-Zawahiri. He was an al-Qaeda hit-man and a long-time scourge of the Mossad security forces.

Like Yousaf and Ibrahim, Ben had been picked up by U.S. troops on a swoop into one of bin Laden's villages. Like them, he had been in possession of no identifying documents. Like them, he had refused to speak. Like them he had faced only the briefest military tribunal, and not one member of the U.S. military could prove who he was, one way or another.

So far as the Mossad was concerned, Ben had constructed the bomb that detonated in Netanya, on Israel's coast, north of Tel Aviv, on March 27, 2002—the one that had nearly blown the Park Hotel in half, killed twenty-seven and injured one hundred and forty, many of them women and children, right in the middle of Passover.

The Mossad, for once, with Middle Eastern peace talks pending, was not anxious just to hunt al-Turabi down and murder him within Israel's borders. And when their INTEL located him in the Hindu Kush, Afghanistan, they tipped off the CIA in Langley and suggested they take over. It took SEAL Team 5 four days to run Ben to ground, and about two hours to manacle him and ship him direct to Guantanamo.

Ben was very nearly as tall as bin Laden himself, and just as malevolent in his loathing of the West. He was not a bad goalkeeper either. He was quick and sure-footed, with the eye of a desert hawk and enormous, powerful hands. His methods of self-survival in the prison were the complete opposite of those employed by Ibrahim and Yousaf. Ben presented a cheerful, sunny-side-up appearance and seemed to be happy to cooperate with both the guards and the interrogators, laughing and shaking his head at the apparent absurd suggestion that he was, himself, a Hamas commander in the cauldron of the West Bank.

Ben's good nature and friendliness toward his captors was, after more than five years, a feature of Camp Five. He had a huge smile, a deep spontaneous laugh, and an almost comic expression of incredulousness whenever it was suggested that he, Ben, had actually blown up the Park Hotel. All these years he had sworn to God he was a back-packer from the University of Tel Aviv, wandering the mountains, and that these weirdos with Kalashnikovs slung over their shoulders had taken him in for a gourmet feast of flatbread, dust, sand, and sour goat's milk.

"Next thing I knew," he would assert, "these huge American guys with beards had sprung from nowhere, shot the guards at the entrance to the caves, and frightened the life out of everyone, including me."

Thus ran the party-line of Ben al-Turabi. Although he was never able to explain quite why, at the moment of his capture, he was carrying a fully loaded machine gun, with ammunition belts slung diagonally across his chest, and four bomb-detonators in the pockets of his baggy Afghan pants. Neither was he clear with his explanation of the gunpowder under his fingernails that the American forensic guys instantly detected. Ben was also somewhat vague as to why the University of Tel Aviv had never heard of him.

The Mossad, Israel's renowned Secret Service, was absolutely certain he was a grade-one terrorist. They had photographed him at the scene in Netanya, and while it was a picture of appalling quality, it was better than three others they had snapped from various other terrorist crime scenes.

According to the hard-eyed sages of King Saul Boulevard, Ben had started off as a young hitman for Yasser Arafat's Palestinian terror group, Hamas, but had been called up to The Base, bin Laden's world jihadist headquarters in the Afghan mountains. He had left the rubble-strewn streets of Gaza on the understanding that he might return for "specialist missions." The Mossad considered he was on one of these when the Park Hotel blew.

The problem for the Mossad was two-fold. One, they did not know Ben's name, or any way to identify him. Two, they had no experience of operating in the northeastern mountains of Afghanistan. Whereas they were more than happy to work in tandem with America's CIA or FBI anti-terrorist squads, they had no fighting force comparable to the U.S. Navy SEALs when it came to mountain combat on murderous escarpments that, down the centuries, had proved beyond the capabilities of both the British and the Russians. No one had to try very hard in order to die up there in the Hindu Kush.

Locating Ben had been largely good luck. A Mossad Intelligence cell had picked someone up on a highly suspicious mobile phone in Netanya in the hours before the hotel explosion. They had swooped on the Mediterranean resort too late. But their surveillance teams had a fix on that cell phone, and they located it again, eight days later, in the middle of a packed football stadium in Amman, on the far side of the Jordan River.

Ben went quiet after that. But Mossad surveillance nailed that telephone again four months later, working in conjunction with the British military: this time in central Afghanistan near the capital city of Kabul. By now Israel's entire Intelligence network believed the man who had killed and maimed all of those people in Netanya was headed up the slopes to rendezvous with bin Laden's high command.

These were innocent days, long before the jihadists wised up to the fact that their cell phones were the most lethal aid to their enemies. Today they avoid the incriminating message. They rarely, if ever, use phones, because the tiny electronic signal can pinpoint the whereabouts of the caller.

In the days when bin Laden was plainly still alive, the National Security Agency in Fort Meade, Maryland, was able to listen in to the al-Qaeda leader on his cell phone, in his cave, talking to his aged mother in Saudi Arabia. They would play the tapes to selected visitors, as a regular party-piece.

Meantime up in the high peaks, Ben al-Turabi was using his phone like a lovesick teenager at an English boarding school, chatting away, checking the football scores, leaving disgraceful messages on his friends' answering machines, and generally behaving in a manner unbecoming for a Palestinian mass-murderer.

The American interceptors picked him up in about five minutes and immediately sent in the heavies, a top SEAL team that crossed the mountains in pouring rain, on foot, slipping and sliding through the gullies, until they fell upon the al-Qaeda redoubt with ruthless efficiency. Somehow or another Ben had managed to smash and then get rid of his cell phone before the SEALs slammed into his cave. The phone was never found and thus another small piece of evidence that might have betrayed his exact identity was lost forever.

The rest fell into place automatically. The laughing goalkeeper wound up, within a week, in Guantanamo, a true no-home, no-name, no-future, pacing-his-cell political prisoner, uncharged but suspected of high treason and murder against the State of Israel and its people.

Despite his "Who? Me?" attitude and joshing manner with his American guards he was listed as a number-one hard-man, unbroken by years of intense interrogation, constantly in shackles, kept in solitary confinement, and regarded as a security risk of the first order. When he played football, armed guards were posted right next to the goalposts. One step out of line, they would have gunned Ben down, no questions asked.

But Ben never stepped out of line. He was a model prisoner despite his "known terrorist" pedigree and obvious connections to al-Qaeda. Several guards over the years had whiled away the boring hours by chatting to the tall Palestinian, whose command of English was outstanding. And although he had zero access to any form of Intelligence beyond the coils of razor-wire that bound up the camp, he gleaned more information than anyone else ever did from the friendlier U.S. guards.

This did not involve specific Intelligence, but it did involve snippets such as U.S. lawyers being involved in protests against the system, advising outfits like Amnesty International. When a newspaper ran a story that a Washington law firm had been retained by a Saudi oil company with suspected connections to terrorist organizations, one of the guards jokingly told Ben he might yet get out of Guantanamo since Left-wing forces in the United States were on the march on behalf of people like himself.

This struck a chord with Ben, because he knew the oil corporation, and he knew bin Laden was related to its president. This latest news suggested to him that The Sheikh was on his case, and he could hardly wait to tell his new buddies Yousaf and Ibrahim.

There was only one other prisoner with whom he might wish to share this information, and that was Abu Hassan Akbar, another former Hamas killer who had trained in the Hindu Kush specifically to become second-in-command to Ben al-Turabi the next time Osama sent in his men to wreak havoc on either the West or Israel.

Abu Hassan was an honest-to-goodness psychopath from downtown Gaza where he had been born twenty-five years previously. Shot and wounded in the backstreets of north Baghdad, he had been hauled into custody by the throat, manacled, and grilled over the deaths of fifteen U.S. Army personnel, who had been killed the previous week by a mighty booby-trap bomb that detonated on the roadside as the troops raced past. He also carried no identity, but Israeli agents, called in to help, ascertained he was Palestinian, almost certainly a Hamas field operative, and one of the principal experts on explosives still at large in that benighted part of the world.

Abu Hassan had been wanted by both the Mossad and the U.S. military for several months, but kept vanishing over the Iraqi border into Iran. When, finally, the SEALs picked him up, it was still impossible to pin an accurate identity on him, but the Mossad swore he was the mastermind behind the Be'er Shiva bombing of a bar mitzvah in 2004, which had left six dead and thirty-five maimed, most of them kids.

Like Ben al-Turabi, Abu Hassan was nailed by poor-quality photographic evidence and the occasional cell-phone location. The Israelis knew him on sight and were happy to take the son-ofabitch off the hands of the Americans and out into the desert to shoot him.

What saved Abu's life, perversely, was his cold-blooded murder of the U.S. Army personnel, because that changed the game. That made him a criminal in the eyes of Uncle Sam, which is not great, but better than being grabbed by the Mossad and the instant death that almost certainly signified.

The Americans spent several weeks trying to pin multiple murder charges on Abu Hassan, but without an accurate name and some form of identity and background it proved impossible. Bin Laden and Yasser Arafat sent in a team of lawyers prepared to lie, beg, or threaten legal mayhem if the Americans harmed one tight, black, curly hair of Abu's head. One U.S. general swore by all that was holy that he would personally wring the neck of one particularly persistent New York–based lawyer, who had stopped about a centimeter short of calling him a liar.

U.S. military INTEL had a thick file on Abu Hassan, with enough circumstantial evidence to hang him from a tall palm tree a hundred times. By one estimate, he was implicated in more than a dozen bombings in Israel alone. He was suspected of launching rockets from Gaza City over the new barrier wall and of blowing up two supermarkets. In the U.S. garrison in Bagram, in the foothills of the Hindu Kush, he was named as the most likely culprit for no fewer than twelve attacks on U.S. personnel involving roadside bombs.

When the SEALs finally grabbed "Abu the Bombmaker" in Baghdad, he was extraordinarily lucky they did not just shoot him right there—but then, so was Saddam Hussein. Abu was, in a sense, in exalted, if notorious, company. Of the four unbroken terrorists grinding out their daily existence in Guantanamo, he was the most likely looking killer, with his unshaven lopsided face, permanent scowl, and jagged scar running down the left side of his jawbone.

An angular character of medium height, with an athletic way of walking, Abu, since a young age had enjoyed killing. Out there in the hot, sandy ghettos of Gaza City he found ample outlets for his talent with knife or gun, while serving a kind of satanic apprenticeship with the hit squads operating on behalf of Hamas, and, of course, Yasser Arafat.

His sorties across the border into Israel were constantly, by his standards, successful. He would kill any Israeli without mercy, man, woman, or child—striking viciously in the darkness with his curved blade or even with dynamite. He went by the name of "Cobra"—and he said it in English, to ensure the Israelis were in no doubt precisely who and what he was.

He had value as a killer, but much more so as a constructor of bombs and an aimer of primitive rockets. Abu had been a nomad among jihadists, answering only to the call of al-Qaeda, moving silently across borders into Iran, into Afghanistan, back into Gaza, and up into the enfolding escarpments of the Hindu Kush. The modern profession of bombmaking is a bit like sailing a yacht. The skilled man can do it anywhere.

Ben al-Turabi and Abu Hassan Akbar knew each other. They had sat side-by-side in those quasi-religious councils conducted by bin Laden in the border country between Afghanistan and Pakistan. Both men were en route to the Tora Bora district when the Americans slammed into the mountains with a barrage of twenty-first-century bombing.

No one at Guantanamo knew for certain the two men had been al-Qaeda comrades in arms, though there were several interrogators who suspected they probably knew each other. There was just something about the way they talked quietly on the football field, as if they did not require quite so many words as normal people. Whenever they met, there was a substantial amount of head-nodding, and a paucity of lip movement. Quite often the interrogators had asked if the two men were acquainted, but neither of them gave an inch. Ben laughed, and Abu Hassan snarled. Neither of them uttered a word.

Proof positive that the two men did know each other would, of course, have been damning evidence against them, because they had been arrested hundreds of miles apart—Ben in the high Afghan caves, Abu Hassan in North Baghdad. Both were believed to be active jihadists by the best Intelligence Services in the world. If they could be proven friends, that would probably be sufficient to guarantee them lifetime accommodation in Guantanamo. Which was, more or less, why Ben and Abu spoke only rarely and, right under the eyes of the guards, created a code of speaking and passing information through Ibraham and Yousaf, which had stood the test of time. The four men were blood brothers in the black art of silence and deceit.

And, somehow, they understood there were forces out there beyond the razor wire that were striving for their freedom, and that in the end they would return to the front line of their holy struggle against the Infidel. Each piece of news came to them slowly and sketchily, by osmosis more than anything else. But it sustained them, and it gave them the oxygen of hope, and it kept alive the flickering flames of defiance and anger.

Throughout their years of captivity, the only form of justice available was that of the military tribunal—a kind of commission for the trial and punishment of any individual detained at Guantanamo. In November 2001, President George W. Bush authorized these "courts" to proceed, and all four men, Ibrahim, Yousaf, Ben, and Abu Hassan had made brief appearances before the military "judges," but none of them had spoken, which made the entire thing a pretty good waste of everyone's time.

Military tribunals can be quite useful for trying members of enemy forces who were operating outside the scope of conventional criminal and civil proceedings. Despite the presence of military officers, serving as both judge and jury, they are distinct from court-martial, which is a fairer and less intense procedure.

The tribunal is an inquisitorial system, based entirely on charges brought by a military authority. Prisoners are prosecuted by the military, and judged and sentenced by military officers. Decisions made by a military tribunal cannot be appealed to federal courts.

In fact the authority granted by President Bush in 2001 was merely a re-awakening of a traditional U.S. tool against adversarial foes. General Washington used military tribunals during the American Revolution. The Union used them during, and in the immediate aftermath, of the Civil War. General Andrew Jackson used one to try a British spy during the War of 1812.

As stacked decks go, the old MT was right up there. And, once more by a process close to osmosis, the fluttering heart of America's political left was touched: In July of 2004, a set of tribunals, the Combatant Status Reviews, were convened to decide whether detainees held at Guantanamo were correctly designated "enemy combatants."

The hearings were exhaustive, the rights of each individual being weighed and balanced. The military, generally speaking, thought the whole world must have gone crazy, as they watched the U.S. legal system turning itself inside out in an attempt to liberate guys who had been hurling bombs, rockets, and other explosives at U.S. troops.

Then, in January 2005, Washington federal judge Joyce Hens Green ruled that the Combatant Status Review Tribunal was unconstitutional, and that detainees were entitled to the rights granted by the Constitution of the United States of America. Yousaf, Ibrahim, Ben, and Abu Hassan were essentially up and running.

Almost immediately two acts were introduced. The first one forbade the inhumane treatment of prisoners, including those at Guantanamo Bay, and laid out tough guidelines for "trials." A few months later, however, the Bush administration forced the Military Commissions Act through Congress. This second act authorized trial by military commission for violations of the laws of war. Yousaf and his cohorts were still up, but not running.

And for two more years they waited for a new breakthrough, confident that in the end, the "soft" western conscience would prevail on their side. And they were right. On June 12, 2008, the Supreme Court, despite being almost deadlocked, ruled by the narrowest of divided margins that foreign detainees held for years at Guantanamo Bay had the right to appeal to U.S. civilian courts to challenge indefinite imprisonment without charges.

President Bush was furious at this third occasion the Supreme Court had repudiated him. Not only did he strongly disagree with the verdict, he actually threatened to seek yet another law to keep dangerous terror suspects locked up.

Justice Anthony Kennedy, whose vote had swayed the decision, acknowledged the terrorism threat that faced the United States but argued that "the Laws and Constitution are designed to survive and remain in force, even in extraordinary times."

He also ruled that petitioners had the constitutional privilege of the writ of *habeas corpus*, the right to appear before a court to protest the illegality of their incarceration without trial. In Justice

Kennedy's opinion, their presence as prisoners in Guantanamo did not bar them from seeking the writ. Nor did it bar them from invoking the Suspension Clause, a civil guarantee that blocks Congress from suspending *habeas corpus*.

And just to stick it to the president and his military staff one more time, the justice referred to the government's argument that this clause affords petitioners no rights, because the United States does not claim sovereignty over the U.S. Naval Station at the eastern tip of Cuba. "Rejected," Kennedy wrote, not adding the word "garbage," though he might have, so certain was he of his ruling.

Chief Justice John Roberts was among the four men who dissented from Kennedy's opinion. The others were justices Antonin Scalia, Clarence Thomas, and Samuel Alito.

Ten days later the U.S. Court of Appeals for the District of Columbia Circuit issued an historic ruling—that a Guantanamo detainee Huzaifa Parhat had been improperly classified as an enemy combatant, thus giving him the chance to win his release. The appeals court ordered the government to release Parhat, or to hold a new tribunal hearing, consistent with the court's opinion. They also gave Parhat's lawyers permission to file a *habeas corpus* petition in the federal district court, as a consequence of the Supreme Court's recent decision.

President Bush almost hit the Oval Office ceiling.

Because right here, in the capital city of the United States, it had been decided that foreign bombers and murderers who had illegally attacked, harmed, and killed U.S. troops on active service, were now to be granted the same rights as peaceful, law-abiding, tax-paying U.S. citizens. Abdul, the blood-thirsty, vengeful, foreign jihadist was regarded as the equal of a U.S. college professor or businessman.

Yousaf and his boys each had one leg over the Guantanamo razor-wire, so to speak.

Deep inside the Pentagon, the service chiefs were appalled. E-mails flashed between the White House and the office of the secretary for defense. Across the bridge at Langley, Virginia, the recently appointed head of the CIA, Bob Birmingham, was speaking on a secure line to the chairman of the joint chiefs. The chief of naval operations was on the wire to the new director of the National Security Agency, Captain James Ramshawe. The question being asked in several different forms amounted to the same one: "What the hell are we supposed to do when some damnfool justice lets these crazy bastards loose?"

Guantanamo's vital statistics were well known to the entire military Intelligence community. Of the 779 suspected terrorists detained in the prison since it first opened, 248 remained. Of these, some fifty had been cleared for release but faced prosecution in their own countries. A further fifty were still being interrogated, and of those, twenty would definitely be charged with a criminal offense.

Estimates were that Guantanamo held perhaps fifty hugely dangerous characters, and of these, fourteen were judged by the authorities to be lethal, and ought not be released ever. All of the principal security chiefs of the United States, both military and civilian, had a copy of that final list. Of the fourteen, four were not identified by name—just by prison number and a short note detailing the circumstances of arrest.

The missing names were Yousaf Mohammed, Ibrahim Sharif, Ben al-Turabi, and Abu Hassan Akbar. The latter two were believed to be former Palestinian "freedom fighters."

Bob Birmingham, who stood six-foot-six, could scarcely believe what had happened. The U.S. justice system was plainly going to be hit by a barrage of lawyers demanding the writ of *habeas corpus* for their incarcerated clients. Each one of these suspected foreign cutthroats/murderers had precisely the same rights as he did, one of them being the right to be heard in an American court of law.

Bob paced his office. *Okay, so a U.S. judge frees these four fanatics—what then? They have no passports, papers, or credit cards. No money, no residences in the United States. What happens now? Do we just release them outside the courtroom? Tell them to get on a bus and then get lost? We can't put them on a civilian air-craft without proper security guards, and we can't send them any-where without informing that foreign government. Equally, we cannot lose them. Neither can we take action against them.*

"Jesus Christ," said Bob. And the big CIA boss knew as well as anyone that in all these cases against suspected terrorists, the advantage rested with the petitioners, not with the U.S. military lawyers who would argue against setting them free. Right now, no one could do much except wait for the appeals to come in from Washington attorneys, who would surely be retained by the al-Qaeda paymasters in faraway Afghanistan or Saudi Arabia.

"Goddamned lawyers," he muttered. "Shameless. Anything for money."

TWO DAYS LATER
PESHAWAR, NORTHWEST FRONTIER, PAKISTAN

ALMOST ONE AND a quarter million souls reside in the ancient city of Peshawar, the world's archetypal frontier town. Half of those souls can scarcely decide whether they are Pakistanis or Afghanis. Pashtuns, Pathans, city dwellers, tribesmen, traders, accountants, goldsmiths and jewelers, farmers and kebab cooks, swarm through this place of romance, intrigue, and danger.

As far as the rest of Pakistan is concerned, the collective heart of these northwestern isolationists lies across the nearby border in Afghanistan. No one else tries to understand them. Not even the NWFP government is suspected of sympathy. Not for the Afghan rulers in Kabul or the leaders of the most sinister elements of the Taliban.

Peshawar has been for centuries the "Gateway to Afghanistan," situated on the only route to the Khyber Pass, the fabled mountain road, which scythes through the frontier and connects the two countries. The Pathans describe Peshawar as the gateway to Central Asia, which of course it is, should you happen to be riding a yak off the heights of the Himalayas.

By western standards, however, Peshawar is the gateway to nowhere. It represents the end of the line for the north-running Pakistani railroad. They all terminate here, big diesel locomotives that have thundered through the mountainous terrain from ancient destinations like Karachi, Lahore, Quetta, and Rawalpindi.

The only train that departs from Peshawar and doesn't head south, back to the "civilized" world, is the old Khyber Steam Safari, which carries tourists west up to the Khyber Pass a couple of times a month—straight up into bandit country, past the lairs of terrible warlords, who have dominated this near-lawless terrain for centuries.

To the north of Peshawar lies the Swat Valley, a steep-sided, 150-mile-long range of towering mountains, running north-south, guarding the river. This is deep Pathan country, defiant of the laws of Pakistan, largely inaccessible, totally unconquerable, and home to the black-hearted training camps of Osama bin Laden's al-Qaeda.

This is the principal refuge of the modern-day jihadists. Hand in glove with the fanatics of the Taliban, the guardians of The Sheikh's terrorist network, they live and train up here in the silence of the mountains along the banks of the great Swat River, and beneath the snowcapped peaks that form the southern escarpments of the mighty Hindu Kush range.

No one in two thousand years has managed to pull this place into any kind of order—not since Alexander the Great turned up in 367 BC, fought four battles in the heart of the valley, and carried on south toward Peshawar, lucky to be alive and thankful to have most of his army still intact. He never went back.

In modern Pakistan, the less people hear about the Swat Valley the better they like it. Its reputation is appalling, even by the standards of a nation so torn by religious and political divisions. Peshawar's divided heart embraces neighboring Afghanistan and the warlike tribes of the valley, the men who nowadays form the soul of the jihad. Peshawar has nothing to do with the economic heartland of Pakistan: that's the mega fourteen-million-strong city of

Karachi, which lies six hundred miles to the south, on the eastern shore of the Arabian Sea.

Peshawar is a throwback to the lawless Middle Ages, cheerful and friendly on the surface, but with the coursing blood of fanatical Islamic warriors raging not so deeply below. No one understands this quasi-romantic, dangerous edge to the historic city. But it's best to remember that even the friendly old tourist train, running visitors up to the Khyber Pass, *never* leaves Peshawar station without its squadron of heavily armed guards. Just in case.

There is no other place on earth where the disciples of the men who smashed the World Trade Center could operate with such freedom, where they could be tolerated, even welcomed, and assisted by the local populace. Such men spell problems for everyone. No one wants them, except perhaps Iran, and the deceptive, secretive politicians and tribal chiefs of Pakistan's remote and forbidding Northwest Frontier.

The Swat Valley is officially closed to all foreigners, since no one can guarantee anyone's chances of getting out alive. And that ban on overseas tourists is probably the only Pakistani law heeded by anyone in Peshawar and its northern hinterlands.

The city itself represents one of the world's most dramatic clashes of the ancient and modern. Motorized rickshaws are all over the place, high-powered modern businessmen abound. Every other person is walking around with a cell phone stuck to his ear. The armada of modern automobiles swamps the camel drovers. You can smell the exhaust pollution on the warm summer winds. . . .

And yet, the heady call of an ancient culture pervades the atmosphere, especially in the teeming bazaars in the warren of the old city. The air at all times is thick with the smell of grilling kebabs, and the majority of people are dressed traditionally in baggy pants and long robes, turbans, and Afghan hats. The presence of women is rare.

Great samovars dispense vast quantities of *qawa*, that delicious green tea with cardamom and lemon, which has refreshed the

Pathan and Pashtun tribes for thousands of years. They pour it into little enameled pots, and fleet-footed boys race through the crowds to deliver these pots to prosperous-looking local merchants.

Some of these families have trading connections established over hundreds of years, stretching as far afield as Shanghai and St. Petersburg. At various intervals there are great houses built around courtyards with overhanging balconies, some of them owned by Peshawar's merchant classes, others are further reminders of the Raj.

Behind one of these high-walled residences on a hot morning in late June 2008, a solemn gathering of five men sat quietly sipping tea beside the fountain on the shady southern wall of the courtyard. The house, approached through a dark alleyway leading directly to the *Andar Shehr*, belonged to Shakir Khan, a ranking government official in the assembly of the North West Frontier Province. He was accompanied by his assistant, thirty-year-old Kaiser Rashid, whose two brothers were both decorated Taliban commanders.

All of them had been born in the Swat Valley in the river town of Madyan, including Shakir Khan himself. The other two men, Ahmed and Gholam Azzan, were brothers, Afghanis by birth, forward commanders and assault instructors in al-Qaeda. Ahmed was thirty-eight years old, the senior brother by two years. He had served bin Laden faithfully through all the years of jihad and intended to continue doing so, whether or not The Sheikh had died in the U.S. onslaught on Tora Bora. Very few people had a definitive answer to that.

The last of the five was Captain Musa Amin, commander of a small Taliban army of perhaps two hundred warriors that operated in the Hindu Kush, harassing, and killing any U.S. military personnel with whom they closed to striking range. The Americans, however, had grown distinctly fed up with the activities of Captain Amin, and had very nearly wiped out his entire force in an ambush conducted in the mountains, ten thousand feet above sea level.

Amin, now forty, had fought valiantly on the ground, but the American bombing and rocket fire, as so often in the high escarpments, had been too tough. Amin had fled the Navy SEAL clean-up parties that swooped down onto the battlefield in the aftermath of the attack. Badly wounded, he had slowly made his way from village to village until, finally, he crossed the Pakistan border, and reached the Kachikani Pass, gateway to the northern end of the Swat Valley.

In the months that followed, his wounds had healed, and he had found his way into one of the al-Qaeda training camps, right here in the cradle of the jihadist movement. What also healed was his spirit, for Captain Amin had been terrified of the U.S. onslaught on his troops, and had doubted whether he would ever fight again.

His search for protection had not been easy, for he could not just present himself, bloodstained and shot, at any village house and demand help. He represented too much of a liability, and the Americans were everywhere. Inevitably he worked his way back into the embrace of his own kind, fellow terrorists who welcomed, and indeed lionized, him.

Such was Amin's celebrity, the camp commandant realized that the Captain outranked him, both in experience and intellect. Within weeks he was appointed by the elders as the camp's commanding officer. And he swiftly slipped back into the old routines, training the young Pashtuns from across the border, and recruiting young Pathans from the Pakistan side.

His new somewhat exalted status brought him into contact with al-Qaeda's high command, and, at least on the eastern side of the border, there was no one much higher than Shakir Khan, who was rich beyond reason, as are many government officials in that part of the world.

Shakir was no warrior, but he was the negotiator for illegal arms from Iran. He was the man who arranged the innocent-looking camel trains to haul the dynamite and the rockets and the Kalashnikovs up the through the passes under the pretence of honest traders.

Shakir too had been bin Laden's banker, receiving the payments from Saudi Arabia, laundering the money, and funneling it through to The Sheikh for distribution, all the while extracting ten percent for himself.

Osama knew perfectly well that Shakir was a villain, but he was priceless in his position as a highly placed member of the government of the Northwest Frontier. His position alone meant cast-iron protection for those training camps, and a complete absence of intruders, including those from the United States armed forces.

Conversation in the courtyard centered around the usual topic, which had more or less consumed al-Qaeda for many years—the crying need for a better officer class. The men who now ran the organization had often been reckless in deploying young lieutenants after the massacre in Tora Bora. And these insurgents had died by the dozen in the hot, dusty backstreets of Baghdad and Basra, Gaza and Kabul, anywhere they decided to launch assaults on the Americans, British, or Israelis.

The result had been a chronic shortage of trained leaders, and, naturally, the lower the standards of military competence fell, the worse al-Qaeda's casualty rate became. They had never succeeded in hitting the United States again in all the years of the Bush presidency simply because they did not have the senior staff officers to pull it off. They kept getting caught, over and over, by either the CIA, the FBI, British MI6, or the Mossad. And without the super-cunning hand of Osama to guide them, things had gone from bad to worse.

They had opened more training camps in the Swat Valley, but as the memory of the World Trade Center began to fade, young men of fifteen and sixteen were turning up with scarcely a memory of Osama's Day of Glory. Like the U.S. Navy SEALs, Osama's army promotes top combat troops into instructors, and the five men in the courtyard had been mulling over this obvious weakness in their indoctrination system for the past three hours.

The critical point was the lack of forward commanders returning from various battlefields. Half of them had been grabbed from the field of conflict and shipped to Guantanamo Bay. The other half died in action, shot while trying to blow up their U.S. enemy. Also, when the men from the mountains were forced to spill the beans in the hot, brightly lit interrogation rooms at Guantanamo, the Americans tended to strike hard, using whatever information they had gleaned.

The result was a series of sudden, merciless rocket attacks on several of Osama's safehouses, and the instant death of literally dozens of al-Qaeda warriors trying to make their way back into the Hindu Kush and the Swat Valley, for the onward progression of the jihad.

Right now there were two camps a few miles south of Kalam, right on the river, which were essentially closed for training owing to this shortage of instructors. The five men talked endlessly about the Valley, and the need for a Big Plan, a major strike against the West. And they talked of the crushing defeats in Baghdad, the disappointments of the Ayatollahs in Iran, and the overwhelming desire they had for another Great Victory.

And, as ever, they talked of the possible return of young leaders still incarcerated in Guantanamo. In particular, Captain Amin had begged Allah, at mid-morning prayers, for the safe return one day of his beloved nephew, Ibrahim Sharif, the only son of his own sister Anandi:

> *Almighty God, to whom all things are possible, we beg of you to rescue your faithful servant Ibrahim—for he will rise up and hold his sword against your enemies, and he will not falter, nor will he lose heart, nor fall into despair, until you, who have power over all things, gather him home unto your kingdom.*

The clock high on the ramparts of the Cunningham Tower stood at two minutes after 1 p.m., and all five men had heard its single resonant chime, the same metallic clang which had tolled out the hour after midday and midnight since the year 1900 when the tower was completed to mark the Diamond Jubilee of the reign of Victoria, Queen of Great Britain, Empress of India, and ruler of the Domains Beyond the Seas, including Peshawar.

The great bell's haughty echo of the old empire had scarcely died away on the warm mountain wind when sound came from the side door of the courtyard that led out into the alleyway— three sharp taps and then a pause, then two more and another pause, then a single crack on the heavy wooden gate. The entrance code was accurate. Whoever wanted entry was an insider.

Kaiser Rashid was on his feet in an instant, drawing his curved combat knife as he walked toward the gate. He peered through a small glass peephole, smiled, re-sheathed his knife, and drew back the two black cast-iron bolts that barred the door. Outside stood an elderly Pathan tribesman, with a hard, nut-brown, wrinkled face, holding the reins of his camel.

He and Kaiser exchanged the traditional Muslim greeting, bowing their heads and touching their foreheads, before bringing down their hands in an arc, the gesture of respect:

"*Salam alaikum* (peace be with you), Kaiser."
"*Wa alaikum as salaam* (and also unto you), Ali."

He handed Kaiser a brown sealed envelope, and added, "From Islamabad, e-mail from the USA. I left last night."

"Will you stay for dinner? You must be tired. I'll have someone take care of the camel."

"I cannot today. I have to keep going, up to the Valley. This is important news."

Kaiser said he understood, and wished him well before closing and bolting the gate.

Shakir Khan opened the envelope and stared at the message. "Allah has heard our cries," he said softly. "And now He has answered our prayers. The Americans have given in to world pressure and allowed our poor brave jihadists at last to be taken from the Guantanamo Hell, to stand before a civilian court of justice and demand either a fair trial or liberty, the rights of every man."

Captain Amin stood up and raised his eyes to the sky. He clasped his hands together and called to the azure blue heavens above the northwest frontier, "Allah is great. Ibrahim and his friends will come home. God has heard our plea. Almighty God, you have saved them from the oppressor!"

Shakir Khan held in his hand a printout of the Supreme Court verdict. Carefully he read out the words of Justice Kennedy, the ones that rendered jihadist terrorists regular rights like any other U.S. citizen . . . the words that had appalled the president himself. Not to mention all of his key military and civilian security advisors.

"Why has this Kennedy person done this? Does he believe in our cause? Is he a traitor to America?" Kaiser Rashid was astounded.

So was the far more sophisticated Shakir Khan. "My son," he said, "the Americans are sometimes difficult to understand. They have big smiles and strike with weapons that would terrify the Prophet himself. They will kill us without mercy. All of you can bear witness to that. And yet there is a side to them that is inexplicable. As if they are ashamed of their own land, and laws, and people. They have fits of conscience, and try to atone for things that cannot be corrected. In the end they must lose our Holy War on them. Because they are soft, and too often they do not have the steel of the true warrior within them. They do not have the stomach for the fight. They are like poor, weak, pitiful women, and now they have invented a way to let loose our top warriors from captivity."

"Does this mean they are tired of the conflict?" asked Kaiser.

"Of course they are," replied Khan. "But we are not tired. This is a long war, and we will not rest until the American Infidel heeds the word of the Prophet and understands that Allah alone is great."

Captain Amin spoke next. "Either that, or he lies dead at our feet," said the uncle of Ibrahim Sharif.

2

THEY PASSED THE COMMUNICATION from hand to hand—five robed native tribesmen staring at the verdict written seven thousand miles away in Washington, DC, by Justice Kennedy on behalf of the Supreme Court of the United States.

No one spoke. The only sound was from the water softly splashing in the courtyard fountain. Ali's camel, which had born the stunning news north through the dangerous mountain passes from the Army city of Kohat, had padded silently away, down the alleyway, and into the streets of Peshawar.

The Azzam brothers and Captain Musa could only ask for clarity, to help them understand the ramifications of the American judgment. Kaiser Rashid, Khan's assistant, who had studied law in London, tried his best.

"The important part," he said, "is the writ of *habeas corpus*."

"Which language is that?" asked Captain Amin.

"It's Latin," said Kaiser. "Most Western law traces back to the Romans."

"How about ours?"

"Older. Much older."

"Did we have *habeas corpus?*"

"I'm not sure we needed it, Captain. We were well organized thousands of years before the Prophet."

"Hmmm," said Amin. "Anyway, I still don't understand what it is."

"It means, literally, *thou shalt have the body,* meaning an appearance in court. The writ requires the person to be brought physically before a judge or a court, with the right to explain why he should be released from captivity."

"And this right would be given to Ibrahim?"

"By the look of this document," replied Kaiser, thoughtfully, "this right has been given to everyone being detained at Guantanamo under U.S. law."

"But surely the judge will listen and then send them right back for what they call crimes against humanity?"

Shakir Khan interjected. "Maybe five years ago," he said, "when President Bush was furious with the entire Muslim world. But not now. Times have changed. The Americans have grown tired of the conflict. And their politicians must listen to the people. They just want it all to be over. And they're starting by getting rid of the prisoners."

"You mean they will just send Ibrahim and Yousaf home?"

"It looks like it. But before they do so, we have much work to do. They need lawyers. American lawyers. And we must make arrangements, both to hire them and then pay them. It must all go through Osama's highest command."

"Can we work directly by phone and e-mail?"

"I don't think so," replied Khan. "Because if they trace us, the Americans will have the government arrest us. It's always better to remain concealed and to move our orders and operational documents on foot. It takes longer, but it's much better."

By now the clerics' call to the faithful was echoing from the minaret high above the glowing white walls of the Mosque of Mahabat Khan, north of *Andar Shehr*. All five men hurried from the courtyard and joined the throng that moved in great droves of devout Muslims preparing to prostrate themselves before their God.

For the next hour Shakir Khan and his men would cast aside the possible release of their heroic brothers from Guantanamo and concentrate on their midday prayers. *Allah is great . . . there is no other God.* There would be time enough to set free Ibrahim and Yousaf during the long hot afternoon.

SHAKIR KHAN outlined his suggestions in carefully coded Arabic and summoned a messenger to transport them on the next camel train leaving the city, laden with the bountiful fruit crops from the lush Vale of Peshawar—apricots, peaches, plums, pears, lemons, and oranges. The communiqué was delivered after a two-day journey to Pakistan's green, leafy new capital of Islamabad, ninety-four miles to the east of Peshawar.

The recipient was a Pakistani government official who kept a private office on Market Road a few hundred yards from the Parliament building. This is the center of the business district, known, curiously, as the Blue Area. Western Intelligence services are unwelcome here, for Islamabad represents the very heart of Islam, as its name suggests.

Shakir Khan's recommendations were e-mailed in private to the most militant group of Sunni Muslim clergy in Saudi Arabia. These were the men who had financed the gigantic Faisal Masjid, the world's biggest mosque, which stands on the outskirts of Islamabad, a religious fountainhead of Muslim learning and history.

From these powerful clerics Shakir Khan sought approval, both financial and spiritual. His message to them read: *New U.S. Supreme Court decision regarding* habeas corpus *for detainees opens the gates of freedom to our brave fighters. Please appoint Washington attorneys to represent them in U.S. Appeals Court. Particular interest Yousaf Mohammed and Ibrahim Sharif. There may be others.*

From here the words of Shakir Khan were faxed from the frantic offices of one of the world's great oil shipping terminals and lost in the daily maelstrom of international tanker communications. When that fax arrived in a small law firm in the City of London, it was utterly untraceable.

Which was how the law firm of Messrs Howard, Marks, and Cuthbert of London Wall came to appoint Epstein, Myerson, and Marsh of 296 12th Street, Washington, DC, as the legal representatives of Yousaf and Ibrahim.

The senior partner of Epstein's, as it was normally known, was a shrewd and legally savvy graduate of Harvard Law School, who had worked for several years as legal counsel to the Texas and Gulf Oil Corporation, based principally in Riyadh and Galveston.

Josh Epstein was sixty now, a big, fleshy man with dark hair and thick spectacles, who had somehow retained an aura of respectability despite grave suspicions among the politicos that he had a stupendously profitable sideline representing some of the most brutal jihadist killers on the planet. Worse yet, his paymasters were Saudi. In a city almost disappearing up its own backside with political correctness and adherence to the most lunatic human rights issues, Josh was, shall we say, a bit of an outsider.

We should also say, perhaps, that Josh did not give a two-cent damn for all that. His God was money, and he was surely in the right profession for that. Dollars, euros, pounds, yen, rupees, rubles, shekels, Josh loved them all in equal measure. But the sacks full of Saudi riyals were his favorites. Because those could be hidden away from the IRS.

And he could hardly disguise his joy when that e-mail came ghosting in from London's cyberspace, appointing him to head up what might be a truly lucrative appeals court team. Hundreds of hours, all billed at a premium thousand dollars per hour, not the normal five hundred, because of the risks to the firm's reputation and all, plus expenses. Not to mention that there would be a massive bonus for success. Josh could barely contain his elation.

Never a man to give much thought to problems that did not directly concern either him or his family, Josh cast aside any flickering concerns about the moral issue of liberating known mass murderers. Outside in the parking lot of the building, a dark blue turbo-charged Bentley bore testimony to the skill and ruthlessness of the senior partner of Epstein, Myerson, and Marsh.

Josh opened up his computer and clicked into Google Instant Messaging: *Thank you, Keith,* he wrote. *I'm sending two appeals court specialists to Cuba tomorrow. Access no problem. We'll file on Monday.* Five seconds later came a one-word reply: *Perfect.*

Josh Epstein summoned his two closest terrorist lawyers into his office. Then he reached across his desk and started the time-clock that counts off the billing hours, per lawyer, per case. In this case, a thousand dollars a tick. Times three.

THE ONLY MINOR blot on the horizon of Epstein's new case was a big Chevy transit van, parked right on 12th Street, maybe forty yards up the sidewalk from the firm's main entrance. On the driver's side was a small decal, two inches across, which bore the unmistakable insignia of the Central Intelligence Agency, with its white battleshield inscribed with a red compass rose. A thin, white line beneath it confirmed this was an operational vehicle, which may not be disturbed. Every cop in Washington recognized that insignia, and the unspoken message: *If we need you, you'll hear, real quick.*

Inside the van, four operatives sat before a bank of computer screens. Each man wore a slim-line headset and a wire-thin microphone. It was stifling hot in their ops-room, and they wore only T-shirts, shorts, and sneakers. And they all spoke in a completely foreign tongue.

They were hooked into the law firm of Epstein, Myerson, and Marsh, through a clandestine network of telephonic wires and carefully planted listening devices, situated throughout the law offices. It had taken months to set it all up, wire by wire, bug by bug, office cleaner by office cleaner, mole by mole.

But now the system was on stream. And the CIA, which had been subversively, and probably illegally, involved in making it possible, had stepped back. The four men in the van worked for the Mossad, Israel's ruthless Secret Service. They were controlled by the vast Intelligence operation that works from the deep basement of the Israeli embassy, three miles north of the city of Washington.

Cooperation between the CIA and the Mossad began to intensify during the first Gulf War and it had, if anything, grown stronger with each passing year. The Israelis have never dropped their guard against the growling threats of Iran, never forgiven Iraq for unleashing Scud missiles at Tel Aviv in 1991, and never forgiven any Western power that offered even the remotest support to the Palestinians.

Since President Bush declared vicious and open war on terrorists, the Israelis, and especially the Mossad, had stood shoulder-to-shoulder with the United States. No country, no organization has ever been braver or more loyal to Uncle Sam.

The CIA trusts, admires, and uses the Mossad on a daily basis, both in terms of information and direct action. Only rarely is a favor judged too great to be asked or granted. The secretive pact between two of the world's greatest Intelligence Services is binding, one to the other, essentially because their interests are usually identical.

The big blue van represented the explicit wishes of the Mossad, wishes honed over decades of study. That van represented conclusions reached after hundreds of hours pouring over court cases and identifying lawyers who had fought for the freedom of jihadists and terrorists, killers who had attacked, London, New York, Madrid, and countless targets in Israel.

The Mossad were the world experts on the links: those in Afghanistan between al-Qaeda and the Taliban; between Hamas and al-Qaeda; between Iran and al-Qaeda in Iraq; between Hezbollah and Tehran. The men from King Saul Boulevard knew beyond any doubt that there were certain law firms, in the United States, the UK, and Riyadh, that specialized in fighting for the liberties of such men. The Mossad had deep files on all of those law firms. Especially Josh Epstein's.

They had been parked in various locations on 12th Street for weeks, ever since Justice Kennedy's ruling. And with CIA backing, they could find out *anything*—particularly if Epstein's men were representing terrorists who had killed and murdered in Israel.

For a start they could trace every incoming e-mail or instant message to its source, because electronic passage through the Internet leaves a trail, which traces Internet activity from the recipient to the user. And the information can be gathered covertly. These techniques of Internet tracking and tracing enable authorities to pursue and identify anyone and anything. The CIA and the Mossad were masters.

As a point of interest, the FBI was not far behind them with a tracking program called "Carnivore," capable of scanning thousands of e-mails with the speed of light. Which was why Josh Epstein could hardly make a move without a red-alert sounding in faraway King Saul Boulevard. It was easy to understand why bin Laden's high command infinitely preferred camels for transmitting sensitive communications.

Within moments, the men in the blue van were able to record that Epstein had just been appointed to represent, legally, inmates of Guantanamo Bay. And a split-second more to learn that he considered that appointment to be "perfect." This caused four wry smiles of amusement, because everyone in the mobile ops-room knew there was a similar blue van parked in a side street off London Wall, conducting an identical operation on the heavily bugged offices of Howard, Marks, and Cuthbert.

There was one big difference: The Mossad guys in London knew the original fax had come from Saudi Arabia, though not the precise location.

There was however one aspect of the operation that bound both mobile ops teams together, and that was the sudden identification of the two men Josh Epstein was charged with freeing—the hitherto nameless Yousaf Mohammed and Ibrahim Sharif.

The Mossad had their names and sketchy biographies because they had wrung the information out of three other terrorist "suspects" before coldly executing them in Syria shortly after their release. They also knew that these two villains, Ibrahim and Yousaf, had befriended two other inmates inside Guantanamo.

They had descriptions and smuggled satellite photographs of the Guantanamo goalkeeper, Ben al-Turabi, and of his fellow Palestinian killer, Abu Hassan Akbar. Only the Mossad knew for certain that these four men were bound together, and that they were all on the CIA list of fourteen lethally dangerous jihadist hardmen.

Now the men in the blue van fed their new information back to the Mossad cell beneath the Israeli embassy as fingers flashed over the computer keyboards, matching the information, fitting names to the images.

Their expressions were grim. Six people in that embassy basement had friends, acquaintances, or relatives who had been killed as a result of Ben and Abu's crimes—at the Park Hotel in Natanya, and the bar mitzvah in Be'er Shiva. As far as they were concerned, Yousaf, Ibrahim, Ben, and Abu, were all the same, and ought to be executed, not standing before a U.S. Court of Appeals.

Tomorrow morning Josh Epstein's legal jackals would begin circling the Guantanamo compound, making their plans, dreaming up well-rounded reasons explaining why the four prisoners had never done anything wrong in their lives, and how American justice had dealt them the cruelest of hands.

There would be countless reasons why poor Yousaf, brokenhearted Ibrahim, blameless Ben, and innocent Abu should be freed instantly, with massive apologies from the White House, and sufficient reparation money to keep them living like rajahs for the next ten thousand years.

At 4:15 p.m. Joshua Epstein summoned his team into the inner sanctum of his office, the most secure room in the entire building—except for the listening device that had been planted in the base of his desk lamp—a mini-bug powerful enough to re-route

U.S. baseball scores to the International Space Station, never mind the blue van parked outside the front door.

James Myerson, a thirty-five-year-old New Englander from Gloucester, Massachusetts, would head up the operation. Myerson had been made a partner after a sensational two years of almost superhuman billing that averaged seventy-eight hours a week, putting him at close to $40,000 a week, or $2 million annually. The incredible ambition of this unmarried graduate of Yale Law School placed him a cut above his peers, and the most important briefs from the Arab world were always offered first to him.

Most people get better with practice, and with each passing month, James had grown to know and understand the Arab psyche more thoroughly. Over and over, James had gained the release of Guantanamo's prisoners, mostly those held on questionable grounds. These days Arab clients usually requested James, and to Josh Bernstein's mind, this was outstanding. And now James was about to be offered the most important case he had ever argued.

"You must get these guys out of that jail, and send them on their way," Epstein told James after a briefing. "Because that will gain us the gratitude and respect of the entire Middle East. Usual rules, low profile, deep research, and iron-clad arguments."

According to the brief, which had emanated in Saudi Arabia, via Islamabad and Peshawar, his concern was with Yousaf and Ibrahim. Only the listening Mossad knew that his client list would soon double, because al-Qaeda would surely demand the release of the two mountain men, plus their Palestinian best friends, Ben and Abu.

The third man in the room was Tom Renton, the twenty-nine-year-old son of a North Carolina Army colonel and a former judge advocate general who had presided as chief adviser over numerous disciplinary cases where standards had apparently fallen short of those required by the U.S. armed services.

Tom's father was an expert on all forms of military legality, had advised the United Nations, and was considered an authority on the Geneva Conventions and Protocols. He understood the complex ramifications of men fighting in civilian clothes, and the illegality of such actions during which they identified themselves neither to their enemy, nor the public at large. Generally speaking, Colonel Renton handed out short shrift to these international hooligans. Tom had attended a challenging law school in North Carolina, but the one at home in Raleigh was even more so, with the colonel drilling into his son the ramifications of surrender, capture, brutal actions against civilians, treaties, legal definitions of armed forces, guerilla fighters, and prisoners of war and their rights. Tom also learned much about military tribunals, courts-martial, and civilian courts involved in military matters.

But Justice Kennedy had hammered out a brand new set of rules, codes, and standards, and both Tom Renton and James Myerson had been engrossed in them for weeks. Tomorrow morning, subject to the acquisition of the correct papers and visas, both would put their considerable intellects and experiences to the test.

There was a wide smile upon the slightly sweaty face of Joshua Epstein as his boys prepared for the opening assault on the U.S. Court of Appeals for the District of Columbia Circuit, right there on Third Street and Constitution Avenue, one block from the Capitol. He handed them the communiqué from Howard, Marsh, and Cuthbert, and warned the two attorneys there may be difficulty in identifying them since several of the most dangerous inmates of Guantanamo had always refused to reveal their identities.

"I think we may assume, James," he said, "that if the jihadists are prepared to spend millions of dollars to free these men, they will be on Guantanamo's equivalent of Death Row. You may have to interview several men to locate them. Also there may be others in precisely the same predicament as Yousaf and Ibrahim. Do not hesitate to increase the client list to three or four, if you can, because that will mean larger fees in the end. These people have endless money. When it suits them."

Epstein told both men he would immediately open up the channels with the State Department to facilitate a trouble-free entry into Cuba, which could still be quite awkward for American visitors.

"Flights to Havana?" asked Tom. "Same as last time."

"Correct," replied Josh. "Washington to Nassau, then Air Cubana or whatever the hell it's called."

"Of course it's still about five hundred miles to Guantanamo," said James. "What do we do? Get a car and drive it?"

"I think we might do a little better than that," grinned Josh. "We won't get any help from the military who, generally speaking, think we're all crazy. But I'm pretty sure State will fix up a local flight from Havana. Tell you what—leave all that to me. I'll get Charlie on the case. We'll meet back here tomorrow morning 5 a.m. That JetBlue flight takes off at eight o'clock. Dulles."

James and Tom headed for the door, but before they exited, James hesitated, and then asked, "Josh, I know the Pentagon doesn't agree with any of this, but are you sure the State Department will help us get there and get us into the prison? You remember all that bullshit last time. Took us nearly a week."

"Things are very different now," said Josh. "This president is a left-wing guy with a big agenda. Guantanamo is an embarrassment to him. He wants the goodwill of the Middle East and he can't get it while all those wild men are banged up without trial. He'd shut it all down and let 'em all out tomorrow if he could."

"I guess the military won't have that?" said Tom.

"Correct. Right now, we're his main hope. So I'm assuming you guys will get a nice ride into Guantanamo, courtesy of the State Department. No problems."

"Leave it to you, Big Guy," concluded James. "See you at five."

CIA DIRECTOR BOB BIRMINGHAM picked up his secure line and requested the Israeli ambassador. Less than thirty seconds later he heard the polished tones of General David Gavron— "Hello, Bobby, this is a nice surprise," he said. "And I could not begin to guess what you need!"

"Well, I am assuming you know a whole lot more about our business than we do, so I'm just checking in. Anything shake loose?"

"Did it ever. The Arabs just hired Epstein's to get two of the most dangerous jihadists in the world out of Guantanamo. Money, I'd say no object."

"You get their names?"

"We did. Try identifying one Yousaf Mohammed and Ibrahim Sharif. We think we know who they are, but you guys have never gotten even a squeak out of them."

"That assumes you guys could have done a better job, eh?" chuckled the big American.

"No, not really, Bobby. We'd have shot them both. A very long time ago."

As far as Director Birmingham was concerned, Ambassador Gavron was the best Israeli ever appointed to the United States. He was a wounded veteran of the Yom Kippur War in 1973, a tank commander who had fought alongside "Bren" Adan in that monstrous battle in the Sinai, when the fate of Israel had hung in the balance.

The scars of that war had never healed for David Gavron, figuratively and literally. The jagged one, slashed down his right cheek, was the result of an Egyptian shell that had blown him thirty feet through the air. The young Lieutenant Gavron had somehow climbed back into his tank and obeyed the immortal command of the towering Israeli hero, General Bren Adan: *"FOLLOW ME!"* Right fists raised, they flung the Egyptian Army back from whence it came.

David Gavron never got over that brief but murderous war. He and Adan had toured the Bar Lev line where they were still removing thousands of bodies of young Israelis who had fought and died. General Adan had famously broken down and wept at this hot and sandy scene from hell, and Gavron had wept with him.

Even today, Ambassador Gavron visibly stiffened at the merest suggestion that Israel should somehow drop its guard. "We tried that in 1973, on our most holy day of the year," was his standard reply to suggestions of compromise with the Palestinians, or the Syrians, or the Jordanians, or Hezbollah, or Iran, and so forth. "It didn't work terribly well then, and I'm not willing to give it another try."

Bob Birmingham, head of the CIA, was talking to the head of the Mossad, and the most uncompromising member of the Israeli government. They were blood brothers, each of whose concern was the safety of their respective countries. The potential freeing of terrorist madmen like Yousaf and Ibrahim was nothing short of pure anathema to them both.

"David, did you get the feeling Epstein's are moving fast on this?"

"Extremely. They're dispatching Myerson and Renton first thing tomorrow. Dulles to Nassau, then Cuba. You want the flight number?"

"It would probably be judged politically incorrect if we took them out, so I don't think we need that," Bob jokingly remarked and then, more seriously. "David, I can't help noticing there is a rather complacent tone to your voice at your obvious success on 12th Street."

"Complacent, Bobby? Me? Never."

"Just don't forget who fixed the bug in that fat bastard's desk lamp."

Both men laughed, but Bob quickly changed his tone. "Seriously, David. What precisely is the Mossad's position if the U.S. Appeals Court liberates these guys?"

"We don't have a formal position," said Ambassador Gavron. "But you may assume we will not like it. Not one bit. It's like liberating a rabid pit-bull terrier onto a college campus."

"I don't think our guys have given a moment's thought as to where this goddamned Yousaf and his pal are going when they leave the courthouse," replied Birmingham.

"Well, they better start thinking, Bobby. Unless you're planning to unclip their manacles right there on Constitution Avenue and tell 'em to catch a bus back to Afghanistan."

The CIA chief was thoughtful. "The real problem is," he mused, "Most countries don't want them and won't let them in, and the airlines won't fly them without massive security, plus guarantees they will be allowed to disembark at the other end."

"Well, if you let them go free, the Mossad will track them. Because we have to. There are people in Guantanamo who have committed shocking crimes against Israel. Guys on that killer list of fourteen."

"David, right now it's more than my life's worth to start impeding our peace-loving president's wish to unload Guantanamo and everyone in it. But come the day, the day of freedom, when some judge lets these bastards loose, there'll be a backlash in public opinion. And from that moment on, we'll also follow them, to the ends of the earth if necessary, anything to keep them out of the USA."

"And for the rest of us?"

"I think the good ole USA will be in your corner, the way we always have been."

JOSH EPSTEIN SMOOTHED the path to Cuba, just as he said he would. Myerson and Renton would fly privately from Havana down to Guantanamo, where the U.S. Navy, with staggering reluctance, would meet them and drive them into the world's most hated prison camp.

On the way to Dulles they had discussed the overwhelming problem of the terrorists' names. James said flatly, "First we have to identify them. Then get them to understand that they cannot set foot in a U.S. courtroom without a goddamned name and address."

"You sure you want them to be in the courtroom?"

"Hell, yes, Tom. We want them in there, dressed like businessmen, looking like responsible citizens."

"What about the friggin' manacles?"

"The military will insist they wear them. And they're still prisoners of the military. But I still want them in court."

"Well, I guess if they won't reveal their names, there isn't going to be an appeal, so the ball's in their court."

"They either announce their identities or the service chiefs will keep them in prison forever. They don't have any choice." James Myerson had it simply worked out.

"Guess not," said Tom. "And that will apply to any other clients we pick up in there. Josh has got his big, flabby hands in that Arabian pot of gold. And he ain't going to let up on these cases, not now, not ever."

"Yup. He got a green light from Riyadh. And we have to maximize the billing. That list of fourteen in your briefcase. They're the ones to sign up. Then we just bang the court with the ole writ of *habeas corpus*—and stand back while the judiciary falls over backward to please the president."

Two cars behind them on Virginia's Hirst-Brault Expressway, the two agents in the Mossad tracking car were listening intently to the conversation, thanks to the bug Bob Birmingham's agents had so carefully fitted inside the roof of Epstein's office car. As the CIA director himself had so shrewdly observed, the Mossad usually seemed to know a whole lot more about the business of the USA than the USA itself. And right now there was living proof of this, moving at seventy miles per hour along the highway to Dulles, transmitting the details of Epstein's bid to set the villains free.

STAFF SERGEANT BIFF RANSOM was hotter than hell, standing out on the sweltering tarmac of Mariana Grajales Airport. Biff, a thirty-five-year-old native of Dallas, Texas, was a guard supervisor at the Navy base on his second tour of duty in Cuba on behalf of the U.S. military.

For an ex-auto worker in one of the General Motors plants in Detroit, Biff was a very smart man. He deliberately tried to befriend prisoners, sucking up every scrap of information, and then reporting it in carefully written e-mails to his colleagues. Ben al-Turabi was as close as he ever got to a friendship with a prisoner, and even Biff did not know the big goalkeeper's name.

Right now he was waiting for a small, private Cessna bringing a couple of Washington lawyers down to talk to a few prisoners regarding legal appeals to free them. And at this particular moment, he was certain of only three things: one, that the lawyers had no right to be fucking around down here and ought to be in the slammer themselves; two, that Justice Kennedy was plainly out of his mind; and three, that if he, Biff Ransom, had been in charge, both these legal nutcases would have been made to walk the five hundred miles from Havana. Also the sons-of-bitches were an hour late, and Biff had a major interrogation in sixty minutes.

"Jesus Christ," said Biff, peering into the crystalline blue skies. "Where the hell are they?"

He would have been slightly more comfortable waiting in the military airport, but that was where the Navy had drawn the line. They could not refuse to cooperate with the State Department, but they could obstruct the forthcoming legal process by refusing to allow a civilian landing, by Cuban pilots, on the military base. "Obvious security reasons," the signal had read when it arrived in the Pentagon.

Which was why Sergeant Biff was hanging around, sixteen miles north of the camp at the little local airport that served the town of Guantanamo, waiting for the two men he sincerely believed were traitors to the United States of America.

To pass the time, he hummed the famous song made popular by the folk singer Pete Seeger, "Guantanamera!" written way back in the 1940s by Jose Fernandez, for the cheerful little town that had now been off-limits to U.S. military personnel for so long.

Biff had been flown over by an elderly marine helicopter, since it was impossible to drive to town through the vast minefield that surrounds the inland border of the U.S. base. There is no land exit or entrance from the base to Castro's Cuba. The helicopter was now parked on the edge of the runway that was so hot, you could have easily fried an egg on the fuselage. "Let 'em work up a little sweat, right?" muttered Biff to no one in particular. Adding, with a flourish, "Sons-of-bitches."

Another ten minutes and the Cessna came in. Staff Sergeant Ransom met the passengers with military precision. Not knowing whether either Myerson or Renton had ever served as commissioned officers in any branch of the military, he saluted them smartly and led the way to the helo, which was right now doing a passable imitation of a metal incinerator.

"She'll cool off in a minute," said the Sergeant cheerfully, "once we get some air flowing." He was wrong, of course. The helo stayed hot. Ferociously hot, and James and Bobby were soaking wet by the time they reached the compound and landed next to the red-brick wall surrounding the white granite slab that proclaimed in big letters: CAMP JUSTICE—Guantanamo Bay, Cuba.

This guarded the entrance to the high-security courtroom, where both pre-trial hearings and military tribunals had been held for many years. Only very rarely did a man walk free from this building—unless he truly was just a school teacher or a wandering naturalist who somehow managed to be caught up in the general panic of Baghdad, Basra, Kabul, or the Hindu Kush mountains.

Tom Renton's father, as a judge advocate general, had spoken and advised in here, almost always in cases where non-military illegal combatants were trying to plead they were as much regular Army as Hitler's Panzers or the Coldstream Guards. Colonel Renton had both thought and said this was nothing more than pure rubbish, and treated it with the contempt it deserved. He always quoted directly from the Geneva Conventions, instructing the presiding officer that no one could be permitted to hurl a bomb into a supermarket or a hotel, kill several dozen people, and then plead they were some kind of a quasi-explosives officer to a modern-day Islamic General Patton, in order to be treated with honor, like a *bona fide* prisoner of war.

It represented, of course, the most profound irony, that Colonel

Renton, a true-blue old school military lawyer, determined to incarcerate all enemies of the United States, should have an attorney son, right down here in Cuba, trying his best to liberate them.

"Times have changed," was the often-stated view of Renton Junior. His father would undoubtedly have kicked him straight in the ass had he known where young Tom was, which he most definitely did not.

Sergeant Ransom walked the two lawyers straight to the office of the Joint Detention Group commander, Colonel Andy Powell, who greeted them coolly, and offered iced tea. Right now, either overheated lawyer would have settled for iced swamp water, and they sat back to hear the restrictions that would be placed on them during their stay.

"First of all, since we do not judge you are here to act in our best interest," said Colonel Powell, "you will stay in the Guantanamo Hotel. The place is surrounded by bars and restaurants, and I've booked you a couple of rooms. Do not, however, go out looking for a cheap native fuck, or you'll probably go home with mold growing out of your pecker."

James Myerson nodded sagely. Renton laughed. "How do we get to the hotel, sir?"

"Same way you arrived. Helicopter."

"Thank you, sir. We intend to stay two nights if that's okay, and then return directly to Washington."

"No problem. I will have two armed guards accompany you at all times, and escort you into the prison block. I have no doubt the men you wish to see are on our highly dangerous list."

"Sir, can you assist us in identifying them, by name I mean?"

"I cannot deny you that. I am ordered by the Pentagon to grant you total cooperation, and despite my natural distaste for your operation, I will help you as and when I can."

"Thank you, sir," replied Myerson.

"I have a suspicion that you have no idea how dangerous these people are. Stay alert, if one of them should ever get his hands on a knife he would not hesitate to slit your throat. My guards are under orders to shoot to kill should anything like that ever break out."

"And has it ever broken out?" asked Tom.

"From time to time, counselor. But we try to discourage it. I expect you intend to file an application for a writ of *habeas corpus*," continued Colonel Powell. "I should just remind you that application will not get out of here under my signature, unless the prisoners are properly identified, names and addresses."

"And will you wish to have those names and addresses verified by a third party?" asked Renton.

"Damn straight I will," retorted the Colonel. "I don't sign off on fucking ghosts. And they don't leave here until I'm good and ready."

"No sir," replied Myerson.

SHAKIR KHAN had called an emergency meeting in the courtyard of his home in Peshawar. In attendance were Kaiser Rashid, and the somewhat mysterious Sheikh Ali al-Sabah, bin Laden's chief of staff, and the mastermind behind the suspect tape recordings released to al-Jazeera, the Arab television network based in Qatar. It was believed that Sheikh Ali was the only man who knew for certain whether bin Laden was dead or alive.

Shakir Khan himself, on a thousand fronts, was operating in the dark. He knew that Yousaf and Ibrahim were incarcerated in Guantanamo. And he knew that, as a general rule, the policy of the true hard-men of the jihad was to say absolutely nothing to their American captors.

Khan was extremely knowledgeable about the ways of the world. He was self-confident and not easily deceived. He had earned a degree in finance from the University of Karachi and done post-graduate work in politics and economics at Brown University in Rhode Island, where he had relatives.

Khan had guessed that the Americans would use the lack of

names and addresses to detain anyone they so wished. The trouble was, neither Ibrahim nor Yousaf any longer had a proper address, and that could hold up their deportation from the United States for months. Where would they go if they were released? As far as Shakir Khan was concerned, they would have to provide their proper names to the lawyers, and to the Guantanamo Bay military authorities. He would provide two addresses, one for Ibrahim and one for Yousaf, where there would be people in residence who would vouch that the men had indeed lived there before their capture.

There was a "safe house" on Flower Street in Kabul over the border in Afghanistan where Shakir could install a field operator and use it as an address for Ibrahim. Yousaf, who had been born in Pakistan, could have an address on Saddar Road, right here in Peshawar, where there were a million friends.

A house servant brought out a silver tray on which was a selection of delicious smelling *chappli* kebabs, a Pashtun classic, with flat spicy bread and jugs of ice-cold fruit juice. The three men sat on heavy wooden chairs around a stone table and each gave his opinion on how the new addresses should be forwarded to the Washington law firm.

Shakir was always wary of any electronic transfer of information from Peshawar because of the known presence of U.S. agents and Israeli eavesdroppers from the hated Mossad. Sheikh Ali's view was that both addresses should be punched into his cell phone and texted from the high peaks of the Hindu Kush, directly to Riyadh where the clerics would take over and find a track into Washington.

Kaiser Rashid also favored this route, and since none of the three men knew the text-message number of the lawyers on the case, Sheikh Ali was elected to make the transmission. Shakir's private government helicopter would take him home, up and over the Afghan border, later this evening.

Thus, through the quivering communications of cyberspace were the hopes and needs of the jihadist terrorists and Josh Epstein married together.

JAMES MYERSON and Tom Renton awakened in their hotel rooms the following morning at 7 a.m. It was 5 p.m. of the same day in the Afghan mountains, and Sheikh Ali had long since fired in the two addresses to Saudi Arabia. In fact, they were already on both lawyers' phones—*Ibraham, 103 Flower Street, Kabul, Afghanistan. Yousaf, 58, Saddar Road, Peshawar, North West Frontier Province, Pakistan.*

Myerson understood immediately what they were for. Renton was about two beats behind him. "Beautiful," he said to himself. "No fucking ghosts. Proper guys, proper addresses. Okay, Colonel?"

At 7:30 on the button, the four-seater Army helicopter landed on flat, rough ground near the Bano River. Five minutes later James and Tom were once more under the resentful eye of Biff Ransom, who marched them straight into the Camp Five Detention Center where all fourteen of the high-security terrorists were held, almost entirely in solitary confinement.

Cell by cell they were led past the prisoners, asking each in turn if his name was either Yousaf or Ibrahim. Through the wire of the fourth cell, Tom Renton could see the prisoner was still sleeping under his standard-issue blue blanket. His instinct took over and he suddenly snapped out a command in a firm but measured voice: "Ibrahim! Get up right now."

Instantly the prisoner swung around to see who was speaking, and Tom Renton asked Sergeant Biff to open the door to allow him and James to conduct their first interview.

"Ibrahim Sharif, I am here to help you, to take you into an American court, which will grant you your freedom. I am here to get you and Yousaf home. My payment is coming directly from your friends in Afghanistan. But, if you do not confirm your name, I can do nothing for you."

Ibrahim demonstrated all the steel that had kept him sane for almost seven years, but he then began to come around, as the thought began to flicker that this American might be genuine.

But it was the warrior's mindset that saved him. *If I don't take this chance I may not get another. I have to trust him because there is no downside. The worse that can happen is they leave me here. The best is that this bastard can get me out.*

"My name is Ibrahim Sharif," he said, finally. "What now?"

Myerson replied, "We have been appointed to act for you in an appeal, which will be made on your behalf in Washington, DC. But first we must hear your story, and prepare our submissions to the chief justice. You will not be required to give evidence in court, and neither will you be subjected to cross-examination."

Ibrahim shrugged. "Will I be on trial for the crimes I am supposed to have committed?"

"Not as such. We will protest your continued incarceration without trial. We are seeking to overturn the verdict of the military tribunal, which decided you had indeed made the bomb that had blown up and killed a truckload of fifteen U.S. Marines and two Navy SEALs in Kabul."

"They had no proof," growled Ibrahim.

"And did you commit the crime?"

"No. I have always been innocent. I've hardly ever been in Kabul."

"Do the Americans have your documents, passports, credit cards, and such?"

"I have no documents."

"What evidence is there you were anywhere near the exploded truck?"

"I don't know. It was never shown to me."

"Were you represented at the tribunal when they heard your case?"

"No. I was all alone. Just Americans, judges, and officers. And in the end they said I should serve a sentence right here in Guantanamo for the rest of my life."

"Where did they arrest you? Obviously not in Kabul."

"No. I was in my home village up in the mountains, hundreds of miles away. They just charged in and took me prisoner."

"Did they take anyone else?"

"Yes. My friend, Yousaf Mohammed."

"Is he a terrorist? A jihadist or some kind of freedom fighter for al-Qaeda or the Taliban?"

"Yousaf! He couldn't fight his own grandma. But they beat him around and then put him in the helicopter with me. They shipped us both together, right here in Guantanamo."

"Did they find evidence against you in your home village?"

"Just a few boxes of dynamite. The Taliban guys leave explosives around all over the place. I've never even touched dynamite. I'd never even been in the house where they found it."

"Where's Yousaf now?"

"He's three doors down from me."

"Was there evidence to convict him of anything."

"I don't know. He had a separate tribunal. Just found him guilty of something. Same as me. Locked him up for life."

"Ibrahim. From now on, we are your lawyers. We're being paid to get you home." Tom handed him a piece of paper on which was written the Kabul address. "This is where you live," he said quietly, out of earshot of the guards. "You'll need that for the court papers. Meantime, we'll see you later. Right now it's important for us to talk to Yousaf."

Ibrahim took the paper and nodded. Biff Ransom unlocked the cell door, bolted it shut again from the outside, and led the way down to the cell occupied by Yousaf Mohammed.

James Myerson could see the lean, hook-nosed murderer standing up at the far end of his cell, and the mere presence of the man made him uneasy. He decided to ask his preliminary questions from the central corridor, just to establish identity and charges.

Yousaf had heard the talking in Ibrahim's cell and had already figured he might as well cooperate. Nothing else could happen to him, nothing much worse than the things that already had. Like his al-Qaeda buddy, there seemed to be an upside, with no downside.

"Are you Yousaf Mohammed?" asked Tom Renton through the wire.

"I am."

"Then take a look at this piece of paper and tell me if you recognize the address."

Yousaf looked at Tom, who smiled and surreptitiously nodded, at the same time signaling friendship and urgency.

Yousaf replied, quick as a flash, "Yessir. That's where I live. In Peshawar, North West Frontier Province."

The trained mind, which had won the Pakistani a degree in chemical engineering, and then gained him entry into the University of London, was still functioning. Almost as well as the intuition that had saved him from death over and over.

James Myerson turned to Staff Sergeant Biff and requested the cell door be opened. Biff obliged and the two armed guards went in first, rifles raised. Degree or no degree, Yousaf's formidable reputation had preceded him into this place. No chances were taken on him, neither would the regime ever relax their unshakeable belief that Yousaf was a terrorist, a killer, a bomb maker, guilty of mass murder in Baghdad, Iraq, and had assassinated a senior U.S. diplomat.

There had been nights when Yousaf had hallucinated and then muttered to himself, partly as a result of extreme sleep deprivation, and partly due to the administration of tranquilizers designed to keep him calm. On these nights, Sergeant Ransom would walk softly in his desert combat boots and stand outside in the corridor with an Arabic interpreter, trying to pick up the gist of Yousaf's rantings as they strained their ears in the silence of the sweltering hot night.

They have ransacked our land of its riches, plundered our oil fields, killed our people. There will be blood, much more blood. America will bleed again as they did before. I will never put down my sword until the Infidel dies. Allah is great. There is no other God but Allah, and death to the Infidel. Let The Sheikh and his followers smash the Americans again and again. . . . Let the towers fall and the blood flow because in the end we must win. Death to the Infidel. Death I say, whatever the cost.

They entered the cell, right behind the guards. The door was slammed shut behind them. Yousaf, standing up now, faced them from the back of the cell, and James asked him if he was prepared to answer his questions. Once more he confirmed that he and his colleague were there to help Yousaf gain his freedom, and that they were in the pay of the Saudi clerics.

The man who had, without question, committed every one of the crimes of which he was accused, had nothing to lose. In truth, the Americans did not know the half of it. Yousaf had been involved in the production of possibly fifty car bombs in the gloomy rubble-strewn cellars of Northern Baghdad.

He had killed and maimed dozens of young U.S. combat troops. He had been a sniper, an assassin, and a rocket operator. Up in the Hindu Kush, he'd been one of al-Qaeda's top battle technicians, planning assaults on small groups of U.S. special forces. Twice he had slammed a Stinger missile into U.S. helicopters and brought them both down with no survivors.

For two bits, Biff Ransom would have shot him right then and there. James Myerson, however, whose principal duty was to keep the Epstein billing clock running hard, was more kindly disposed toward his bearded meal-ticket.

"Yousaf," he said, "I have to ask you this. Are you guilty of any of the crimes with which you have been charged?"

"No, I am not," replied the terrorist. "They have always said I shot some American official and bombed a hotel in Baghdad. I've never even been to Iraq. I've always lived in Pakistan, around the Swat Valley, or Peshawar, near the border."

"Papers? Documents?" asked James. "Passport, credit cards?"

"I've never had a passport. I never left the area. And I'm too poor to have a credit card. I'm just a farmer."

Biff rolled his eyes heavenward. James pressed on. "Did you live in the village where you were arrested?"

"No. I was just visiting Ibrahim. You don't need passports in the mountains. There's no checks. It's hard to know whether you are in Afghanistan or Pakistan."

James nodded. "Did the military tribunal find you guilty of any crimes?"

"I think so. But I didn't know what they were saying. I heard the officer recommend that I could never be let out of here. And I've been here ever since."

"Have you had contact with your family?"

"I've lost touch. I'm alone now."

At this point Biff Ransom could restrain himself no longer. "Speaks pretty good English for a poor mountain farmer. Guys who've never been out of the fucking peach groves."

"I imagine there's a lot of English spoken in a city like Peshawar," replied Tom Renton patiently. "He could have learned. The Brits ruled the place for generations, right?"

"Have you read the tribunal report on this guy and his pal?"

"Not yet."

"May I ask you a couple of questions?"

"Sure, Staff Sergeant, go right ahead."

"Do you think we're all stupid? Do you think it was some kind of a fluke that the SEALs went in and hauled out a couple of goatherders who just happened to speak fluent English in one of the most remote, backward, and illiterate areas in the fucking universe?"

"Staff Sergeant," interjected James, "We can't answer that. We have no idea whether it was a fluke or not. And, I suggest, neither do you."

"Just checking. Sir," answered Biff, who was appalled, as ever, at the dogged literal minds of visiting lawyers, men who probably earned more in a year than he would in a lifetime.

"Yousaf," said James quietly, "I am going to review the evidence of your case. And then I am going to file an application in Washington for a legal appeal on your behalf. I anticipate you may be free to return to Pakistan within four months. Maybe sooner."

"Thank you, sir," said Yousaf, trying to affect a facial expression that was both grateful and ingenuous.

"And just one more thing," said James quietly, "Do you have any other friends in here who might also be released under the same system we are using for you? That's the obvious illegality of locking people up without trial for the rest of their lives, even though there's no proof of guilt."

"Ibrahim and I have two friends in here. Number Eleven and Number Fifteen. They are innocent and have never been to a proper courtroom, just the one full of military officers."

"I need to know their names," said James, "Otherwise we can do nothing."

"I don't think they have ever revealed their names," said Yousaf. "And they have no documents. Like me."

"Then I guess they'll have to stay right here," said Tom.

"Sir," replied Yousaf, "the man in cell number eleven is Ben al-Turabi. Number fifteen is Abu Hassan Akbar."

"What were they charged with?"

"I don't know if they were ever charged. They're both just here, forever. Ben was only a student when he arrived."

"Yeah, and I'm the quarterback for the Cowboys," growled Biff.

James Myerson grinned good-naturedly, and said, "I wonder, Staff Sergeant, whether you could take us along the corridor to visit Mr. al-Turabi and Mr. Akbar."

"No problem."

By now the word had whipped around Camp Five Detention Center that two hotshot lawyers from Washington were in Guantanamo with a brief to secure the release of jihadist prisoners. The Great Osama had come through at last, with heavy sums of money and top attorneys to speak for the Muslim warriors.

By the time Myerson and Renton reached al-Turabi's tiny cell, the excitement in the air was intense.

"Welcome to my humble world," beamed Ben.

Renton formalized his identity, confirming Ben's name, and that he had been briefly accused by the tribunal of having committed various crimes against humanity before his arrest in the mountains.

But that was several years ago and since then Ben had been held without charge or trial.

The two lawyers went through the same broad-brush procedures with both Ben and Abu Hassan Akbar, who strongly denied he had ever fired a rocket or a bomb at anyone, did not know how to make one, and had been in Baghdad helping the Red Cross when he was arrested.

"They mistake me for very bad men," he assured them.

"Holy Shit," breathed Staff Sergeant Ransom.

Akbar told Renton and Myerson there had been lawyers here before to try to obtain his release but nothing had worked. The military had neither tried nor released him. He had almost given up hope of justice.

James Myerson told him there was now hope, since Akbar could not be denied his day in court, and it would be a civilian court at that, presided over by a civilian judge. He and his colleague would argue the appeal, and there was a real chance of freedom for Abu Hassan.

Cutting short the interviews, James and Tom established that both the prisoners had been born in Gaza City and had cut their teeth with Yasser Arafat's terrorists. They told both men they would be furnished with proper addresses, and from now on would use their proper names.

The lawyers then retired to the offices of Colonel Andy Powell to request access to the files on Ibrahim, Yousaf, Ben, and Abu Hassan. This was formally granted, but the most difficult part came when the files were produced. These four men were accused with some of the most shocking crimes of modern times, particularly Akbar, whom Tom remembered "had killed all those kids at the Be'er Shiva bar mitzvah."

Even the ruthless James was slightly shaken by the level of criminal he was being asked to liberate. But the image of Josh Epstein stood stark before him, and he made his copies, studied the documents, and resolved to keep that billing clock ticking above 12th Street, no matter what.

THEY ARRIVED BACK in Washington the following evening and began work immediately on filing for the writ of *habeas corpus*. When the documents were completed, they were dispatched to the Pentagon and on to Guantanamo for the signatures of all four prisoners, plus those of the Joint Detention Group commander, who was required to sign off on the releases of the detainees.

The case was filed and allocated a slot on the appeals court calendar for Monday morning, February 19, coming before Chief Judge Stanford Osborne, who would be assisted in his deliberations by Judge Art Cameron and Judge Merrick Rosser. These details were expedited with zero delays.

The appeal would be heard in Court 11, on the fourth floor of the E. Barrett Prettyman Courthouse, named for the brilliant Truman-appointed chief judge, the man who was selected to decide whether Frances Gary Powers had handled himself correctly after his U-2 spy plane was shot down over the Soviet Union in 1962.

This monumental courthouse also contained judicial officers and staff, the probation office, the circuit library, and circuit executives offices, all guarded by squads of hard-eyed U.S. marshals. It is a cathedral to the majesty of American law, and on February 19, within its massive gray concrete walls, a ruling would be made upon a truly stunning application for the release of dangerous men. It was an appeal that was in danger of causing Harry Truman to rise up in fury from his grave in Jackson County, Missouri.

Proceedings were conducted in the lowest possible key. The left-wing bias of the United States media ensured the minimum was written about the appeal, and neither did the op-ed pages spend much time discussing the wisdom of granting these astonishing human rights to foreign terrorists whom the military believed were guilty of murder, mayhem, and other dreadful crimes against the United States, who ought not to be alive, never mind freed.

But the law of the land had been decreed. Justice Kennedy had decided that the moral and fair standards of justice practiced for centuries by the United States ought not to be put on hold just because a bunch of Middle Eastern maniacs were running around killing people. America's rules of just and equitable behavior must be seen to be enacted at all times. Most of the judges believed that, and the president really believed it. Which was why, at 0730 on the morning of February 19, a military night flight from Guantanamo Bay, Cuba, touched down lightly at Andrews Air Force Base northeast of Washington, DC.

Disembarking, still in manacles, surrounded by armed Army guards, were the four terrorist killers, Ibrahim Sharif, Yousaf Mohammed, Ben al-Turabi, and Abu Hassan Akbar. A military prison van awaited them, and they were taken immediately to 12th Street for a final meeting with their lawyers.

At 0943 they were led to the bank of elevators in the great appeals court building on Constitution Avenue, and from there they were escorted up to the courtroom on the fourth floor.

They would not be permitted to speak during the hearing. The petitioning lawyer, James Myerson, would plead his case for the release of the men, and the military, formally objecting, would be granted just five minutes to make their case. Their view was simply stated, that Ibrahaim, Yousaf, Ben, and Abu should be returned to Guantanamo and locked up immediately, with their cell keys hurled into the sprawling minefield to the north of the compound. Biff Ransom would probably have gone one step further.

Cases such as this were essentially unknown territory. There was, as yet, no tried and tested formula. An appeal was not a trial. There would be no witnesses. And each side was permitted two lawyers maximum. In this instance, only one would speak for each side.

The judges had already read submissions from each side, and accepted the writ of *habeas corpus*. The format for the hearing had been worked out only on the previous evening by the clerk to the court, and he acquiesced to the request by James Myerson that the appeals by the four petitioners should be heard jointly and severally, rather than in four separate hearings.

There were, however, many people occupying the seats behind

the hub of the courtroom, and the entire fourth floor was in the iron-grip of the U.S. marshals, off limits to the public, out-of-bounds even to the legal profession.

Inside Court 11, there were probably a dozen military officers, three politicians, and six members of the CIA. The four petitioners, smartly dressed in jackets and ties but still manacled, were seated with armed Army guards both between them and on the flanks.

The most unlikely group in the entire courtroom were four anonymous representatives from the Israeli embassy, and you needed to be a real insider to understand the purpose of their attendance—that Israel wanted Ben al-Turabi and Abu Hassan at least as badly as the Navy SEALs wanted Ibrahim Sharif and Yousaf Mohammed.

If necessary the Mossad was quite prepared to take over and haul them off to Israel for execution. What terrified them was this American judge was about to liberate Ben and Abu—liberate the two men who had killed and maimed so many people in two of the worst atrocities ever committed in Israel. The Mossad's oft-stated motto is, *We Never Forget*. The unwritten one is, *We Never Forgive*.

Captain Al Surprenant, the top lawyer for the Navy in the San Diego base, had flown in the previous day in company with three senior SPECWARCOM commanders.

The SEALs had spilled a lot of blood bringing down men like Ibraham and his buddies, and each one of the U.S. Special Forces in that courtroom was hoping the steely, silver-tongued resolve of Commander Surprenant would compel the judges to see reason. Military reason, that is, which is not always the same as civilian reason.

"All Rise!" The court officer called the room to order as Judge Stanford Osborne led the justices in. All the principal figures in the appeal were familiar with the facts.

And the justices understood the enormous difficulty for the military to provide proof, *civilian court proof*, that these obvious scoundrels who were petitioning had indeed committed the crimes of which they had never really been accused.

That of course was not the issue. Could it be fair and reasonable for the United States to act like some banana republic and lock up these men, indefinitely, without trial, without reasonable proof of guilt, and without appeal to anyone? They were, after all, members of the human race.

James Myerson was invited to begin, and he stood before the court and argued that, despite the beliefs of the military, there were massive issues here about the burden of proof. "Maybe these men had committed crimes," he said. "But no one saw them. No one bore witness to anything. And each of these men swears by his God that he is innocent.

"I am not here to protest their innocence. I am here to plead that never, in all the annals of United States law, from the Founding Fathers to the twenty-first century, has it been acceptable, has it been regarded as legal, fair, or even reasonable, for a court in the United States of America to declare that it does not care one way or another whether the accused are guilty or not.

"That's not America, your Honor. That's Stalin. That's Pol Pot or whatever the hell his name was. That's a banana republic. Not us. No, sir, not us at all. And whatever the rights and wrongs, these men have spent many years of pure hell in one of the cruelest prison camps in the Western world.

"And with every passing month, while they endured forms of torture and deprivation, their very presence on that Godforsaken outpost of U.S. civilization has tarnished and dishonored our great nation. It has sullied us, reduced our reputation in the world, poisoned opinion against us.

"Your honor, this cannot be right. And I beseech you to end this most terrible stain on the name of American justice. I'm imploring you to free these four men, allow them to return home, and help the world to understand that we are indeed the bright City on the Hill, the shining hope of the human race. That we are Americans, to whom a lack of fair play is nothing less than abhorrent."

Myerson sat down next to Renton, who subtly patted him on the shoulder. Judge Osborne nodded his appreciation of the manner in which Myerson had delivered his case. And the clerk signaled for Captain Surprenant to proceed with the motion for the military.

The Navy attorney stood and briefly reminded the justices that the U.S. military had tracked and grabbed Ibrahim Sharif from the remotest of Afghani mountain villages, where Yousaf Mohammed was also hiding out. There was plainly no doubt that these men were bomb makers. With assistance from another Middle Eastern Intelligence Service, they had been identified with no reasonable doubts. Well, almost.

The other two were high on the list of Israel's most wanted mass murders, and they were both from Gaza City. "I understand," said the captain, "that the evidence was not one hundred percent decisive, and that it was, in a sense, circumstantial. But no one would dispute it was ninety-eight percent decisive. Circumstantial or not."

He outlined the crimes and the continuing dangers posed by such men. The scale of the mayhem that might break out if such men were free to return to the lands where they plotted and launched the 9/11 attacks.

"Your Honors," he continued, "these men are disciples of Osama bin Laden. All of them are members of the most sinister terror groups in the Middle East. The world has changed. These men do not fight in uniform, they do not represent Nation States. They are secretive, underhanded killers, who strike indiscriminately at both military and civilian targets. They have loyalty only to fellow jihadists. They observe no national borders. No nation even recognizes their organizations, with the exception of the pariahs of Iran and the West Bank.

"There are no standards in the world today by which such men can be judged. They render, by their own actions, the Geneva conventions and protocols obsolete. I am not pleading for them to remain in jail to justify some ephemeral and hopelessly outdated sense of fair play. There is no fair play left in our fight against terrorism. That ended around 9 a.m. on a Tuesday morning in September 2001.

"Your Honors, I cannot believe you are prepared to grant this appeal, to liberate these men who will surely come at us again. Every military expert in the country understands that they cannot, they must not, be freed to fight again. We might be the City on the Hill, the beacon of freedom and fairness, but those four men, the ones in manacles in this courtroom, would surely flatten it, given even a semblance of a chance. I ask their appeal be denied."

The clerk immediately declared a recess for the judges to retire to consider their verdict. A timeframe that would, unusually, be announced within the hour.

It was soon announced that the decision would be at 3 p.m., and when it came, the entire law enforcement and security forces of the United States of America understood that this was the appeal that was decided before it was heard.

"We have listened to the arguments," the judge said. "And we have studied the evidence exhaustively. We are unanimously drawn to the truth that the moral standards of the United States of America are being examined here, and that Captain Surprenant offered the most compelling case to cast them aside.

"However this great nation's sense and reputation for what is right, respectable, and fair, must always be paramount. Otherwise, we should perhaps ask ourselves, who indeed are we? But it was with some misgivings that we nonetheless reached an irrevocable decision.

"We could not bring ourselves to abandon the light that has guided this nation for so long—the light carried down the centuries, and first illuminated by Adams, Jefferson, and Franklin. The simple light of fairness, for everyone.

"That is the most important thing in all the world for us. And holding men in endless incarceration without even a trial, without giving them a chance, crosses that line, and it takes us into the darkness, which lies on the other side of decency.

"Therefore this court finds unanimously for the petitioners. The appeal is granted. Ibrahim Sharif, Yousaf Mohammed, Ben al-Turabi, and Abu Hassan Akbar, you are freed this day by the Court of the United States of America to go about your lawful business."

The words of Judge Stanford Osborne seemed to echo throughout the corridors of the Pentagon, ringing through the grim offices of the CIA and the FBI. Republicans were stunned, and a new era of caution began to waft through the ranks of the stone-faced Navy SEALs training in Coronado.

One of the SPECWARCOM commanders jolted back in his seat, as if he had been shot. And all four of the men from the Israeli embassy instantly stood up and left the courtroom.

3

NEWS OF THE JUDGMENT in Court 11 ripped around the nation. The Army major in charge of the four men's security hit the cell-phone line to the Pentagon and asked blandly, "What do I do now? Unclip the manacles, say goodbye, and wait for something to blow?"

An Army colonel on the other end suffered a complete collapse of his sense of humor, and growled, "Keep them under DC Superior Court control. Get 'em back in the prison van.

"Then take them direct to the U.S. marshals' cell block, down in the basement of 500 Indiana Avenue, Washington Northwest. They got a big holding pen in there. And don't let 'em out 'til we fix flights out of this country. We don't want 'em back."

CIA Chief Birmingham, with three of his senior officials, stared in horror at the CNN newsscreen. It seemed like every phone in Langley was ringing. What the hell was going to happen?

Birmingham hit the line to the State Department, direct to the secretary's office.

The call was only just on the south side of panic.

"Jesus Christ! They've got to go somewhere."

"Pakistan's the most likely country, but they don't have a flight out of here until tomorrow."

"Well, get 'em to France."

"Unescorted?"

"Hell, no!"

"Someone better call Sarkozy."

"We'll put four agents on the plane."

"Same guys to track 'em onward to Karachi?"

"No. We'll change the guard at Charles de Gaulle."

"Then what? Chase 'em into the fucking Himalayas!"

"No, but we can't let 'em loose."

The message came through to Langley that the four terrorists were being transferred to the cells in Indiana Avenue. From that point on, State, the CIA, and the Pentagon moved quickly and aggressively.

"We need four clear rows in coach class. Then you'll have to throw people off the flight. You want to go on flying in and out of the USA, you'll clear those four rows. If I have to I'll have the president call Sarkozy right now."

The Air France agent finally understood that this had nothing to do with tickets, and bookings, and cancellations. Right here was something that looked like a national emergency. And whatever it was these lunatics from the American government wanted, it was obvious they were going to get it. The ticket agent told the CIA official that someone would be back within a few minutes with detailed seat allocations for the flight to Paris.

Bob Birmingham himself put in a call to an old friend, General Michel Jobert, commander-in-chief of the French equivalent of the U.S. Navy SEALs. General Jobert's headquarters was in the outer suburbs of Paris in Taverny, home of France's Commandement des Operations Speciale (COS).

Jobert answered his private telephone and smiled at the sudden sound of the voice of his old friend and golfing partner Bob Birmingham, who was, so far as Michel was concerned, the most useful man in the United States. "*Bon jour, mon vieux!*" he exclaimed.

"Hey, Michel," replied the CIA boss. "We need to talk. The U.S. Court of Appeals just liberated all four of those killers from Guantanamo . . . "

"I know," interrupted the General.

"You do? It only happened five minutes ago."

"I knew five minutes ago."

"I should have guessed. But anyway, we now have the problem of getting these guys out of the USA. They're going to Pakistan, Dulles to Paris, Air France, then Paris to Karachi, Pakistan International Airlines."

"And you want me to organize CDG security."

"Well, I know your slightly hysterical government will take more notice of you than anyone else."

"You will have an escort on board from Washington to France?"

"Yes, two U.S. marshals, and two of my top guys."

"Will you keep the prisoners in handcuffs?"

"Well, that's the point. I don't think we can, not on a foreign airline in international airspace."

"Well, why not use a U.S. airline as far as France? That way you can do what you like."

"So can you . . . "

"I'm sorry?"

"French customs or immigration could refuse to let them step out onto French soil—then they'd have to come right back to the USA, on their American aircraft, and for us, that is not an option."

"You mean if they arrive on Air France, we really have to let them out, and then get them back on a foreign airline as fast as possible?"

"Correct. And it has to be PIA because Pakistan is the only nation, so far, which has agreed to accept them."

"A little cooperation, eh? And the problem goes away."

"Precisely. But we shall ask for your help in boarding four CIA men on PIA to track the prisoners into Karachi. We'd like to exchange agents at Charles de Gaulle. The first four will return immediately to the United States."

"Bobby, I will take care of it. I'll send you an e-mail with a couple of contact phone numbers. But it's all on one condition . . ."

"Shoot," snapped Birmingham.

"You're not going to assassinate these characters on French soil, nor will you blow up the aircraft?"

"You have my word."

SOMBRE "COUNCILS OF WAR" were regular in the Mossad's situation room in the basement of the Israeli embassy on International Drive, Washington NW—as regular as Friday evening prayers for the Shabbat or Rosh Hashanah. There was always something, an atrocity, a Muslim rally or demonstration, hundreds of fanatics pledging loudly their support for Hamas or Hezbollah.

Sometimes the threat was worse. Sometimes, like tonight, even Ambassador Gavron was in attendance. To the nine men gathered informally in this nuclear bomb–proof room, sipping tea, the U.S. courts had done the unthinkable. Judge Osborne and his colleagues had liberated two of the worst mass murderers in Israel's recent history.

These men were very close to being mercenaries, except they killed not for money, but for their God, which made them maniacs rather than professionals. The Mossad knew them both to be members of the hated Soldiers of the Companions of God, an operation born of madmen who believed Hamas was neither tough enough, nor sufficiently effective, to batter a surrender out of Israel.

Both Ben and Abu had fought Palestine's Holy War and joined

the war being conducted by Osama bin Laden. They were also happy to fight and kill for the Taliban, as comrades-in-arms in the Hindu Kush. This cross-pollination of fighters between jihadist groups these days gave the Mossad the chills, as these highly dangerous commanders moved from Baghdad, to Gaza, and then Kabul.

And, in their judgment, Ben and Abu were among the most worrying, having been caught for their crimes thousands of miles apart, and yet plainly operating on the same side, striking quite separately against Israeli civilians.

"Of course," said Ambassador Gavron, "the problem is the American lawyers. If they refused to represent these scum, this would never have happened."

"Well, if they didn't, surely the sheikhs would simply bring in foreign lawyers?"

"They can't," retorted Gavron. "To try a case in New York you have to be a member of the New York Bar. Same with Washington or anywhere else. They would always need American attorneys—especially to file for a writ of *habeas corpus* to be heard in a Washington circuit courtroom."

"Can't we get some Republican Senator to make it illegal for a U.S. attorney to represent a foreigner accused by the U.S. military of crimes against the State?"

"Probably could've done it if President Reagan was in the White House," replied the ambassador, "or President Bush. But not with this guy. He *wants* these guys freed and sent home because he wants the Middle East to love him when he shuts down Guantanamo."

"You mean we have to just sit here and watch these murderers being liberated by U.S. judges because of powerful arguments assembled by U.S. lawyers."

"Well stated," said the ambassador. "That's exactly what I mean."

"Unless of course we were able to discourage them ourselves," interjected Israel's military attaché, a cousin of the beloved former prime minister, General Arik Sharon. "Perhaps somehow we should let them know there are powerful world forces that do not approve of their antics in either the prison camp or the courtroom."

"They already know that," said David Gavron. "But the money for their services is enormous. And there have been unscrupulous lawyers since time began."

There was a sudden silence in the room, until Itzak Steiner, the youngest of the Mossad cultural attachés spoke up and ventured, "That summation by James Myerson blew the U.S. Navy's attorney out of the water. That speech made it easy for the judge to find for the petitioners. All that stuff about decency and the American sense of fair play. If he had not done that . . ."

"It may not have gone through," said Gavron. "I agree with you."

THE LIGHTS BURNED late into the night at the offices of Epstein, Myerson, and Marsh. Josh Epstein was there as midnight approached. James Myerson and Tom Renton were drinking cups of coffee with him, waiting for word, any word from the underground cell block at 500 Indiana Avenue. And all the while, the other clock ticked on at three thousand dollars an hour.

The marshals had denied them access to the holding pen under the cast-iron excuse of "national security," but they had given their word that all four of the petitioners would be on Air France's morning flight to Charles de Gaulle. This was, of course, news of a mixed blessing, because it meant the billing clock was running down fast.

Midnight came and went. The billing clock bleeped its special little digital bleep to signify the start of a new day, and the steady accumulation of a new pile of Saudi riyals. That bleep would be the last sound they ever heard, however, as just then, a truly stupendous explosion blew 296 12th Street right off the face of the earth.

It began in the basement and blasted upward, slamming the building to smithereens, floor by floor, before detonating yet again up near the roof and hurling concrete hundreds of feet into the air.

It was an explosion sufficiently powerful to have almost knocked down the Capitol building.

Shattered gas mains lit up the street like the Fourth of July. And yet there was something professional about the blast. It was narrow, shaped, causing mostly superficial damage to the adjoining buildings, but blowing its target construction to hell and back, essentially vaporizing it.

The final act on this night of massive destruction took place in the parking lot, when a colossal hunk of masonry came hurtling down from the stratosphere, and smashed straight through the dark blue roof of Josh Epstein's Bentley. The bodies of Josh Epstein, James Myerson, and Tom Renton were never found. Indeed it was three days before it was definitely established that they had been in the building at all. No one had even noticed the big Mossad transit van leaving the area at around 11:45 p.m.

And, on the other side of the Atlantic, most of London was asleep at approximately seven minutes after 5 a.m. (local), when an entire office block on London Wall was blown to high heaven in another gigantic explosion, which obliterated the law offices of Howard, Marks, and Cuthbert.

But no one died, and there were no injuries on the deserted winter streets of England's capital. The incident seemed isolated, pointless, and utterly random. Nothing appeared to connect the London explosion and the one in Washington, and all evidence had been incinerated. There was not a single document from either law firm that would cast light upon the motives for the destruction.

Meanwhile a large reception party gathered at 6 a.m. at Dulles Airport to await the arrival of Ibrahim, Yousaf, Ben, and Abu Hassan. Bob Birmingham was there in company with a dozen CIA personnel, two of whom would travel on the Air France flight to Paris. Two of the U.S. marshals escorting the four terrorists to the airport would also travel as far as the French capital.

There was a group of six officials from the State Department that had provided documentation for the terrorists—tickets, temporary passports with identification, plus cash, Pakistani rupees. The idea was to eliminate mistakes and unforeseen hitches.

There were several military personnel, four officers from the Pentagon, plus a platoon of armed U.S. Navy SEALs, flown in from Virginia Beach, just in case someone tried something, well, unusual.

General Jobert had plainly put a rocket underneath Air France and the French government. The airline was insisting the four terrorists remain handcuffed, and three French security guards from the Washington embassy were also booked on the flight. The changing of the guard at Charles de Gaulle was formally in place. The French had insisted and Pakistani Airlines cooperated fully.

Just after 7:30, the black prison van from the U.S. marshals' building arrived under police escort and was driven directly to the base of a stairway leading to the rear door of the gleaming white Boeing 777-300 jetliner. The prisoners were led out and their ankle manacles removed. State officials handed them each a brown envelope with their cash and documents, and the CIA men led the way up the staircase.

There were four complete rows, right at the rear of the aircraft, set aside for the U.S. government group. A blue curtain had been drawn across the area. The four terrorists were ordered into separate rows, and then manacled to the armrest. One guard would sit with each man. Already Ben al-Turabi was joshing and laughing with his man, and, to an extent, so was Ibrahim. The other two remained sullen, their eyes filled with hatred and loathing just as they had been for five long years.

At this point the regular passengers were boarded, and finally the huge doors were closed, and the Boeing taxied down to the end of the runway for its top-priority take-off.

Bob Birmingham and his team waited on the hard top and watched the plane rise into the overcast skies. Within moments, it was out of sight. There should have been a brief interlude of pure relief, but there was only a suspended atmosphere of profound foreboding. *What now? Where will these guys end up? And how do we prevent them from striking at us again? And perhaps again?*

As far as the SEAL commanders were concerned, there was only one solution to that, and the CIA men agreed completely. But that solution was unmentionable, either in public or in private.

THE CIA TOP BRASS, with their inviolate connections to paramilitary operations in the more troubled parts of the globe, needed to speak, to make contacts, and discuss the ubiquitous worry of the four freed killers.

There was a certain amount of criticism in Washington surrounding the recent promotion of thirty-five-year-old Jimmy Ramshawe, a career Intelligence officer, to the director's chair at the National Security Agency. Jimmy had been moved to the Fort Meade complex several years ago, and his rise had been meteoric, thanks mainly to a God-given capacity to bring even the most elusive issues to the ground. He spent more time lost in thought than rampaging around the various ops rooms, more time pondering than speaking, and much more time drawing correct, cast-iron conclusions than making wild speculations.

He was every Intelligence officer's ultimate alter-ego, a natural, with a gift for examining wide-ranging international conundrums. American-born to Australian Naval and diplomatic parents, Jimmy had never lost his Aussie way of speaking. His office was, according to the recently retired ex-NSA Chief Admiral Arnold Morgan, where the "Man from Snowy River meets James Bond."

With the retirement of Admiral George Morris, the service chiefs had recommended almost unanimously that Commander Ramshawe be given his shot in the Big Chair, mostly because if he was passed over and left the agency, it would take about ten years for anyone else to catch up.

The young Aussie American had a colorful background. His father had been an admiral in the Australian Navy, who had risen to military attaché in the Washington embassy, and became a friend of Admiral Arnold Morgan.

The tall, lanky, young James had been schooled in Connecticut, where he became an outstanding baseball pitcher, later following in his father's footsteps and enrolling in the Naval Academy in Annapolis. From that point, he began to excel. His stratospheric IQ and capacity for the most infinitesimal detail made him a warship commander in the making. In a way, it was his brain that set him apart, and his brain that tied him up. One of his instructors famously observed, "Ramshawe could end up a second Captain Queeg, counting the fucking strawberries while all hell was breaking out."

But the U.S. Navy is masterful at channeling talented people, and it swiftly noticed that Ramshawe's meticulous and tireless approach to his academic work were the God-given natural talents of an Intelligence officer.

Jimmy was furious because he saw himself as a potential battle commander, not, as he phrased it, "Fucking George Smiley, friggin' around at that bloody Kremlin in the middle of Maryland, with a bunch of right weirdos."

But the Navy was not joking. A couple of very senior admirals had a surreptitious word with his father, and the Selection Boards offered James a rare three-year tour of duty at Fort Meade, with a gilt-edged promise that if he hated it, his career would be reviewed with the intention of sending him to sea with the rank of Lt. Commander. Ramshawe senior told his son he would be crazy to turn that down, and Jimmy duly reported to the National Security Agency, where it took the Director Admiral George Morris only two months to recognize him as probably the best young Intelligence officer he'd ever met.

Ramshawe had just been slotted into the world's largest and most powerful Intelligence agency: a gigantic global listening center, fluent in ninety-five different languages, plus every possible dialect of Arabic, including Iraqi, Libyan, Syrian, Saudi, Jordanian, and Modern Standard Arabic.

There were thirty-nine thousand people on the payroll in the NSA, all spread around the sprawling spacious campus, where people operated behind bullet-proof glass walls, in buildings set inside a razor-wire perimeter. There were enough guards to hold back the Red Army, and the military assessed that life expectancy for anyone who broke in was somewhere between twenty-five and thirty-five seconds.

And today, sitting in the Big Chair, was Commander James Ramshawe, the rookie from Annapolis, who had started out as some kind of "teacher's favorite," and then earned the profound respect of the entire military Intelligence world for his relentless, shrewd and brilliant pursuit of the truth.

His unassuming Aussie manner made him one of the most popular directors ever, likely to address anyone from a five-star general to the gardener as "mate."

Right now, Director Bob Birmingham wished to caucus with Jimmy more than anyone else in the country because this was Jimmy's kind of problem: keeping tabs on four dangerous but low-profile tribesmen, who would shortly be journeying north through Pakistan, almost certainly heading toward the al-Qaeda training camps in the Swat Valley.

The questions rained down on Bob: *Do we track them? If so, who does the tracking? Do we stay with them? Or do we wait until they head back west, for an operational hit on the Great Satan? Do we get a spy, or a mole, in there? Or do we concentrate on satellite observation? Do we tip off the SEALs to take them out as soon as they cross the high border into Afghanistan? How about a rocket hit with a Predator?*

Bob's helicopter touched down at Fort Meade. He was driven directly to the office of the new director, where he tapped on the door and entered.

"G'day, Bobby," said Commander Ramshawe. "Thought you might be on your way up the bloody Khyber Pass by now!"

Bob Birmingham laughed. "They're on their way now, nonstop to Paris, then Karachi."

"We following them?"

"Damn straight we are. We have to—far as we can. You read their personal dossiers? The ones containing the stuff from various guards? Jesus, they'll be working on a new 9/11 before you can say highjack."

"I've read it all," said Jimmy. "And I'm with you. That bastard Yousaf Mohammed, what a right bloody treat he is. You read that report by the supervisor? *Let the towers fall and the blood flow . . . death to the infidel.* Fuck that."

The CIA boss smiled. He always smiled at Jimmy's way of speaking; that famous irony of the outback. But what mattered was Jimmy's diligence, the fact that he had plainly read every word of that massive dossier.

"Well, maestro," said Birmingham, "What do you think?"

"Me? I think we need to take the bastards out. Because any other kind of action lacks logic. We already know they want to nail us again. We also know al-Qaeda never succeeded without guys like this. So why wait until they've knocked down the Empire State Building. I think we should nail 'em sooner rather than later."

Bob looked nervous. "Any chance this room is bugged?" he asked uneasily.

"Hell no, it gets swept every day."

"Well, I'm going to give you a lot of reasons why we cannot just order their assassinations. For a start, we can't ask the police, we can't ask the military, we can't do it ourselves, and we dare not ask a foreign government."

"Why not?" said Jimmy.

"Because these men were granted their freedom by the Court of the United States, and we'd be asking them to act in flagrant defiance of U.S. law. I wouldn't ask them, and if I did they'd have to refuse."

"Hmmmmm," said Jimmy. "I suppose they would. But this must have happened before. When it was obviously in the national interest that a small group of foreigners be removed from circulation."

"I suppose so. But as the current head of the Agency, with its enormous responsibilities to the president and government, I cannot risk openly breaking the law."

"Nor can I, mate. But I'm still going to do it if I believe it will save thousands of lives. They might have dressed me up like a fucking bureaucrat, but deep down I'm something different."

"It's because half of you is Australian and you just don't feel the same way about this country and its traditions—not like we do."

"Bullshit. I'm just a lot less scrupulous than you guys. Aussies are frontiersmen, you guys have gone soft. Whatever it takes, right?"

"Okay, smartass. Now you can outline for me how we unload Ibrahim, Youssaf, Ben, and Abu without ending up in the slammer."

"No worries. We get a small group of private guys and pay them to do the deed."

"Thus leaving both us and our nation open to the most tawdry kind of blackmail 'til the end of time."

"Good call, Bobby. Back to the drawing board!" Ramshawe grinned. "Want a cup of coffee?"

"I need a cup of coffee after five minutes with you. We playing golf this weekend?"

"Sure we are. Sunday morning. Eighteen at Bull Run with my father-in-law and Al Surprenant."

Jimmy poured the coffee. And then he said with mock solemnity, "Bobby, we're basically looking for a bloke with the skills of a Navy SEAL commander. But he can't be a Navy SEAL because we cannot ask him to break the law, and he wouldn't do it anyway. We need an ex-Navy SEAL. That's precisely what we need."

"No such animal, Jimmy. SEAL Commanders don't leave. They become instructors or admirals. And they treat Coronado as if it's the Vatican."

"Well, how about a retired SEAL?"

"Oh yeah, right, a guy of almost sixty to get into armed combat against a bunch of friggin' wild tribesmen at the ass-end of the Himalayas. He'd last about ten minutes."

"I guess that leaves a hit with a rocket-armed Predator, just as soon as we locate where they're living."

"Maybe it does. But even that's not ideal. And first we have to track them into the mountains. And then be prepared to fend off allegations that we deliberately and willfully murdered four men who had been exonerated of any crime by a superior Court of the United States of America. Don't like it much."

"Nor do I, mate. But at least we're agreed on one thing. We have to take the bastards out. And no error."

"Shut up, Jimmy, for Christ's sake. You make me nervous. You sure no one's listening?"

"Not here, old mate. But I'll tell you somewhere they were listening."

"Oh?"

"Yup. Right outside those law offices that were eliminated this morning."

"Who was listening?" asked Birmingham, ingenuously.

"The bloody Mossad. Who do you think."

"How do you know that?"

"Because I swiftly worked out there must have been a connection between the blowing up of two law firms, one in London, one in Washington, simultaneously, and apparently for no reason. Using precisely the same method. Classic Mossad, big bang, no chance of missing, evidence totally destroyed."

"So what did you do?"

"I called the bloody Mossad in Tel Aviv about two hours ago and asked Charlie. Took him about ten minutes to call back and tell me they'd been keeping tabs on both law firms for several weeks. He also told me the CIA knew all about it. So did MI6 in London."

"And then?"

"I checked with your Middle East desk and got a confirmation."

"They could have been lying."

"Bobby, old mate, no American lies to the National Security Agency. No American."

"So, I suppose you now think the Mossad blew up both of those law firms for daring to help al-Qaeda to free four mass murderers."

"I know bloody well they did, old mate. They were absolutely furious. And I'm not sure you didn't give 'em a helping hand."

"Yes, to the first. We gave 'em a hand to bug the place. No to the second. We had no idea they would go to those lengths. And no one will ever prove it anyway."

"And I'll tell you something else. The guys who blew the buildings were on their way home in a private El Al Boeing five hours before the explosions. Timed detonators. For what it's worth, they're all in King Saul Boulevard right now. How do you like them apples!"

Bob Birmingham was temporarily shaken. "Whatever you think, that was a pretty extravagant reaction by the Mossad."

"Bobby, for Christ's sake, they didn't just want to wipe out a couple of lawyers. Matter of fact they didn't care one way or another whether the attorneys died or not. They were formally issuing an international warning, that if any law firm in future played a prime role in assisting terrorists to get their freedom, that law firm may not survive to talk about it."

"Jimmy, has it ever occurred to you that the Mossad may be getting way above its station?"

"Yeah. Often. But they're too good, and too important a friend to us for anyone to start issuing reprimands. And I suppose we ought to remember those little bastards Ben and friggin' Abu nutcase killed or maimed over two hundred people, mostly women and children, with just two bombs."

"Maybe we should get the Israelis to take 'em out."

"In a funny way, the law firm explosions made that even less likely. Because if the four terrorists died, and the Mossad were suspected, they'd sure as hell be suspected of getting rid of the lawyers. And that might be a bit too hot. Even for them."

"Even they won't do our dirty work, right?"

"No, Bobby, they won't. Not this time."

FOUR HOURS LATER the Mossad leaked the story to the al-Jazeera television news network in Qatar, which has always been slavishly followed by America's left-wing media. It pointed out the sinister connection between two "gigantic bomb blasts," which had occurred simultaneously in Washington and London in the dead of night.

The killer-message did not emerge until the fourth paragraph on the al-Jazeera website story, which stated, "Sources say this was a warning to both American and British law firms that they should not continue to assist known terrorist killers to obtain their freedom under the new U.S. *habeas corpus* law."

Al-Jazeera then quoted the senior partner in a Saudi law firm with strong connections in Washington: "This firm has never partaken in cases that involve the freeing of terrorists. And this latest outrage makes it unlikely that we ever will."

The story was scarcely in print and on the airwaves when the security forces of the UK and the United States went into a collective reign of terror, because they believed both blasts were state-sponsored, and that it was probably the same state doing the sponsoring.

The CIA immediately began demanding answers from a diverse collection of foreign embassies, from officials unused to being grilled in such a manner. MI6, Great Britain's overseas Intelligence agency, working in tandem with Scotland Yard's antiterrorist squad, caused havoc in Her Majesty's Court of St. James's, to which more than 150 foreign embassies are accredited.

Everyone wanted answers, and, in both capital cities, literally hundreds of embassy officials and attachés were questioned. But no one knew anything. And the curious thing was, there was only one embassy in London and one in Washington where no one was even approached—the embassies that represented the State of Israel.

MEANWHILE THE FOUR most closely guarded men on the planet had landed in Paris. One of the CIA's top field operators in

Europe, Phil Denson, had flown in from the London station as the designated U.S. tracker. Phil's job was to stay in the deep background, but not to let the terrorists out of his sight.

Phil, a forty-six-year-old southerner from Georgia, had worked in Baghdad, Tehran, Riyadh, and Islamabad. On this mission he would be assisted by twenty-nine-year-old Ted Novio, a six-foot, five-inch ex-baseball pitcher from Massachusetts, a tower of strength who had made the Yankees triple-A but had to retire with a shoulder injury.

Ted had been assigned as a bodyguard for Phil, but he had been very successful himself, exposing an amateur terrorist cell in southeast London before the leaders could set up a rocket site on the edge of a swamp, west of London's Heathrow airport.

Now Ted and Phil caucused on the tarmac at Charles de Gaulle Airport. They had already befriended the French police, and Phil had had coffee with General Jobert.

Also on the tarmac were six armed members of the First Marine Parachute Infantry Regiment, France's prime special-ops unit, which has been at the forefront of almost every antiterrorist move made by the French in the past ten years. These men formed the guard that would escort the former Guantanamo prisoners on the central leg of their journey, out of the Western world and into a major Islamic Republic.

At the request of the Pakistani government, the French military escort would travel on the new PIA A310 Airbus from Paris to Karachi, since the four freed men would no longer be required to wear handcuffs.

Pakistan Airlines had nothing personal against these brand new celebrities, who would most certainly be worshipped in a large part of the Pakistan nation. It was just that PIA valued its fleet of airbus passenger jets sufficiently to try and avoid the highjacks and high explosive that often accompanied such men on their travels.

Phil and Ted would travel incognito, as would two other CIA men—four Americans still on duty, when finally Ibrahim, Yousaf,

Ben, and Abu arrived in the land that would be, at least temporarily, their first proper home for five years.

Also on the flight, and also incognito, were two al-Qaeda "freedom fighters." These two, Nawaz Salim and Fahd al-Ghamdi, had both arrived on the aircraft but had not disembarked. Their task was to scour the passenger seats on the journey to Karachi, searching for any American or French undercover agents who might be tracking the ex-prisoners.

So far, Ibrahim and his cohorts had been silent, eaten very little, and requested only water. Well separated from each other, they had slept most of the way, and would probably do so again as the aircraft flew across the eastern Mediterranean, and then high over the Gulf of Iran, before landing on the eastern shores of the Gulf of Arabia.

The changeover at Charles de Gaulle took a couple of hours, as everything in airports is apt to do. And it was a very relieved General Jobert who noted everyone was in place, and then watched the white airbus, with its green livery, climb away to the southeast and out toward the distant peaks of the Alps. General Jobert did not care where it went, just as long as it flew the hell out of France, taking with it those four Islamic maniacs, and their neurotic American escorts.

THE GENERAL PERFORMANCE of the four earnest high handicap players on the notorious uphill 448-yard fourth hole at Bull Run probably would not have caused Tiger Woods to announce his retirement. Bob Birmingham had almost hit a long, straight drive down the fairway, but it had veered into the first-cut rough on the left. Jimmy Ramshawe, from the same rough, stepped up to take a tricky, angled long-iron to the green. The NSA director slashed it straight into the trees, swore like a Queensland sheep-shearer, and questioned the sanity and the parentage of "whoever the hell invented the bloody game."

On the other side of the fairway, the Navy attorney Al Surprenant rifled a perfectly angled high four-iron onto the front of the green. The full majesty of the moment was only slightly marred by the fact that it was his sixth shot, having driven out of bounds into the dried-up creek in front of the tee, and then put a second ball in there, this one landing in a clump of bushes that should have been growing in the jungle of Borneo.

Out there this morning, in a cold but glorious landscape, just a few miles from the scene of some of the most formidable fighting of the Civil War, each member of the foursome struggled with his game, the way ultra-busy men do after weeks with scarcely any practice.

And when Ambassador Peacock, Jimmy's father-in-law, three-putted the sixteenth green from seven feet, the pure humiliating nature of the royal and ancient game sprung into sharp perspective. Jimmy changed the subject and talked about work, and the long hours he seemed always to put in, which, incidentally, had prevented him from becoming the natural successor to Greg Norman.

When the round was completed, Al and the ambassador had won fifty bucks apiece from Jimmy and Bob, who shared a ride back to Washington in defeat. On the way they talked not of golf, but of a game involving much higher stakes.

"I hear they landed in Karachi," said Jimmy.

"Sure did. But God knows where they're going. Our guys followed them to a train headed north up to Lahore. It's the Karakorum Express, and it takes darn nearly eighteen hours to get there. Arrives in Lahore tomorrow morning, their time. From there on, we don't know."

"Our guys on the train?"

"Uh-huh. Four of them."

"You still agree we need to eliminate them?"

"Of course. Because we all know they will seek revenge for those five years of incarceration and the torture they think they suffered."

"Bobby, you know what I think we should do? I think we

should arrange a private meeting with a senior Navy SEAL commander and get his input. He might not have anyone who could pull this off right now. But I bet he knows someone who might."

"You sure we haven't done enough betting for one day?"

"Almost. But you know what these bastards are capable of. And I just don't want 'em on the loose for much longer. In those court papers there were about four U.S. Army guards who swore to God those fanatics were taking vows to get out and start killing Americans. We need to stop them. And we can't recruit the Mossad to do it for us."

"I know, I know," said Bob. "It's just that the whole darn thing is so goddamned illegal."

"Then we better look bloody sharp about it," replied Jimmy. "Before some interfering bastard finds out what we're up to."

THE RETIRED HEAD OF SPECWARCOM in Coronado, Admiral John Bergstrom, was mildly surprised to receive a summons to the National Security Agency in Maryland. He had left California to retire to a beautiful family home on Albemarle Sound in North Carolina for a couple of reasons. One was that it had belonged to his mother, so it was essentially free. Two was that it was very close to many friends who had served with the SEALs in their east coast headquarters at Virginia Beach. Today it was very close to the National Security Agency, and "young Ramshawe," as the admiral referred to him, had dispatched a helicopter right to his front door to deliver him to Fort Meade in person.

When he arrived he was mildly surprised to find the CIA Director Bob Birmingham awaiting him. Also in attendance was Admiral Mark Bradfield, the ex-Carrier Battle Group Commander who now occupied the Chief of Naval Operation's chair in the Pentagon. Also sitting in was Rear Admiral Andy Carlow, Commander, SPECWARCOM, Coronado.

Commander Ramshawe introduced everyone and announced

that as far as he was concerned, Admiral Bergstrom was about to have a chat with four of the sanest people in the entire nation. He added the short and slightly mysterious rider that this particular group did not include many judicial figures from Washington's appeals court system. Everyone chuckled, except Admiral Bergstrom, who had not the slightest idea what Jimmy was talking about. But it took him about twelve seconds to realize that they were discussing the fate of those four Islamic fanatics, which some judge had let loose from Guantanamo Bay.

"Where are they?" he asked

"On an express train in Pakistan heading up to Lahore in the Punjab. And, if we are not gravely mistaken, on to the Swat Valley where al-Qaeda are training their forces to strike at us again."

"In case any of you had forgotten," said the admiral, "I actually did retire about fourteen months ago. I also got married to a somewhat dashing Beverly Hills widow, fifteen years my junior, and still elegantly assembled. And I no longer command the finest fighting force this world ever saw."

Bergstrom had a way about him, and everyone laughed at the ex-SEAL commander's wry mode of delivery. Finally, Director Ramshawe said, "John, this meeting requires the utmost discretion. But we all believe these characters need to be, er, eliminated. Before they do something shocking.

"Trouble is, they're not a small group of mass murderers running around while we hunt them down. These cats were officially liberated by the one of the highest judicial authorities in the United States legal system. We cannot go against that. So if anything is to be done, it has to be one of the greatest secrets this country ever had."

"Otherwise we might all end up in the slammer," said the admiral, echoing the fears of Ramshawe himself.

"Precisely," said Birmingham.

"Well, I'm not doing it personally," said the admiral, without a smile.

"No," said Jimmy. "We asked you to come here to try and think of someone who might. Someone one hundred percent trustworthy, honorable, and capable."

"Any one of my SEALs would fit that," he said. "But I do see the problem very clearly. Because he cannot be a serving officer, and then act in total defiance of the laws of the nation, and indeed against the expressed wishes of his commander-in-chief."

"And there you have it," said Rear Admiral Carlow. "We simply could not make such a request of any serving U.S. officer to carry out such a mission. If we did and someone was caught, there would be a case for treason, and that still carries the death penalty."

"Christ, they might execute us all. Nice." Ramshawe was very obviously baffled.

It was John Bergstrom who marshaled his thoughts quickest. "Look," he said. "Let's not make this more complicated than it is. We got four murderers we need to eliminate in the most efficient and secretive way, for the highest possible motive. That's the safety of our country. And there are plenty of guys out there who would do it for the right money."

The admiral paused, and asked, "May I assume money is no object?"

"You may," said Bob Birmingham.

"Okay, I'll make a few calls. A lot of ex-SEALs are in private security firms, operating all over the world, protecting heads of state. Maybe the best way is to look for a foreign-based outfit."

"Just so long as they never know who hired them," ventured Admiral Bradfield.

Rear Admiral Carlow spoke next, very slowly. "Look," he said, "the guy we want needs to be ex-Special Forces. He also may need some experience in mountain warfare against the Taliban or al-Qaeda—just because he may end up there. He needs to be a top-class marksman, an expert in unarmed combat, proficient with a knife and high explosives. We're looking for a warrior, right?"

"Close," said Jimmy. "But he's also got to be a man of honor. A guy who understands the totally clandestine nature of the mission. A man who is conducting this operation on behalf of the nation—yes, for a big financial reward, but this man needs to be a cut above the rest. He's actually gotta be a fucking saint!"

Everyone laughed. But the deadly serious edge to the meeting would not go away. Rear Admiral Carlow, the United States Special Forces commander, spoke again. "It's running through the back of my mind, but a year or two ago, I recommended the court-martial of one of my officers for murder and reckless conduct in the face of the enemy, during which he totally flouted the Geneva Conventions."

"Sounds perfect," said Jimmy, sarcastically. "He could probably start World War III, if he concentrated."

"Actually, I'm not joking. He never was guilty, and he was just about the best officer on the base."

"Who did he murder?" asked Bob Birmingham.

"A group of a dozen al-Qaeda killers, right there on the banks of the Euphrates River."

"What for?" asked Jimmy.

"They'd just wiped out twenty of his guys in a missile attack."

"And he let 'em have it, right?" recalled Admiral Bradfield. "Opened fire while they were trying to surrender. I remember the incident."

"That's it," said Andy Carlow. "He just let 'em have it . . ."

"The court martial found him not guilty on all charges. I remember that as well," said Admiral Bradfield.

"That court martial should never have been brought. And I'll go to my grave regretting my part in it," replied Carlow. "All the way to my goddamned grave."

"He got off with an officer's reprimand," he added. "But it finished him. He left the Navy immediately. Everyone stood at the gate to say goodbye, I mean the whole base stood at the gate. People were in tears, guys who'd fought with him in the backstreets of Baghdad. I was ashamed of the Navy that day. Ashamed at the injustice of it.

"No one who was there will ever forget it. I mean, watching him walk out to the car. At the last second he turned around and saluted us all. I damn nearly wept."

"Jesus," said Jimmy, "Some kind of a man. What was his name?"

"Lieutenant Commander Mackenzie Bedford, SEAL Team 10, Foxtrot Platoon."

IT TOOK DIRECTOR RAMSHAWE'S researchers approximately fifteen minutes to track down Mack Bedford. He was working in a shipyard in the little town of Dartford on the Kennebec Estuary in Maine. The six-foot-three, former SEAL team leader, now thirty-five, was a native of the town, and his family had known the shipyard owners, the Remsons, for generations.

Harry Remson had given Mack a position commensurate with his high status in the U.S. Navy. He had his own office and secretary right next to Harry. He was Remson's only salesman, and his task was to acquire orders for warships, guided-missile frigates.

Mack's territory was the globe, and in his first six months he had landed a major order from the prime minister of an African nation—a man who was anxious to spend the international food-aid money on the kind of modern weaponry required to conquer the peace-loving but wealthy nation next door.

Mack knew what the smiling Homba Bomba was up to, and he did not especially approve of it, but the Remsons were paying him a comfortable $250,000 a year, and he was duty-bound to bring in the orders. This one was worth $500 million, and the Africans had put down a $29 million deposit, non-refundable.

Director Ramshawe had declined to call Mack, preferring instead to travel to Maine, without prior warning, in company with Bobby Birmingham and Rear Admiral Andy Carlow, Mack Bedford's old boss. All three men arrived in a marine helicopter at around 10:30 a.m. the following morning.

They circled the snowy landscape above the little town on the river around thirty miles northeast of Portland, then landed in a windswept, frost-covered field right opposite Mack's white clapboard home, where he lived with his strikingly beautiful wife, Anne, and their son, Tommy.

Anne stepped out onto the porch wearing a heavy-duty sheepskin coat, and waved to them. The helicopter contained only one word on its fuselage, **NAVY,** and after twelve years of marriage to the former lieutenant commander, she guessed there could only be one man in this town such an aircraft might be coming to visit.

Rear Admiral Andy Carlow, in full Naval uniform, climbed out before the rotors had stopped spinning, and he waved reassuringly at Anne Bedford, whom he had known briefly while Mack and his family lived in Coronado. Ramshawe and Birmingham disembarked next and walked the short distance across the field to the house where Andy introduced everyone.

Not many days went by when Andy did not find himself wondering about Mack Bedford. And that applied to a number of senior officers who cursed the day they had agreed to find him guilty of something even so minor as an officer's reprimand—anything to placate the politicians and their goddamned useless peace talks.

The officer in charge of the court martial was haunted by that infamous day, and, even now, Andy Carlow remembered that final moment when Mack had turned around and saluted, plunging a dagger of remorse, regret, and sorrow into the hearts of them all. There were a thousand guilty men at the gateway on that day, and not one of them was Mack Bedford.

The question hung in the air for months. Why had someone not run forward and stopped it? Why not Carlow? Why not the goddamned president of the United States? Why not indeed?

"How's he been?" asked Carlow.

"Not too bad, Andy," replied Anne. "Considering everything. We're okay. Do you want to see him?"

"May we?"

"Sure, I'll call him. He can be here in five minutes. Come on in, I'll make some coffee."

She still was very beautiful, Andy thought, and the consummate officer's wife. Calm, assured, and confident.

Inside the house, the big room was heavily beamed across the ceiling, with broad, polished, wooden floorboards, colorful rugs, and a log fire. The furniture was Americana but comfortable. Andy noticed the newest U.S. Navy magazine, *Proceedings,* on a side table.

Within minutes they heard a car come sweeping into the drive, and shortly thereafter, Mack Bedford came through the front door. He'd shaved his beard now, but Andy would have recognized him anywhere. The big ex-SEAL commander entered the room and exclaimed, "Andy Carlow, hello. Welcome to the great state of Maine."

The two old buddies, who had once roamed the rubble-crushed streets of north Baghdad together, now embraced, slapping each other on the shoulders, remembering things said during Mack's final days, and things that could never be said.

Andy introduced his traveling companions, head of the CIA, head of the National Security Agency.

"What happened?" joshed Mack. "Chairman of the Joint Chiefs busy?"

Just then Anne arrived with a large pot of coffee and mugs, with a pitcher of cream and a sugar bowl. She placed it on the sideboard and instantly beat a tactful retreat. Mack walked over and closed the door to the front hall. "Okay, what do you need? I doubt that chopper in the field was on loan for a social call."

Jimmy Ramshawe opened the proceedings. "Lieutenant Commander," he said, carefully granting the SEAL the full respect of his rank, "I wonder if you read recently that under a new Supreme Court ruling some of the most dangerous inmates of Guantanamo Bay are now being released by the U.S. appeals court?"

"I did. And I should tell you that a couple of years ago I thought the world had gone crazy when my own career was shattered. I now think it's gone a lot crazier. I'm sure you understand just how dangerous some of those characters are. I used to hunt them down, up in the Hindu Kush. They'd slit your throat as soon as look at you."

"Well, there are four guys in question right now. The appeals court let 'em loose a few days ago, and as we speak they're in Pakistan heading north across the Punjab on a train."

"Up to the Swat Valley, I guess?" said Mack. "There always was some serious shit going on up there—training camps and all. Probably preparing another hit on the U.S. mainland. Better stay on 'em. Seems just about every last fanatic who got out of Tora Bora headed for the Valley."

"You ever go there?" asked Bob Birmingham, who was always rather in thrall to the military, and loved their stories.

"I never did get right in," said Mack. "But I observed it a few times from the steep walls of the escarpments that run alongside it. I remember one time some hairy fucking tribesman walked up on me, carrying this curved dagger. Said he would cut the throat of the Infidel. And he meant it."

"Christ, what happened?" asked Bob.

"Nothing really. But I had to kick him in the balls, then break his wrist, then his neck. Mad bastard."

"I'm guessing a kick in the bollocks from a bloke like you would have shot his eyeballs straight across the Swat Valley, like a couple of bullets," said Jimmy.

"Got his attention," Mack replied, chuckling at the Aussie's knack of reducing even the most violent confrontation to a scene from a cartoon.

"Well, anyway," said the NSA director. "We are now facing a problem that may repeat itself. Right here we've got four of the most dangerous terrorists ever captured, and they're all on the loose. We cannot re-arrest them because they just got freed by the U.S. Court of Appeals.

"Equally we cannot forget about them because they all have the most diabolical records of mass murder and violence. And they've sworn revenge on the United States. The Mossad wants them worse than we do, but daren't move because of U.S. law."

"So you want to take them out?"

"Precisely."

"Good luck."

"Thanks."

"And may I ask the purpose of your visit?"

"Of course. We came to ask you if you could help in this mission."

Mack Bedford stood up and walked to the sideboard. "At this moment," he said, "I have two very simple questions."

"Fire away . . ."

"Would everyone like some coffee? And, do you think I might be insane?"

"Yes, to the first," said Ramshawe, "Not bloody likely, to the second."

"I am not quite clear on one thing. Are you suggesting I very quietly go out and murder these four characters?"

"Well, we were not going to put it in quite that way," interjected Bob Birmingham.

"Any way you phrase it comes to the same thing," replied Mack, "Shoot, blow up, cut throats, poison, or throttle. You want them all dead. And since all four of them are now, apparently, innocent men, that would come under the general heading of 'murder.' So the penalty for me would be life in prison or a death sentence."

"The way you say it, no one would dream of taking on the mission," said Andy Carlow.

"Well someone might," replied Mack. "But he'd have to be a professional, someone who would do it for money. You might locate one of those somewhere. Ex-military, highly paid, for certain unusual skills."

He passed around the coffee, and through the closed door Mack could hear Anne talking animatedly, just catching the phrase, "Well, they definitely wanted something very important."

What he didn't know was that Anne was talking to Mack's father, and that they were both concerned in many ways about Mack's recent demeanor. Plainly he missed the SEALs, missed the hugely fulfilling role of commanding men who had a higher calling than mere cash. Men who had a touch of the noble savage about them. Americans, who, when the bugle sounded, would come out fighting, for honor and patriotism, and would die for their country. Mack missed it. Missed every last vestige of his far-lost command.

And he treasured every memory. There were nights when his dreams were filled with elation. Nights when he was scared, waking up, breathless, reaching for his rifle, shouting out to Lieutenant Mason, leading his men into unknown territory, way up in the mountains, or in the hot and dusty ghettos of Baghdad.

The trouble was, Mack was a SEAL, from his boots to the top of his head. For months and months he'd tried to enjoy his new life, enjoy his big salary and time with his small family. But the black-top grinder where they trained, out in Coronado, was never far from his thoughts. He'd even had a flagstaff constructed in the front yard, in the same position as the SEALs' flag, back on the shores of the Pacific.

Every morning he hauled up the Stars and Stripes, and every evening as twilight descended upon his home, half a world away from SPECWARCOM, Lt. Commander Bedford hauled it down. When he thought no one was looking, he came to attention, and saluted. And whenever he did so, there was the faintest tremor on his upper lip.

Anne usually knew what Mack was thinking. And right there, when he stood rigidly beneath his personal flagstaff, she understood he was recalling the lines from the creed of the SEALs—lines she considered utterly magnificent. Lines for heroes:

> *My SEAL Trident was bestowed upon me by those who have gone before. It embodies the trust of those whom I have sworn to protect. . . . I humbly serve as a guardian to my fellow Americans—I will always defend those who are unable to defend themselves. I must earn my Trident every day.*

On the rare occasions when Anne caught a glimpse of her husband enacting this private ceremony, it almost broke her heart. Just to see this strong and powerful warrior, a man born to lead troops in battle, so utterly alone, so solitary, yearning for the only life he could never have. She always pretended she had seen nothing.

But these past few weeks, both she and his father had noticed an ever-increasing change. Mack was becoming more within himself, reading more, watching the History Channel and the Military Channel. She was secretly thrilled that Andy Carlow and his friends were here, especially when she heard Mack's great shout of laughter at one of Ramshawe's more absurd metaphors.

And he was plainly flattered at being selected by an old friend to commit a quadruple murder. "Sets you apart, old mate," said Jimmy. "We could probably make you more famous than Jack the Ripper!"

"Well," said Mack, "What price do you put on it?"

"Ten million bucks," said Birmingham, instantly. "Cash. Half up front, if we get the right guy. No taxes."

"Just tell us. Are you interested?"

"Not really. I was never cut out to be a mercenary. Killing for money. It just doesn't feel right. And with a crime like this, well, you gotta live with yourself. And I don't think I'd like it much. And Anne, if she ever knew, would hate it."

"How would you feel about $20 million?" asked Ramshawe.

"Same."

"But could you do it? If no expenses were spared, and you could make all your own rules and arrangements?"

"Probably. With some backup in locations. I guess I probably could."

"But, Mack Bedford," said Rear Admiral Carlow, "there is no price we could put on it, that would tempt you to perform this service for your government and your commander-in-chief?"

"Well, that's not quite accurate, Andy. Because there is a price."

"Name it," said the SEAL boss.

"I want my commission back in the United States Navy SEALs. I want my name cleared of any wrongdoing, and I want my rank back, as if I'd stayed in the Navy."

"Jesus," replied Carlow. "That would take a Board of Inquiry . . ."

"Quite frankly," replied Mack, "I don't really care if it takes an Act of Congress. They say every man has his price. And I guess that's mine. Because for that, I'd do anything."

Rear Admiral Carlow stood up and told them he needed to call the Pentagon, and speak to Admiral Mark Bradfield, the head of the United States Navy. He walked out of the room and then out of the house to make the call on his cell. He had been gone for only around six minutes when he walked back into the room. "It's done," he said. "Welcome back, Commander Bedford."

"Steady, Andy," replied Mack. "I'm still only a lieutenant commander."

"Not anymore, you're not," replied the SEAL boss.

4

T HE STUNNING EVENTS of those six minutes in the Bedfords' white house in snow-swept Maine took everyone by surprise.

By way of explanation, Andy Carlow told them a board of inquiry was being convened right now, with orders from the highest possible authority that the dreaded GOMOR—General Officer Memorandum of Reprimand—that had had been issued against Mack was to be overturned and struck from the record as from this day.

All further matters, regarding pay, pensions, benefits, and promotions, would be retroactive, backdated.

"If anyone's interested," said Andy with a broad grin, "Bradfield's precise words were 'This should have been done months and months ago, as soon as the stupid, know-nothing Middle East peace talks went down.'

"He also said he never could remember any action in any

court-martial ever to cause that much bitterness and resentment, especially among the SEALs. He mentioned that even the god-damned janitor knew Mack should never have been sacrificed like that, especially as the court-martial had just found him not guilty on all counts."

"Will I need to complete the mission successfully in order for all of this to kick in?" asked Mack.

"Absolutely not," replied Carlow. "Your word and your hand-shake are good enough for us. Everyone knows you will either take out those four mass murderers. Or die in the attempt."

THE OLD NAVY BASE at New Brunswick, Maine, was still func-tioning, even though its days were numbered. They flew Mack Bedford out of there, direct to the Quantico Marine Base in Vir-ginia. From there he was flown into the Central Intelligence Agency's helicopter landing pad, a short walk from the New Head-quarters Building situated on the main Langley campus on the western bank of the Potomac. The entire building sits beneath a giant copper-grid of a roof designed and structured to prevent lis-tening devices from penetrating the atmosphere inside the walls of the Agency.

Mack arrived under escort, the steel heels of his polished black shoes echoing on the sixteen-foot-wide granite CIA seal inlaid into the lobby floor. Heads turned to look at him; even the sound of Mack Bedford was not like that of other men.

Mack strode to the North Wall of the lobby and stood for a few moments staring at the eighty-three engraved black stars set into the white marble, each representing a member of the agency who had perished in the line of duty.

In the nearby Book of Honor, however, there were only forty-eight names revealed, the others still classified. Mack had known some of these fallen senior INTEL agents, having forged close friendships with them, both in Baghdad and at the Bagram Base in Afghanistan.

Their skills, observations, and strategic plans were often life-and-death for the U.S. Special Forces. The combat SEALs, in all of the world's trouble spots, damn near worshipped their hard-eyed guides from Langley, Virginia. Mack glanced up at the wording on the wall, the stark black letters, which immortalized them all:

IN HONOR OF THE MEMBERS OF THE CIA WHO GAVE THEIR LIVES IN THE SERVICE OF THEIR COUNTRY

The memories of lost friends stood before him, and for a few brief seconds he was transported back to the hell-holes where he had fought an often unseen enemy. And he thought again of those guides and their consummate skills, and the terrible dangers in which they operated, undercover and behind enemy lines.

And he remembered the fear and the brutality, the death and destruction. And, here in this great wide and tranquil hall, standing in front of the flag of the United States, he bowed his head in private remembrance. He was unaware that every eye in the place was upon him, although no one knew who he was. He just seemed like someone who really mattered.

Finally, he walked across to the guard station where an escort had already arrived to take him down to the CIA's situation room, one of the most secretive conference rooms in the United States. They took the elevator down and walked along the great curved concrete tunnels, which made electronic intrusion impossible.

Four guards stood at the entrance to the bomb-proof, sound-proof, phone-proof situation room, where every last law of classified military "Black Ops" was observed. For meetings like this one, there were no cell phones, no communications to the outside world, no visitors, no secretaries, no assistants.

There would be just the principal operations personnel, men who made big decisions and had the power to make them without reference. In this case, reference might have put them all in jail.

Rear Admiral Andy Carlow, the SPECWARCOM commander, was already in the room. And so was Captain Ramshawe. Mack

Bedford entered and stared around him. The space was plain, with white walls and no windows. But there were two giant computer screens set into the wall and one giant television. On the huge, polished central table, there was a massive world atlas and several Navy charts and maps.

There was a white encrypted telephone, which had instant access to the Pentagon and the White House. Two of the armed guards came in and placed a coffee pot with mugs, cream, and sugar on a long antique sideboard. Security clearance at the highest level was required, even to cross the threshold of this place. The guys who brought in the coffee had sufficiently high security clearance to protect the president.

Even the master of all this, Bob Birmingham, towering above his guards, came down that reinforced curved passage and into the room under escort. He was accompanied by the Chief of Naval Operations, Admiral Mark Bradfield, who was reputed to become the next chairman of the joint chiefs.

Only one other high-ranked official was invited, Birmingham's deputy, John Farrow, who, at forty-five, was regarded as a kind of civilian Jimmy Ramshawe. A career CIA man, he had a degree in economics from Georgetown and had served undercover in Arabia and India for many years. The slim, athletic Farrow had served in Peshawar for six months three years ago, and almost got himself killed by Shakir Khan's tribesmen, out on the rebels' road up to the Khyber Pass. Farrow operated right at the frontline in the fight against terrorism and had been brought in from the warmth by the CIA high command who were concerned that he would be assassinated. But now he was back, and regarded as a world authority on terrorism. And this particular operation had his name written all over it.

Bob Birmingham introduced Farrow as his 2I/C and the doors to the room were closed. The six men seated themselves at the table, and their "host" proceeded to issue a quick progress report. "The four liberated terrorists have arrived in Lahore and are taking the late mail express up to Peshawar," Bob began. "They're ten hours in front of us, and it leaves at 10 o'clock tonight. My guys are on the case, and it looks very much as we discussed. They're on their way up to Swat Valley, returning to the fold of terrorism. Gentlemen, we have to eliminate them at any cost, except for discovery."

Bob Birmingham placed five folders on the table and pushed one toward each man. "In here is the criminal record of Ibrahim Sharif, Yousaf Mohammed, Ben al-Turabi, and Abu Hassan Akbar. The charges listed against them include those we know perfectly well they committed, those which, in addition, the Mossad says they very definitely committed, and those we very much suspect they committed.

"You will notice they almost entirely involve bombs and high explosives. All four are skilled bombmakers. Colonel Powell, the Joint Detention Group commander at Guantanamo Bay, says they are, in his opinion, probably the four most dangerous men ever to be held in U.S. antiterrorist incarceration."

He stared across the table at the man who had volunteered to solve this enormous problem. "I'm going to start calling you Mack," he said. "And so is everyone else. It's important we remember you are not in the military at present. Wherever you are in the world, if you have to call in, you do so as Peshawar Mack, or Hindu Mack, or, if you go skiing, Aspen Mack.

"Admiral Bradfield has a document with him that sets out the terms of your new career in dark blue. At present it lacks a start date, which you understand. You will also understand why it cannot be released to you right now. The only thing this mission lives or dies by is its secrecy. No one here doubts you will accomplish it."

"Thank you, sir. I'll try not to let anyone down." Mack Bedford was pensive, but unafraid. "I would just like to mention the subject of backup. Can I count on anything?"

"Mack, you can have anything you like, armed assistance, weaponry, documents, transportation. Just name it, and it's done. I have right here your credit card, which has the backing of the United States Government, Triple-A, and no limit.

"With this magic plastic, you can go anywhere, stay anywhere, eat anywhere, pay for anything—cars or even camels if you have to. And of course, cash, however much you need. There will be no questions asked. You are trusted implicitly.

"Remember, nothing matters except that you take these four bastards off the face of the earth, before they strike again."

"Who's my main contact if I need to call in?"

"We thought you'd prefer military Intelligence, so it's Captain Ramshawe. That factory of his in Maryland is probably the most secure building on earth, except for here. And you will have Jimmy's numbers, e-mails, whatever you need, which will make him available twenty-four-seven for any kind of emergency."

"If I have to call in, it will be a real emergency," replied Mack. "You can count on that."

"Do you intend to go to Peshawar right away?" asked Admiral Carlow. "Start tracking them early?"

"I need to talk to Jimmy about that. Because I don't think these guys will hang around for long. I've studied the court papers on the way down here, and Jesus, three of them have stated publicly their desire for revenge. I think they'll be heading right back to the West as soon as they have a plan."

"Remember, we have accurate photographs and full sets of fingerprints now," said Bob. "Plus names and birthdates. They needed all of that to get into court. And it's all in the immigration system. They won't find entry easy."

"I guess not," said Mack. "But several billion Mexicans made it."

Jimmy Ramshawe chuckled. "With a bit of luck we'll get a fix on them long before they reach our points of entry.

"We've got real good coverage all through the Hindu Kush, and along the western side of the Swat Valley. There's about a hundred people on the case every day in Fort Meade alone.

"And it won't take me long to get the Brits onside either. They're more bloody jumpy about these four characters than we are. Mostly because they've got shocking leaky borders. And they seem especially vulnerable to Pakistanis every bloody time."

"For the moment," said Mack, "I intend to work long-range, with Jimmy, and with Bob's guys in Peshawar, try to establish a fix. Right now the prisoners don't have cell phones, but they soon will. Guys like this operate on direct links to their high command. And that North West Frontier is one hell of a big place. I have a ten-times bigger chance of success when they move out, back into the Western world."

"Did we circulate their photos, details, and fingerprints to the Europeans?" asked Mark Bradfield.

"A week ago," replied Birmingham. "But none of their major airports are a hundred percent secure. We actually think al-Qaeda guys have infiltrated some of the immigration authorities, probably the Brits, and they're getting people through the net."

"Beautiful," said Ramshawe. "That's just bloody super." At which point he raised his voice to mimic those of . . . well, an effeminate persuasion, and squeaked, "Here in our lovely multicultural society. . . ." And then he went back to his normal tough Aussie tones and added, "Where you can't tell for the life of you who's bloody well who."

THE MAIL EXPRESS was running late all along its hundred-mile journey from Islamabad to Peshawar. It finally came rumbling into the Peshawar City Station an hour and a half behind schedule, and late for morning prayers. Literally hundreds of people cascaded out onto the platform after their all-night ride from Lahore. It was 8:30 in the morning, and the old city of the British Raj was slowly awakening.

But there was nothing slow about the seething action taking place among the terrorists. Ibrahim, Yousaf, Ben, and Abu emerged from the station, and a chauffeur stepped forward and hustled all four of them into the back of a stretch limousine, windows darkened.

Ted Novio came running out of the station just in time to see the huge black automobile pull away from the sidewalk. Instinct told him the four terrorists were in that car, and he instantly memorized most of the license number. There wasn't a taxi to be found, but there was, however, a line of native Pakistani auto-rickshaws, those little three-wheeler engine-driven transports that zip around almost every city in the country, driven by men who regard themselves as the permanent keepers of the nation's urban culture. Much like London cabbies.

Ted hurtled toward one of them and dove headlong into the rear seat, terrifying the driver, who was generally accustomed to being asked, "*Rickshaw khali hai*" (is rickshaw empty) before anyone got in. He was so astounded he leapt out of the driver's seat.

"FOR CHRISSAKES GET THIS WRECK MOVING!" yelled Ted. But by now there was chaos. A dozen other rickshaw drivers had rushed to help their colleague whom they assumed was under attack by a giant American. It took five minutes for everyone to calm down, by which time the limo might have been on its way to Rawalpindi. "Fuck it," said Ted resignedly, as Phil Denson and the third CIA agent, Fred Zarcoff, arrived with the suitcases.

"They moved very fast," said Phil. "Any clues?"

"They just took off in the biggest goddamned car in Pakistan," he replied. "I have the number. Black stretch. Dark windows. A U.S. Lincoln, I think."

"If it's in the city we got a chance. If it's on the road to somewhere a much less chance."

Phil wrote down the number, walked over to a policeman, and inquired if he spoke English. The reply was affirmative, and Phil explained he was looking for a car that was supposed to have met him and gave the policeman the license plate number.

"That's a government registration, sir," said the policeman.

"Well, they said it would be a black Lincoln limousine."

"Yes, sir. I think I saw it leave about ten minutes ago. Maybe it's coming back."

"Okay. Thanks, officer. Does that car live in the city?"

"No, sir, Islamabad. But it might be here for the day. Maybe with

Mr. Shakir Khan, a very high-ranking official. Very high rank, indeed."

"Yes, we're supposed to be seeing him," lied Phil. "Any idea where he lives?"

"In the old city somewhere. And he works in Islamabad. I don't know any more."

"Thanks, buddy."

Anxious to avoid another rickshaw riot, Ted, Phil, and Fred headed for a taxi. The fourth CIA man stayed at the station to wait for the next train to Islamabad. From there he would fly home to Paris.

"Just take us for a ride around the old city," Phil told the driver. "To see a few sights." For the next twenty minutes they moved slowly along streets chaotic with the raucous shouts of vendors and mule drivers, clogged with horsedrawn carts, rickshaws, motorbikes, and people.

They were just running north of Andar Shehr, close to the great Mosque of Mahabat Khan, when Zarcoff spotted the car, parked to the left of a small group of street traders trying to lay out peaches, plums, and apricots on three narrow trestle tables. It was easy to see the limousine, illegally parked among the produce and causing a sensational traffic hold-up, which was threatening to bring the entire city to a halt.

Fred guessed that no traffic cop would be writing out a ticket for the limousine, not if he wanted to go on working for the police department. An expert on police cooperation, Fred was a native of Romania and a former member of one of the largest, cruelest, most brutal secret police regimes in the old communist eastern Europe. He had been a young officer in Securitate, the notorious KGB-modeled force that operated out of Bucharest, on behalf the Romanian dictator Nicolae Ceausescu. Fred had seen the writing on the Berlin Wall, and with some alacrity had jumped ship, over to the CIA, for whom he had worked as a loyal and brilliant agent since 1989. On this particular mission he had been extremely agitated since they had left City Station, peering around, checking the rearview mirror, concerned they might be followed.

Phil had been asking, quite reasonably, who the hell could possibly be following them, since even they had no idea where they were, and no one from America could, by any stretch, have tracked them here. Phil was certain they were fireproof. Fred was equally sure they were not.

Yet neither of these vastly experienced CIA field men had noticed an old blue rickshaw chugging along close by, sometimes ducking down side streets, but always popping out right behind or dead level with their yellow cab.

Phil paid off the cab driver, and the agents walked toward the fruit stalls, checking out the limo from about forty yards away. There was little they could do, short of a house-to-house search, except to hang around and wait.

Ted stationed himself on a busy corner of an alleyway crammed with silversmiths. Phil chose to wander up and down the street, checking out the jewelry. Fred found a clothes store and proceeded to dress himself like Ali Baba in baggy pants and shirt, with a colorful waistcoat and black turban. He then headed to a sidewalk café and ordered tea from a brass *samovar*. Which he never tasted.

The first bullet from Fahd al-Ghamdi's silenced rifle ripped out of the enclosed rear of the rickshaw and caught Fred full in the chest. The second smacked into his skull, three inches behind his left ear, blowing out his considerable brain. Fred catapulted over the back of his chair and died, messily and instantly.

Nawaz Salim, the other al-Qaeda killer who had followed the CIA men by air and by train, took Phil Denson by the throat from inside the beaded curtain of a silversmith's and plunged his dagger deep into the American's heart. Phil, too, was dead before he hit the ground.

It took Ted Novio a full ten minutes to realize something was wrong. By that time, Fred's body had been cleared, but Phil had simply vanished. Ted raged up and down the alley looking for his boss, and encountering nothing but blank looks, especially from the silversmith's.

BOB BIRMINGHAM almost hit the ceiling when he got the news. "What d'you mean dead?" he snapped into the phone. "Are you telling me that Yousaf or one of his pals killed two of my agents? And where's Ted?"

Captain Ramshawe put down the telephone and stared at Ted Novio's message.

Jimmy knew it was hopeless to leave Ted Novio in Peshawar on his own. If these lunatics could kill Phil and Fred, they could kill Ted. They could also kill Mack Bedford, though, thank God, they did not yet know of his existence.

Long-range surveillance was the speciality of the National Security Agency, and they'd tuned into the most dangerous terrorists before. In Ramshawe's opinion, Bob Birmingham's boys could cast a blanket electronic survey all over the North West Frontier. They could activate their moles and spies, and sooner or later the names Yousaf, Ibrahim, Ben, and Abu would come popping out of the ether.

Jimmy called the Willard Inter-Continental Hotel on Pennsylvania Avenue and asked to be put through to Mack Bedford. He informed him of the missing CIA men and arranged for the ex-SEAL commander to come to Fort Meade that afternoon for a strategic discussion. Mack was unsurprised at the outrage in Peshawar.

"You have to meet these guys to understand their hatred of us," he said. "Sounds to me like the assassins had been following our guys since Paris."

"Then you don't think Ibrahim and his buddies killed Phil and Fred?"

"I doubt it," replied Mack. "They wouldn't risk an uproar that quickly in the middle of a city, and for no reason. I'd guess al-Qaeda were on our case as soon as that PIA flight left Paris."

"But they didn't get Novio," said Jimmy.

"Was he seated separately?"

"He was. As a bodyguard he wanted a longer view of the group, just in case anyone made a tricky move. He was sitting by himself, four rows back."

"Then they may not have noticed him."

"He also left the train station in Peshawar way in front of the other CIA guys, so they never connected him to them."

"Lucky guy," said Mack.

BACK IN PESHAWAR'S OLD CITY, Shakir Khan sipped fruit juice in his wide, stone courtyard, now bathed in the warm noontime sun. He sat with his assistant Kaiser Rashid, the Taliban combat captain Musa Amin, and, from the nearby Grand Mosque, a black-turbaned imam, who smiled through a white beard and solemnly wished peace and blessings on the Prophet Mohammed. Before them, on a stone bench, sat Ibrahim, Yousaf, Ben, and Abu.

This gathering was in the nature of a military debriefing, but it was not a nuts-and-bolts plan of action. It was an informal talk about life in Guantanamo Bay, and a kind of high-minded forecast of the wrath to come, the terror to be inflicted on the West. And, of course, the glory to Allah, which would surely follow when the Great Satan and its Zionist allies were driven from the Middle East forever.

"We will strike soon, and we will strike hard," said Ben al-Turabi. "It's important that they remember us. That we, who would be martyrs if necessary, had come back from the dead, and raised the Sword of the Prophet against our enemy, and smashed into them, as we did in 2001."

The imam continued to smile indulgently. "I am so proud of all four of you," he said, "because, among us, you alone have understood that al-Qaeda and the Taliban will never be defeated, and that the more the Americans kill and humiliate us, the more we will expand as brothers in the cause of Allah."

The other seven men in the courtyard all intoned together: "Allah is great. There is no other God but Allah."

And the imam continued, "A peaceful and happy life is a distant dream for us—and the false promises of the West will never be of any good to us. Ibrahim, Yousaf, Ben, and Abu Hassan, you have kept alive the light of Allah in the darkest place on this earth, and now He has brought you home."

The four ex-prisoners bowed their heads in respect, and then Shakir Khan spoke for the first time. "My friends," he said, "we already know of the treachery of the Americans. Even as they cast goodwill upon us, and liberated our bravest warriors, they were already acting with venom and dishonesty, sending those two killers all the way to Peshawar to slaughter you all.

"Thanks be to Allah that His brave and gallant servants Nawaz and Fahd were able to cut down the American assassins before they could do us more damage."

"Brave and gallant," was a somewhat colorful description of the actions of Nawaz, who had hidden behind a curtain while stabbing Denson in the back, and Fahd, who had shot Zarcoff dead from the heavy cover of a rickshaw parked forty yards away—while the police turned a deliberate blind eye.

Nonetheless, there was an element of pride in the courtyard as everyone congratulated everyone else, and the imam wished peace and blessings upon them all.

More to the point was the plan formulating in the mind of Shakir Khan, whose task it now was to return Captain Musa and the four heroes to the al-Qaeda training camp up at the north end of the Swat Valley, in the mountains beyond the town of Kalam.

His government chauffeur would drive them out of the City at 10 p.m. in the limo, north through ancient towns, like Mardan, and then up through the passes through Madyan and Bahrain to Kalam, which straddles both sides of the river and is joined by a wooden suspension bridge. From this point on, you need a four-wheel drive with a strong engine and little value, or an ox cart, or a mule, or decent hiking shoes. The terrain is almost impassable, but the men of al-Qaeda knew what they were doing when they built their main training base up here. The land is cooler and the scenery spectacular, with massive snowcapped peaks rising above fertile farmlands, miles of blossoms in spring, and bounteous peach crops, plums, and oranges, even rice fields.

Tourists are banned, travelers are wary, and the locals suspicious. No one walks alone up here. And in the last hundred years no one ever could. Except for The Sheikh, who was nowadays in hiding or dead.

Shakir Khan's driver would end his journey at Kalam. He would attend morning prayers at the picturesque wooden mosque, and then drive back to Peshawar. Ibrahim, Yousaf, Ben, and Abu Hassan would change into tribal clothes and continue their journey over this rugged country, well-armed, and in a well-supplied mule cart, accompanied by two bodyguards from the training camp.

They would take the route that leads northward from Lake Mahodand, over the Dardarili Pass, and then down to Handrap on the Gilgit-Chitral road. Yousaf had relatives here, but he would not attempt to join them until his rehabilitation in the training camp with al-Qaeda's highest officers. Many people had waited a long time to see the young warrior who had somehow gotten out of Guantanamo.

Shakir Khan mapped out all of this in the courtyard, and every now and then, touched on the revenge they would surely take on the Great Satan who had imprisoned the four men for so long without trial. The one aspect of this revenge upon which everyone agreed was that it needed to happen very soon.

The four ex-prisoners, out of touch for so long, had no progressive ideas on a new and sensational attack on the United States. Indeed, they had not the first idea about a new target, a new strategic plan, or a new workable network of fundamentalists in America. The absence of bin Laden in recent years was, to al-Qaeda, like the Roman Legions without Caesar, or France's Grande Armee without Napoleon. There was no big thinker, and al-Qaeda's lower ranks had been terrified by the pulverizing attacks on them, launched by President George W. Bush and his cohorts Cheney and Rumsfeld.

Since then, the jihadists had made sporadic attacks on a night-club, a Spanish railroad station, and a London bus—but nothing on the U.S. mainland, and nothing which truly made the United States sit up and take notice. It was time, and the powerful Shakir Khan, a devout Muslim fundamentalist to his fingertips, was considering taking over the role of principal al-Qaeda strategist. This was a position that would sit nicely with his Taliban roots and his clandestine support for this extremist religious organization, which had granted sanctuary, a haven, assistance, and military support to Osama and his men in the first case.

Shakir was a Machiavellian figure. He was secretly to the fore-front in that ever-growing section of the Pakistan military that believed fervently in an Islamic State ruled by Sharia Law. He was constantly attempting to encourage a huge ideological division in the ranks of the Pakistani military. Indeed, he was widely suspected of being the leading figure in the background when the fundamentalists shot down Benazir Bhutto in December 2007.

Indeed it was Shakir's friend, the al-Qaeda commander, Mustafa Abu al-Yazid, who claimed responsibility for the attack, describing the Harvard-educated Ms. Bhutto as "the most precious American asset." The Pakistani government also stated that it had proof that al-Qaeda was behind the assassination, and swore to God the killers belonged to Lashkar i Jhangvi-zan, an al-Qaeda-linked militant group blamed for hundreds of killings, including an attempt to assassinate former Prime Minister Nawaz Sharif.

There were those who believed Shakir Khan was the secret leader of that formidable terrorist organization. And now, right here in the courtyard, he was expanding his vision on the major "hit" on the United States he intended, one that would attract world attention and implant a new fear of the rising Muslim brotherhood—a fear that would prove, beyond doubt, the Islamists were back to their pre-2001 strength.

"Only by our actions, can we regain respect," he said. "Actions, not words. And that leads directly to the subject of our new target, one that cannot be too heavily fortified by the American military.

"Quite simply, they are too strong both in weaponry and manpower. Therefore anything even remotely connected to their armed forces is out of the question because we cannot afford to fail. Also we could not undertake a major hijacking program because, again, their airport security is too strong.

"I refer you all now to the events of September 1, 2004, to an incident that still ranks as one of our finest triumphs—the successful attack on School Number One in Beslan, North Ossetia-Alania, the autonomous Russian republic in the North Caucasus."

Shakir Khan outlined the brutal attack on the school, which had ended in violent explosions, fire and destruction, and the deaths of perhaps three hundred and eighty-five people, many of them students. A further seven hundred eighty people were wounded when a huge section of the roof caved in.

"The immortal brotherhood of the Riyadus-Salikhin Reconnaissance, financed and trained by al-Qaeda, led by our departed Muslim brother Shamil Basayev, held the great Russian Army at bay for three days. We stormed and then dominated the school, and the town. No military operation since 2001 ever brought such endless glory upon our jihadist revolution. And such world attention. Gentlemen, I say to you now, Beslan was only a dress rehearsal."

"But why, sir," asked Ben al-Turabi, "have we never attempted a repeat of the operation?"

"Ben," said Shakir Khan patiently, "after that, both U.S. security and Russian security were increased drastically, against us. Putin used it to tighten his grip on the Russian satellite republics, and the tyrant Bush continued to crush and humiliate us at every turn in the road.

"But the tyrant is gone from the White House. And the United States grows softer. Now is our chance to take them by surprise. And there is no place where surprise is simpler. Nowhere less heavily guarded than U.S. schools and colleges."

"Are you suggesting that we four, within months of crossing the wire out of Guantanamo, should lead the highest-profile armed

Muslim attack on the United States in a generation?" Abu Hassan was visibly cautious.

"If you were willing, I can think of no greater honor we could bestow on four of our finest young commanders, and no greater irony for the United States. That they should have stretched out some insincere hand of friendship for their usual political reasons, only for the jihadist warriors to spit at it, and then show them what we think of them."

"Last time I spat at a U.S. combat soldier, he very nearly killed me," said Ibrahim. "It was just before I was captured. He was a huge man and strong as a bear."

"But these were proper U.S. troops, not security guards, which don't exist in U.S. colleges."

"The men who took Yousaf and I were Special Forces," replied Ibrahim. "You could tell by their beards. They're the only U.S. troops permitted to wear beards. It's for working among us, in the mountains."

"Well, you won't find men like that in U.S. colleges," said Shakir Khan. "And there you can effect the most terrible revenge on them for what they did to you and Yousaf, and to Ben and Abu Hassan."

"When Shamil Basayev and his men took the Russian School, did the Army come against them with full artillery and infantry?" asked Yousaf Mohammed, sternly.

"Oh yes," said Khan. "The Russians deployed tanks and heavy armor against them, blasting holes in the walls of the school, killing indiscriminately, children, parents, and our brave fighters. But it still took them three days to defeat the small Islamic force. Though in the end we had many martyrs."

He paused, and bowed his head, then looked up and added, "It was appropriate. *Riyadus-Salikhin* means 'Garden of the Martyrs.'"

"And how did the al-Qaeda men get into the school in the first place?" asked Yousaf.

"Oh it was very simple," said Khan. "They planted workmen in a team, which was in the school during the July holiday. We understand they concealed weapons and explosives in an unused area of the basement. We also heard they were able to walk into the school unannounced on September 1 because this was the traditional start of the Russian school year, their Day of Knowledge. The place was swarming with parents and other relatives of the children, and no one took a blind bit of notice of a few workmen wandering around the building.

"The preparation was so important in that mission. And it ended in worldwide headlines and praise for the brave jihadists who accomplished their mission. That day, the *amir* of the Muslim force was very proud of them all. As indeed was Allah, for Allah is great, and He welcomes into His arms those who die in His service."

Shakir Khan did not offer any examples of the outraged Western media, neither did he elaborate precisely on why Allah so desired the mass slaughter of several hundred Russian schoolchildren.

"Do you have a list of possible targets?" asked Abu Hassan.

"Not really," said Khan. "But we can easily make our selection near strike time."

Kaiser Rashid, Khan's thoughtful former London law student assistant, spoke for the first time. "Sir," he said, tentatively, "I have been putting together some kind of a dossier on the events that surrounded the Washington court's decision to release our four brothers.

"It seems both law firms that assisted us were blown up on the very night of the court's decision. Two bombs, detonated simultaneously. No accident."

Shakir Khan, normally the very picture of calm, literally gasped, "Then someone has penetrated our communications system?" he growled.

"Epstein's work on the case was public," said Kaiser. "They had two lawyers in court, both relatively well known on the legal circuit. However the London firm, Howard, Marks, and Cuthbert, who passed on the request from the Saudi clerics to Washington, was not."

"Was anyone killed?"

"No one in London because of the late hour. But Josh Epstein and both the lawyers who argued our case are dead."

"Any conclusions?"

"Yes," said Kaiser, somewhat darkly. "It must have been the Mossad. I have checked it out as thoroughly as I dare. And the conclusion is inescapable. The mere fact that they used a bomb, is pure Mossad. No chances taken, no assassinations, just a massive detonation on a Washington side street that destroyed their enemy, plus every last vestige of evidence.

"I am told the FBI in Washington is scarcely bothering to search for the culprits, simply because everyone knows who did it. But no one wants to know. The whole of the U.S. security force, military and civilian, is furious that Ibrahim, Yousaf, Ben, and Abu Hassan have been released."

"Zionist pigs," muttered Khan. "But they will surely pay for that crime."

Captain Musa Amin had been silent during the explanations, but now he spoke and, for him, rather slowly. "It would be almost perfect if we could find a large college in the United States that was predominantly Jewish. That way, we could kill several hundred pigs with one stone."

"Are there such places in the USA?" asked Ben al-Turabi. "I did hear of a couple in England—I think it was King David's High School in Liverpool."

"I had a classmate in London who went to a Jewish school, but I don't recall the name," added Kaiser.

And then Shakir Khan joined in the conversation. "There are more Jewish schools and colleges in the United States than there are in Israel. One of the most famous is called the Yeshiva University, way uptown in New York City.

"But I think we might seek somewhere more peaceful. The New York police and security forces are completely trigger-happy at the slightest suspicion, after the Day of Glory.

"No, gentlemen, we need a large, tranquil college in the American countryside. I'll have Kaiser prepare a short list. East Coast preferably, where we are still better organized, but we should explore the Midwest, but not Chicago with its terrible, tough police force.

"Meanwhile, we should have supper after evening prayers, and then you all will be on your way. Because I have a feeling this place may very shortly be full of U.S. agents and spies, who will surely not like the fate that befell their assassins. Praise be to Allah, for He is great."

AT 10 P.M. IN THE DARKNESS of the alleyway beyond the wall, Shakir Khan's official Mercedes Benz was running softly. The courtyard door was silently opened, and all four of the former prisoners slipped through the entrance and into the black automobile with its North West Frontier government plates.

The chauffeur closed both the rear doors, with Abu Hassan in the front passenger seat, and set off through the town heading north, up to the Grand Trunk Road, which is a slow-moving traffic nightmare all day, but a very decent stretch of highway at night. The chauffeur drove fast, only slowing up through the passes. It was almost 1 a.m. when they reached the banks of the tumbling Utrot and Ushu streams, which combine in Kalam to form the mighty Swat River, flowing south down the valley.

Four tribesmen, al-Qaeda fighters, greeted them. They had brought tribal dress for the four men, and there were three mule carts, laden with supplies, weapons, cushions, and rough blankets. Ibrahim, Yousaf, Ben, and Abu, the conquering heroes, were given a warm and enthusiastic welcome.

But night was passing and they still had miles to go under the cover of darkness. The six mules began to move softly into the deep, uncharted regions of the Upper Swat Valley, into the northern mountains, back into the warm embrace of bin Laden's jihadists, a place where each of the four devoutly believed he belonged.

And visions of that triumphant three-day siege of Number One School, Beslan, stood starkly before them. The pictures in their minds, relayed so powerfully by Shakir Khan, were magnified by their imaginations and made more vivid by the specters of dying Infidels. These were the visions of the coming Days of Glory.

All four of the rescued terrorists felt safe now as they moved slowly into the uplands. They were almost in sight of their own Promised Land now. They all could sense the majesty of the place where warriors trained, where the dream of Muslim domination still thrived, and where that dream would never die.

Each of them knew the terrorist training camp to which they were headed was an integral part of the al-Qaeda organization. All nineteen of the 9/11 hijackers, as well as the operatives in the USS *Cole* attack, had attended Afghan or Pakistani training camps. Following every successfully executed attack, there was a spike upward in recruitment and enrollment.

The training was diverse. Most recruits received conventional warfare training, but al-Qaeda needed foot soldiers, heavy machinery operators, and individuals who could bomb embassies or hijack planes. Specific terrorist training was given only to top recruits personally evaluated by bin Laden's successors.

The overall plan was to encourage recruits to develop creative ways to conduct mass murder. The curriculum was unswervingly based on the ideology that Israel and the United States were evil. Martyrdom was the highest honor, and many recruits had volunteered for suicide missions.

The Iranian and Pakistani governments knew and disregarded the influx of al-Qaeda operatives moving through their respective countries, but the lines of communication were never down between them, and the twenty thousand individuals involved in this vast and determined network moved freely around the Middle East.

Only a select few would receive the ultimate specialized terrorist training, and for the next few weeks, Ibrahim, Yousaf, Ben, and Abu Hassan would provide it, passing on their combined knowledge, practicing their own skills with the young recruits, and preparing for the next strike against the American/Zionist Satan.

They continued on through the night, sometimes sleeping on the cushions in the back of the mule carts, sometimes staring up at the night sky. They reached the camp at around 3 a.m. and were greeted by the commandant, Captain Musa Amin, who had been flown up by helicopter.

Like almost every one of the al-Qaeda camps, there was no accommodation block. Instead there were small, square, single-story houses, dusty, walled spaces, to provide protection from wind and rain. It occurred simultaneously to both Ben and Ibrahim that accommodations had been slightly more comfortable in Guantanamo Bay.

They unloaded their few possessions and retired to one of the dwellings as two hundred miles above them, the massive ten-foot-wide digital imaging mirror on America's KH-12 CRYSTAL satellite swiveled ominously in the sky. This incredible, billion-dollar piece of flying hardware had trouble photographing only objects under five inches high, but three mule carts and a group of full-grown men were kid's stuff. It had cost $400 million to get it up there, firing it into space with a Titan IV rocket from the Vandenberg Air Force Base northwest of Los Angeles. Now swiftly orbiting the earth at Mach 25, the KH-12 was a spymaster's dream come true. It probably could not reveal the number on the front door of your house, but it could tell if there were a couple of bikes in the front yard.

Known as the Keyhole Class, the KH-12 was so secret, the National Reconnaissance Office in Virginia never even referred to it as number twelve. In fact, all these supersonic spy satellites were known only by random numbers like KH-362, to confuse foreign spy operations—and most of Washington.

The KH-12 had been programmed to pass over the camp in the upper Swat Valley the day the four prisoners were released. There were actually six satellites up there, making a total of twelve passes a day, or one every couple of hours. This meant that Ibrahim and his boys had been photographable for at least two hours, if you count their approach and the unloading of the carts.

The near-permanent frown of Abu Hassan's face came up in ultra-sharp focus in the NRO after the stark black-and-white image was flash-transmitted through the relay network of communications satellites. They caught a couple of good ones of Ibrahim too, snoring like a B-52 bomber in the back of the mule cart in the still of the mountain night.

The NRO, located in Chantilly, twenty-five miles west of Washington, had been matching images of arriving and departing terrorists in the upper Swat Valley for several days, but when the group on the mule carts showed up, there was no doubt in anyone's mind. The high-quality prison photographs, matched with the brilliant digital pictures taken from space, made identification simple. The findings of the NRO matched precisely those of the CIA's National Photographic Interpretation Center, and were placed on the link, instantly relayed to the National Security Agency.

When the images came up on Captain Ramshawe's screen, he was filled with conflicting emotions. Loosely translated into the poetic turn of phrase so natural to his Aussie forebears, this came out as, "Well, at least we know where the bastards are, but we can't start bombing in Pakistan, and we can't go in and grab 'em, so we'll have to bloody wait 'til they make a move."

Bob Birmingham arrived at the same conclusion. So had Rear Admiral Andy Carlow and the CNO Admiral Mark Bradfield. There was nothing else to do except wait. But the wait did not last for long.

Six weeks after KH-12 took the space shots, Shakir Khan's plans were in position. The four veteran al-Qaeda killers—Ibrahim, Yousaf, Ben, and Abu Hassan—would strike against the United States, by blasting a Jewish school or college, and preferably on the East Coast, from where it was quicker to escape.

Because entry into the United States would be impossible, Khan decided the four would join the hundreds of Mexican peasants trying to break in across the southern border with Texas, perhaps over the Rio Grande. Khan knew that scores of Mexicans were caught and sent back after crossing that infamous strip of desert. But the same rules would not apply to Ibrahim and his men, because they would have modern weapons and endless money. Also, they were ruthless killers, who would stop at nothing to get across, fighting under the unassailable banner of the Prophet Mohammed, in the name of Allah.

Shakir Khan would now set about awakening the "Sleeper Cells"—the terrorist groups already in place in the United States, which President Bush once assessed as about five thousand separate groups. There were not that many these days, but there were still plenty, and any one of them would move forward with limitless high explosive for the right attack on the Great Satan.

Final selection of the target would be made when Ibrahim's squad reached Mexico. And that was another problem, because the tried and tested way out of the badlands of Afghanistan and the Hindu Kush was through the soft left-wing underbelly of the United Kingdom, where the thirteen-year socialist government had almost bankrupted the country, and needed its Muslim voters to love it still. The UK's border officials would have let Osama and his best buddies in, just so long as they had official papers confirming their enrollment at the Pakistan Culture and Commonwealth Centre for Advanced Literary Studies, with its sprawling "modern campus," situated in one room above a Bradford fish-and-chip shop.

The scandal of these fraudulent universities has seethed for years, not to mention the ludicrous English laws that let in *anyone*—terrorists, tribesmen, jihadists, fanatics, lunatics, guys whose great-grandfathers had served in the Bengal Lancers, mullahs, snake-charmers, camel-drovers, bombmakers, fakirs, fuckers, and God knows who else. At the last count, to the fury of the police, Britain's absurd Labour Government was issuing ten thousand student visas to Pakistanis ever year; between 2004–2008, they allowed 42,292 Pakistanis to enter the UK on these visas.

Even the notorious Abdul Rahman, jailed for six years in 2007 for recruiting British Muslims to join the Holy War, entered the country on a student visa. He lived in Cheetham Hill, Manchester, where in April 2009, police arrested in an Internet café eleven suspected terrorists who had entered the UK on student visas, and discovered only one of them was attending a "reputable college."

There are an estimated two thousand fraudulent educational institutions in the UK, bogus colleges with big websites, many located in specific ethnic areas in big cities. And they have very grand names: Oxford and Cambridge World Scientific College; UK Harvard Advance Studies; Commonwealth Literature and Engineering School; and London Language School. This latter organization offered a £250 course in "door supervision"—an interesting euphemism for training students to become nightclub bouncers.

Even the embarrassed Pakistani High Commissioner in London complained to Britain's unelected prime minister, Gordon Brown, that the UK authorities were hopeless. Mr. Brown argued, defensively, as one might expect from a man whose political antennae have been compared to those of a song-thrush. At around that time it was discovered that the PM's car was being officially guarded against terrorist booby traps by an illegal immigrant from Pakistan or somewhere.

Shakir Khan knew the way into the West. Ibrahim, Yousaf, Ben, and Abu would fly out of Karachi, back to Europe, probably Amsterdam, and on to Leeds-Bradford International Airport. They would fly on Pakistani passports and student entry visas to the UK, issued with Islamabad support. They would then settle in the Pakistan-dominated city of Bradford for a few weeks before setting off for Mexico, probably via Madrid.

It was time-consuming but foolproof. If the guys made the border crossing into Texas, they, backed by the Sleeper Cells, would be home free to kill and maim U.S. citizens. The overall objective of the al-Qaeda quartermaster was maximum death and destruction, national and world outrage, international attention, and glory to al-Qaeda from all Muslims, all 1.4 billion of them.

Shakir Khan intended to run Pakistan one day. And he had cast his lot with the extremists, the Taliban, the Islamic fanatics who despised the center-left government the country now had. Shakir Khan wanted the fundamentalists to take over both the government and the military. That way, come the inevitable insurrection and the creation of an Islamic State stretching from the Horn of Africa to the Atlantic, he, Shakir Khan, must surely be in line to rule it; to rule half of the world, to become the second coming of the immortal bin Laden.

He could hardly wait to leak the news to the al-Jazeera television network when the U.S. college blew, that al-Qaeda now formally claimed responsibility for the latest atrocity. That the powerful North West Frontier politician Shakir Khan was believed to have been the mastermind, following in the giant footsteps of the Great Osama. Because surely after this, the Godless Americans unwelcome in the Middle East would pack up and be gone forever, leaving him, Shakir Khan, descendant of the Prophet, to rule the greatest empire the world had ever seen.

And he was going to enjoy this, especially when the time came to tell the U.S. authorities in an untraceable message that the perpetrators of the enormous crime against their people were the four men they found not guilty in a Washington courtroom, released, and then tried to assassinate.

MACK BEDFORD HAD RETURNED to Dartford, Maine, to wait for his four targets to emerge. He had decided to say nothing about his new mission, or the consequences should he be successful, to his wife. He knew that Anne had been happy in California, and that a return to Coronado, with its glorious oceanside weather, would probably delight her, but he needn't worry her with the rest.

Meanwhile he took great comfort in the fact that the entire machinery of U.S. Intelligence was working in the background, trying to locate Ibrahim, Yousaf, Ben, and Abu Hassan.

By day he continued to work at Remson's Shipyard, making contacts with various foreign Navies, and by night studying the ever-growing documents relating to the prior activities of the four terrorists.

Only in the early morning, at first light, did the ironman former SEAL emerge, pounding along the coast road down the Kennebec Estuary, up hills, down steep gradients, through the rain and wind, finishing with the uphill sprint home that usually leveled him on the wet lawn. Right after that, he climbed to his feet and underwent his morning pull-ups on the steel bar he had rigged between the branches of an apple tree.

He had to stretch upward to grasp the bar, and the idea was to keep pulling his chin above the level of the steel until he had no more strength left. An average person might manage two or three, a trained athlete, possible eight or nine. Mack Bedford could do thirty-eight.

Four evenings a week he drove down to a small, hidden cove right on the estuary, stripped down to his wetsuit, and plunged into the river, swimming six hundred yards out to a line of rocks and back at full power. On evenings when he knew the current would be running hard, he wore big SEAL-issue flippers and powered his way through the entire twelve-hundred-yard training swim.

Ever since leaving the SEALs Mack had stayed with his ironman regime. Somehow, somewhere in the back of his mind, Mack Bedford never stopped hoping and praying that one day he would return to Coronado. And now he had his chance.

As each day passed, Mack was attaining an almost unprecedented level of fitness, more animal strength than human. Mack Bedford packed the fighting qualities of a Bengal tiger. He was still a SEAL to his fingertips, and even measured against that illustrious brotherhood, he was one of the very best there had ever been.

He understood the dangers of his new mission, and he did not underestimate his task. However it was incomprehensible to him that anyone in the entire world could defeat him in combat.

Mack studied the Guantanamo pictures of the terrorists, tried to asses their characters. Mostly he drew some kind of a blank, except for an obvious hard-edged evil expression common to all four. There was also defiance and hatred, common to most terrorists.

But there was something about Ibrahim Sharif, something distantly familiar. But Mack could never put his finger on it. The U.S. authorities had made the Afghani shave his beard during his incarceration in Cuba. Every Islamic fanatic Mack had ever seen wore a beard, so identification was just about impossible.

And yet, Mack still wondered whether he had ever seen Ibrahim Sharif before.

NOT EVEN MACK BEDFORD understood the intensity of the U.S. and British sweep of the Hindu Kush mountain airwaves. The United States had installed powerful ground and satellite surveillance from Peshawar to the area north of the upper Swat Valley, and then covering the lands to the west, to Afghanistan, across the passes, over the towering peaks, and down to the scattering of villages clinging to the almost sheer escarpments.

They could intercept almost any call, and while this was a gigantic task, there were specialists looking for the rare conversation or signal that might have been military or terrorist based. And they were good at it. Too good for quasi-amateurs like Shakir Khan.

The Pakistani who would be king needed to inform the al-Qaeda leader in the UK, Sheikh Abdullah Bazir, of the pending arrival of his most holy and exalted four-man fighting force. He had it planned, and, so far as he could tell, he had no alternative but to use the telephone. But there were excellent codes between the Hindu Kush and the Islamic Sleeper Cells in England, and Khan was confident he could slip easily through the system. However, it was a system he did not fully understand.

From the hub of his government office, he dialed a private number way up in the mountains on the Afghan side of the border. It was answered by an al-Qaeda commander, who did not speak, but wrote down precisely what Khan told him, and hung up. The man then dialed a number in the UK, and Sheikh Bazir answered from his office in a mosque in Bradford, Yorkshire, a town where there were eighty thousand Muslims in residence. The al-Qaeda man spoke only his message: "The chosen ones shall kneel before the Prophet in Hanfia. Blessings upon Allah who will guard them by the stone cattle RV."

The call was as swift as any call could be. The line was cleared instantly. Sheikh Abdullah never even had one second to reply. Speed was everything, and that was understood by everyone in bin Laden's organization. But they were not quick enough.

British Army sergeant, Shane Collins, a specialist signals expert from one of the UK tank regiments, was at his post on a quiet morning in the British Intelligence listening post in Cyprus, located up in the hills north of the military base in the UK sovereign territory of Dhekelia, in the southeast of the island. Geographically this was a major crossroads of east and west, a British hub that intercepted satellite messages, phone calls, and transmissions emanating from all over the Middle East. To the north lay Turkey; to the east, Syria, Israel, and Iraq; to the southeast, Jordan and Saudi Arabia; to the south, Egypt.

This secret listening post was known in the trade as JSSU, and it was manned by the cream of British electronics interceptors from all three services. They maintained a relentless watch, monitoring communications around the clock, each of the operators a highly qualified linguist trained to make literal translations of intercepted messages and conversations as they were transmitted.

Faxes, e-mails, coded signals in a hundred languages were all recorded on a long-running tape for later analysis. Conversations that sounded particularly intriguing, however, were written down by the listening operator as they were spoken and instantly translated.

Sergeant Collins chose to record this message because it pushed the exact right buttons: (1) it was excessively brief; (2) there was no response from the other end; (3) there was no personal greeting; (4) no recognition; (5) it made no sense; (6) and it contained references—in this case, "stone cattle."

Sergeant Collins, whose grandfather was from Pakistan, understood Pashto, the language in which the communication had been spoken. But he needed a more accurate translation. In moments, he had it. He already knew the call, made on a cell phone, had come from somewhere fifty miles west of Peshawar, somewhere in Afghanistan.

And now he flashed a signal through to a second British listening post in the UK to retrace and track the line on the frequency he had in front of him. When the message came back it specified the line bisected the city of Bradford in West Yorkshire, probably the town center, but could go no closer.

Sergeant Collins immediately called over his duty captain and reported he had a satellite signal, cell phone, one which, in his opinion, bore the hallmarks of secrecy, probably military. The captain agreed it was unusual, and passed the text straight through to Government Communications (GCHQ) in Cheltenham, Gloucestershire, for detailed analysis.

GCHQ is the jewel in the crown of Britain's espionage industry costing $1.5 billion a year to run. The NSA in Maryland willingly pools all of its Intelligence with Cheltenham, where the staff of four thousand operates in blast-proof offices under an armorplated roof. It was a huge building, absolutely circular, with a round center courtyard. They called it "the Doughnut."

Within five minutes, GCHQ had completed its search. Its computerized system had made several trillion calculations and had arrived at the irrevocable analysis that this was not code. It was veiled speech, with military overtones. They agreed that this was a signal, not a conversation.

And, as ever, the critical question stood starkly before them. Had JSSU in Cyprus just tapped into an al-Qaeda Command Headquarters? Was this as vital as their greatest triumph years before, when they had tapped into bin Laden and his henchmen high in the Hindu Kush?

This was also a call made from the nearest big city to the same Hindu Kush. GCHQ admitted being baffled about motive, culprit, and recipient. They were not however in any way confused by the innate importance of Sergeant Collins's signal.

Shortly before noon, they relayed the message to the National Security Agency in Fort Meade, Maryland—For Your Eyes Only, Captain James Ramshawe—in big red letters **FYEO**.

Shakir Kahn had, essentially, been intercepted.

5

CAPTAIN RAMSHAWE STARED at the incomprehensible note, now designated as "veiled speech."

"Peshawar," he muttered. "Gateway to Nut Country." *Now where the hell does it say that phone call went? Bradford, England, where they've got more bloody Muslims than Mecca.*

Jimmy read and re-read the signal: *The chosen ones shall kneel before the Prophet in Hanfia. Blessings upon Allah who will guard them by the stone cattle RV.*

"Now what in the name of Christ is that all about?" he said to his empty office. "Hanfia? Where's that? And who's RV when he's up and dressed? Ravi Vindaloo? Or does it mean rendezvous, military rendezvous? As for the friggin' stone cows, beats the hell out of me."

The British spooks in Cyprus believed the word "guard" had definite military overtones. They also thought the RV meant rendezvous. There should have been a period after the word "cattle," if there was a signature. Could have been a mistake. But the sender made no mistake with the other two periods, one after "Hanfia"—another at the end. And there was no greeting.

Jimmy Googled "Hanfia" and instantly came up with a burial site in the middle of the Punjab, which Jimmy knew was also home to about eighty million Pakistanis.

As problems go, this one seemed more or less unsolvable. Riddles like this preyed on the mind of the young director of the National Security Agency, and he could not stop wondering about the "chosen ones," *and their trip to the bloody graveyard, even if it was eight thousand miles away.*

He called the Middle Eastern desk at the CIA but detected no progress. And then he settled down to his Internet link, researching terrorists with roots in Peshawar or the Punjab, looking for a link, trying to find a connection.

His new wife, the surf goddess from Sydney, Jane Peacock, daughter of the Australian ambassador, had called him twice on the general subject of lateness, before he decided to give it one last shot. He Googled "Bradford," and hit pay-dirt in the first twenty seconds. Zooming in on the city center, he instantly spotted the Hanfia Mosque, situated right on the edge of the Pakistani area of Manningham.

The chosen ones shall kneel before the Prophet in Hanfia. "That," stated Jimmy loudly, "looks like four Pakistanis headed right for England and reporting to some mullah in the old Hanfia Mosque. Beaut." He put a signal on the link to Bob Birmingham's office in Langley, suggesting a very fast alert to Scotland Yard's Antiterrorist Squad in London.

Before leaving for home, he zoomed out of the city of Bradford and scanned the surrounding area, glancing at a few Yorkshire Towns and villages, searching for clues. But there was little to the south and east of the metropolitan area, and nothing much on the great plateau of the Pennines. In the north, the Pennines divide the counties of Yorkshire and Lancashire, which in the fifteenth century fought the Wars of the Roses—white for the House of York, red for Lancaster. Jimmy knew that Lancaster won.

Right now he was strictly with the losers, and he scoured the Yorkshire moors above the village of Ilkley, zooming in, consulting local ordinance survey websites. But then his cell phone rang. "Jesus Christ," he muttered. "I'm on my way, sweetheart. On the highway."

"Liar," snapped Jane. "If you're not here in fifteen minutes I'm going to Dad's place for dinner."

Jimmy was always amused at his spectacular-looking wife's propensity to refer to the Washington embassy of Australia as "Dad's place." But he got her drift and swore to God he'd be there. And in that split second he spotted a place on Ilkley Moor marked down as Cow and Calf Rocks.

It's the friggin' stone cows, he breathed. And then he weighed up the conflicting merits of "nailing the towelheads, against the wrath of Jane," and the willowy blonde from the sunlit harborside suburbs of Sydney won, hands down. He switched off the "ole Apple" and fled from his office, murmuring an old Aussie victory mantra, all the way down to the front lobby. . . . *You bastards, I've got you dead to rights!*

At home, Jimmy was greeted with a chilled rosé wine from the Barossa Valley, near Adelaide. For dinner, he and Jane enjoyed two supreme New York strip–sirloin steaks, which, Jimmy guessed, were testimony to her outrageous flirting with the seventy-year-old head chef at the embassy.

Jane announced she was getting ready for bed at 10:30 and walked sassily from the room. Jimmy then raced into his study, where his fingers flew over his computer keys as he punched in "Cow and Calf Rocks, Bradford."

There they were, high up on the moors above Ilkley, one massive squarish stone a hundred feet high, the other only forty-five, and neither looking anything even remotely like a cow or a calf. The text suggested their name originated in the mists of time, probably prehistoric, the smaller rock having broken off from the main one.

Whatever the history, Jimmy surmised that these were indeed the "stone cattle" where the chosen ones would meet, fourteen hundred feet above sea level, high on the vast and desolate moors, less than nine miles from downtown Bradford. Jimmy made a note of the GPS numbers.

He switched off the computer and headed for bed, already looking forward to the new day, but not as much as he was looking forward to the night in the arms of his gorgeous new wife.

MACK BEDFORD WAS JOGGING south along the Kennebec River estuary at seven the following morning when Captain Ramshawe called to inform him of what had been learned.

"All I can do, mate," said Jimmy, "is to remind you to travel light, conceal weapons until you need 'em, and to stay in touch with Britain's SAS. They understand the mission. Whatever you need."

"Roger that, Captain. Bedford to Bradford. Messages via Stirling. Over and out."

The former SEAL team leader headed home immediately. He sat on his front stoop and called the British military attaché at the embassy in Washington. Using his new code name, "Black Bear," fashioned after the sports teams of the University of Maine, he requested a ride, as quickly as possible, on a military aircraft headed to England. The attaché was back on the line in five minutes. The Royal Navy had a Hercules going to RAF Lyneham in the English County of Wiltshire tonight. They would make a stop at the U.S. Navy Base at Brunswick, Maine, around midnight and pick him up. There would be an unmarked black Jaguar sedan awaiting him at Lyneham, but no driver. As requested.

Mack spent of the rest of the day reading up on the Internet anything he could find about the Bradford area of Yorkshire. He'd never been there, and tomorrow he would arrive incognito and check in with West Yorkshire Police, one of England's toughest and most efficient antiterrorist forces, located on the edge of one of the largest Muslin enclaves in the Western World.

Mack would travel with no documents. His journey would be, in and outgoing, on military transport. His all-encompassing government credit card featured no name, just an indecipherable code number. There were only two such credit cards in the world, the one issued to the President of the United States, the other in the possession of Mack Bedford.

Presented to any credit-card machine, anywhere on earth, the words pop up: *"OK Visa. U.S. Govt."* Uncle Sam, of course, has never defaulted on one dollar in its entire history. Mack did not represent much of a risk to anyone.

U.S. and UK police and the British military were aware he was on a clandestine Black Operation, but he was unrecognized by any government.

Should he be killed in the line of his duty, no organization anywhere in the world would claim to know either him or anything about his mission. He would die, as so many others have in war, an unknown soldier, known only to God. His death would represent one of the most mysterious exits from this planet, ever.

Mack dug out an old Afghan tribal disguise he once rescued from the Hindu Kush, white baggy pants, long shirt, and headdress. He crammed it into his waterproof leather duffel bag, along with a few pairs of pants, regular shirts, jeans, combat boots, and camouflage trousers and top. Hidden in a secret compartment beneath the floor of the bag was his SIG-Sauer 9mm service revolver, six magazines, his combat knife, and fifty thousand dollars in cash, drawn on his credit card from four different banks.

He wrote a short note to Anne—*I'll be away for a few days. Don't worry. Tell Tommy I'll bring him a new rugby shirt. And whatever happens, remember you're always on my mind. I love you forever, Mack.*

He placed it on the hall table, under his cell phone, thus confirming there would be no contact until he returned. Anne's heart missed about seven beats when she arrived home and read it. But she'd been married to a member of America's Special Forces for a very long time. And she had always known precisely what that meant.

Mack traveled by taxi a dozen miles to the north and checked into the Parkwood Inn, in the little town of Brunswick. The Inn was surrounded by the secluded ocean peninsulas of Bailey and Orrs Islands and the long waters leading down to spectacular Casco Bay. He had arrived in the early afternoon and settled down in front of the computer, checking data on the Swat Valley, Peshawar, the Hanfia Mosque, Bradford, the Muslim enclaves of Manningham, and the Cow and Calf Rocks, which Jimmy Ramshawe had sworn were an integral part of this operation.

Mack cast to the back of his mind that he was expected to commit four murders, but when the iron truth of his mission elbowed its way forward, he justified everything by confirming to himself that all four of these men had sneakily killed and murdered his brothers-in-arms, slaughtered innocent women and children, and deserved not one shred of mercy, certainly not his. Bastards.

And because the men he planned to take out were most certainly working on a vicious and terrible revenge on the United States, he even started to feel good about the operation. As always, Mack was protecting his fellow citizens, and some of the most important men in the entire nation were backing him. For the ex-SEAL commander it would be as it had always been, accompanied by an unending reminder of the creed of the United States Navy SEALs:

> *I humbly serve as guardian to my fellow Americans, always ready to defend those who are unable to defend themselves. I do not advertise the nature of my work, nor seek recognition for my actions. I voluntarily accept the inherent hazards of my profession, placing the welfare and security of others before my own . . . the ability to control my emotions and my actions, regardless of circumstance, sets me apart from other men.*

As he sat on the wide veranda of the Parkwood Inn, he recalled when he had first heard those words, when they had pinned the golden Trident high on the left side of the jacket of his dress uniform. No one ever forgets that moment, the day of indoctrination into the world's greatest fighting force. They had never tried to take that Trident away from him. Because no one ever could. That was his gift. Goddamnit, that was his life, and it always would be. The solemn words still seared through his brain:

> *My Trident is a symbol of honor and heritage, bestowed upon me by the heroes who have gone before. It embodies the trust of those I have sworn to protect. By wearing the Trident, I accept the responsibility of my chosen profession and way of life. It is a privilege I must earn every day.*

Mack had lost his commission. But he had never lost the soul of the Navy SEAL commander. And now he was within reach of regaining his old life. And he stared at the 8x10 glossy photographs of Ibrahim, Yousaf, Ben, and Abu Hassan, mass murderers. "If I pursue you to the ends of the earth," he murmured, "I will find you. I will stop you doing whatever the hell you are doing. And you will die."

THREE HOURS AFTER DINNER, the hotel car dropped Mack at the gates of the historic World War II Naval Air Station, and the guards nodded him through. No documentation was asked or offered. A staff car driver transported him in absolute silence to the end of the 8,000-foot runway and, without a word, Mack climbed out and stood in the shadows.

The car drove away, and Mack checked his watch; still fifteen minutes early. It had just started to rain, and he buttoned his trench coat and turned up the collar but stood bare-headed in the hard southwesterly wind that slashed across the airfield directly off the Gulf of Maine. Like all local Down Easters (seaward natives of the state) he took a perverse pride, like desert bedouins, that they alone could easily stand the harsh climatic elements of their homeland. And Mack stared doggedly to the northeast, watching for the landing lights, when the gigantic Lockheed Martin C-130 Hercules came howling over the 3,000-foot lighted runway approach.

Right now it was pitch dark beyond the markers, and the big ex-SEAL found his thoughts wandering to the last time he had been here, the shattering day when he had left the Navy. It might have broken a lesser character, but Mack Bedford turned his head sideways to the wind, as if daring the gusting squalls even to attract his attention.

Visibility was not so hot, but he'd been in worse. Then suddenly, maybe a mile from where he stood, he spotted two pinpoints of light, like twin stars sliding slowly toward the ground. The huge turbo-prop freighter was losing height quickly as it came thundering down the approach, landing wheels lowered. Mack watched all twenty-three wheels hit the blacktop with a sharp squeak as the plane's massive wings flared out and then leveled.

One minute later, the aircraft taxied to where he stood and pulled up within thirty yards. From out of the darkness, a mobile flight of stairs emerged. Mack, holding his bag, loped across the runway and bounded up the steps, through the open door and out of the rain.

Mack heard the great aircraft door slam behind him as he was led to a wide seat made of netting. It was time for his 3,400-mile journey to begin in one of the noisiest aircraft ever to wend its way through the stratosphere, an enormous echoing steel cave, designed strictly to transport heavy military gear. No one spoke, and no one offered help or instructions as he stripped off his coat, slung it with his bag on the next seat, sat down, and buckled himself in.

The flight crew knew he was no ordinary former SEAL, that this was the fabled Mackenzie Bedford, the ex-frog who had once led SEAL Team Ten's Foxtrot Platoon to the sensational and ruthless capture of one of the biggest offshore oil rigs in the Gulf of Iran (Proprietor S. Hussein). Eighteen armed troops were killed that night, none of them American.

The entire crew was under orders not to converse with their passenger—to merely bring him coffee, whatever food there was, and anything else he needed. But there would be no communication. They were transporting the closest thing to a ghost any of them were ever likely to encounter.

At the north end of the blacktop the Hercules made its turn, never braked, and, with its Boeing engines howling, screamed down the runway, shaking and rumbling as it gathered speed. It thundered into the night sky, through the coastal rain clouds and up into the clear air. It rose up through the pale rays of the almost-full moon, which glinted along its portside, as it made its way across the Atlantic Ocean.

AS THE U.S. HERCULES TOOK OFF, the Pakistan International Airlines flight from Lahore to Amsterdam, a Boeing 777-300ER, was heading northwest somewhere over the eastern Mediterranean, preparing for its long swerve up over the Balkans, right across the old Soviet territories of Eastern Europe, and on to Amsterdam. Ibrahim, Yousaf, Ben, and Abu Hassan were seated in first class, each wearing a tailored Western suit and traveling on impeccably forged student visas.

They were confident, fit, and cheerfully reading Western magazines and newspapers, looking forward to their meeting with the rabid Bradford-based al-Qaeda leader, Sheikh Abdullah Bazir.

The big Pakistani passenger jet came in low over Holland's flat country and sprawling network of canals, around the time of the morning rush hour. At Schipol Airport, nine miles south of the city, they were first out of the aircraft. They moved quickly through the line for transfers, the Dutch officials showing scant interest in passengers who were not remaining in their country.

One hour later they boarded a busy Air Iran charter flight bound for Leeds-Bradford, the final one-hour lap of their 4,500-mile journey. They landed mid-morning and now faced the most dangerous part of the day, the moment of truth where a beady-eyed customs official could spot a flaw in their student visas and start demanding explanations. At least that would have been true in the United States, or Australia, or even France or Germany, certainly Japan. But not in England. The officials stamped the entry documents, giving the green light to the "University of British Literature and Law."

One by one, Ibrahim, Yousaf, Ben, and Abu, walked right through, out of the airport, and boarded separate taxis. Each gave the driver the same instruction: "Please take me up to the Cow and Calf Rocks on Ilkley Moor."

The cabs completed the seven-mile drive at five-minute intervals, and for ten minutes the four terrorists from the Middle East stood in a huddle beneath the largest of the two stones. Shortly before midday, a black Range Rover with darkened windows pulled up alongside them.

A young Indian-looking man wearing Western clothes jumped out of the driver's seat and opened the rear door. A character who might have stepped off the back-lot at Universal Studios in Burbank emerged, the robed figure of the most dangerous man in England, the al-Qaeda mastermind and recruiter, Sheikh Abdullah Bazir.

The white-bearded mullah, unsmiling beneath a black turban, offered the traditional Muslim greeting, his right hand making a wide arc from his forehead to a point level with his waist. He said, quietly, "Welcome, my sons. Allah has delivered you safely, and I would like you all to join me in prayer."

Without another word, he walked to a point on the north side of the giant stone. He stared heavenward to ensure the sun had passed its peak. Then, firmly, he spoke the words of imams across the world, calling the faithful to prayer from a thousand minaret towers. Sheikh Abdullah had no minaret, but his words still rang with fervor, echoing across the bright and otherwise deserted Moors:

> *God is most great.*
> *I bear witness there is no god, but God.*
> *I bear witness Mohammed is the Prophet of God.*
> *Come to pray!*
> *Come to wellbeing!*
> *God is most great.*
> *There is no god, but God.*

And then he turned to the east, toward the ancient West Yorkshire village of Burley-in-Wharfedale. But his gaze was elevated and it carried far beyond that, beyond the Moors and the North Sea, beyond Europe. It was focused to the east, toward the Ka'ba Shrine, in the Holy City of Mecca, with its massive symbolic presence in the minds of the most devout followers of Allah.

Suddenly, Sheikh Abdullah cried out the sacred word, *"Takbir!"* And Ibrahim, Yousaf, Ben, and Abu responded in unison, *"Allahu Akbar!"* God is great.

There, on the dry heathers of Ilkley Moor, the five men prostrated themselves before their God, and the imam murmured the mantras of the Prophet Mohammed—ending once more with the cry, "Allahu Akbar," the phrase written so sternly on the national flags of the Islamic republics of Afghanistan, Iraq, and Iran. They would also be the last words uttered by the four terrorists whenever their next bomb detonated, bringing, as it always did, blood, sorrow, and destruction to so many innocent lives.

And now Imam Abdullah Bazir took each one of the four men by the hand and spoke to him, as his leader. "My sons," he said, "the agents of the Infidels are conducting surveillance upon my mosque throughout every day. They watch for my visitors and especially for my warriors. I dare not allow you entrance and therefore we must meet only here on the high moors. But don't be afraid, for we are closer to Allah."

Ibrahim thanked him. And the Sheikh continued. "Either I or my representative cleric will be here each evening at 7 p.m. It's a lonely place, and we shall not be disturbed. It is not necessary for you to attend when your minds are clear, but when you need the guidance of the Prophet, we will be here for you."

"And, Imam, will you pray with us?" asked Yousaf.

"Either I or my cleric will conduct prayers here each evening when you arrive. But each day wherever you are, you must make the recitations—that Allah is the one who deserves to be worshipped, that praise and thanks be to Him, the owner of the world.

"Remember, He is the Owner of the Day of Judgment. From He alone we dedicate worship and seek help, which is the ultimate subjugation. You must repeat again, *'O, Allah, we pray You keep us on the straight path, and not the path of those who went astray.'*"

The imam then turned and walked back toward the Range Rover, signaling for the others to climb aboard. "I will not come with you," he said, "but you will be taken to a safe place, and you will never be far from me. I alone will know your new address.

"Shakir Khan has entrusted you to my care. But when it is time, you will be told. And you will continue your long journey to the United States of America, where you will conduct God's work. You will be here as guests of the al-Qaeda High Command for several weeks while arrangements are made for your new mission."

Each man thanked Sheikh Abdullah, who now stood apart from the black vehicle, alone in the shadow of the giant rock. And the young Muslim driver set off without him, across the Moors, heading south toward the Islamic area of Bradford.

DETECTIVE SERGEANT OWEN THOMAS, lying flat in the heather about eighty yards east and slightly elevated from the rocks, watched the Range Rover leave, and finally put down his camera.

He and his younger colleague, Constable Tom Wainright, had

been watching the downtown mosque all week from a small, un-marked, dark blue patrol car.

When Sheikh Abdullah moved, they moved. And they had driven up onto Ilkley Moor about three hundred yards behind him. As soon as the holy man disembarked, they pulled off the road and half-walked, half-crouched into their current hiding spot.

Sergeant Thomas had an excellent set of finely focused shots, taken through a powerful old-fashioned "long-Tom" lens. He had no idea who the four visitors were, but he had perfect identification of everyone who had prayed at the rocks.

Within five minutes, another vehicle arrived to collect Sheikh Abdullah, and they watched it head back toward Bradford. Tom Wainright immediately called in, and reported that he and his boss would return to HQ immediately to develop the film. The next two-man shift would take over the endless night watch on the mosque.

That afternoon in the West Yorkshire Police bureau in Brad-ford, events moved rapidly. The 8x10 glossies delivered by Ser-geant Thomas at 9 p.m. to the desk of Detective Superintendent Len Martin were almost immediately sent for transmission to Scotland Yard's Antiterrorist chief, Ronald Catton, in London.

He had them wired electronically across the Atlantic to the CIA in Langley for possible identification. It was 4:15 p.m. in Washing-ton, and Bob Birmingham's boys took only moments to identify Ibrahim Sharif, Yousaf Mohammed, Ben al-Turabi, and Abu Has-san Akbar. The four most wanted men on the planet had plainly moved into Bradford.

Len Martin asked Sergeant Thomas a relatively simple ques-tion: "Did we track the four guys to their address?"

"Nossir."

"Why not?"

"That's not our job, sir. We're detailed to track Sheikh Abdullah at all times. Nothing else."

"Jesus Christ, Owen," exclaimed Martin, "according to this signal from both Catton and the CIA, the four men on the Moor, the ones you just photographed, are convicted terrorists, ex-Guantanamo Bay."

"Sir, if we tracked everyone the imam spoke to, we'd need another three hundred cars and six hundred officers."

"Apparently half the antiterrorist squads in the free world are trying to locate these four characters."

"Do the Americans have names for them?"

"Just arrived, in a signal from Catton. The usual, Mohammed, Abu, Ibrahim, etcetera. And we're forbidden from entering any of their names anywhere in our records."

"Any point checking with immigration?"

"None. Guys like that can't even remember when they last used their real names. Still, they can't be far away. Tom and I saw them leave in Abdullah's car, and one of the boys just called in to say it was back at the mosque, and so is the Sheikh."

"So it must be in Manningham, maybe a few streets away from the mosque."

Moments later another surveillance signal came in: "Range Rover spotted parked north end of Darsfield Street, passengers disembarking. No further surveillance."

"We got four suspect houses in Darsfield," said Len Martin. "Guess it's one of them."

"We still can't pick anyone up," said the grim, tough-looking Sergeant Thomas. "So far as I know it's not really against the law to speak to a Muslim cleric in the middle of a bloody field."

"No. But it should be, when it's that particular Muslim Cleric," snapped Len Martin. "He's a bloody menace. Should've been sent home to the Punjab years ago."

THE FOUR-ENGINED J-model Hercules freighter carrying just Mack Bedford, instead of its usual load of 156 troops and twenty tons of hardware, was well over the United Kingdom by dawn, heading to its home base of RAF Lyneham.

It came lumbering in over the chalk hills and touched down hard on the west runway. They had the big steel staircase at the aircraft door open within sixty seconds, and Mack Bedford ran lightly down the steps, directly to a waiting Jaguar. He slung his bag onto the front passenger seat and settled behind the wheel. No one acknowledged him.

He switched on the SATNAV system and headed for the exit gates, aiming across the Cotswold Hills to Cirencester, Gloucester, and then Ross-on-Wye, a distance of seventy miles. The last leg of his journey took him up an old familiar road, the one which led to Hereford, the former home to 22 SAS, the Brits' top Special Forces regiment, with whom he had trained many times.

The SAS had moved recently, and now occupied the most secretive HQ—the instantly fabled Stirling Lines, set in deep, wooded countryside outside the tiny village of Credenhill, four miles north of the 930-year-old Hereford Cathedral.

Here, in total seclusion, the SAS, often in company with U.S. Navy SEALs, worked and trained their way through the most searching brutal routines ever dreamed up, including those of Attila the Hun, Genghis Khan, Alexander, Geronimo, and Conan the Barbarian.

Stirling Lines housed Mack's only point of contact, his old friend Lt. Colonel Russ Makin, who, having done such a good job in command of the regiment, he hadn't been promoted further to a job in the Defense Ministry in Whitehall.

Russ was a combat soldier at heart. He had served with distinction in Great Britain's Falklands War in 1982, and again in the first Gulf War. In 2003, at the age of forty-one, he had attacked the oil rig in the Gulf with Mack Bedford. In a joint SEAL/SAS operation, the two had taken the high platform after a firefight with twelve Iraqi commandos, none of whom survived.

Russ half expected to see his old colleague today, but the signal from U.S. military Intelligence had been deliberately vague. He had no idea what Mack was involved in, but it was sure as hell secret. He sipped his afternoon tea in silence, watching the twenty-four-hour news channel on a large flatscreen television. He learned two more guys he knew were dead, blown to bits by a roadside bomb in Kabul, another British Army jeep with insufficient armored protection.

Russ could never quite work out whether he should feel sorrow or fury, regret or anger, whether to play all hell in Whitehall, or resign forthwith, and get out of the entire dirty rotten business. He was worn down watching kids get killed for nothing, because of dumbass politicians, who put budgets and their own pathetic careers before the lives of his troops.

"Fuck it," he muttered, not caring a damn whether anyone heard him or not.

Right now, Mack was in the city of Hereford. He'd taken a detour from the main road to drive the Jaguar down memory lane, past his old haunt, the four-hundred-year-old Green Dragon Inn, where he and Russ, along with three other SEALs and the SAS guys, had attended an Iraq reunion in 2006.

He drove over the fifteenth-century six-arched stone bridge, and into the old town before heading out on the A48, which runs through rich pastures and past herds of some of the finest beef-cattle in the world, the red-coated, white-faced Herefords.

Mack reached the gates of SAS Headquarters at 6:30 p.m. The guards spotted the Jaguar's registration plate number and waved him through. They knew who had arrived. Again, no one spoke.

He parked the car, and walked up to the unit's majestic and somber Clock Tower, which had been rehoused in the barracks memorial garden in front of the Regimental church. Engraved on the memorial were the names of SAS men who had lost their lives; the heroes who had willingly "gone beyond that last blue mountain barred with snow"—the sacred and avowed aim of SAS personnel, should the battle, the safety of their team, or the plain call of duty, have demanded it.

Mack walked to the Clock Tower and stared at the memorial as the memory of three lost friends washed over him. He bowed his head briefly and then turned and walked away toward Russ Makin's office.

The CO of Stirling Lines saw him coming through the window and walked out to greet him. They shook hands warmly, and the British officer grinned and said, "I heard about your antics along the Euphrates, now what are you up to?"

Mack Bedford laughed, and replied, "Couple of minor tasks, kind of thing you give a guy who's unfit for command."

Russ slapped him on the shoulder and led the way back to his office. As they walked in he called to a young SAS trooper, "Tell someone to bring some *hot* tea, will you, Harry? And a few biscuits."

They walked inside and Lt. Colonel Makin picked up a message on his desk that read, "There's an e-mail for you, sir. Military Intelligence. It's on your machine."

He tapped a few keys on his keyboard and asked Mack to excuse him briefly as he picked up the message. Then he looked up and said, "Christ! Are you Visiting Black Bear?"

"Shouldn't be surprised, buddy," said Mack.

"Well, you'd better pay attention. It says here, 'Tell Visiting Black Bear—for future ref. VBB—the chosen ones reached Stone Cattle as predicted. Suggest proceed there this day. Police DS Len Martin briefed. Tracing.' Who the hell's the chosen ones?" asked Russ.

"Bunch of jerks who might try to blow us all up."

"You trying to find them?"

"Uh-huh."

"Then what?"

"Maybe a little negotiation."

"You mean you're going to take them out?" edged Russ.

"Who me?" said Mack. "Steady on, old buddy. I'm just planning to have a chat."

"Of course," said the CO. "Just a little chat."

The tea arrived, hot, along with officers' mess Royal Crown Derby cups and saucers, a curved milk jug, a sugar bowl, and a plate of biscuits. Mack sipped gratefully. He loved tea when it was made by the British. And he liked Russ Makin as much as he had ever liked any serving officer anywhere in the world.

"Okay, Mack," said Russ. "Since you're plainly on your way to the bloody Stone Cattle, in the kind of car they routinely give to any old messenger boy, I'd better tell you my brief."

"Shoot."

"I am your contact and your link. You will not be moving signals through any other source. This office is effectively your command post. I have written down my private cell phone and my e-mail. This is my personal land-line number, and, if all fails, you know the main number of the base. Any time you need to, grab a phone and reverse the charges to my office. Also I am forbidden to admit to one living soul that I have ever been in contact with you since we left Iraq."

"How about the Green Dragon?"

"Screw the Green Dragon. And, before you ask, no, there isn't a chance in hell this office has been, is, or will ever be, bugged."

"How do you know?"

"Because this is the toughest, most brutally efficient military base in the world."

"Second."

"Who once saved your life, *Lieutenant* Commander Bedford?"

"Same guy who was darn near captured by the Iraqis, and I had to shoot all three of them and then throw their boss off the top of the oil rig."

"Well, we can all have a bit of luck," replied Russ Makin, laughing. "I wonder if we could be serious for a moment."

"Okay. Let's give it a shot."

"Right. I am briefed that you are no longer a serving officer in the U.S. armed forces?"

"Correct."

"However, your mission is classified to the highest possible degree. Your contacts, through me, are heads of department only—CIA, NSA, Pentagon, Navy, and Scotland Yard antiterror. And that

Detective Superintendent West Yorkshire Police. That's my brief."

"And mine."

"I understand I may not know the nature of the mission?"

"Correct."

"But I can guess."

"Very possibly."

"I am also instructed to provide you with any and all assistance you may request. Actually, Mack, they did not use the word 'request.' They used 'demand.' Whatever it is you're working on, you'd better not screw it up."

"How about rescue? Should I end up in deepest excrement?"

"I am ordered to activate an entire platoon 22 SAS and get you out at all costs."

"Comforting."

"You want to tell me what's happening?"

"Hell, yes. But I cannot."

"Well, you have to tell me where you are going. Or I can't effect a rescue."

"Guess so. But only when I demand it. Right now, I'm Secret Mack."

"Okay. You staying for dinner?"

"If I get invited. No point arriving in Bradford in the middle of the goddamned night."

"You going straight to the old Stone Cattle tomorrow, right after you leave here?"

"I don't think so. I'll need twenty-four hours to get my bearings. But there's quite a lot of stuff I'd like to check out with you before I leave. Can I have another cup of that tea?"

RUSS AND MACK DINED TOGETHER in his private house, away from the other officers. There was a ripple of curiosity throughout the base as to the identity of their guest, but no one could find out who he was.

Mack had breakfast in his own room and then spent the

morning working with Russ on his big computer screen, familiar-izing himself with the Yorkshire Moors and the access roads that led to and from one of the loneliest parts.

Right after lunch, he started his 125-mile journey to Bradford. He headed west, up to the M5 motorway, a very fast stretch of road leading on to the M6, and then the M62, a six-lane highway carv-ing straight through industrial Lancashire to the southern ap-proaches to Bradford.

He arrived in Bradford at 8 p.m. totally unaware of the chaos his presence in the UK had caused the previous evening. Detective Superintendent Len Martin had considered he might become a laughingstock if he had admitted the four terrorists had slipped clean through his net, probably within hours of landing in York-shire. So ordered Sergeant Thomas literally to ransack Darsfield Street, forcing entry into houses listed as "occupied by known Is-lamic fanatics," on the pretence of searching for drugs, weapons, or bombmaking equipment.

"I don't care if it takes all night," Martin told Detective Sergeant Thomas. "Find those four guys who met the mullah up by the rocks this afternoon."

"I can't arrest them, can I?" said Thomas. "They haven't actually done anything."

"I don't want them arrested yet. I just need to know precisely where they are living in our city, all right?"

And so Sergeant Thomas and a heavy hit-squad, comprised of twenty-four armed officers, two big police vans, four tracker dogs, three police photographers, and an ambulance (just in case), had swooped down on unsuspecting Darsfield Street just before dark.

They had kicked down two doors, hit another with a sledge-hammer, dragged sleeping Muslims out of bed. They shouted, in-timidated, threatened, and generally played hell, for two hours, until they reached the last of the seven houses on their roster.

Right there the game changed. The entire street by now was aware that something was happening, and there were lights on in number 289, which now had six officers guarding the back door, with another eight at the front, machine guns leveled.

Sergeant Thomas himself had banged on the door. And it was answered immediately by Ibrahim Sharif. Behind him stood Yousaf Mohammed and Ben al-Turabi. All eight of West Yorkshire's finest came charging into the house. They lined up the three Islamists at gunpoint against the wall. Then they searched the entire place, finding no explosives but a large bag of chemical fertilizer and several detonators, plus wired batteries. Any experienced policemen, especially in Bradford, knew precisely what this meant. Bombs.

Then Sergeant Thomas discovered Abu Hassan Akbar locked in the bathroom. He'd found all four of the men he'd photographed; all four at once. Bloody good night's work that.

He handcuffed and arrested them immediately on suspicion of attempting to make IEDs (improvised explosive devices). He was taking the law into his own hands, knowing it would be a hard charge to prove, and that he could only detain them in Yorkshire for forty-eight hours. But he also knew someone, somewhere, would be bloody grateful to him. He ordered them to bring their passports, documents, and visas, and to get into the police van, right away.

With blue lights flashing, the dark blue paddy wagon was flung open to admit the four recently arrived killers, and they stumbled into the wide mobile rear section, uncertain of the fate that awaited them.

They arrived in the holding cells, just before Mack Bedford touched base by phone with Len Martin. He announced himself as "Black Bear," as arranged, and informed the detective superintendent he was calling from SAS home base. He also told him he would arrive the following evening, and requested that someone check him into the agreed hotel.

Martin told him he would provide clear information when he arrived. He and Sergeant Thomas had already issued the legally required warnings to Ibrahim, Yousaf, Ben, and Abu. Photographs confirmed there was no doubt whatsoever about the identification of the four men they were detaining.

Ibrahim had asked permission to make one call, to Sheikh Abdullah Bazir, since he guessed he needed to speak to a lawyer. Martin denied this permission for a period of twelve hours while they examined the confiscated bombmaking equipment. He made the excuse that he may elect to release them all, subject to this examination.

He was, of course, breaking the law. In England, even terrorists are permitted immediate access to a lawyer. But Martin reasoned if any trouble ensued, he could always nail them on student visa irregularities.

BY THE TIME Mack actually checked into the Cow and Calf Hotel, Len Martin had had the Chosen Ones under lock and key for twenty-four hours, and he was beginning to feel a little jumpy, since that was an inordinate amount of time to prevent any suspects, never mind terrorist suspects, from speaking to a lawyer. So Martin was relieved when Mack called in from the hotel, announcing that he would like to meet the four terrorists alone, up near the rocks, the following evening at 9:30 p.m. Mack told Martin to drive them up there, inform them a friend was meeting them at the base of the small stone, and then liberate them.

"That's the outside limit of my holding time," he replied. "Will the result be as we expect?"

"Yes," replied Mack. "I'll call in with details for the clean-up before I leave."

"SAS?"

"Affirmative."

AS MILITARY STYLE operations go, this one was proceeding smoothly. Mack called Russ Makin and alerted him to have a Chinook helicopter ready to come in with body bags around 2130 the following evening. The SAS boss placed one on immediate stand-by at the British Army garrison at Catterick on the edge of Hip-swell Moor, forty-five miles and fifteen minutes north of Bradford. Martin entered his data on his desktop computer and e-mailed everything to Lt. Colonel Makin in Credenhill, as ordered by Scotland Yard.

Four hours later, he sent the four prisoners coffee and sandwiches, which he hoped would shut them up. Then he left for the night.

For the past eight months, the Bradford HQ of West Yorkshire Police, had harbored a "mole"—a twenty-five-year-old Pakistani janitor named Freddie, who worked three nights a week. He was a cheerful young man, who studied—sometimes—by day, in one of the myriad of "universities" situated in the borough of Manningham. Everyone liked Freddie, but there were two things about him that no one knew. One was that he held a master's degree in Internet Technology from Cornell University. The other was that he was a skilled bombmaker, who planned to blast the Bradford Police HQ off the map.

Freddie worked for Sheikh Abdullah. His father had died in the American bombing of Tora Bora, close to where bin Laden lived. Freddie was an Islamic extremist, right on the cusp of pure fanaticism.

And now he moved stealthily, standing in the shadows as Len Martin and his driver exited the building. With his mop slung over his left shoulder and bucket of hot soapy water in hand, he walked down the long corridor to the superintendent's office. He took out his key chain and carefully selected a master key from the bundle, letting himself into Len Martin's office.

Without turning on a light, he booted up the computer and waited for the screen to light up. He opened the e-mail window, as he'd done just about every night, and scrolled through.

He stopped at the one tagged "SAS Contact," which he opened and read:

> VBB requests Chinook backup with four body bags
> 2300 tomorrow Ilkley Moor GPS 53.195N 1.450W. VBB
> rendezvous Chosen Ones Stone Cattle 2130. No reply
> required.

Freddie quickly wrote down notes on Len Martin's pad, then scanned the list again until he found one called "Chosen Ones." He opened that and found the names identified by U.S. Intelligence, against the photographs—Ibrahim Sharif, Yousaf Mohammed, Ben al-Turabi, and Abu Hassan Akbar. This computer was the only place in the station where their names were written down.

"By the Prophet! Body bags! SAS! They're going to murder my brothers," breathed Freddie. "Tomorrow night at 9:30 up at the two rocks."

He ripped out his cell phone and called Sheikh Abdullah Bazir, who answered sleepily, but snapped into high alert quickly. He grabbed a pen and paper and wrote down the details, not understanding for one moment how the Yorkshire Police could possibly know the Chosen Ones were in the country, nor how the police had correctly identified them, with accurate names, in so short a time. He thanked Freddie, who then switched off Len Martin's computer and carried on mopping the station floor.

Sheikh Abdullah then proceeded to telephone three of his most ruthless assassins, men who had been fortunate not to have been sentenced to life imprisonment after their suspected involvement with the August 2006 plot to blow up seven passenger jets over the North Atlantic with liquid bombs.

That was a plot planned in the Swat Valley to be carried out by al-Qaeda associates based in England. Several had subsequently received massive jail sentences, and several had worked directly for Sheikh Abdullah Bazir.

Britain's antiterrorist forces had done spectacularly well to foil this outrageous scheme to kill possibly 2,800 transatlantic passengers, a number eerily close to the total death-count at the Twin Towers in 2001.

Three of the culprits were still free, and now Sheikh Abdullah had them on the line, detailing their next mission. They were told to report to the Cow and Calf Rocks at 8:30 p.m. tonight, and then seek and kill without mercy the man who would try to murder the Chosen Ones at around 9:30 p.m.

"He is probably very dangerous," said the Sheikh. "Go well armed and shoot to kill. No need to hide evidence. You will leave for Pakistan before the body is found. Bradford Airport. Iran Air charter jet."

"Consider it done, master," the assassins replied. "We will not fail you."

"Go with Allah," said the Sheikh. "For He will go with you. Allahu Akbar."

SHEIKH ABDULLAH SOUNDED CONFIDENT, assured, determined. In truth, he was not. Someone was going to die out there. And the Sheikh wasn't sure who that someone might be. There would be someone out there, maybe alone, maybe not, but almost certainly a professional killer hired by either the Americans or the Brits—someone who truly knew the track record of the Chosen Ones. He could only hope that his trusted assassins, all from Pakistan, would locate their enemy and put him to the sword. Three against one seemed to favor his men. However, three against two was less appealing, and he hoped the government's killer would come alone. He resorted to prayer, imploring Allah to grant him justice, and to lead his servants out on the moors tonight along the path of light.

The second great puzzle that faced him was, why were the Chosen Ones expected up at the rocks at 9:30? He had made no arrangements to rendezvous, and they would have no reason to go there without at least informing him. Which meant the police, or the Army, was taking them up there to murder them, to rid the Western world of the problem, and then deny all evidence of wrongdoing. Sheikh Abdullah knew that governments were good at that, especially the Americans, the Great Satan.

Therefore he had but one task this day: to prevent the Chosen Ones being taken up to Ilkley Moor. But, short of blowing up the police station and probably killing everyone in it, including the Chosen Ones, he had no ideas on how to proceed.

Except for one.

ACROSS THE YORKSHIRE BORDER in Lancashire, deep in the northern suburbs of Manchester, lies the heavily Muslim-populated Cheetham Hill. And right there, on Cheetham Hill Road, lived Dr. Ahmed Kamil, a forty-year-old somewhat-shadowy figure, known to be involved in a labyrinth of legal actions involving terrorists, but never a man to take center stage in a trial.

Dr. Kamil had a doctorate in law from the University of Cairo. He practiced in the UK as a consultant and advisor, not an advocate. His business was entirely terrorism, but he had never even taken the final exams that would permit him to speak in even a Crown Court, far less the High Court where terrorists tend to wind up.

Born in Pakistan and a familiar figure in major police headquarters all over the north of England, Ahmed Kamil operated from an elegant suite of offices in Manchester's Deansgate—a relatively snazzy address for an unqualified attorney whose clients were apt to be unshaven potential killers and amateur bombmakers. No one really knew who paid him for consulting, but someone valued him highly: Dr. Kamil drove a brand new Rolls Royce.

And right now, that particular dark red Phantom drop-head coup was making short work of the long escarpment up Lakewood Moor on the western edge of the steep Pennines. At the wheel was Ahmed Kamil, frowning, speeding to do the bidding of Sheikh Abdullah in Bradford. His paymaster.

He knocked off the forty-two-mile journey in half an hour and pulled into the private parking lot next to the mosque shortly after 11 a.m. Swiftly he made his way down to the Sheikh's office for his briefing.

Dr. Kamil made a note of the allegations that would probably be made against the men. And he requested the full names and addresses of the previous residents of 289 Darsfield Road. He also wanted to know the name of the official owners of the property, but Sheikh Abdullah ruled that would not be helpful. After three hours, Dr. Kamil set off to do battle with West Yorkshire Police. In his attaché case he carried copies of law-book pages detailing the new Acts of Parliament that specified the precise number of days permitted to hold suspects without trial.

There had been, quite recently, almost riot conditions in the House of Commons before they arrived at a twenty-eight days maximum. But that required warrants from judges and much other technical data. The golden number was forty-eight—the precise number of hours any suspect could be held without being charged with anything. Thanks to the diligent Freddie, Dr. Kamil knew the record would show the four prisoners had been held since 7 p.m. on the night of their arrest.

Kamil pulled into the police private parking lot and drove into an empty space, on the basis that no one ever doubted a Rolls Royce's rights, because the owner was probably extremely important. He walked into the police station, marched straight to the front desk, ignoring a small line of waiting people, and announced himself as the lawyer representing four prisoners who had now been in custody for almost forty hours. "Please take me down to them immediately," he said, knowing his request would be denied.

The station sergeant picked up the telephone and informed DS Len Martin there was someone to see him—"Lawyer representing the four Pakistanis downstairs," he added.

Len Martin was not pleased. He was already skating on thin ice, and this intruder might make things extremely awkward. He instructed that Dr. Kamil be brought to his office.

"Sir," Kamil said, "I have been retained to represent all four of the men, and I understand they have been held, so far without charge, since approximately 6 p.m. the night before last. My question is, do you intend to charge them, and if so with what?"

Len Martin thought quickly. "I am almost certainly going to charge them this afternoon with attempting to manufacture IEDs with intent to kill or maim citizens of the city of Bradford."

"Have they been questioned?"

"Not yet."

"Then how can you possibly know what their intent was? Also I need to know whether you have evidence that any of them were making anything that might explode. Was there TNT or dynamite in the house?"

"There was no actual explosive, but there were several electrical detonators and substantial quantities of industrial fertilizer, which can be quickly turned into high explosive."

"My question, superintendent, is, were they in the process of turning it into high explosive?"

"Well, not precisely at that time."

"Did they own the industrial fertilizers, or indeed the electrical detonators?"

"That we do not know."

"Then we are dealing with the purely circumstantial evidence that placed these four men in the same house as certain ingredients of certain types of bomb."

"I cannot easily dispute that."

"Superintendent, do you know how long my clients had been in residence in number 289 Darsfield Street when your officers swooped on them?"

"No. I do not know that."

"Less than five hours. They arrived from Pakistan that morning. Which means that my four clients were seized by the British police almost immediately after they moved into their residence. That they were handcuffed, thrown in jail, never questioned nor spoken to, and held without charge, all under an entirely false time of arrest?"

"What do you mean false time of arrest?"

Dr. Kamil took a chance. "Your record shows they were booked in here at 7 p.m., and therefore you are entitled to hold them for forty-eight hours, until 7 p.m. tonight. I am saying they were held in police custody from 6 p.m. not 7."

"It was 7 p.m. when we checked them in," replied Len Martin.

"But it was only 6 p.m. when you arrested them, handcuffed them, and subsequently ordered them into the police van, thus depriving them of their lawful liberties."

"That's not the way it works," replied Martin. "Their time of entry into police custody is the time they arrive here. 7 p.m."

"Then you dispute that to handcuff a man, and imprison him in the back of a police holding van with barred windows, under armed guard, is to deprive him of his liberty? You think he's still free to go about his lawful business?"

"Well, not exactly . . ."

"I am afraid the law is an exact business, superintendent," replied Dr. Kamil. "And I challenge your right to hold my clients for one moment after 6 p.m. this evening without charge."

"And where do you propose to make this challenge?" said Martin.

"Oh, I have already requested a magistrate and a hearing, subject to an unsatisfactory conclusion to our meeting. Mr. Martin, I am afraid you must either charge them or release them at precisely six today."

"You may assume we will charge them."

"That's your right. But I hope, for your sake, you are able to reconcile the alleged bombmaking materials with the presence of my clients. Because I believe the previous residents of 289 Darsfield Street were convicted of bombmaking offenses after they were arrested in London.

"My clients will deny vigorously they even knew the stuff, or anything else, was in the house. They'd only just arrived, and you most certainly will find none of their fingerprints on anything except a few mugs of coffee.

"I think you'll be very lucky to locate any judge or jury to find them guilty of anything. At which point, of course, I will have you charged with making wrongful arrests, and deliberately failing to grant my clients their legal right to a lawyer for more than forty hours. Our legal team will demand substantial damages."

From a police point of view, this was going stupendously badly. Every aspect of the operation had swerved in the wrong direction. There was the threat of publicity, damage to police reputation, and a couple of criminal charges that could not possibly hold up. Not to mention the oncoming fury of the Ministry of Defense, Scotland Yard's Antiterrorist Squad, the CIA, SAS and God knows who else. One word in the media could bring the bloody roof down on his head. Len Martin stood. "Dr. Kamil, I think we understand each other. Allow me to consult with my colleagues, and perhaps we can reconvene later."

"I would appreciate that," said Dr. Kamil. "Perhaps around 5:45 this afternoon?"

When he saw the Rolls pull out of the parking lot, DS Martin opened up his line to Lt. Colonel Makin, who wished to consult with the Americans. It was well after 5:30 p.m. (local), when the parties were all agreed that the operation would have to be put on hold, temporarily.

And at three minutes before 6 p.m. the al-Qaeda killers, Ibrahim Sharif, Yousaf Mohammed, Ben al-Turabi and Abu Hassan Akbar, for the second time in three months, walked free from police custody with no further stain on their character.

More importantly, they would not face Mack Bedford, who was already surveying his own personal killing field, up there on windswept Ilkley Moor.

Dr. Ahmed Kamil had, once more, earned his fee.

6

B Y 6:30 THAT EVENING, the weather on these high Yorkshire plains had deteriorated rapidly. The moors were famous
for sudden storms, high winds, and fog, but in autumn, they
were at their most capricious, with both the temperatures and the
wind direction subject to swift, almost hourly, changes.

Mack Bedford, like all combat members of the Special Forces,
especially SEALs and SAS, required about four times more reconnaissance than anyone else. All through the late afternoon, he had
stood at his hotel window watching the light grow darker, and the
winds begin to rise.

The rain set in, right after he had watched the BBC's six o'clock
news, at which point Mack decided to leave and begin his recce
down by the two rocks, which he could now see, stark against the
lowering sky. He wore his rainproof, camouflage trousers and over
a polo-neck sweater, his cammy top. He pulled on waterproof

combat boots, black leather gloves, and black balaclava hood. He loaded a magazine into his SIG-Sauer 9mm service revolver and jammed it into his leather belt, on the opposite side of his sheathed combat knife.

In the specially tailored inside pocket he placed a hand grenade sufficiently powerful to blow up the Cow and Calf Hotel. This was courtesy of Lt. Colonel Makin, "In case of a minor emergency." He also carried a slim SEAL night glass telescope, but nothing to identify him in the event of his death.

Unavoidably attired as Public Enemy Number One, Mack Bedford opened the window of his ground-level room and stepped through it, out onto the rapidly darkening Ilkley Moor. He missed Len Martin's call, postponing the operation, by twelve minutes.

Swiftly he ran clear of the light-field caused by the hotel, and moved into the wild country, where he was still able to pick out the distant outline of the stone cattle. He'd been in several creepy places in his life as a combat SEAL. But none more so than this.

The wind made a faint moaning sound, rising and falling, and the light rain beat on his outer clothes. He sensed the air should have been clear, but the altitude and the low cloud created mist, and the feeling of bleakness enveloped everything. Also it was goddamned cold.

So far as Mack could tell there was almost no chance of cover or shelter. Although he could rapidly become invisible by lying prostrate in the wet heather, he did not look forward to that. But SEALs like to claim their territory, becoming experts on the terrain, its feel and its sounds, long before their enemy arrives.

It was well after 7 p.m. when Mack reached the rocks, and he was amazed at their size. They towered above him, black satanic walls of stone, the largest one, an outcrop from the land, was not climbable without proper mountaineering kit. And it was surrounded by flat, rocky terrain, with just a little mountain grass. He walked around and then moved to the smaller boulder, about forty-five feet high, jutting out across the heather.

The road was a hundred yards away. From the enormous main outcrop, the Cow, to the nearest stretch of high heather was thirty-eight yards, a five-second sprint in an emergency. Mack was not thrilled about that—not on this wet, slippery terrain in the dark.

He continued to pace out distances. Checking visibility, watching for more deterioration. And within twenty minutes he noticed it was growing appreciably darker. The cloud was right over the moor. There would be no stars and no moon. For an attack, this was darn near perfect. For defense, it was not so good. If he had an enemy out here, that enemy could, in SEAL parlance, "walk up on him." In his long experience not many people could achieve that, the one exception being those friggin' mountain men in Afghanistan. *Those Afghan bastards could really nail you, creep right up on you, and never even snap a twig, or slip on the stony escarpment. Like goddamned goats they were, same sure-footedness, same goddamned smell, the only thing that might give 'em away.* Mack Bedford chuckled in the darkness.

So far as he knew, he was waiting for his four "targets," who were being delivered by the police and then walking up to the rocks for their rendezvous. As far as he was concerned, there would be no predictable enemy. The coast would be permanently clear for him to strike as and when he wished.

And yet, no SEAL or SAS man has ever settled for that mindset. They are so often in overseas territory, so often surrounded by enemies, they assume instinctively that every man's hand is turned against them. Out here on the pitch black moor, danger could lurk anywhere. Every sense, every ounce of intuition, every nerve in his body was urging Mack to be goddamned careful.

Once more he walked back across the ground, pacing out distances, listening, searching for the one spot in which he could hide, and watch for the arrival of his targets, or, alternatively, his enemy. It was almost eight o'clock when he finally made his decision.

He did not want to be too high, but certainly not at ground level. His SEAL telescope gave him fabulous vision no matter how dark. But he needed elevation; just sufficient to allow him to leap to the ground, and to provide an all-around view of the dark, wet moorland.

On one side of the biggest rock, there was a "shoulder" jutting out, probably fifty feet up. But below that, there were cuts and hollows and breaks in the stone. Mack could see a crevasse, almost like a crow's nest in a ship. It was maybe fifteen feet above ground level. But there was a rocky platform maybe six feet wide about halfway up to it. If he had to, Mack could hit the ground in two bounds from there, one onto the platform, one onto the grass.

Mack climbed the rock, and hunkered down, right in the lee of the wind. He aimed his glass down at the road and scanned the area. There was not a movement anywhere, just the rain sweeping across Ilkley Moor on a stiff, rising northwester.

SHEIKH ABDULLAH'S three cutthroats left the mosque armed to the teeth. They slipped out of a side window and crept down a long wall to a narrow side street, where a black car and a Bangladeshi driver awaited them. Out of view of the police, they piled through a rear door, and set off for the moor.

Theirs was a difficult task. They had no idea who they were looking for, no idea where he would be, and no idea how they would nail him. Also they had no idea how dangerous he might be; though Sheikh Abdullah had warned that if the assassin worked for the U.S. Government, he was likely to be lethal.

They had one advantage, the element of surprise. The assassin would not be expecting them. Aside from that, all three of them—Mustapha, Jamal, and Sachin—were scared stiff, even though the latter two were carrying fully loaded Kalashnikovs, inaccurate, but fast, powerful, high-speed weapons.

Also, they understood that if they were caught, the Brits would throw the book at them, probably demanding they face re-trial for their role in the seven-jetliner plot in 2006. In the end they all knew the consequences of apprehension by the British authorities.

Only their terror of the Sheikh, and their lifelong belief that Allah loved his martyrs, and that they would be welcomed into paradise should they die on this mission, had kept them going.

They had been provided with top-class weaponry, including combat knives and service revolvers, recently stolen by an associate from a nearby police department. But they lacked night-sight and training—and they were going up against a master.

Mustapha, their leader, had a very pessimistic feeling, but they only had to kill one guy, after all. And they were sufficiently armed to take on a small platoon.

Back in police HQ, Len Martin had no knowledge of the leak from his office, no clue that his station harbored a mole, and thus considered that VBB, whoever and wherever he was, would just give up and return to his hotel when no one showed up for the assassinations on the moor. No harm done.

Twenty minutes after Mack took up position in the crevasse, Mustapha's driver arrived. Mack had seen several cars drive by, but this was the first one that had stopped. One by one, he watched the al-Qaeda men disembark, counting them, uncertain whether the driver was one of the four he was expecting.

But then the driver stepped back into his vehicle and left, driving a short distance further on, turning around and heading right back toward the city. Mack froze. That left only three, and that was all wrong. He wanted Ibrahim, Yousaf, Ben, and Abu. SEALs *hate* variation in commands, loathe inaccuracy, detest even the slightest deviation to a plan.

Mack's hair-trigger brain told him these were different guys. And why had they not arrived in a police cruiser as arranged? There should have been blue lights flashing, the final signal that these were his "targets." Mack did not like what he was seeing, and he sensed screw-up.

The three men were walking toward him, but then they fanned out, one running to the smaller rock, one heading around to the north side of the large one, and the other positioning himself against the wall of his crevasse, fifteen feet below. He could see two of the men carried light machine guns, but not the guy right below him. And he could see them taking up obvious battle stations, rifles raised to waist level, peering into the darkness.

Mack didn't know for sure who they were awaiting, but he had an uncanny feeling it was probably him. He surmised that there had been a leak somewhere. That the police had been unable to deliver the Chosen Ones. Even through his glass, he could see plainly that these were not the right guys.

It occurred to Mack that they had come to kill him, and that meant he might have to kill them instead. Or at least take them out of the game. Then one of them spoke, in a half-whisper, across the sloping, wet ground. The words were muffled by the rain, but they were still intelligible: "What this terrible bastard look like?"

The language was unmistakable to Mack's trained ear. It was Pashto, the official language of Afghanistan, the language of the mountain men. "Fuck," said Mack under his breath. "Those goddamned little creeps, all over again."

He knew he could not stage a gun battle up here. Sounds, especially gunfire, carry in wide open places like this, rain or no rain. If they really were after him, he must take them out silently. He waited for a reply to the first question.

"No information," someone called, "except he might be American, and that means very big and very horrible."

"Well, where is he, Jamal?" asked the third man, in English.

"Not here yet," came the reply. "English police say he meets our brothers at 9:30. It's not even 8:30."

So there had been a leak. The Chosen Ones weren't coming. And this crowd was up here specifically to get him.

"Better get the ole' ass in gear," muttered Mack to himself. "Starting with this little sonofabitch right below me." Through the glass, he could see the long, curved tribal knife, in the man's right hand. Quietly and carefully he climbed to the rocky platform. Then he debated whether to jump and attack, or to climb slowly down and kill in total silence.

Mack chose the second option because he did not want one sound from his first victim. The man below Jamal had his dagger drawn. Mack could see the glint even in the rain. He slowly inched down the rock until his left foot felt the wet ground at the base of the Cow.

Now he was four feet from Jamal, who was busy trying to light a cigarette. As his match flared he caught sight of the masked giant just as Mack rammed his left fist across his mouth like a manhole cover. He tried to yell, tried to bite the hand that gagged him, all in the hundredth of a second before Mack slit his throat from end to end, and the tribal knife slipped onto the soft ground beneath the giant rock.

Mack lowered the body softly, and then straightened up to spot his next target. Through the glass, he could see Mustapha leaning against the smaller rock, trying to make himself an impossible target. He heard the man call out, "Jamal! Jamal! Can you hear me?"

Mack needed to get behind him, fast, and that required a run across the open ground, thirty-eight yards and into the heather, the bit he had slightly dreaded. He tried to mimic the man he had just killed, "Jamal, Jamal here!"

He took off into the darkness. He tried to keep quiet but the pounding of his boots betrayed him. But it also confused his two enemies.

Mustapha now yelled out, "Jamal, where you going, man? You can't run out on us now."

By this time Mack Bedford had dived headlong into the high heather, and was lying completely still as he made an infinitesimal adjustment on his glass, just so he could see Mustapha with total clarity in the soft green glow of all night-vision equipment.

The silence of Jamal completely unnerved his leader, who opened fire in blind panic—just one burst aimed toward the biggest rock. The third man standing in total shadow on the far side of the Cow suddenly yelled, "What's going on? Mustapha, where's Jamal? Is anyone here?"

That yell betrayed him. Mack swiveled the glass and focused on Sachin. He drew his pistol and shot him dead at forty yards range, four SIG-Sauer 9mm bullets fired right into his upper chest.

Mustapha still had no idea who was doing the shooting. He screamed out, almost hysterically, and all the while Mack Bedford was coming through the heather, in the grim terrifying elbow crawl of the trained Navy SEAL sniper.

"Where are you? JAMAL! SACHIN! ANSWER ME!"

Mustapha had no clue who was alive or dead, or if there was an intruder. Were they still alone? Why was Jamal no longer answering? Again, in a kind of fiendish desperation, he opened fire into the darkness, three volleys, echoing over the moors. But now there was only silence. Mustapha was petrified.

And he did not have long to wait. He slumped back against the rock, his rifle held loosely by his side. At which precise moment Mack Bedford came out of the night.

Mack grabbed the barrel of the rifle from Mustapha's astonished grip, leaned back like a baseball slugger, and swung the butt with home-run force straight into the Afghani's face, obliterating the nose, both cheekbones, the jawbone, and the front area of his skull. Mustapha, his head caved in, died as he slithered backward down the Calf. Mack's unscheduled night's work was almost done.

He dragged Mustapha's body over to the big rock, retrieved Jamal's dagger, and placed it in the leader's right hand. Then he jogged over to Sachin, dragged him over to the other two, and placed that rifle firmly into Mustapha's grasp. Now they were just three immigrants from a primitive tribal culture, who'd had a somewhat nasty row.

He picked up Mustapha's rifle and hurled it with all of his force, far into the heather. Then he began his mile-long walk across the moor, in the rain, back to the hotel, where he would change, shower, and get into dry clothes.

He would check in with Russ Makin and leave cash in an envelope in the room to pay the bill. He would then head south, back to the iron-security of the SAS base, where he could regroup in peace and quiet. Mack presumed Russ would have the SAS clean up those bodies long before anyone else realized they were even dead.

And only a few locals had heard the steady beat of the helicopter's rotors when four SAS men landed on the moor two hours later and efficiently removed the three dead Afghanis.

SHEIKH ABDULLAH was still walking around free, thanks mainly to an instinct for survival that, in modern times, ranked second only to that of the impeached U.S. President Bill Clinton. And right now he had but one thing on his mind. He had to get Ibrahim, Yousaf, Ben, and Abu the hell out of the UK before they all ended up in the slammer, himself included.

Dr. Kamil had driven them back to Darsfield Street and had agreed to remain with them, for his usual astronomical fee. But the Sheikh was unnerved by the entire set of circumstances. He already sensed there was big trouble out on Ilkley Moor, and that the Americans were in league with the British government in their determination to eliminate the Chosen Ones, the Holy Warriors of Allah. He had to get them away, in the obvious interests of both Allah and the Prophet. But even more significantly in the interests of the blood brothers of al-Qaeda, the disciples of bin Laden.

He guessed it would be a matter of hours before the West Yorkshire Police came up with another reason to arrest Ibrahim and his men. And he decided to move immediately. He picked up the phone and instructed Dr. Kamil to drive them out to Leeds-Bradford airport, where the chartered aircraft from Air Iran was waiting.

The Sheikh, dressed now in Western clothes, would meet them there and supervise their exit from Great Britain. "Tell them to bring passports, visas, and all other documents," he said. "They cannot stay here."

Before he left he called his main contact at Air Iran in Tehran, and deposited the problem with him—the problem being, of course, what to do with the Chosen Ones and how to find a place for them to land in another country, any country, except the UK.

When he arrived at the airport he was met by an Air Iran official who informed him they could take off immediately. The four passengers were on board, and Dr. Kamil had left for Manchester.

The sixteen-seater turbojet was fueled and ready, and the Ayatollah in Tehran, with whom the official had consulted, had arranged for the flight to go into Alcolea, a rural Spanish airstrip outside the picturesque Andalusian city of Cordoba. There they would be transported to a Muslim safehouse in the city at first light.

This pleased the Bradford imam immensely. Spain was becoming increasingly important to Europe's network of Islamic extremists, and nowhere was more important than Cordoba, with its Great Mosque, which had been turned into a Cathedral in 1492, when five hundred years of Muslim rule in Spain had ended. But it was still one of the largest mosques in the world, with nineteen aisles, eight hundred and fifty red-and-white striped Moorish arches, and epic Muslim simplicity.

For centuries it had been neither one nor the other. And periodic uproars were apt to break out over the ban on mass Muslim prayer meetings. The massive mosque/cathedral had two warring hearts, with Spain's one million Muslims seized by romantic nostalgia for the lost paradise of al-Andaluca, and the Caliphate that had ruled the country for so long.

It was the perfect situation to breed resentment, indignation, anger, and that brand of religious loathing that sits so easily upon the shoulders of the Islamic faithful. There are hundreds of mosques in Spain, and many of the population, not to mention the Catholic bishops, believe they are funded by undemocratic countries promoting radical Islam, particularly Saudi Arabia.

They cite the undeniable truth that the Pope was permitted to make an act of prayer at the Blue Mosque in Istanbul, which is open to Christian worshippers. And, in apparent exasperation at the obdurate attitude of the Catholic clergy, there were now plans to build a completely new half-size replica of the Cordoba Great Mosque.

The Islamic intention was for the new structure to stand as a site for Islamic pilgrimages from all over the world. And this truly alarmed Spain's bishops, who resolutely opposed any such building being constructed in the former heart of the ancient Islamic Kingdom. Opponents of the mosque swear by all that's holy the bombing of the Madrid Railroad Station in March 2003, in which 191 people were killed, had lines of evidence, and overtones of hatred, leading directly to Cordoba.

Twenty-nine Islamists were charged over the railroad massacre, and most of them were found guilty, with two of them creating such a spectacularly bad impression on the judge, he sent them to prison for a combined total of forty thousand years.

The very word "Cordoba," with its new modern revolutionary connotations, made Sheikh Abdullah's heart sing. And he waited to see the Iran Air charter take off, over the Yorkshire moors, heading south, before he returned to his office in the basement of the mosque. It was almost midnight when he arrived, and a little after midnight when his cell phone rang, the numbers on the caller ID indicating Peshawar, Pakistan, where it was 5 a.m.

He knew immediately the caller was Shakir Khan. The Sheikh waited for his voicemail to pick up, and then pressed the button to retrieve the message, spoken by a female, "The four sons of Allah have been blessed by the Ayatollah and taken into his care. The path to Satan leads to the mezquita where the Prophet slew Janus, then to MCM in Avenue Colonia del Valle."

For a quasi-military signal plainly packed with information, that one moved quickly. Not, however, quickly enough. The British Pashto signals expert Shane Collins was again at his post listening. And once more he was onto the unusual aspects of this call. Again, he needed a more accurate translation, and in moments, he had it.

He already knew the call, made on a cell phone, had come from somewhere fifty miles west of Peshawar, somewhere in Afghanistan. He now flashed a signal through to a second British listening post in the UK to retrace and track the line on the frequency. In minutes, it came back and revealed that the line bisected the city of Bradford in West Yorkshire, which was all too familiar.

He called over his supervisor and reported his immediate findings, confirming this had many of the hallmarks of a previous coded call from the Hindu Kush. The young British captain agreed, and sent a report into GCHQ Cheltenham, England.

They ran their tests, confirmed Sergeant Collins's findings, and relayed the full report directly to Captain Ramshawe.

Once more, Shakir Khan had been badly intercepted.

SHEIKH ABDULLAH BAZIR, in common with almost every senior Islamic cleric in the world, was a man of great learning. And like Ayatollah Khomeini, Sheikh Abdullah, had studied for fifteen years in the sacred Shi'ite city of Qom, home of the gold-domed Astane shrine. As a theologian he was first-rate, steeped in the extraordinary history of his religion, familiar with the rules and nuances, the teaching and the taboos. He could not put his followers directly in touch with Allah, but he could show them the path, teach them how to beseech the one and only God to hear their prayers, and to guide them in His holy and righteous ways.

But for all his education and training, Sheikh Abdullah was unaware the Brits were on to him as he deciphered the signal. *The path to Satan leads to the mezquita where the Prophet slew Janus. . . .* Mezquita is Spanish for mosque, and "Janus" shot the word "Cordoba" right to the front of his brain. Every Muslim cleric knew the legend of the Cordoba Mosque, when the Moorish conquistadors in 785 AD discovered the sacred site of the temple of the two-headed Roman God, Janus, in Cordoba, and had slammed the gigantic edifice of the Great Mosque right on the spot where Janus had once occupied prime position, which was a very major deal in those days.

Therefore, there was no doubt in Sheikh Abdullah's mind. Ibrahim, Yousaf, Ben, and Abu were heading due south, straight for Andalusia, and the safety of the Islamic embrace in the radical heart of restless Cordoba.

Then to MCM in Avenue Colonia del Valle. The rest of the signal was crystalline clear. For years Muslim clerics in Europe, North Africa, and the Far East had tacitly supported the stop-go growth of their religion in Mexico because everything there was right for them. Mexico was metaphorically begging for the *dawa*, conversion, owing to its current situation of mass poverty, waning Christian religion, and a rebellious heart second to none in the Free World.

Aside from Islam, the great revolutionary surge in Mexico was the rise of the Zapatistas, named for the great revolutionary leader Emilio Zapata, the National Army of Liberation. Based in the jungle wilds of Chiapas, Mexico's southernmost and poorest state, the Zapatistas represent a severe cultural unrest and an open door for a Muslim dawa.

Mexicans had for centuries leaned on the Catholic church for religious comfort, but there was too much prosperity for the Americans, and too little for them, and millions of Mexican peasants were ready for the dawa.

They were so poor and disorganized, there was a time when the Pakistani ambassador to Mexico allowed converted Muslims to use a prayer room at the Mexico City embassy on Hegel Street, since they had nowhere else to go. But then, in the late 1990s, a serious Islamic organization was founded, the Muslim Center of Mexico, which rapidly expanded to build mosques, libraries, and classrooms in fifteen Mexican cities, the most beautiful complex being, unsurprisingly, in the Pacific coastal region of Chiapa.

Every Islamic cleric knew of the rise of Allah in Mexico. They all knew the surge of interest, the hundreds of daily conversions taking place, the brilliant success visiting Muslim clerics had in summoning the poor and the helpless to the Koran.

The Muslim Center of Mexico was possibly the fastest growing Islamic study center on earth—a kind of sprawling controversial madrassa, the Islamic Religious School system. The Center is known throughout Islam as the MCM, headquartered at Avenue Colonia del Valle in the Mexican Federal District.

So Sheikh Abdullah understood precisely what was going on, that the Chosen Ones would enter the United States through Mexico. At evening prayers, he thanked his God for delivering them and for setting them on a safe and correct path to set in motion the longed-for follow up to the Day of Glory, September 2001.

CAPTAIN RAMSHAWE could not for the life of him wrap his mind around the slain Janus. He punched the name into Google, and came up with the double-headed Roman God of Gateways who was able to look both backward and forward at the same time. "Two-faced bastard," he muttered to himself. But he still couldn't make the connection. The Romans, in his mind at least, had been around at the time of Christ, whereas the Prophet, whom he assumed to be Mohammed, did not get going until six hundred years later. *So how the hell did the Prophet nail this bloke with the two heads?* Jimmy put that aside for a moment to look up the MCM in the Avenue Colonia, and found about ten thousand Avenue Colonias all over the Spanish-speaking world. And the MCM reference was impossible; his search had turned up an electronics company, then a brand of upmarket handbags, then music. The list was disparate and endless.

Meanwhile the Chosen Ones were heading for the southern coast of England, flying low-level at around 10,000 feet. There was nothing to eat on board, and it was touch and go whether they would need to stop and refuel somewhere over central Spain. The entire journey would be twelve hundred miles, much of it over the ocean. The charter would clear the French coast somewhere west of St. Malo, flying around fifty miles over Brittany's Atlantic headland, before heading three hundred miles down the Bay of Biscay to a point west of Bilbao. From there it was a straight four-hundred-mile journey across Spain to Cordoba.

At least three Sleeper Cells had been alerted in Cordoba, and there would be no shortage of help for the four terrorists once they landed.

MACK BEDFORD had no idea what had gone wrong, but it seemed to him that there had been an information leak inside the police station, which had prevented the four Islamists from being delivered to the right place. As a result, he had been the hunted, rather than the hunter. And the four proposed victims had somehow gotten away. All bad news, since now his task was on hold, until they could be located again.

He gunned the Jaguar through the night, racing back through Lancashire, and heading south through Cheshire and Shropshire to Hereford.

Lieutenant Colonel Makin was pouring himself a medicinal Scotch and water, and wondering where the hell Mack Bedford was when the former SEAL showed up just after midnight demanding food, drink, shelter, and information. Russ Makin had an abundance of the first three, almost none of the latter. But both men were agreed it was imperative Mack leave the country right away. "Right now there's no chance anyone will ever find out anything," said Russ. "But we need not take chances. Those air-heads at West Yorkshire Police have a very dangerous spy right in the middle of their operation. And he blew our plans apart, left no clues. I spoke to that detective superintendent a half hour ago and he says they are conducting an investigation."

"I should think they fucking well would be," said Mack, uncharitably. "I could have been killed out on that goddamed moor."

"You? Not likely," replied Russ. "How many did you say there were, three?"

"That's all I saw."

"Were you scared."

"Well, no. Not really. But I knew I'd better stay sharp. Can I have a drink?"

"I'm getting it, I'm getting it."

"No one gave a shit if I stopped a round of Kalashnikov bullets—and I don't suppose you give a shit if I die of thirst!"

Russ handed him a long Scotch and soda. "I have a Navy Merlin helicopter picking you up at 0630 and taking you to RNAS Culdrose in Cornwall. There's a freighter leaving from there, which will drop you off at Brunswick, Maine, on its way down to Norfolk."

"Outstanding," replied Mack. "I was hoping I wouldn't have to fly commercial. Especially since I haven't got a passport or any documents with me."

"Jesus. You're more highly classified than even I thought," said Russ. "My orders are to get you home without trace—no signs that you were ever here."

"That's me," said Mack, tipping back his drink. "The SEAL who never was."

IBRAHIM, YOUSAF, BEN, AND ABU remained in hiding for forty-eight hours and then made the two-hundred-mile car journey north to Madrid, crossing the three-hundred-mile range of the Sierra Morena Mountains and then Spain's hot pine-and-oak miles of the central plateau.

They reached Madrid's Barajas Airport in time for Iberia's nonstop flight to Mexico City leaving at 0120, using the same passports on which they had flown into England. The Spanish are routinely slack about checking people leaving the country, and not terribly exercised about those coming in.

The flight took off on time, with the four terrorists traveling business class and eating rich Spanish paella in the smooth temperature-controlled Airbus A340. It was an eleven-hour flight, and they landed in Mexico City's Benito Juarez International Airport at 6:30 in the morning.

Meanwhile, Intelligence officers throughout the UK and United States had spent the entire night desperately trying to make sense of that intercepted cell-phone call from Peshawar to Bradford, and only Jimmy Ramshawe, punching his computer keys until they almost melted, came up with anything. He had found a short list of temples built in honor of Janus, and one of them was the original in Cordoba. Jimmy even found out many of the breathtaking Moorish arches were constructed out of jade, marble, and granite from the original temple. That was when he connected the mosque, which had landed on top of Janus. Jimmy deduced that the Chosen Ones were in Spain, in Cordoba, except he was about twenty-four hours too late.

The "MCM" section of the signal remained, for the moment, a complete mystery. Bob Birmingham's CIA team was on the case, and so were the Brits in GCHQ Cheltenham. However there was no break yet. The mindset was still Europe—Bradford and Cordoba—known cradles of potential revolution. And nothing was shaking loose.

By the time Captain Ramshawe returned to work, two hours in front of Mexico City, Ibrahim and his men were having breakfast and settling into the sparse accommodation in the MCM complex on Avenue Colonia del Valle. They were made welcome, but there was an innate suspicion that these four men were not all that they seemed.

There was a strong feeling of brotherhood among the imams who lived, worked, and visited this fountain of Islamic progress, for they saw themselves as pioneers, bringing the great religion of the world to a land that was crying out for spiritual help. These four Pakistanis had been recommended, and a wire transfer of money had been made to the Center, from a source that emanated in Tehran. But there was something of the night about these four, who spoke rarely to anyone else. They attended morning prayers and requested that they be served lunch and dinner.

By any standards, the scarfaced, scowling Abu Hassan Akbar gave the impression of villainy, both in appearance and attitude. Not one of the resident imams believed their names were genuine, and they would be extremely glad when they left.

Late on that first afternoon a package was delivered to the

Muslim center, marked for the attention of Ibrahim. He opened it to find four air tickets from Mexico City to the northern city of Chihuahua, a distance of almost seven-hundred miles. It also contained around ten thousand in Mexican pesos, and a note that specified all the details of the night-crossing. Ibrahim swiftly realized this would be a perilous mission. The U.S. border patrols were sick of being made to look foolish, with hundreds of Mexican peasants streaming, illegally, across the border, night after night. They were also sick to death of drug cartels, criminals, and God knows who else, charging through the wire, digging tunnels, knocking down steel fences, and ram-raiding U.S. property. Those U.S. guards were likely to open fire, especially if they suspected they were being assaulted by international criminals.

These days they were heavily armed. They were sweeping the entire border with radar, and American satellites had cameras trained on the border. They also had high-speed vehicles that were armored and equipped with searchlights. Their communications were state of the art. Lately, the patrols were increasingly successful, which did not especially appeal to Ibrahim, since a return to Guantanamo was not in his immediate plans.

He comforted himself with the undeniable knowledge that thousands broke out of Mexico every year and were never located in the United States, and he cast to the back of his mind that 660,000 people were stopped, apprehended, and sent back every year.

His new itinerary required he and his three fellow terrorists reach the city of Chihuahua, and then take a bus northwest up to El Bajio, a small town some five miles short of the border in the middle of the endless wastes of the huge Chihuahua Desert—a place with no water, and no hope for those who collapsed in exhaustion while attempting to cross it.

The instructions specified they were to rendezvous with a guide, who would provide them with food and water for the journey. But they would first have to walk the five miles across the desert, which is almost too hot for survival in the day, and very nearly too cold at night. A vehicle was out of the question because it could be tracked by U.S. radar, was and would also be open to attack from the many gangs of Mexican brigands who drove around the desert at night looking for victims to rob. They were also instructed to buy cowboy boots, because snakes would be out at night, some of them rattlers, and most cowboy boots made in this part of the world are snake-bite proof.

The only way across that border was by pure stealth, dropping down to the desert floor at the slightest suspicion of an intruder, staying below the radar, and making as little sound as possible.

Despite their nickname, "coyotes," the guides had a very good reputation, though more out of necessity than goodwill. The human cargo and escort border business was so lucrative, no one would dare to shoot, harm, or rob a guide because of the damage it would inflict on the entire "industry."

One reckless bandit did indeed shoot a guide and then robbed and murdered his paying clients, and it was just about the last thing he ever did. The man's body was found two days later in a hotel room in El Bajio with multiple machine gun wounds, and a dagger sticking out of the left-hand side of his chest.

Ibrahim's coyote, Miguel, would locate the four al-Qaeda men in El Bajio, in the main square. There would be four Kalashnikovs with magazines in the back of his truck, though Ibrahim's al-Qaeda officer sincerely hoped that a shootout could be avoided. Miguel would also bring them curved combat knives of the kind wielded by the Special Forces of the Taliban, and four cell phones pre-programmed with all the necessary numbers. There would also be one hand grenade, in case of real trouble. Three different al-Qaeda Sleeper Cells would be awaiting them on the U.S. side of the border, all with vehicles.

Ibrahim felt better once he realized they would be well-armed for the crossing. All four were hardened freedom fighters, veterans, and they had been unarmed for too long. Abu Hassan especially longed for the comfortable grip of those light and deadly Kalashnikovs, the weapon that had kept him safe in combat zones like Baghdad, the Left Bank, Kabul, and in the mountains.

They landed at Chihuahua's General Fierro Villalobos Airport just before noon and boarded the bus into town, a distance of eight miles. They changed at the main Aldama Street terminal and set off across the hot, dusty cactus-strewn wasteland for El Bajio, a deeply unimpressive place peppered with tin roofs and several abandoned stone buildings. There was one shop and one bar, apparently made of driftwood. And a large town square where the bus stopped.

In Ben al-Turabi's opinion it was hotter in the still of the late afternoon than it had been in the bus depot on Aldama Street. And he was right. Chihuahua is a mountain town, situated on the high foothills of the Sierra Madres. Out here, further north, the land flattens out as it descends to the floor of the desert, and that cooler mountain air is left behind.

Dusty El Bajio simmered in a dying afternoon wind. The sun beat down, and there was a heat-shimmer off the tin roofs. One or two Mexicans were sitting quietly on the veranda outside the ramshackle bar. It was too hot to talk, too still to walk, and too unutterably boring to think.

"As far as I am concerned," said Abu Hassan, in Arabic, "this is the worst place I ever went, and that includes Camp Five. But this is hotter."

The four men slouched across to a wooden bench in the middle of the main square and watched as the rickety bus that had transported them across the desert was disappearing to the northwest in a cloud of dust.

There was no shade, but the arrangement was to meet the coyote on the bench in the square. Ibrahim would have done anything to get out of the sun, but like his enemies in the SAS and the SEALs, he could not tolerate even the slightest deviation from a mission plan. And he ordered the other three to join him.

Abu said he wasn't going to sit under that sun and that he

would wait outside the bar under the veranda. Ibrahim spun around on him. "What happens if this coyote drives into the square looking for four Arabs, and sees only three people on the bench? Maybe drives away, and doesn't come back. Sit down on that bench."

At that moment, Ibrahim became the leader. The powerfully built al-Qaeda warrior was the expert bomb maker and a man who had been groomed for the high command of bin Laden's platoons. And in the previous two minutes, he had shown wisdom and thoughtfulness, the instincts of a trained strategist. He had made Abu Hassan look like a child, and the Palestinian accepted it. Without another word, Abu sat down on the bench, and Ibrahim, like the natural leader he was, offered him the last of the cold-water bottles, a gesture of friendship, and the action of a man who wanted the best for his troops.

They sat there in the heat for more than an hour before they saw a truck approaching the town, kicking up dust, bouncing and bumping at high speed over the sandy shale of the Chihuahua Plain. It came hurtling into the main square and skidded to a halt, turning as it did. A dented, scraped, battered wreck, driven by a maniac.

"We're not driving with him, are we?" asked Yousaf. "Allah would not wish that upon us."

"Unless he wanted us to become martyrs," said Ibrahim. But by then the driver was out of his cab and walking toward them. He was a Mexican kid, early twenties, with a large high-caliber revolver stuck jauntily into his wide leather belt.

"I'm Miguel," he said, "your guide to the border."

"We're walking, right?" asked Ibrahim.

"No other way," said Miguel. "It's five miles, and we need to arrive there by ten o'clock for the border patrol's shift change. That's when there's a gap, and the fence is unguarded."

"How do we know when that's happening," said Ibrahim. "It'll be very dark, right?"

"You leave that to me. That's why I get paid."

"Okay, boss," grinned the Afghani. "What happens to us now?"

"I got a little work. You need better clothes. It gets real cold out here, very sudden. I'll get blankets—ponchos, you stick your heads through like proper Mexicans, okay?" For some reason this floored Miguel, and he threw back his head and laughed. "You Mexicans for one whole night! I got guns for you in truck. You have rich friends."

"I just hope we don't need to use them," said Ibrahim. "We're looking for a quiet crossing."

"You don't use guns," said Miguel. "They are just for emergency. Your people tell me that. Only if we are attacked in the desert, or a guard opens fire on us. Then we kill him quick, before he kills us."

"I tell you what I do notice," said Abu Hassan. "The temperature just dropped maybe twenty degrees. You're right about those blankets."

"I done this before, hey?" said Miguel. "This is my profession. For a few more years. Then I go to medical school. Doctor Miguel before you know it. Maybe I fix that scar on your face. Big money, for plastics, eh?"

For a few moments all five of them laughed out there in the square. Four mass murderers and a kid with a huge pistol, falling about laughing, before attempting to breach the most heavily guarded U.S. border, the one that sealed off West Texas, New Mexico, Arizona, and California.

Tonight they would storm the symbolic barricade that led into the U.S. State of New Mexico, where forty-five percent of all the population was Hispanic, thanks in part to Spanish Colonial settlers, but also to the droves of Mexicans who made it over the border in the early years. Not to mention their friends and relatives who still keep trying.

"We need to get away by eight o'clock latest," said Miguel, "Which gives us two hours to cover the five miles. That ought to be simple, but if we get any kind of a hold-up on the journey, we'll be glad of the extra time. I want to be in position at the border by around nine thirty."

Miguel headed off to fetch the ponchos and water and was

back in thirty minutes. The men gladly put on these deceptively warm outer garments and their new cowboy boots, and prepared to face the desert.

Miguel took them to the back of the truck and issued the rifles, magazines, combat knives, cell phones, and the hand grenade. They had all bought Stetsons in Chihuahua, and, with their Kalashnikovs tucked into their belts under the ponchos, they endeavored to look as little as possible like renegades from Emilio Zapata's revolutionary army.

Night fell swiftly, and the desert grew suddenly colder. Without another word, Miguel gave a jolt of his head toward the northwest, and began to walk. The others fell in line behind him. "Do not talk," Miguel said. "We travel in silence all the way."

Ibrahim thought this said much about the safety of the place, reminiscent of days in the Hindu Kush when the American SEAL patrols were on the warpath. But he had not expected a vast and desolate Mexican outback to be anything similar.

One thing that was not similar was the terrain. The desert was as flat as a pool table, all rough shale and sand, with a surprising number of plants somehow thriving in one of the harshest, driest climates on earth. The lemony scent in the air was from the plentiful creosote bush that opens its pores at night. The agave plants, the thick-leafed cactus-like giant from which tequila is made, and which can grow as high as thirty feet, were everywhere.

There were sundry cactus, ocotillo, and yucca bushes, all rough and spiky, and painful when you blundered into them in the dark. Ben al-Turabi stabbed himself on a cactus and let out a yell that might have been heard at the border. "No noise," Miguel hissed. "No noise at all."

They covered the first mile in a little over twenty minutes, but found the next mile slower. It was impossible to walk fast because of the desert bushes, and Miguel, who seemed to be able to see in the dark, led them at a steady pace, steering them away from the impediments and making the occasional murmured call on his cell phone.

They were midway through the third mile, freezing cold and

getting tired, when they spotted the lights of two vehicles heading directly toward them. Miguel sensed all four of his clients were reaching for their rifles. "Don't shoot anyone, because if you do we'll have to go back," he whispered. "There are patrols, Mexican, and even my money won't buy them off if there's bodies on the ground."

The two vehicles veered off, one left, one right. But suddenly they changed direction and were once more headed for the group, now from different directions.

With headlights blazing and spotlights on the roof, two Jeeps came screaming to a halt. One man, a big, powerful character in a sombrero and holding a heavy machine gun, stepped down from his cab, and called, "Okay everyone. No one gets hurt. Just give me all your cash, watches, and jewelry. Because if you don't, I'll blow your heads off."

Miguel stepped forward, and shouted, "Hey, Tony, what the fuck are you doing. I'm trying to make a living over here."

"*MIGUEL!* You crazy kid. What's going on."

But now Miguel's voice hardened. "You wouldn't dare shoot me, would you? Because you'd be dead yourself in twenty-four hours."

Tony said nothing. Miguel drew his pistol and aimed it straight at the bandit's head. "You got five seconds to beat it. Otherwise I'll blow your head off and a lot of people will thank me, you fucking nuisance. Now *FUCK OFF!*"

The bombast and swagger seemed to drain from the would-be bandit. He said nothing. Just turned around, climbed back into his jeep, and left, followed by the second vehicle.

The border-crossing game was big business in this part of the world, and tearaways like Tony Morina were merely tolerated, just so long as they paid off the Mexican police. However, Miguel mattered more. Because he paid them off much more, very regularly. And there were dozens like him. Tony and his thieves were just scavengers, mere jackals in the high finances of the Chihuahua Desert.

By now it was really cold and the men wrapped their ponchos around themselves as they walked forward in the pitch dark. There was no rising moon, and the sky was overcast. They just kept following Miguel, sometimes swerving past the cactus and spiky bushes. By nine o'clock they were approaching the final mile, and there were distant lights far up in front on the horizon.

"We stay slightly left from here," whispered the guide. "There's a group of hills up there, not very high, but good for reception on phones. I got a man up there, watching."

No one answered. They were all tired, and Ben al-Turabi's cowboy boots were killing him. All four just kept walking, and slowly the lights drew nearer. The ground began to rise, and up ahead, through the wire, they could see two patrol jeeps, both green, both with the livery of the State of New Mexico on the doors.

They hunkered down behind a clump of bushes, and the border wire was about two hundred yards in front. They could see the patrol officers gathered in a small huddle, laughing. There was no other movement.

Miguel, hidden just off to the left, pulled out his GPS and hit the buttons on his cell—"Hey, Pedro . . . yeah, it's me. I'm at thirty-two spot four zero north, one zero seven spot five zero west. We got a gap?"

The others heard him repeat, "One hundred yards west of those two jeeps right ahead. Wires cut one side to the right, five feet high, four feet wide. My guys just shove it open. Any paint? Okay blue line at the base. Okay, Pedro. What time? Okay, fifteen minutes when the two jeeps leave. How long we got?"

The others did not hear Pedro's reply—"Last night they went early, night before ten minutes late. Who the hell knows? Gringo bastards. Keep watching."

"Watch the jeeps, guys," he said. "Shift change very soon. They will both leave. Both going right. One new jeep will be back from the left about twenty minutes later. That's your window. You run to the wire. I'll be right out in front, find the cut."

And so they waited. Miguel's phone vibrated in his pocket. "It left already? That means fifteen minutes and the others are still here. That's all we have. Otherwise we try again tomorrow? Okay."

At that moment they all heard both jeeps start to rev up, and the first one moved forward, turning hard right, and then accelerating down the rough road toward the West Texan border city of El Paso. The other one instantly followed. And now there was not a single light along the long, twelve-foot high wire fence.

"THAT'S IT!" yelled Miguel. *"COME ON! RIGHT NOW! GO! GO! GO!"*

He rushed out and began racing over the ground, straight for the point where he knew the wire was cut. He reached the fence twenty yards in front of the others, who were now running hard.

"Hit the ground!" he yelled, diving forward. "They got radar and trip-lights everywhere. Stay down while I find the gap."

Miguel crawled forward using a tiny flashlight. When it beamed on the low, blue-painted strip, he stood up and heaved, and the sliced tennis court wire ripped apart. Miguel hauled on it, and it came back like an opening door.

"GO! GO! WE'RE THROUGH AND THERE'S NO LIGHTS. RUN! FOR CHRIST'S SAKE, RUN!"

And even as he yelled his last command, a pair of blazing headlights came hurtling over the slight rise in the road to the west, some four hundred yards away.

Ibrahim and Yousaf were through, and Ben al-Turabi was five yards short of the entrance. The big Palestinian came charging through, pounding after the leaders. Abu Hassan was ten yards behind him, and everyone could now see the oncoming patrol car. But it might not yet have seen them.

"Cut right," bellowed Miguel. "Cut right. There's trees, then get down!"

Ibrahim and Yousaf heard him, and swerved. But even as they did so, the headlights suddenly went on full beam, and now the jeep was headed straight for them. A guard with a bullhorn stood up from the passenger seat and bellowed to them both, to *"STOP! IN THE NAME OF THE GOVERNMENT OF THE UNITED STATES!"*

The jeep came to a halt and the two guards disembarked, one

aiming a pistol straight at the two terrorists from the Afghan mountains. The second man caught sight of the charging Ben and aimed his revolver straight at him. All three of the arrested men held their cool, and made no attempt to reach for their Kalashnikovs.

Meanwhile Miguel, safe on his side of the border, had backed off and hit the deck in some bushes. Abu Hassan, with the wild animal instincts of the trained killer, rolled through the gap and pressed down on the ground next to the wire, watching the action. Quietly, he loaded a magazine into the breach of his rifle, and began to move behind the lights of the jeep, gaining cover from the vehicle as he went.

Neither guard saw him, because by now they had herded Ibrahim, Yousaf, and Ben into a group, and were busily checking them out. They asked them to remove their ponchos and hats and to produce documents just as Abu Hassan, his scarred face glowing with excitement, moved slowly out from behind the jeep. He shot the two American security officers dead, straight through the backs of their heads. Back in the cold darkness of the Chihuahua desert, they all heard a sharp burst of laughter, followed by "So long, gringos! They told me you could shoot straight!"

Now Ibrahim took the lead, walking due north, guided by his small pocket compass, toward a point on Route 9, just west of the New Mexico town of Columbus, on the southern slopes of the misleadingly named Florida Mountains.

THERE WAS SILENCE now in the rough, wooded ground where the four Islamic killers walked. The two patrol guards lay dead in the dust some two hundred yards behind them, and, as if unnerved by the sudden and dangerous events of the past fifteen minutes, Ibrahim began to run.

Circumstances were closing in on him. He and his cohorts were ultimately still free, but they were plainly wanted men: they were four illegal immigrants, wearing Mexican ponchos, Stetson hats, cowboy boots, and each carrying a loaded Kalashnikov. Not to mention the hand grenade, and the two cold-blooded murders.

Ibrahim understood that if the getaway vehicles were right where they were supposed to be, it might be okay. But if anyone else saw the four men, they had about an hour before they were on their way back to Cuba. They had documents and passports with false names. But the American authorities had excellent prison photographs of them all, and they'd probably fly that bastard Sergeant Biff Ransom in from Guantanamo to identify them.

In Ibrahim's opinion, dressed and armed as they were, they were doomed in the United States. They did not have the knowledge or the experience to evade the law indefinitely. He himself had attended Harvard, but that was years ago.

Ibrahim hoped they'd have their moment of revenge sometime in the not-too-distant future, but right now the cards were stacked against them. Because sometime in the next couple of hours, they would all be wanted, nationwide, for murder.

They could not just hide their rifles because their fingerprints were all over them. They would just have to keep jogging forward wearing their ponchos to hide the weapons. Ibrahim considered that prayer was the only answer, and as he jogged through the scrubland, he begged Allah to grant them safe passage toward the Islamic brothers who waited for them somewhere a mile up ahead. He also decided he would regrow his beard, in the Islamic tradition, after the years of enforced clean-shaving in a U.S. prison camp.

They ran on for another ten minutes. There were lights, car headlights, traveling fast along Route 9. Ibrahim was searching for a grain elevator, his landmark. Somewhere to the left of that was his rendezvous spot, where there should be three cars so they could split up as the police would be looking for a group of four, not one single person or two.

Ibrahim was slightly out of breath now, but he still managed to tell Yousaf, Ben, and Abu they must get rid of their ponchos, hats, boots, and guns as soon as they reached the rendezvous point—to throw them into the trunks of the cars and instruct the drivers to lose them. Abu Hassan did not want to give up his Kalashnikov, but understood the foolishness of trying to keep it.

They reached the road, found the cars, and shook hands with their drivers. Then they piled their gear into the trunks, separated, and set off for the railroad station at Albuquerque, 267 miles to the north, straight along New Mexico Interstate 25.

Ibrahim and Yousaf traveled individually, both in fast Ford

sedans; Ben and Abu in the back of a Buick. All three drivers wore jeans and cowboy shirts and boots, standard American gear for this part of the world.

Ibrahim understood there were many things that now mattered, which had not mattered before—their appearance, their avoidance of being seen together, the destruction of their old clothes and rifles, their constant unobtrusiveness. Everything was now heightened, and everything now mattered. Their eating habits, their dress, their newspapers. They needed to be seen as Americans.

Ibrahim, however, was keenly aware of what really mattered. And that was the undeniable fact that they had breached the U.S. border. They were back in the United States and they were ready to attack. Shakir Khan's al-Qaeda network was already helping them. The Sleeper Cells were active.

They were on their way to the East Coast to prepare for the next great Islamic assault on the Great Satan, in the name of Allah, and under the banner of the Prophet. That was what really mattered. Ibrahim slept the calm and tranquil sleep of the righteous, as his young driver, Abby Gamal, formerly of Lahore, gunned the Ford north.

THE BODIES of the two patrolmen, Officer Ray Carrol and Officer Matt D'Arcy, were discovered by the incoming shift around one hour after the murders, just after eleven. The headlights of the jeep were still on and the engine was still running.

There were shootings and deaths quite often along this side of the border, but the killing of security guards was rare. Mexican peasants seeking only a safe crossing were not often armed, and most of the gun-fighting was conducted against drug-runners and other villains, who attempted to storm this back door into the United States.

Within an hour of the discovery of the bodies there were six New Mexico police cruisers at the scene, blue lights flashing in the night, a dozen state troopers, several forensic guys, and various homicide detectives from both the cities of Deming and Las Cruces.

If the bodies had been those of Mexicans, the authorities would have moved heaven and earth to keep things quiet at least for a few days, while the diplomats tried to calm down the Mexican government. But this was different. In the opinion of the police it was Mexicans who were the perpetrators, the Americans the victims, brutally slain while conducting their lawful duties on behalf of the State. This was an outrage.

Back at the Deming Police Department, twenty-three miles north of the crime scene, the public relations officer had already been called in at midnight to issue an immediate press release to every newspaper and television and radio station in the country:

> **With immense regret the Police Department of Deming, New Mexico, announces that two state border patrolmen, Officers Ray Carrol and Matt D'Arcy, both of Columbus, New Mexico, were shot down and killed on the United States side of the border fence with Mexico at approximately 10 p.m. last evening.**
>
> **The incident occurred at a point on the wire two miles southeast of the city of Columbus. Both men were shot from behind. It was an hour before the bodies were found.**
>
> **So far there have been no arrests, but the police are treating the deaths as murder in the first degree. The FBI have been informed, and unusually, the CIA have announced they are sending investigators to the crime scene, direct from Langley, Virginia.**

The shootings had happened too late to make it into the morning papers on the East Coast, where they were two hours ahead of New Mexico. But the release was perfectly timed for the twenty-four-hour rolling news channels. The *New York Daily News* revamped its front page in the small hours, hitting the street the following morning with:

U.S. PATROL SLAIN ON MEXICAN BORDER

The *Chicago Sun-Times*, with an hour more to prepare, was just as brash:

MURDER ON MEXICO BORDER:
MANHUNT FOR KILLERS OF U.S. PATROL

All through the night CNN, Fox News, and the rest were running and building the story, conducting interviews with half-asleep people, trying to get ahold of the families of the dead men, who were currently under the rigid protection of the Deming police department.

From a media point of view, the trouble with this type of story was that in the middle of the night, no one wants you either on the phone or standing outside the front door. But the reporters kept going, probing, trying to find out the number of bullets fired, from what kind of gun, who had been first on the scene, and if there were any suspects, motives, or angles.

There was a groundswell behind this story, merely because so many people wanted answers and there were none. There was no sign of a gun battle. The guards' pistols had not been fired. There was no sign of a struggle, and thus no one knew why the Americans had died. There were zero witnesses and no suspects.

By lunchtime the CIA agents had arrived by helicopter, and were given unhindered access to both the police and local detectives. Subsequently they filed the best report, but only back to their own Langley headquarters.

Bob Birmingham read it thoroughly and passed it on to Captain Ramshawe. Both were intrigued that the guards had been shot from behind. They had fallen forward, both of them holding aimed, loaded revolvers. This suggested there were at least two, and possibly three men standing in front of them, probably being told to raise their hands high. The man who had killed them was a third or fourth person, and they plainly had not known he was there.

That person had shot each of them in the back of the head, twice, using a Kalashnikov rifle, which is the weapon of choice for professional criminals, especially foreigners, because it's relatively easy to purchase on the black market via Russia. It is also much less likely to be traced back to a specific gun shop by its U.S. serial numbers.

In Captain Ramshawe's initial opinion, that gave the authorities probably four armed criminals, trying to cross the Mexican border into the United States. They had somehow been sighted by the guards, and apprehended; except for one of their number, who had hidden himself in the dark, and then crept around the parked jeep, with its engine running noisily, and shot the two guards who were about to arrest his mates. Ultimately, however, he decided that four made more sense than three because his own investigations into the disappearance of the Chosen Ones had led him to Mexico City about an hour before.

Ramshawe had ordered a massive computerized search for every Muslim organization in the world that had recognizable acronyms. There were of course thousands. But then the researchers asked for addresses, and fed, into the program, the Avenue Colonia del Valle, and out popped MCM (Muslim Center de Mexico), located on Avenue Colonia, a middle-class area of Mexico City.

Not only that but it had a massive website, accessed from all corners of the world by people planning to visit Mexico. The intercepted message from Peshawar suggested the four ex-Guantanamo Bay inmates were right there, in one of Mexico's newest mosques.

Jimmy was back on the line to Bob Birmingham in moments, and two CIA station field officers were dispatched to the doorstep of MCM to make inquiries. They learned that the four had made no friends in MCM, mostly because of their aloof and unsociable attitudes. No one liked them, especially the one with the scar.

One friendly imam was only too pleased to confirm they had been there, but had now left. He identified the photographs, confirmed the four men had been in residence for only twenty-four hours, and then left for the airport. He had no idea where they were going. This motley group of facts was presented to the director of the National Security Agency, and Jimmy instantly connected the missing Muslims with the border killings.

"Gotta be the same blokes, right?" muttered Jimmy to himself. "They've been helped by a national organization on every bloody step of their journey. Travel plans immaculate. Money no object. And we've been about five steps behind, all the bloody way."

Jimmy Ramshawe was certain the cold-blooded shooting of the two guards must have been the work of Ibrahim Sharif and his team. It was the exact right day and the exact right time for these four professional terrorists to breach the border. "And now where the hell are they? Right back in the USA, of course. Everything that made us nervous on the day they were released, just came true."

Jimmy knew the guys who had checked into the old MCM in Avenue Colonia, and the gang who had just blasted their way into the United States were one in the same. *We have to find these characters because they are planning something terrible.*

He picked up his secure phone and dialed Mack Bedford in Maine. The ex-SEAL commander was surprisingly sanguine about the situation, saying simply, "Ever since last February, when that Judge Stamford Osborne kicked 'em out of the front door, I always thought they'd come right back in, through the back."

THE *SOUTHWESTERN CHIEF* came thundering into Albuquerque's First Street station four minutes late from Los Angeles. The massive diesel locomotive, now bound for Chicago, was a deafening presence in the quiet, sunlit, adobe New Mexican city.

Abrahim, Yousaf, Ben, and Abu Hassan stood separately on the departure platform, some fifty yards apart. They had purchased new clothes and now stood dressed for a city. No neckties, but white shirts with sport coats and regular black loafers. No Stetsons or ponchos. Definitely no Kalashnikovs. Each now carried a briefcase: brown leather for Ibrahim and Yousaf, black for the others.

Their tickets had been pre-paid under the names on their passports. They each had a reserved seat, and they boarded the great American passenger train without even a flicker of recognition, seated far apart but with reservations in the dining car that placed them within conversational distance.

Yousaf thought the whole thing was, in a Western phrase, pretty nifty. Which was understandable since his normal family train rides had often involved carriages packed to the gunwales with rural farmers, and sometimes their livestock, with others riding on the roof carrying baskets of live chickens.

And the four gazed through the windows in awe as the mighty locomotive pulled out at 12:40 p.m. sharp, speeding through the manicured suburbs of Albuquerque, on its 550-mile journey along the old cattle routes, to Dodge City: ETA a half-hour after midnight.

The route took them through vast expanses of the fabled American West, from New Mexico through wheat fields, past ranches and missions, across mountains and deserts, and sometimes thundering through curving canyon passages only a few feet wider than the train itself.

They dined on roast beef and ice cream, and rolled into Dodge City at 12:34 a.m. They were booked into separate sleeping cars, and slept as the *Chief* hammered its way across the great flat bluestem prairies of Kansas.

They were all awakened as the train echoed its way into the gigantic Union Station in Kansas City, Missouri, for its scheduled twenty minute service stop. Ben and Abu went back to sleep, but Ibrahim and Yousaf headed out onto the breathtaking concourse and gaped at the almost hundred-foot high ceiling, with its three massive 3,500-pound chandeliers, and six-foot-wide clock hanging over the central archway.

Neither of them had ever seen anything like it, anywhere, never mind in a train station. And they forgot about not knowing each other as they stood there gazing around them, staring at the ornamental plasterwork completed in the 1999 renovation. It would, of course, have meant nothing to them, but the spectacular moldings in the ceiling were crafted by Hayles and Howe, fresh from restoring the ceilings of Windsor Castle after the 1992 fire.

Ibrahim and Yousaf walked back to the train and headed to the dining car for breakfast, speaking softly at adjoining tables as the locomotive pulled out of the Taj Mahal of railroad stations at a quarter to eight in the morning.

They were still sipping coffee as the train hauled over the 135-foot high steel bridge that spans the Missouri, America's longest river. From there it set off on a three-and-a-half hour journey across the plains of northern Missouri, and then made a twenty-mile dash through southern Iowa. But just after the scheduled stop at Fort Madison, right on the Illinois line, the train came to a shuddering halt, for no apparent reason, in the middle of nowhere.

Ibrahim, raised on a lifetime of old, mostly pirated British and American movies, half-expected a squadron of Hitler's Nazis to come jackbooting along the corridor demanding papers. American Nazis, of course, but nonetheless officers who would seize him and his pals and bring them back to the concentration camp of Guantanamo Bay.

He turned to a young man sitting right next to him reading the *Kansas City Star* and asked, "Why this hold up? Is this official?"

"Official! Hell no," the kid replied. "We just reached the Mississippi. We got river traffic coming under the bridge. It happens sometimes. Probably make us twenty minutes late getting to Chicago."

Ibrahim Sharif had not felt such relief since Judge Osborne had freed him. He had no idea why a ship could shut the bridge, since he thought ships went under bridges and trains ran over them. He'd certainly never seen a bridge where the center span pivots to make a gap. And he sat patiently until the *Chief* moved forward again, and rumbled over the world's longest double-decked swing-span bridge, high above America's second longest river.

They reached Princeton, Illinois, at one o'clock and Chicago at twenty minutes after 3 p.m. Right on time at the end of the line, with 1,340 miles behind them. They had been on that train for almost twenty-seven hours, and no one in the United States had the slightest idea of their whereabouts.

The CIA suspected they were hiding out somewhere in the endless scrubland desert of New Mexico. Captain Ramshawe thought it more likely they had cleared the datum, and possibly taken a plane to God knows where.

But the FBI had alerted every airport security office and issued photographs of the four men, top-class photographs taken both in Guantanamo and in the Washington Court. They had e-mailed the images nationwide. Every airport guard was on the lookout for the four murder suspects. In Albuquerque's International Sunport, a force of twenty reinforcements had been drafted in.

Every highway patrol in the country had the four photos on their cruiser screen. State troopers scanned every vehicle as they drove past. In New Mexico and the adjoining states of Arizona, Texas, Colorado, and the Oklahoma panhandle, any vehicle, car or truck, was pulled over if it carried more than four people. There were unprecedented traffic jams on the freeways of the southwestern states.

The murder of the two border guards was being treated like an assault on the very manhood of the United States. Who the hell were these little creeps, come busting in here, and opening fire on Uncle Sam's finest? Left to the public and the media there could be a good old-fashioned Wild West lynch-party before sundown.

Except no one knew where the murderers actually were. And the gigantic manhunt taking place was having no luck whatsoever. Ibrahim, Yousaf, Ben, and Abu were having coffee at separate tables in the Chicago station, trying not to look at each other, waiting to board Amtrak's famous *Cardinal* for the 1,145-mile journey to New York City, partway along the historic old lines of the picturesque Norfolk and Southern Railroad.

And so, while the entire southwestern sprawl of the United States was consumed with their capture, the four former Guantanamo prisoners were casually reading the afternoon newspapers, which by now were splashing with the photographs, big, on the front page, of the men who were wanted for the double murder.

It's a strange phenomena in the United States that the railroads, which opened up the lands to the west, and played such a massive part in forging the nation, are not considered as mainstream long-distance transport. Everyone flies. So if a police force seeks out fugitives from justice, they go for airports and roads. Which left Ibrahim and his guys more or less in peace until the *Cardinal* reached New York City.

And once more, the four terrorists stayed separate, uttering no word about their current notoriety, but each of them wishing there had been another way across that Mexican border, a method that might have prevented Abu Hassan blowing Ray and Matt's brains out.

They boarded the *Cardinal* at 5 p.m. ready for the 5:45 departure. Ibraham had looked up the timetable and discovered the huge locomotive would haul the train for more than twenty-eight hours, with thirty-one stops, before it pulled into New York's Penn Station, tomorrow night.

Ibrahim had no idea who the al-Qaeda mastermind was who was arranging their travel. But when he had reported to the ticket office in Chicago, everything was ready. Under the same false names, which required passport or driver's license photo identity, there were travel tickets, vouchers for the dining car, and reserved sleeping berths. There would be no need for any of the four to speak one word throughout the long journey.

The *Cardinal* pulled out on time and headed south-southeast through the flat wheat fields, past the soybeans and fruit, hay, hogs, and oats, two hundred miles, running in the dark, all the way to the Ohio border. They reached Cincinnati in the small hours as the men from the Middle East slept soundly in the sleeper car.

In the relatively short run along the northern edge of Kentucky, dawn began to break, and still the presses were pounding out newspapers, demanding the police find the men who had murdered the border guards, almost two thousand miles behind the train.

The sun rose over the banks of the mighty Ohio River as the *Cardinal* prepared for its final swing to the south from the West Virginian city of Huntington. From there it rolled on toward the southern end of the Allegheny Mountains. It stopped at White Sulphur Springs at 11:30 a.m. And when it left, it headed directly toward the high slopes of the Virginia Appalachians.

For Ibrahim and Yousaf, it was hard to believe this was all the same country. And now they were in some kind of wonderland, crossing the majestic Blue Ridge Mountains and the Shenandoah Valley, where another revolutionary, General Stonewall Jackson, had once nearly driven the government armies crazy.

If Ibrahim and Yousaf had understood the slightest vestige of U.S. history they would probably have sensed an affinity with that great southern warrior, and the Valley where his ghost haunts to this day. But they knew nothing. And when they reached Charlottesville, home of President Thomas Jefferson, they also knew nothing. Even when the conductor announced the significance of the stop, they stared blankly and separately, unaware of the revolution the third president had so influenced more than 230 years before—an even greater rebellion than their own.

They were, in a sense, kindred spirits passing in the mountain mists. Because they were men for whom a flame of righteousness could not be extinguished. The difference was, the Americans were highly educated, sure of their truths, sure of their intellectual ground.

Ibrahim, Yousaf, Ben, and Abu Hassan were little more than rabid dogs of war, fanatics who would kill and maim, without one thought about the ultimate outcome, the futility of their efforts, or the shocking consequences of staging a four-man war on the United States.

Right now, they rode in peace, heading to Washington and then New York. It grew dark again as they left the nation's capital, and it was almost 9:30 as they pulled into Penn Station.

Ibrahim had slyly informed them to meet him outside the main entrance where the taxi queue was located. He had an address, to which they should report. He also had a phone number, and all four still had their cell phones given to them in Mexico but connected to an American network.

Everyone was calm and confident, except for Abu Hassan, who was the most distinctive of them. All the way from Alexandria, he had been conscious of a fellow passenger staring at him. Every time he looked up, the man, a middle-aged, balding guy in a city suit and necktie, was looking directly at him. Abu also noticed the man was reading the *Washington Post*, which had photographs of all four of them splashed on its front page. The Palestinian had been on the run for most of his life, either from the Mossad, the Israeli Army, or the U.S. armed forces. And right now he smelled danger, not because of who the man might be, but because it didn't matter who he was. Anyone in this country could betray him with one phone call. It would not take much more than that for all of them to find themselves under tight arrest.

Abu could not talk about it, nor could he indicate he suspected he was being watched. Instead he kept his head down and watched for the moment when the guy moved or left the carriage. If he made a phone call, Abu believed he would have to act.

Abu decided to play it quietly, and all the way into New York, the man never moved, just read his newspaper, and periodically spent time staring at Abu, who was pretending to doze quietly.

The train came out of the tunnel and slowed as it entered Penn Station. Abu made certain he was behind his quarry as they walked down the platform, separated by about twenty feet. From this slender indication of amateurism, Abu Hassan understood the man was not a real detective or an undercover policemen. He was just a concerned, observant individual.

They traveled up the escalator, and Abu could see the man was heading directly to the men's room, which was off to the right, from the main drift of the passengers heading for the street exit.

Aside from the arrival of the *Cardinal,* the station was quiet. New York was going in other directions. The commuters had gone home for the night, the young crowd was out in the bars, and the swells were concluding dinner.

Abu's man entered the men's room, which was virtually deserted. And at that point he took a cell phone out of his pocket and opened the door to one of the cubicles. Abu watched him from the corner, watched the door slam shut, and heard the lock click into place.

In the accepted sense of the term, Abu was unarmed. What no one knew, even his colleagues, was that he still had the hand grenade, which he'd slipped into his briefcase and carried three quarters of the way across the United States at truly stupendous risk.

Abu reached into his briefcase and pulled out the heavy, round shell. He ripped out the pin and rolled it under the outer wall of the first cubicle. It rolled noisily, through four more cubicles, but no one was listening, except perhaps the man now calling the police from his cell phone.

Abu spun around and walked steadily back into the crowd heading for the exit. Now he could see Ibrahim, Yousaf, and Ben, and he tried to avoid converging with them. But suddenly there was an earth-shattering explosion, as fifteen toilet-bowls and twelve sinks were blasted clean through the ceiling of the men's room.

The entire edifice shook. Above, Madison Square Garden shuddered at probably the biggest single bang heard in that 125-year-old arena since Smokin' Joe Frazier's fifteenth-round left hook temporarily flattened Mohammed Ali on March 8, 1971.

Below in the men's room it looked like a scene from Hiroshima. There was nothing left, and there was a twenty-foot gaping hole in the obliterated ceiling. High pressure jets of water were scything in every direction, rapidly causing a flood. It was probably the longest and most powerful toilet-flush in recorded history.

There was no possibility of survival, not in that tightly enclosed space, surrounded by heavy marble in the walls and floor. In fact that heavy-duty structural material had contained the blast, driving it upward, causing serious damage directly above in the arena.

Meanwhile, Abu and Ben piled into a yellow cab, while Yousaf and Ibrahim jumped into another and took the lead. Ibrahim asked the driver if he knew where number 300 East Seventy-Sixth Street was, and with the second cab following, line astern, they made their way through light city traffic to the Upper East Side. They disembarked, and Ibrahim, who had the money and the address, paid for both cabs.

"Hey, nice apartments," said Ben looking up.

"Guess so," replied Ibrahim. "Pity we're not going in."

"What d'you mean?" asked Ben.

"You don't think I'd have two New York cab drivers running around knowing the precise address where they dropped off four Arabs, do you, right after Abu nearly knocked down Penn Station? Sorry. We have to walk south to Sixty-Ninth Street. That's where we're staying."

Abu looked momentarily chagrined, and he said, "Ibrahim, I'm telling you, that guy knew who I was. He was reading the paper, and my picture was all over the front page. He kept on looking at me."

"I just wonder if you might not have taken him out with maybe less of a national catastrophe?"

"We are all unarmed, so I couldn't shoot him," replied Abu. "I couldn't risk a fight because I might have lost, and I couldn't risk the chance he might have been a cop or a detective, carrying a gun. I had just one chance to kill him, and I knew I could get out of that railroad station without being noticed. Those grenades got a twenty-second lead-time after the pin gets pulled. I cover a lot of ground in twenty seconds."

"You were not supposed to have the grenade. It could have put us all in danger."

"If I hadn't had it, we might all be in jail by now, and jail is worse than danger."

"Abu Hassan," said Ibrahim, "it was very brilliant of you to spot that guy. And correct to take him out before he could use his phone. But now we must lay very low, because every person in the United States is going to be looking for us, not just half of the country like they were earlier today."

"With our luck," said Ben, "the guy Abu removed will probably turn out to be the Mayor of New York or someone like that."

"Mayors don't shit in Penn Station," retorted Abu.

"How you know that?" demanded Yousaf, who was quite shaken by recent events.

"I never heard of even one mayor in all the world who ever took a shit in Penn Station. I never even heard of a mayor who farted in Penn Station. Ha! Ha! Ha!"

"Shut up," snapped Ibrahim. "And separate. Walk farther apart, and cross the street at the next light."

They covered the next two blocks in silence, drifting farther away, one from the other, on the way downtown to Sixty-Ninth Street. When they reached it, Ibrahim gathered everyone together in the shadows, and told them, "This is a very important man we are seeing. He will tell us not to go out together at any time. Everyone should do as he says, okay?"

No one argued, and Ibrahim ordered two of them to go back across the street, and then enter the building one at a time at ten-minute intervals—"Me first, then Yousaf, then Abu, then Ben," he said. "You will each buzz Apartment 21D, three quick, two slow. That way we know it's you. The man's name is on the directory on the wall, next to the buzzer. He's Faisal al-Assad, a Saudi."

"Is that his real name?"

"It is so far as we're concerned. He works for his government. Finance, oil, and construction. He's a close friend of Shakir Khan."

NEWS OF THE PENN STATION "bomb" broke on the 11 o'clock television news bulletins. The police had instantly cordoned off Seventh and Eighth Avenues for five blocks, north and south, and closed the cross streets from West Twenty-Ninth to West Thirty-Third, all the way from Ninth Avenue to Sixth. They evacuated several buildings because of a general fear that this was 9/11 all over again and that there would be more bombs.

The media leapt immediately to the conclusion that the Penn Station bomb was the work of a terrorist cell operating in Manhattan. The slug line on Fox News quickly became: *Terrorists Hit New York All Over Again*.

All through the night the media attempted to make sense of the bombing. They were waiting for someone to step forward and lay claim to the disaster, as terrorists usually did.

By the time New York's *Daily News* came out at dawn, the media were treating it as a full-blooded mystery: "*Was it Al-Qaeda that bombed Penn Station?*" "*Was the Evil Hand of Bin Laden Behind This?*" "*Police Baffled by Bombers' Silence.*"

Because there was as yet no death toll, the *New York Post*, predictably thought it was marginally amusing, their front page reading "*Who Bombed the John?*"

The police confirmed that twenty-seven people had been injured, most of them Amtrak and Penn Station staff. The only serious injury was caused when a member of the cleaning staff was flattened by a hunk of flying masonry.

No one knew whether anyone had been in the men's room when the bomb detonated. Right now the place was just a heap of rubble, with three feet of water being pumped out by the fire department, while emergency crews tried to halt the flow from dozens of fractured waterpipes.

As the morning wore on, the reality of the story set in. There was no proof of terrorist involvement, but New York had ground to a halt in the central midtown area during the night. The morning rush-hour traffic was affected, but a vast squadron of police, security guards, and tracker dogs had found nothing after a twelve-hour search. The city was expected to return to normal before the afternoon rush-hour was underway. They even had Penn Station functioning again that morning, mostly because the blast had gone upward, and Madison Square Garden was dark that night.

Nonetheless, there remained the suspicion of terrorism, based on the simple truth that in this modern world, aside from half-crazed jihadists, not many people walk around midtown Manhattan with bombs in their briefcases.

The FBI and the CIA were called in and both reached the same verdict: *The key lies in knowing the precise identities of anyone who died in the men's room through DNA, if human remains were found.*

In addition, there was the possibility of people calling in to report that their relatives or loved ones had been in Penn Station at the time and had not been heard from. The bomb-thrower had plainly vanished, and there was little that could be done until forensics turned up evidence and the missing were identified.

Seventeen hours after the blast, Mrs. Susan Harvey, of West Thirty-Six Street reported the disappearance of her husband, Michael, a coal-mining executive who had been traveling back to New York on the *Cardinal*. As far as she knew, he had boarded the train at Charleston, West Virginia, at around 8:15 in the morning, and arrived in New York just before 10 p.m. She told them that Michael preferred the train to flying because it gave him time to work, rest, and think, and deposited him just a few blocks from home.

Mrs. Harvey had not heard from him since he left Charleston, and had been assuming he either missed the train or changed his plans. Now she was beside herself with worry.

The second person to call in was a Miss Irena Seaford, of East Eighty-Second Street. Her father was missing. He had taken the late Amtrak from Penn Station to Philadelphia to visit her sister— or at least that's what she thought. But he never arrived, and the entire family was now concerned that he had somehow been injured in the station bombing.

The police could only say they had no reports of anyone dying in the blast, and that the names of Michael Harvey and Thomas Seaford were not on the injured list. It would be two more days before gruesome body parts were recovered and examined, and the police laboratories confirmed both missing men had indeed died instantly in the men's room explosion.

In a sense, this made the investigation even more difficult, because there was not a single shred of evidence to suggest that either Michael or Thomas could possibly have been a target for an al-Qaeda jihadist.

Interest in the Penn Station bomb began to wane. Even Captain Ramshawe, whose paranoia for terrorist activities was all-consuming, began to veer toward the "nutcase" theory as there was no rhyme or reason to the explosion—two non-entity New Yorkers killed, neither with any connection to politics or terrorism.

THE CHOSEN WERE NOW comfortably installed in the six-bedroomed duplex apartment of Mr. Faisal al-Assad, the tall, dark-skinned Saudi who acted as Shakir Khan's right arm for all of al-Qaeda's operations in the United States. These operations had been somewhat limited during the past few years, while an angry George W. Bush prowled around the White House threatening to eliminate half the Himalayas if anyone from Afghanistan or Pakistan dared even to let off a firecracker in the United States during his watch.

And predictably no one did, which put the Saudi financier on hold for a few years. But Faisal al-Assad was a fanatic along with the rest of them. And the flame of injustice burned within him. He had earned the admiration of his colleagues in the mountains above the Swat Valley by his superlative, and secretive, handling of the Islamic treasure chest in the West, especially during the preparations for 9/11. He somehow managed to remain the acceptable face of Middle Eastern capitalism, while working in tandem with the totally unacceptable Osama bin Laden.

But now things had changed. There were key al-Qaeda men being freed from Guantanamo, and al-Assad was ready to go back to work. And it was with genuine warmth and friendship that he welcomed Ibrahim, Yousaf, Ben, and Abu into his home, laughing and clapping when he heard that Abu had blown up the men's room at Penn Station.

He told them they should not venture out onto the streets of New York together under any circumstances. But they could of course go out separately within two or three days, as long as Abu Hassan promised not to take any more hand grenades for a walk.

Al-Assad would be passing a signal through to Peshawar this evening to inform Shakir Khan that the Chosen Ones had arrived safely according to plan, and everything was in place for the next attack. He believed this would involve the total destruction of an American Judaic school with an estimated twelve hundred people inside it—children, teenagers, parents, and the college faculty.

"Will everyone know afterwards they had just witnessed the revenge of the Islamists?" asked Ben al-Turabi.

"Oh yes," said Faisal al-Assad. "They will understand that very well. We will make absolutely certain that they do."

"And can we know where our target is?" asked Ibrahim.

"Right at this moment, that is a state secret. But maybe I can tell you tomorrow. And then we will have much preparation. Places to go and money to spend. There will be no mistakes."

THE FIRST BREAK in either case came shortly before midnight. The forensic reports predictably confirmed the remains of two dead men were in the Penn Station rubble. DNA confirmed one was Michael Harvey, the other Thomas Seaford. Mrs. Harvey and Miss Seaford were at a downtown precinct. There were no complete bodies to identify, but there were scraps of clothing.

The second part of the report was dynamite, so to speak. The men's room had been blasted by a hand grenade, an identifiable military hand grenade, produced by the world-famous Swiss arms manufacturer, RUAG, registered in Berne, a huge European-wide organization with an Aerospace Division and some of the biggest small-arms plants in the world.

RUAG manufactured millions of 9mm bullets for weapons like the German Luger, and it was the world's specialist in hand grenades. The one that blew the men's room was quickly identified as RUAG's classic HG-85, which the Swiss ammunition masters supplied to armies all over the world. In precisely which plant the grenade had been manufactured was neither obvious nor relevant. But the fragments of the outer casing found in the rubble were critical.

Had the detonation been caused by a regular Improvised Explosive Device (IED) typical of those in Baghdad and Kabul, that would have been one thing. But a hand grenade was entirely different. They were strictly military, unavailable on the black market. Whoever had hurled the grenade had some kind of connection to a national army.

Captain Ramshawe was awakened in the small hours of the morning, and jumped straight out of bed with excitement. Because that hand grenade changed everything. Because you would need to be a proper terrorist to get your hands on one of those. And that rushed the Chosen Ones right back into an intricate equation.

Captain Ramshawe's afterburner kicked in as he headed for his study and looked up the train schedules from Albuquerque to New York. "I just wonder," he pondered, "if those four bastards traveled across this country by train, and found some reason to knock out those two New Yorkers with a proper terrorist weapon—a goddamned hand grenade."

By any standards the link was a long shot, but Jimmy had been obsessed with finding the four men, and he was suspecting anything and everyone who might have a connection to the Middle East. If he'd spotted a three-year-old colt named Desert Sheikh running at Belmont Park, he'd probably have had it arrested.

Eventually he located the two trains anyone would have used if they had been trying to travel from Albuquerque to New York on the morning after the two murders on New Mexico's southern border. There was no choice, no other station, no other route.

The first of them, the *Southwestern Chief* left at around lunchtime, ran through the night and arrived in Chicago in the middle of the following afternoon at 3 p.m. The next one, the *Cardinal* left Chicago, a deliberate link, and ran all the way to New York, arriving the following evening just before 10 p.m.

> *And right there this fucking Ibrahim Towelhead jumps off the train and blows up the bloody Penn Station shithouse at 9.55 p.m.—the exact right time. Makes no sense.*

Jimmy Ramshawe's brain was in some kind of a high gear, and he was thinking and muttering in pure Australian, which he always did when he was over-excited. "*What have I proved?*" he demanded of himself. "*Nothing, right? Except that the Chosen Ones could have done it, if they'd ridden the precise two trains I just found. Odds: About a billion to one. Screw it.*"

He closed down the computer, and stood up, resolved to return to bed and cast the problem to the back of his mind until he went to work at 7 a.m. But then he had a new idea. *The next major hit on a U.S. target is to be Penn Station, scheduled for a time when most of the workforce and passengers are not there—like the World Trade Center. The Towelheads pick up a stash of hand grenades from the Mexican Army and rush through the border, killing a couple of American guards who got in the way. Their mates pick 'em up in a car, and drive them to the nearest long-distance train terminal—Albuquerque. They board the* Southwestern Chief *for Chicago and New York.*

They head up to the main Penn Station concourse, but one of them is spotted handing out the grenades. A passenger, probably ex-military, shouts and runs toward them.

Yousaf Cameldung runs for the men's room. The passenger charges in after him. Yousaf trips him, pulls out the pin, and blows

the place up. Towelheads stack away their grenades, and bolt to a
waiting car outside Madison Square Garden.

Jane Ramshawe never even stirred while Jimmy delivered this soliloquy two rooms away. And she was up and making coffee and toast at 6:30, prior to leaving for Georgetown University, where she was completing a course in American history. She was actually reading the final pages of a chapter on the army of General Stonewall Jackson when Jimmy asked her, "Do you think the bomb at Penn Station was an accident?"

"Probably," she replied. "There's no motive. No logic. No gain for anyone. Huge risk, and for what?"

"How about I tell you it wasn't a bomb. It was a military hand grenade."

"A hand grenade! Where the hell did they get that?"

"Good question," said Captain Jimmy.

IT WAS SHORTLY BEFORE MIDNIGHT in Shakir Khan's government office in Islamabad. Aside from the security guards, he was the only man in the building. His chauffeur awaited him outside in the courtyard.

He sat at his desk, checked his watch, and picked up the telephone, a phone that engineers had spent hundreds of hours making as secure as any land line in the world. The new Pakistani system was fully encrypted, and it protected classified government conversations to an incredible degree. It was effectively spy-proof. Well, nearly.

Right now it was three o'clock in the afternoon in New York. Faisal al-Assad was alone in his study waiting for the phone to ring. His guests were all watching with rapt attention the continuing adventures of the *Terminator*. The phone rang at two minutes past the hour. Faisal picked it up without a word. From the other end of the line came a voice: "Back to nalseb because King Saul's boys are top-class one in Abe's Place. It's a go for the former caged songbirds but be sure they can see the mountain. Sleepers one, three, and four-zero are awake. Canst proceed?"

Faisal said: "Affirmative." And the line went dead.

The Saudi link man understood every word of the veiled speech that had been transmitted to him. He now knew the target, selected from a short-list of ten different colleges. Right now, he needed to deposit $2 million in small country bank accounts he must open—finance for the high explosive, and their operational headquarters.

This was a very fine plan, which would most certainly reflect more glory and notoriety on the fighting forces of al-Qaeda than anything else that had been achieved since the Twin Towers. This gigantic strike against the Great Satan might cause the Americans and their cohorts to pull out of Afghanistan altogether, leading that great tribal nation back to where it belonged—in the sacred hands of their holy brothers of the Taliban.

Al-Assad knew it would probably lead to the death of the four young men in the next room, and by that he was saddened. But Allah loved those who were martyred in His name, and would call them unto Him, across the bridge to the sound of the three trumpets. There were worse fates, he decided, but that particular one was certainly not in his own immediate itinerary.

THEY WERE ONLY a couple hundred miles from the Syrian Desert, these sovereign British lands on the coast of Cyprus. But, just like home in the UK, it was pelting rain tonight, and had been for five hours. The rough, sandy ground outside the JSSU ops room had already become a quagmire. The huge German Shepherd guard dogs were wet and bedraggled. The guards themselves were soaked, and the rain lashed onto the big wooden warning sign that declared trespassers would be shot on sight. "British Sovereign Territory," the sign proclaimed. But tonight they need not have bothered. It was British alright, chilly, windswept, wet, and miserable. The satellite and radio aerials and masts that jutted from the roofs of the stone building, swayed in the gusting south-wester, and the night was as black as a terrorist's heart.

Inside the ops room, lit only by the flickering screens and the backlighting of the keyboards, the cream of Great Britain's electronic Intelligence interceptors were at work, ready to translate any message, signal, or coded transmission into any one of a hundred languages. They watched and listened for the one careless communiqué that would betray the terrorists, and leave them at the mercy of the security forces of the West.

Sergeant Shane Collins was on the evening watch, assisted by a Royal Navy Lieutenant, when he picked up a call on INTELSAT: "Back to nalseb because King Saul's boys are top-class one in Abe's Place. It's a go for the former caged songbirds but be sure they can see the mountain. Sleepers one, three and four-zero are awake. Canst proceed?"

That was definitely Arabic. And then there was a brief delay of maybe nine seconds, and before a distant voice replied: "Affirmative." Nothing else, and then the line went dead.

This was routine for an experienced operator like Shane. The message was plainly military because of two words "proceed," and "affirmative." The sergeant swung around and called for a supervisor—"Captain, over here, please. Station Five."

Army Captain Alec Simon, aged thirty-two, came quickly and asked, "What's going on?"

Scribbling quickly, without looking up, Shane Collins replied, "Telephone intercept. Possible government encrypted India or Pakistan, but not very good. Seems military, but not in code. More like veiled speech. Fourteen-second transmission, then a very short reply. I have a rough translation." He handed his headset to the supervisor and pressed his "listen-again" button.

Seventeen seconds later, Captain Simon nodded and picked up a telephone, saying quickly, "Satellite COMM two-three-zero-six translate and prepare text for immediate transmission to GCHQ for detailed analysis."

Sixty seconds later, more than two thousand miles and two timezones away, a screen lit up in the operations center at GCHQ, a huge brightly lit room, staffed by civilians, night and day, GCHQ was the opposite environment to the stark military ops room in Cyprus. Also it was not pouring with rain outside, and there were no public signs bearing threats to shoot anyone who stepped out of line.

And yet this place, both historically and practically, represented the very heart of the most sinister aspect of the United Kingdom—the frontline muscle of MI6, the hard-eyed secret police force, which glares at the world's problems, eavesdrops on the world's villains, and never drops its guard in its relentless surveillance of rogue states.

This massive circular building is both the successor and custodian of the secrets of Bletchley Park, the great English manor house in which they cracked *Enigma*, Hitler's World War II military codes, evoking the everlasting gratitude of the Allied Commanders.

The hardware has moved on after sixty-five years, but the ethos endures. GCHQ is still staffed with people whose gods remain those studious mathematicians and cryptologists who silently rendered the Nazi war codes useless; who pinpointed the Panzer Divisions, identified the armadas of German fighter bombers, and nailed down the routes of the Atlantic U-boat packs.

In recent years, the staff of GCHQ struck a large gold badge that was presented to each one of the few survivors of the sainted members of Bletchley Park's old WWII *GC and CS (Government Code and Cipher School)*. The front emblem is a stylized rendering of the great modern surveillance dragnet, the Doughnut building on the outskirts of Cheltenham. The rear of the badge, behind the fastener, cannot of course be seen. It reads, with momentous British understatement, "We Also Served."

And now the words of the plainly unbalanced Pakistani fanatic Shakir Khan, followed in the pathways of signals written long ago by Hitler's generals. And those words stood before the thoughtful gaze of a British cryptologist, a young civilian woman, who called out, "JSSU request detailed analysis on intercept."

The supervisor called back, "Put it on my screen, would you?" Moments later, he picked up the phone and said, "Satellite COMM two-three-zero-six from Cyprus. Please establish a line on the frequency and check for code. I'll hold for the tracker."

Seconds passed and the response flashed back, "Frequency line Cyprus to a point beyond the Hindu Kush range, Northeastern Afghanistan. I'm still checking . . . maybe Peshawar . . . no, beyond that. I'm getting somewhere in Islamabad . . . still checking . . . trying to pinpoint."

A full minute went by, and then a clear message came through: "That frequency line crosses Syria, Iraq, and Iran into Afghanistan. No further information for onward transmission."

Back in Cyprus Captain Simon was waiting. He knew the information would be coming, because he had always believed there was an especially strong frequency between his own ops room and Pakistan, probably something to do with the fact that they almost shared a link along the thirty-fourth parallel.

The GCHQ supervisor turned back to the young operator who first fielded Captain Simon's signal. "So far," he said, "we know for certain that someone in Islamabad around midnight placed this call to an unknown destination. Request a second frequency line, will you? Alert stations Saudi Arabia and Pakistan. Get a fix where the lines bisect. Thank you, Lindy."

One minute later, the operator was back on the link to Cyprus, and she reported to Captain Simon, "Sir, they're certain it's not coded. And we agree it's military. We just got a fix on that 'Affirmative' reply, but it was too brief for a second frequency line.

"Right now we're definite North America East Coast. But the rest is vague . . . somewhere between Washington and Maine. We transmitted to U.S. National Security Agency, Maryland. Still searching."

"Will I hold or will you come back? . . ."

"Just a moment, sir. We're getting something. U.S. authorities pinpointing a government building in Islamabad, protected system. No number, but the call came from somewhere inside the Pakistani main administrative building, called Pak Secretariat."

"Thank you," replied Captain Simon. "Any more on the U.S. end of the call?"

"Not much. But NSA trackers are nearly certain it's New York rather than Boston or Washington. Still trying. We'll come back."

At this point the full translation jumped onto the captain's screen, with broad suggestions.

"First line may refer to Jewish special forces, or even Mossad. *Top-class one* euphemism for 'very important.' *Abe's Place* unknown. Could be anywhere. *Caged songbirds* possible Pakistani ex-inmates of Guantanamo Bay. There are many. *The mountain* indicates some address. *Sleepers* could be reference to al-Qaeda sleeper cells, bin Laden's favorite subject. See references. '*Canst proceed*' obviously military shorthand."

It wasn't much, but it was a start. GCHQ confirmed they had sent the signal through to the U.S. National Surveillance Office, the NSA, and the CIA. There was a cryptic note from the NSA requesting both Cheltenham and Cyprus to update Fort Meade throughout the night at the first sign of a crack in the signal.

Nailing down that phone call to a major government building in Islamabad was critical because Pakistan is a powder-keg of hidden nuclear weapons, which Taliban and al-Qaeda dissidents covet with all of their hearts.

A national military, of the power and efficiency of Pakistan's, should have been more than a match for a turbaned rabble trying to cause some kind of a world war in the Middle East. But it was not. And it kept proving it.

Alex Simon stared out of the door of the Cyprus surveillance bunker. In his mind he held his usual visions of evil jihadist cut-throats, in their mountains, in their caves, handling their high-explosives, and now, apparently, hunkered down in clandestine government offices. It occurred to him that killers like these would ultimately be stopped by the thoughtful space-age detectives in England's damp, green Cotswold Hills; men and women whose predecessors had located much darker forces and far greater villains than any of these modern Holy Warriors.

8

CAPTAIN JAMES RAMSHAWE had an uncanny feeling he was breaking one of Admiral Morgan's cardinal rules: *Kid, never waste your time chasing goddamned shadows.*

Before him was his ever-present, lined legal pad upon which he recorded his thoughts, theories, facts, and strategies. Right now the page that stared up at him resembled the ramblings of a madman.

He had tried to assemble all the clues and evidence that had surfaced since those four terrorists had been freed. And he had to admit the trail had more or less gone cold.

They'd gone to England and somehow gotten out. They'd also gone to Andalucia in Spain, and also gotten out. They'd most definitely shown up in Mexico, and *may* have killed two border guards while re-entering the United States. This Penn Station bullshit in New York was a total red herring without yielding one scrap of evidence.

And now there was this quasi–Mata Hari signal from Islamabad to some contact who *might* have lived in Manhattan, droning on about King Saul and God knows what else. Okay, there may have been something in it, but that was someone else's task, not his. *Call in the bloody cryptologists,* he muttered, *but don't bother me till there's something tangible.* In his heart he knew that Admiral Morgan would have laughed at him if he'd sought advice on this one.

Also he had a whole lot of far more important matters to deal with. The Chinese were again suspected of being involved in Pakistan's nuclear agenda; both countries were secretly speaking to Iran, which was infuriating the Pentagon; and the Russians were refusing to admit they'd mislaid a Typhoon-Class ICBM submarine somewhere in the North Atlantic.

There was also intense pressure on the NSA to tap into the SATCOMS systems of the stupid Brits, who were once again threatening to abandon their expensive Trident submarine fleet.

And yet, Jimmy Ramshawe could not dismiss the activities of Ibrahim, Yousaf, Ben, and Abu Hassan from his mind. He believed they were somehow in Manhattan, mostly because of the hand grenade.

He e-mailed Mack Bedford the signal from Islamabad and then called him. The two men spent a half-hour exploring the ramifications. *Was it them? Are they in New York? What if they are? What if they're not. And, as the* New York Post *so succinctly wondered, Who Bombed the John?*

At the end of their talk, Mack Bedford made one crucial observation. "That signal from Islamabad," he said, "came, likely as not, from a person associated with the rebel forces in Pakistan—Taliban or al-Qaeda. Those nutters from the Swat Valley who have a lot of government support.

"And whenever those guys start talking about anything connected with Israel, they're never peaceful objectives. I can't decipher that conversation. But I'd bet the Mossad was interested. Remember the Israeli Secret Service was right in the thick of it on the night those guys were last in court.

"It's not the worst thing in the world to play a hunch. I've saved my own life a few times doing that. And right now I think I might move down to Manhattan for a few days. See if I can locate those guys again—before they do something real bad."

"Will you check in?"

"Uh-huh. Coupla days. Lemme know if anyone cracks that stuff from Islamabad."

MACK CHECKED INTO the Waldorf Astoria the following day. He needed a place more like a city than a hotel, somewhere he could get lost. At lunchtime he strolled three blocks over to Second Avenue and then walked down to Forty-Third Street to the Consul General of Israel.

He walked through security and reported to the desk holding a small sealed envelope he had prepared at the hotel. The name on the outside was Colonel Benjamin Shalit, and old friend with whom Mack had served in Afghanistan.

Ben Shalit had been recruited to the Mossad five years ago, and had served in the Israeli Secret Police both in Tel Aviv and in various sections of the Middle East. They had appointed him to New York a couple of years before. Mack knew he was there but not what the former commando was doing.

He understood it would have been pointless to ask to speak to him because the Israelis would never dream of admitting there was a Mossad field officer anywhere near their sunny tourist front office. Number 800 Second Avenue was strictly for passports, advice, hotels, visas, and tourist destinations.

Men like Ben Shalit operated in the shadows, watching for danger, locating threats, observing suspected terrorists who might wish his nation harm. They had their own network, and in this building, even their own doorway, around the back of the building, because you never knew who might be watching.

Mack Bedford had simply left the envelope at the desk and asked the doorman to have it delivered. Inside was simply a note asking Ben to call the Waldorf. Then he strolled back to the hotel and waited.

At 4 p.m., the front desk called to inform him Mr. Shalit was here to see him, and to meet him at a table on the cocktail terrace.

Mack's former comrade-in-arms was a medium-sized man who was heavyset with a swarthy complexion and an unmistakable twinkle in his dark, deep-set eyes. Ben Shalit, now in his late thirties, had never married, having lived a life of constant upheaval in the service of his country.

"I'll say one thing, Benny," said the American, "you look a whole lot better than you did last time I saw you."

"So do you," replied the Israeli. They both recalled the bomb blast on the roadside in Kabul, which had capsized their jeep and flung them both out, leaving them covered in blood and dust but relatively unhurt, considering that four other men had been killed.

Neither touched alcohol during working hours, so they settled for tea over a long talk about the situation in the Middle East, which neither of them thought was great.

It was almost a quarter to five when Mack told his old buddy what he'd come for. "Benny," he said, "I need to plug into the Israeli network that deals with national or local threat right here in New York."

"Well, I guess you're in the right spot already," the Israeli replied. "That's my watch. My life, actually. What's on your mind?"

"I am, unofficially, on the lookout for four former prisoners recently freed from Guantanamo."

"Funny," replied Ben. "So am I. But I have a special interest in two of them."

"You mean Ben al-Turabi and Abu Hassan Akbar?"

"Correct. Two terrorists who committed two of the worst crimes in our history. And many more."

Mack nodded carefully. "They are traveling with a couple of guys in whom we have a special interest."

"That'd be Ibrahim Sharif and Yousaf Mohammed—coupla

bombers from the mountains over there. Guess you guys were thrilled to bits when those judges let them go free."

"Oh, sure. Trouble is we think they are planning to take their revenge. And we think they might be here in New York."

"Did you pick 'em up in Mexico?"

"We did. And we think they shot those two guards at the border."

"So do we. Which I guess brings us to the Penn Station bomb?"

"We haven't made much progress with that. But we now have a transcript of a phone conversation that linked up Islamabad and New York."

"Yup. Cyprus copied us on all that. We're their nearest allies if push ever comes to shove. And you can bet when we saw the words 'King Saul' we stepped it up a few notches."

"Any luck?"

"No more than you, I imagine. But we're working on it."

"What are you planning to do with them if you find them?"

"Us? We'll take 'em out, no questions asked. All four. Save a lot of trouble. How about you?"

"Same."

Mack poured more tea for them both. And then said, "How can I plug in? Follow you down the same road."

"Well, we're not very far along. But, Mack, when you suspect there is a major terrorist hit being planned, there's always a trail that leads to a big hunk of cash. These operations cost money. And you sometimes run into property deals. Because big plans need some kind of HQ.

"And then there's phones, air transport, other transportation, maybe cars to be bought and registered, meals, hotels, pay-offs, purchases of chemicals and electronics. It all adds up, 'specially if there's four main guys and several assistants involved."

"How can I get into that trail?"

"It's hard for you. Easier for us."

"Will you give me a hand?"

"Sure. We don't care who kills them."

"What do I do now?"

"You have to contact the Sayanim."

"The who?"

"The Sayanim."

"Who's he?"

"Mack, it's the world-wide Jewish brotherhood, the Friends of Israel."

"They got offices right here in New York?"

"Not quite. It's probably the most secretive network in the world. They don't have offices anywhere. And they don't speak to anyone except when they are spoken to. They don't even speak to each other."

"Sounds like a quiet group."

"That it is. It's our global organization, private Jewish people who hold positions of power, or wealth, or authority, or maybe just responsibility. They are people who live abroad but are still devoted to Israel and what it means to all of us."

"Okay," said Mack. "But what do they do?"

"Mostly nothing. But they are always there, prepared to do everything in their power to help Israel, no questions asked. Like us, they work in the shadows."

"Then they are a secret society?"

"They are much more secret than that. They have no structure. They are unknown soldiers fighting for a common cause, treasured by the Mossad, priceless to Israel's government."

"How do we find them?"

"By being careful. There are two thousand of them in New York City alone. Someone always knows someone."

"Are you a member of the Sayanim, Benny?"

"I am still a serving officer. They have not invited me—yet. But in time they will."

"And what would happen if you refused?"

"No one's ever refused."

Mack sat in silence for a while, profoundly impressed by the enormity of Ben Shalit's words. He'd served in Israel, worked with the Mossad, and he'd seen firsthand the atrocities committed against the nation of Israel. He understood their heartbreak and determination to live, and, if necessary, die, standing shoulder to shoulder against the Arab world.

But to him, that whole scenario had often seemed remote and isolated. Everyone knew Israel had its back to the wall. But the brotherhood, the Sayanim, well, that was amazing. No wonder Israel managed to get its own way almost all of the time.

"I am going to put you in touch with someone," said Ben. "But you must be completely guarded in your questions to him. Remember, he will have only my word that you are safe and that we all fight on the same side against the scum of Gaza and the Afghan mountains."

"I am grateful for that," said Ben. "But I'm not sure what to ask him."

"The man you will meet, right here in the city, will know more about a possible attack on New York than anyone else. The signal from Islamabad suggests a Jewish target—that bit about King Saul's boys, and Abe's place. Our man will have many lines of inquiry out there. If anyone can help, he can."

Mack stood, and Ben told him he would call in one hour with a name, place, and time. They shook hands and parted.

IT WAS 8 P.M. and Mack climbed out of a taxi on West Houston Street, Lower Manhattan, as instructed, and headed toward Wooster Street, a boutique, art, and restaurant throughway in trendy SoHo.

There was a buzz about the place but it was dark and the buildings, former industrial places that are now occupied as enormous loft apartments at astronomical rents, were tall and, to Mack, somewhat foreboding. But he was not a city boy. Indeed, he rarely went to cities without an express purpose of blowing out someone's brains or capturing some restless, troublesome district by force of arms. Tonight he was not even armed, but as he stared up at the massive concrete and iron structures, he wished he were.

Nonetheless, he strode fast down Wooster, heading south, seeking the address Ben Shalit had given him. When he found it, he was surprised. The sign above the door and steel-meshed picture window read BANDA FINE ARTS. For a moment Mack thought he was in the wrong place, but he re-checked the number and this was it.

As far as he could tell, the art gallery was not even open. There was a single light somewhere in a back recess, but no one could call it inviting. Mack turned the handle and pushed open the door. He stepped into a gloomy, half-lit showroom, where, at the far end, behind a low desk lamp, he could see someone sitting.

The lamp lit up the man's chest and jacket, but his face was invisible. One hand was gently holding a drawing of some kind, the other was gripping a Browning automatic pistol, which was aimed straight at Mack's head.

Mack glanced left and right, and debated the best way to kill this faceless gunmen. But then a soft, refined voice said, "Are you Mack Bedford?"

"Yup. You planning to shoot me or something?"

The gunman laughed and put the offending weapon into his desk drawer. "I'm afraid you can't be too careful these days," he said.

"You're telling me, pal," said Mack.

From behind the desk, the man turned on another light and then walked out to shake Mack's hand.

"Good evening," he said, "I'm John Strauss."

His grip was hard, and so were his brown eyes. Strauss was tall and athletic-looking, with well-cut, curly black hair. There was something about his bearing that Mack instinctively sensed was military. He also had a slight accent, and Mack guessed Israeli. Ben Shalit had the same intonations.

Strauss walked over to the door and locked it, pulling down an inside blind. He led the way into a big room behind the art gallery, which was probably the finest room Mack had ever seen.

There was something classic about it, although it had no windows. It had a wideboard polished oak floor with teak paneling on the walls. The beautiful Persian rug was patterned in deep red and blue. Mack was no expert on carpets, but he knew "sure as hell" that it had cost more than his car.

A small log fire crackled in the wide brick fireplace, and a fine French sideboard, which Mack was sure cost more than his house, rested against the wall. He was not absolutely clear what this Strauss character really did for a living, but he sure got well paid for it.

On the wall above the sideboard there hung three exquisitely framed sketches, and Mack had no doubt they were valuable. He stared at them for a few moments while Strauss walked to a decanter on the sideboard and poured two glasses of chilled white wine. Mack hesitated but accepted. "Come on, Mack," said the art dealer. "Even a Navy SEAL can have a glass of Israeli dessert wine with a new friend."

Mack chuckled. "Those are really great drawings, John. I was just admiring them."

"Preliminary sketches for Titian's *Bacchus and Ariadne*," he said. Mack didn't have any background in art, but he'd heard of Titian, although he would not have recognized his work. All he knew of the artist was that all the girls he painted had dark red hair.

"He's one of the easiest artists to recognize," said Strauss, "because of the amount of bucolic landscapes he almost always used, no matter what his subject. Do you know why that is?"

"I'm sorry, John. It's not really a subject I know anything about."

"Well, I know you did not come here to buy a print or a drawing, but I'll tell you anyway. Titian was born in the Dolomite Mountains—that's the last jagged peaks of the Alps, where they sweep down to the plains north of Venice. They influenced his work till the day he died."

"Funny, isn't it," said Mack, "the way we never forget where we come from."

Strauss nodded and sipped his wine. "And now, Mr. Bedford," he said, suddenly slipping into a wryly formal mode, "you better tell me what you want."

"First thing I want is to know who *you* are. I'm guessing Benjamin told you all about me."

"He told me what you are working on. And I have to say you are right to be concerned about the four hoodlums who got out of Guantanamo Bay. You think they are in New York?"

"Do you?"

"Yes."

"Can I know why?"

"Well, who the hell else would be in Penn Station with a hand grenade? And where else would you be if you were planning a major hit on the USA? Also, one of my most reliable men thinks he saw one of them, that Ben al-Turabi, coming out of a bookstore on Fifth Avenue, midtown. That's the sonofabitch who bombed the Park Hotel in Netanya. We had him once, and then you guys found a way to release him."

"Did your man get a chance to follow him? Were there any clues?"

"No. He was across the street on the east side of Fifth Avenue. And al-Turabi came out and jumped into a black limo, which headed west at the next light. But our man was quite certain it was him."

Mack sipped his wine. "You keep speaking as if we are somehow separate. Come on, John, who are you?"

"Because I have been told I can trust you with my life, I will tell you. I'm the head of the Sayanim in New York."

"Ex-Mossad?"

"Affirmative."

"Some art dealer."

"It's my hobby. And a useful front for my real activities."

"Can I know what they are?"

"I'm involved with the relentless pursuit of those criminals who have committed crimes against my country. Killers who have blown up supermarkets, buses, synagogues, and hotels. Many of them end up here in New York, either temporarily or permanently. My task is to hunt them down."

"And then?"

"To ensure they do not repeat their crimes. *EVER!*" John Strauss uttered that last word with such venom Mack was actually startled.

"You mean, you do the deed?"

"When I find them? No. I have a man to carry that out. A trained killer whom I trust more than I ever trusted any man."

"Benny?"

"Affirmative."

"Christ, John, I'm talking to the new Simon Wiesenthal."

"Well, there are similarities, I admit that. But Simon was a pure Nazi hunter, a scholar, who scoured the old records, and tried to bring them to justice, publicly to expose and humiliate the Germans."

"You mean your basic objectives are different?"

"Most certainly. You see, terrorists do not represent a State. They represent a loose operation delighted to be publicized as killers and murderers. So there's nothing in it for us, trying to humiliate them. They cannot be humiliated. Our objectives are simply to eliminate those who have killed and murdered on Israeli soil. And there's a lot of them."

"So the only similarity between you and Wiesenthal is you are both hunters—but he basically displayed his prey, you kill it."

"Nicely stated. But remember, the Vienna bookseller was not averse to an execution, if the wheels of justice moved too slowly."

"I guess not. Did you ever meet him, John?"

"No, to my great regret. I spoke to him a few times on the phone. But never in person. If I had met him, that would have been the greatest honor of my life."

"He is not such a major figure in the United States," said Mack. "But I know he's a real big deal in Israel."

"I think about him every day," said Strauss. "Just imagine. He's the man who captured Karl Silberbauer, the Gestapo brute who arrested Anne Frank. He also captured Franz Stangl, Commandant of the Treblinka death camp. He tracked and located Adolf Eichmann, head of Hitler's extermination camps."

"Simon was old when he died?" asked Mack.

"He was ninety-six, and he said his work was done."

"Except that you're carrying it on."

"We think those who maim and murder Israeli citizens are the same as the Nazis. Stangl, Eichmann, al-Turabi, Abu Hassan— what's the difference? They all deserve to die. And they all will."

"Are we going to catch these four in New York?"

"I think so. And it will be my pleasure to guide you wherever I can."

"Where do I start?"

"With the money. I have my ear to the ground on that. Soon as something suspicious happens, I'll call. Meantime, we need to make sense of that Jewish target they allude to in that conversation."

John stood up and informed his visitor that he had an appointment in the next fifteen minutes, and would have to terminate their discussion. "But I've enjoyed it," he said. "And I think we'll have a break in this case soon. If those characters are in the city, they can't stay hidden for much longer. One of my people will spot them. I've circulated all their photographs. We'll find 'em."

Mack stood up and shook his hand.

"By the way, Commander Bedford," said Strauss, "my friends call me Johnny. Try to remember that."

Mack laughed. "G'night, Johnny," he said, and he headed back into the dark canyons of New York.

IT WAS 2 A.M. in the Cotswolds when the cryptologists made their first break in the phone conversation between Islamabad and New York. Deep inside the Doughnut, they decided the word "nalseb" did not exist. There was no place in the world with that name, no trace of anything like it in the dictionary, and the two words before it, "back to," suggested an anagram.

It took someone about forty-five seconds to come up with Beslan, and they all turned their attention to that town in Russia's North Caucasus region, where, on September 1, 2004, there was an incident that still ranks as one of al-Qaeda's most brutal achievements. The attack on School Number One ended in violent explosions, fire, destruction, and the deaths of perhaps 385 people, many of them students, with a further 780 people wounded when the roof caved in.

The jihadist leader Shamil Basayev had stormed and then dominated the school and the town, and then held the Russian Army at bay for three days. The night-shift operators at Cheltenham, not necessarily military historians, read with disquiet that the operation had been financed and the leaders trained by al-Qaeda, and that, in their opinion, "No military operation since 2001 ever brought such endless glory upon the jihadist revolution. Or such world attention."

They also read the unnerving rider, placed at the conclusion of the report, that three senior U.S. Navy SEAL commanders considered Beslan only a dress rehearsal. They placed their own conclusions about the wording on the link to the CIA and the NSA, knowing the hour was much earlier in the United States. And they added that the words "top class" and "Abe's Place" may indicate some kind of an educational establishment with Jewish connotations.

They had run a search for a school or college in America with the word Abraham in the title, but they'd drawn a blank, even though there were more than eight hundred Jewish schools, colleges, and universities in the States.

The emergence of the word Beslan was unnerving, and Britain's Joint Services Signals Unit had gone on high alert for any new telephone contact of a military nature between Islamabad and New

York. But no one was holding their breath. Breaks of that quality were rare and valuable.

And the al-Qaeda command was getting shrewder every year, rarely repeating a mistake. Captain Simon, for a start, would have been amazed if they did not by now understand they had been intercepted—*the buggers had moles everywhere.*

FAISAL AL-ASSAD did not have a high profile in New York, but neither was it low. He occasionally attended diplomatic and charity events, and socialized with oil industry heavies. What Faisal al-Assad did not need were the four most wanted terrorists on earth hiding out in his luxurious East Side quarters. And that night, in the small hours of the morning, he received new and welcome orders, delivered via a landline phone call from Boston, Massachusetts: "Move your guests to temporary HQ somewhere close to Norfolk, Northwest Connecticut. Buy or rent small house ASAP. Also open two bank accounts town of Torrington, also NW Connecticut."

"Roger that, caller," replied Faisal, as instructed. And with that, he awakened all four of his guests to inform them that they would be pulling out at 7 a.m. sharp, and it was essential they be ready for the long journey ahead.

Meanwhile they were each to leave a passport with him, because it was essential they all be legally stamped into the country with the small, blue, oval crest of U.S. immigration, which showed red stamps for date of entry, and another for compulsory departure after six months. Faisal needed to get this properly forged if they were ever to get out of the United States without a million questions.

MACK BEDFORD, also working in the dead of night, called back Captain Ramshawe at home in response to a message on his hotel phone—that Cheltenham had made a firm connection with the message from Islamabad and the massacre at Beslan Number One School in 2004.

A SEAL team leader, who had personally captured two al-Qaeda hard-men, had once told him the next major assault on America would be a college or university—the soft, unguarded heart of the United States. And the team leader had been definite. The Russian op, he insisted, was just a rehearsal.

And now, Captain Ramshawe was telling him this recent intercept confirmed those words. Mack was silent for a few moments and then said, "Jimmy, our guys have suspected this for a few years. And the trouble is, these fanatics are never joking. We better get on the case."

"We're on it," said Jimmy. "Checking out Jewish colleges because there's a definite Jewish intonation in that phone call. You know, Abraham and King Saul. But it's tough. There is no Abraham College except for some agricultural place in Georgia, and it was only the first name of the founder. But we're searching, and everyone's waiting for a new intercept."

"Jimmy, I made a few inquiries myself last night. And I may have tapped into a decent lead. I'll keep you posted. But I guess this Beslan bullshit has turned up the pressure a bit."

"You could say that, mate. Talk to you later."

AT SEVEN THE NEXT MORNING, Faisal al-Assad and his four guests headed north in his black SUV. From Manhattan he'd taken the Cross Bronx Expressway and then the Hutchinson River Parkway. From there it had been a straight shot up to the Connecticut border, and directly through Danbury and Waterbury. By this point they had covered a hundred miles and were deep in the New England countryside, with the terrain growing more and more hilly as they made their way up toward the distant Berkshires.

Their new highway was Route 8, and there were no more towns, just rolling hills leading into the mountains, thirty-five miles of woodland and farmland, a bucolic green joy for tired New Yorkers' eyes. Except city-boy Faisal hated it, and his passengers could not have cared less if they were driving through a ghetto. They had other things on their minds.

It was almost 10:30 when they ran down the steep hill to the old mill town of Torrington, which lies in the heart of the Naugatuck River Valley up in the far Northwest part of the state. The outskirts of the town stretch right up into the hills, and driving from one side to the other feels like a U-shaped section of the Rockies.

But it's a thriving little town, with a great amount of redevelopment and surrounded by spectacular countryside and mediumrange mountains. It is also home to a large number of banks and real estate offices, which are apt to spring up in these progressive communities within striking range of New York.

Faisal found a parking place in one of the town's open lots. He instructed his team to find breakfast on Main Street, and that he'd join them in an hour. He gathered his brief case and set off across the street to the Connecticut State Bank, where he opened a new account. Faisal explained he was planning to buy a farming property in the area, and then produced his social security number, New York address, driver's license, U.S. passport, and printed stationery from his place of business, the *Anglo-Saudi Oil Corporation* of which he was a director, listed on the headed paper. He showed two credit cards and the name and phone number of an eminent Saudi Prince in the embassy in Washington as a reference.

He pulled out $300 in cash with a banker's draft from Citibank for a further ten thousand dollars. He filled out the official signature card, adding one more name, for which he would take a spare card and have it delivered back to the bank. The name was Ibrahim Sharif, whom he explained was a colleague from Saudi Arabia who was transferring to New York for a year.

Faisal collected a temporary checkbook and details of his account number that would allow him to wire a substantial sum of money in during the next few days. Faisal concluded the transactions and walked further down Main Street to the newish offices of the Bank of New England. There he conducted the exact same operation, walking out with a second bank account in the town of Torrington, a place that was somewhat richer since his arrival from along the banks of the swift-flowing Naugatuck River.

At this point he went in search of Ibrahim, Yousaf, Ben, and Abu, who were ensconced at the Sugarloaf Café, drinking coffee and eating blueberry pancakes with Vermont maple syrup and bacon. Faisal joined them and ordered fruit salad, dry toast, and black coffee. Faisal explained to the men that he needed to find a real estate office, and that it would be inappropriate for them to be seen anywhere near such a place, or indeed a bank. He told them to return to the car and wait for him, and no one opposed this cautious approach. Faisal paid the check and walked out onto the sidewalk alone.

So far as Faisal could tell, there were more real estate offices in Torrington than there were diamond dealers on West Forty-Seventh Street. He looked in the windows and noted that many of them were principally involved in the new developments in the downtown and outlying areas. The one he chose was Cutlers and Sons, the oldest (established 1903), which displayed pictures of country houses and farmland.

Faisal entered and introduced himself. He told the broker, a cheerful young girl of about twenty-two, he was looking for a small farm in a specific area, up to perhaps two hundred acres. He was given a local map and asked to detail the area he wanted. Faisal drew a circle around a stretch of land close to the 1,700-foot-high Haystack Mountain near the village of Norfolk.

"Sir," asked the girl, who turned out to be Miss Aimee Cutler, great-granddaughter of the founder, "do you want to farm the land or just own it for privacy? Because farming up here is difficult."

"It is?" replied Faisal, who had never even seen a plough or a wheat crop in his entire life. "Why is it so hard?"

"Do you know Norfolk's nickname?" asked Aimee, smiling. "It's called the Icebox of Connecticut—very high elevation, freezing winters, and cool summers. It's the last bit that people like."

"That's the bit I should like," said Faisal. "I'm used to the heat, but New York is stifling in July and August."

"I'm sure you understand that property around here is surprisingly expensive, although it's a lot cheaper now than it was four years ago. Right here we're talking millions. We have a 160-acre farm in your area, with an eighteenth-century farmhouse for $1.5 million. And a real nice contemporary house standing in twenty-two fairly isolated acres for $1.3 million. Others run up to $3.5 and above, if you're looking for a grand residence."

"Actually, it's more the privacy I'm looking for," he replied. "And since I own a large part of a construction company I'm happy with an unobtrusive residence that I can develop. But I do need outbuildings."

"Almost everything around here with land has outbuildings, so that's not a problem. You really can't leave stuff out in the winter because of the cold and snow."

"I won't be here in the winters, I assure you," said Faisal. "But I expect I'll have equipment—mowers and tractors—and I would like them locked up."

"Exactly," said Aimee. "Now let me take down your details, and I'll give you some brochures to look through. And then we can fix a day, and go out and see a few properties. How much of a hurry are you in?"

"Big," said Faisal. "I plan to make some decisions very quickly on this trip. Perhaps we could do something this afternoon or tomorrow morning."

"Of course. Will this be a cash sale, or do you need to sell first, or arrange a mortgage?"

"Cash," said Faisal, utilizing the magic word that is apt to put a rocket under the backsides of all real estate brokers.

"Can I ask why the hurry?"

"Of course," replied the Saudi financier. "I have a daughter going to the Canaan Academy in the next couple of weeks. Flying in from Riyadh. I would like to have a place near her, for her mother and I to visit, and for her to entertain her friends."

Aimee Cutler could scarcely believe her luck. Big sale, big hurry, big commission. The broker's paradise.

Leave it to me," she said. "Please sit down over there by the fire and I'll bring you some coffee and reading material."

Faisal sat facing the window. He stared out to the west, toward the distant peaks of the Canaan Mountains, which towered over the same academy about which he had just told such a thunderous, and, in a way, deeply ironic lie.

FAR AWAY FROM the evil unfolding below the Canaan Mountains, one of the midtown branches of Gotham National was moving its daily mountain of wire transfers. And, as in all major banking organizations, there were senior bank officers keeping a careful eye on those transfers.

Generally, they were searching for stuff like obvious money-laundering, drug money being ferried around between suspected dealers and banks in Colombia and Panama. They noted big amounts of cash being deposited, and they watched for U.S. nationals moving heavy sums to tax havens on various tropical islands.

They were not especially keen to make reports to the FBI, except in cases of blatant dishonesty or danger to the population of the United States. But they liked to know what was going on, principally because it suited them to be particularly helpful when the big government agencies came trawling for information.

The current financial climate did not encourage bankers to risk looking ridiculous, or unaware, or too greedy, or even furtive. These days it was necessary to be right up front. And the scions of Gotham National, which had darned nearly gone bankrupt in the Crash of 2008, were making absolutely certain they had their fingers on their own pulse. At all times.

There was something striking about a transfer made this morning, which had been phoned in to the most senior banking officer in the building, Jarvis Goldman. Goldman took personal care of this major account, which was utilized by the Saudi businessman, Faisal al-Assad, a client known personally to Jarvis.

Faisal had instructed the sum of $2 million to be wire-transferred—$1.5 million to a small branch of the Connecticut State Bank in Torrington, and $500,000 to the Bank of New England in the same town.

This was not corporate money. This was money from Mr. al-Assad's own deposit account, into which $3 to $4 million was deposited every few months from the Anglo-Saudi Investment Bank on Olaya Street, Riyadh.

It was not unusual for large sums to be moved around the country, or indeed the world, by Mr. al-Assad, but these were bigger amounts than usual. And Jarvis Goldman wondered what was going on in the mountains of NW Connecticut, which was proving so very costly.

Still, it was not really his business if a multimillionaire Saudi businessman was buying something expensive up in the cool mountains on the New York–Massachusetts border. Nonetheless he made a note of the transfers, and entered them on his personal computer file, the one labeled, simply, "Unusual."'

He formally authorized the wire drafts to go through to the two modest Torrington banks, but then he called the Connecticut State Bank and verified the basics of the account—that it was a personal deposit in the name of Faisal al-Assad, and that the personal details matched those in the Gotham files. He checked the social security number and verified Mr. Faisal was the sole signature on the account. The Torrington officer said at present this was so, but that a new signature, Mr. Sharif, from Saudi Arabia, was expected to be added in the next couple of days.

Jarvis Goldman knew there was no other signature permitted on the other al-Assad accounts. And he had never heard of anyone named Sharif, except for Omar in *Lawrence of Arabia*. Again he made an entry in his "Unusual" file. And still he wondered what the smooth and sophisticated Faisal al-Assad was buying up in the remote and chilly mountains of northwest Connecticut.

He probably would not have bothered so much had that second signature been an obvious American. But there was a general terrorist alert in New York City after the bomb at Penn Station. And John Strauss had e-mailed a page to hundreds of people detailing the names and identities of four Arabs he wanted located.

Among those hundreds was a select group of around thirty New York bankers, including Goldman. He could not remember offhand the precise four names. But Jarvis Goldman was a devoted member of the Sayanim. Four minutes later, the phone rang in the front showroom of Banda Fine Arts.

SHORTLY BEFORE NOON, Faisal checked his four-man team into the Royal Inn in Torrington. He ordered chicken sandwiches and coffee to be delivered to them at one o'clock, and asked them to stay in their rooms and watch television for the afternoon. They should not under any circumstances be seen around town.

He walked back to the real estate office and waited for Aimee Cutler, who drove her car around to the front and picked him up. Aimee headed for the Norfolk area by a direct but narrow network of passes and country lanes, never even seeing a main road. She covered the distance pretty quickly, too, before stopping at a large farm on the south side of the village.

"This is the one you liked in the brochure," she said. "It's a very nice house, and sits in eighty acres of farmland. They're asking $2 million plus, but they probably won't get it," she said.

Al-Assad feigned interest, but this house was to close to a group of houses on the edge of Norfolk. He wanted seclusion, a place where comings and goings would not be noticed. He did not care particularly about the price, but it ought not to be ostentatious.

The next property they saw was ideal except for the entrance.

The house itself was situated at the end of a long driveway, and more or less surrounded by mature trees. Its outbuildings were perfect, and it had four bedrooms. But that driveway emerged onto the principal road in and out of Norfolk, less than four hundred yards from the start of the built-up area. And it had enormous black wrought-iron gates with gold-painted tips on the upright struts.

The price was $1.4 million, and if it had had a rough old post-and-rail farm gate Assad would probably have bought it. But these gates were only a couple of ticks short of neon-lit, and they were electrically operated. Traffic in and out of that house would be too public, and there would be a lot of waiting around for the electric mechanism to kick in. Aimee and Faisal waited for almost a minute to drive in.

The sale died in that minute, and they moved on to the next house, which Aimee had warned was a little run down—real estate code for "absolute wreck." Mountainside Farm stood in the foothills of Haystack Mountain, which rose to its north.

The house was within thirty acres of the south bank of the Blackberry River, which could be crossed by road from West Norfolk, and it was less than two miles from Canaan Academy.

The property met all of Faisal's requirements. For a start it did not even have gates. Its entrance was on a lonely road, through a gap in the woods onto a cart track. The woods were probably fifty yards deep when you drove in, and from there the drive was black-topped and ran another three hundred yards to the house, which was, as suspected, a wreck.

Aimee explained it had been used for years by a New York scientific writer who specialized in botany, and only came on weekends in the summer. He plainly had never painted the place, and he had put it on the market to include its entire contents, furniture, and pictures, carpets and curtains, which Faisal assessed must have been worth all of twelve dollars and forty cents.

But it had a couple of sofas, a three-hundred-year-old television, a dining room table, and eight chairs that had seen better days. The kitchen was the best room in the house, with a fairly modern stove and fridge and a tiled floor. Aimee said the hot water system had been renewed recently, "definitely since the Vietnam War."

Outside, the outbuildings were spacious if run down. There was a big, high barn in which there was still a line of cattle-feeders, suggesting someone had once run a herd up here. But that must have been long ago, because there was an outside machine room, which contained a tractor that dated back to the 1930s. The asking price was $900,000, plus $25,000 for fixtures and fittings.

"I'd need to spend a lot of money to fix it up," mused Faisal. "When can I have it?"

"This afternoon if you like, for a cash sale. My brother is the local lawyer representing the client. And I have him on standby."

"I'll offer $875,000 cash, payable immediately with a local banker's draft, Connecticut State. No further questions or checks."

"Let me call Danny," said Aimee. "He's been a friend of Roger's for years. He has power of attorney and can do the deal right away. The place has on the market for almost a year."

She walked outside the barn and dialed her brother's number. Faisal could see her speaking into her cell phone, smiling. He caught the sound of the word "cash," and then, "I'll do that," and then, "See you in an hour."

Aimee returned to her client and told him the deal was done, and that they should return to Torrington immediately. On the way, he should call the bank, and she would call her office to have the final documents prepared.

The bank manager was a little surprised to have received $1.5 million that morning and then have $875,000 of it spent three hours later. But he moved quickly. The draft was prepared, and by 4:45 p.m. that afternoon, Faisal al-Assad was the owner of Mountainside Farm, with annual property taxes of $2,400, payable in advance.

Faisal knew the recce of the area around the academy had been made by members of the Sleeper Cell in Boston, a group that had been very nearly moribund with fear and trepidation since American Airlines Flight 11 had smashed into the World Trade Center's North Tower on that September morning in 2001. His memorandum from Boston had stated clearly the new property must have clear views of the Haystack Mountain, otherwise it would be too far away from the target.

Well, he had located and purchased the precise, correct farmhouse, with privacy, seclusion from the road and the village, and plenty of barn space. Aimee handed him the keys and told him to visit her office the following morning to pick up another set of keys, plus instructions and warranties for kitchen equipment. Meanwhile she would leave him to run out and inspect his new house in peace. Faisal al-Assad thanked her and stepped outside, walking down the street to the Royal Inn to pay the bill and collect his team.

Before stopping at the house, they drove to an agricultural dealer, where Faisal ordered five hundred bales of hay to be delivered next day.

"You got a decent-sized barn?" asked the salesman.

"No problem," said Faisal. "Mountainside Farm on the East Norfolk Road." He paid with his American Express card and drove to a supermarket, where he told Ibrahim and the team to get out and get whatever they wanted, and that he'd meet them at the checkout to settle the tab.

Next, they set off for East Norfolk using main highways, rather than Aimee's labyrinth of country lanes. It was growing dark when they arrived at Mountainside. But they unpacked swiftly, checked out the upstairs rooms, checked the hot water, found some dry logs in the wide brick fireplace, and settled in.

Faisal told them they would be receiving an old farm truck in the morning, and that he would return in two days. He said his good-byes and left.

Faisal headed south toward New York City. He would, he knew, not pass this way again. His work was done.

JOHN STRAUSS spent only three minutes on the phone to his fellow Sayanim, Jarvis Goldman. He respected the Park Avenue banker and had received useful information from him before. And if Jarvis was exercised about this Arab's $2 million that was suddenly headed out of Manhattan into the wilds of the Connecticut mountains, then he would continue the investigation.

He called Mack Bedford at the Waldorf and summoned him to the world headquarters of Banda Fine Arts. There he informed him about Goldman's suspicions, suggesting that Mack head up there and check it out.

Mack's own brand new black Pro4X Nissan Titan truck was a vehicle gazed upon with awe in rural Maine, but was regarded as the transport choice of a plumber in Park Avenue, New York. And Mack had never forgotten a SEAL instructor stopping him in Anne's Pontiac out in the SPECWARCOM base in Coronado.

"What the hell are you doing in that red faggot car?" he'd demanded. "Men drive trucks, boy. SEALs don't drive anything else."

Mack grinned at the memory, and then he told Johnny Strauss he had a vehicle parked in the Waldorf garage. Right now he needed to take down whatever details there were about the money transfer. And he'd be in Torrington tomorrow morning, hard on the track of the Arab, Faisal al-Assad. He wasn't sure what there was to find, but if it was there, he'd find it.

THE AL-QAEDA attack on Canaan Academy had been masterminded in Peshawar by Shakir Khan and three senior bin Laden commanders, one of them Captain Musa Amin. As ever, their problem was drafting personnel into the United States. This was the main obstacle to every terror attack attempted during the years of President George W. Bush, when every last one of them was thwarted by security forces. And the ports of entry were still slammed shut. Al-Qaeda's planners either had to sneak their killers over the border from Mexico, or use personnel already in residence in the States. A border crossing from Canada was more certain to end in failure and capture, than taking Osama for a walk along Fifty-First Street at Lexington, past the Seventeenth Police Precinct.

More Sleeper Cells were active now than at any time since 9/11. Calls were being made in and out of the States to the Afghan mountains, to Tehran, and Peshawar, because jihadist personnel in the United States needed to be supplied, paid, and armed.

Two trucks carrying five of these cutthroats were headed down from Boston to Connecticut, expressly to assist Ibrahim and his men. They would act as bodyguards, servants, drivers, and, in the final stages, armed terrorist combat soldiers, forging what they considered to be a brave and gallant attack on the unguarded, predominantly Jewish American students at Canaan Academy.

The trucks were deliberately old, each with assorted bumps, dents, and scratches. At first sight they looked like a couple of props from *Creatures from the Black Lagoon,* so caked was the mud on the wheels and bodywork. This had the effect of deflecting the fact that each one was equipped with a brand new Dodge-Chrysler engine, and a new set of heavy-duty Goodyear tires. Beneath the flatbed rear section of each truck, fastened with industrial clips, were four AK-47 Kalashnikov rifles, and the toolboxes were packed with ten fully loaded SIG-Sauer 9mm pistols.

Stacked in the rear of the lead vehicle were forty white plastic 25kg bags of the industrial fertilizer, ammonium nitrate, which, when mixed with either No. 2 fuel-oil, diesel, kerosene, or even coal dust, develops into high-explosive of majestic proportions. The complete mixture is usually referred to as ANFO, at least it is when being used for peaceful purposes like blowing apart hillsides and quarries for mining purposes. In the modern world, it's normally known as an IED (Improvised Explosive Device), and universally prized by the very worst kind of terrorists, the guys drawing a sneaky bead on serving U.S. or British military or diplomatic personnel.

Of course these villains have found various ways of increasing its explosive power, like using a "booster" in the form of a couple of sticks of dynamite, or, even better, mixing in powdered aluminum, which increases the blast to the extent of knocking down an entire office building rather than merely blowing out the front wall.

Powdered aluminum was once used widely in mining, where experts are still employed to make their ANFO on site. But recently this became too expensive and has been largely discontinued except in the case of well-funded, state-sponsored terrorists. So of course there were two large bags of it behind the seats of the second truck.

This vehicle contained all the paraphernalia required for a large scale IED. In fact it contained all the paraphernalia for several large IEDs—bundles of dynamite, electronic detonators, detchord, and, in the rear, twelve empty wooden reinforced packing cases, three feet long by two feet wide and a foot high, roped together in the back.

Later, six of these would be packed with ammonium nitrate, mixed generously, 50 pounds to three quarts of fuel oil, and reinforced with the powdered aluminum, plus a couple of sticks of TNT to hasten the deadly explosion. This would give the Chosen Ones six very special high-velocity devices, sufficient to flatten a Manhattan skyscraper.

But the second six would be even more special, because these were being packed with the most powerful weapons-grade ammonium nitrate available. Nitromethane was the substance packed into the fertilizer truck-bomb that Timothy McVeigh, with one principal assistant, used to completely destroy the Alfred P. Murrah Federal Building in Oklahoma City in April 1995. That blast killed 168 people, and injured 680 others. It damaged or destroyed 324 other buildings and burned out 86 cars.

It was a fertilizer bomb, in a Ryder truck, which detonated under the World Trade Center in 1993—as was the IRA car blast in the City of London, a concrete-shattering one-ton bomb, that same year. The Bali nightclub blast in Indonesia in 2003 was a fertilizer bomb, and that same month, another knocked down two syna-gogues and the British consulate in Istanbul. One of the biggest raids on Islamic radicals was carried out by the British Police in London and Bradford, and among other things, and people, they rounded up a half-ton of ammonium nitrate.

The biggest blast of all, however, was an accident, when the French merchant ship, SS *Grandcamp*, packed to the gunwales with 2,500-tons of heavy ammonium nitrate fertilizer, suddenly ran too warm and blew up on the wharf in Texas City 1947. The explosion of this massive industrial time-bomb was heard 150 miles away and sent a black mushroom cloud more than two thousand feet into the air.

Great white-hot hunks of the ship crash-landed into the gigan-tic petroleum and petro-chemical holding tanks hundreds of yards away. These secondary blasts leveled buildings. The ship's anchor, which weighed one-and-a-half tons, was blown off its shackles and flung two miles away into the Pan-American refinery, where it buried itself ten feet into the ground, like an asteroid from outer space. The Texas City blast remains the most catastrophic industrial disaster in United States history.

And yet, ammonium nitrate is not taken very seriously by U.S. authorities, not even considered a high-risk item in terms of road transportation. You need a license to buy it, but it's not even classi-fied as dangerous, and it's labeled just an "oxidizer" when traveling from place to place.

The lead truck driver, who traveled by the name of Mike, even though he had been named Mustapha long ago in a village in the Punjab, made his southern turn about twenty miles before the state line. From Springfield, he had only thirty miles to go along Route 57, and then down a narrow mountain road, straight across the border to Norfolk, Connecticut.

He found the house with ease, leading the way through the woodland at the entrance, and up the long blacktop drive to the barns. Ibrahim and Yousaf were waiting outside, and they greeted their colleagues warmly, offering coffee, and questioning them about their cargo.

Making bombs is a highly skilled business, with little room for error, and obviously dire consequences for those who fumble in making them. Yousaf knew a lot, and Ben and Abu were competent. But Ibrahim was a master. He opened the wide doors of the barn and signaled for the trucks to drive inside.

"How's the security?" Mike asked immediately.

"I think very good," said Ibrahim. "The house cannot be seen from the road. And cannot be spied on except from its own private woodland."

He turned and pointed to a long line of trees on the north side of a former cattle pasture. "Even then it's not possible to see into the barns because they both have a solid wall at the back facing those trees.

Mike nodded. But he was frowning. "What can you see from the woodland by the gate?" he asked.

"Too much," replied Ibrahim. "I walked the property this morning early. We could not do much about anyone standing in there with a pair of binoculars."

"But we're not expecting anyone even to know we're here," said Mike. "That is correct, right?"

"Certainly. So far as I know we have not been observed."

"I would suggest an armed guard with a cell phone at the gate. Not to stop everyone with deliveries—just to watch from a hidden position if anyone shows up unexpectedly."

"I haven't had the manpower for those kind of luxuries," said Ibrahim. "We've all been killing ourselves this morning building straw castles."

"Building what?" said Mike, laughing.

"Come and see," chuckled Ibrahim. And he led the way to the next bigger barn and slipped in through the narrow gap between the almost-closed doors. Inside was a construction made of four-foot long bales of straw. Two twelve-foot high walls, around fifteen feet apart, came out twenty feet from the back wall and formed a kind of three-sided box.

At the end nearest the barn entrance was a third wall, fifteen feet long standing crossways and twelve feet high. But this wall was not joined in any way to the other two. It was freestanding, blocking the way into the box, shielding what might be scheduled to go inside.

Mike was amazed. "Wow!" he said. "What's going in there?"

"One large yellow American school bus," replied Ibrahim, tapping the right-hand side of his nose with a forefinger. "Very nice fit in the straw garage," he added. "That way we can work in peace."

"Where's the bus coming from?" asked Mike.

And again Ibrahim went into his forefinger tapping routine. "Not far away," he said. "New York State, near here. Car, truck, and bus auction held every Saturday. There's two coming up. Excellent make, Blue Bird, out of Georgia, around ninety thousand miles on the clock."

"Once we get it here, how far does it go?"

"A couple of miles."

"And that's it?"

"Probably," said Ibrahim.

MACK BEDFORD'S Nissan Titan rolled along the Naugatuck River Valley into Torrington about two hours before Mike and his Islamic dynamite squad turned south for Norfolk. It was around 10:30 in the morning when he pulled into the same parking lot where the jihadists had parked the previous day.

Mack was not precisely laden with overwhelming evidence. He knew only that a wealthy forty-two-year-old Saudi oil executive, Faisal al-Assad, of East Sixty-Ninth Street, New York, had transferred $2 million out of his Gotham National account on Park Avenue, and moved it to a couple of small banks in the old mill town of Torrington in northwestern Connecticut—$1.5 million into the

Connecticut State and $500,000 into the Bank of New England. Standing on the sidewalk in front of the parking lot he could see both banks on the far side of Main Street.

He understood the pure futility of walking into either of them and asking what this Faisal al-Assad was up to, moving his own money around like that.

Strauss had grilled Goldman and had established there had been some urgency in the transaction, and had a distinct feeling that his client was already in Torrington when he made the call. He had not, however, checked.

So far as Mack could tell, Faisal had already spent, or was quickly preparing to spend, a large hunk of this cash in Connecticut, suspecting perhaps setting up a base from which to conduct an attack. The New York Sayanim boss had pointed out that al-Qaeda always set up bases, not necessarily close to their target. The 9/11 attack was masterminded and carried out from Boston, from a network of city-center apartments owned by bin Laden's relatives. The very name al-Qaeda meant *The Base* in Arabic.

Mack strolled down the sidewalk taking in the storefronts he passed. He was struck by the volume of real estate brokerages, almost all exclusively involved in the development of commercial property. If Faisal al-Assad was making a big investment, or even buying into an office block or some kind of industrial real estate, well, Mack surmised there would be nothing suspicious about that. After all, Faisal al-Assad was an executive director of a Saudi oil construction outfit in Riyadh and New York. An investment interest in an up-and-coming area like Torrington, where they were hoping to reconstruct even the railroad down to New York, surely made good business sense.

But Mack had a hunch there was more to it. He needed to find out whether the Saudi had started writing checks of an unusual nature, whether he was trying to finance a new base. Looking into the window of an old established local real estate office, Cutlers and Sons, he decided this was the place anyone might go to look for a remote country retreat, which would make for a great base.

And he was already wondering if there was a sizeable Jewish College situated anywhere in this picturesque corner of Connecticut.

He pushed open the front door, closed it carefully behind him, and was greeted by Miss Aimee Cutler.

9

AT HIS BUDS CLASS eleven years ago in Coronado, young Mackenzie Bedford had three times been announced Honor Man, the Navy SEALs' most coveted accolade for the outstanding member of a training course.

Mack had been Honor Man at Sniper School. He'd been Honor Man in the murderous section for Unarmed Combat. And Honor Man, Class of 234, the overall outstanding student among that group of eleven young iron men, the only ones left standing out of 163 starters.

Right now Honor Man was standing before a twenty-three-year-old real estate broker named Aimee, giving serious thought as to whether to tell the biggest lie of his entire life, or the second.

He could tell her he was a close, personal friend of Faisal al-Assad, and wanted to know if Faisal ended up finding a place to buy in this area, but that could leave a trail. Better would be for him to pretend he was also looking to buy, and could she show him some properties that recently sold so he could get a better sense of what his money could buy.

Aimee Cutler was looking at him kind of quizzically, as if he might be a bit slow-witted. Mack grinned and went with lie number two.

"I'd be glad to," she said with a smile and rummaged in a file cabinet for her sales brochures. She then punched a set of numbers on her keyboard, which swiftly lit up a large computer screen on the wall. She beckoned for Mack to sit down on the opposite side of her desk and asked him what price-range he was considering.

"Well, I'm looking for some land, something to give me a little seclusion, and protection from development on adjoining lots," he replied. "So I guess I'm looking at around one to one-and-a-half million dollars."

"Oh yessir," said Aimee with more enthusiasm than she intended. "I'm sure we can find something very nice for that. Right now it's a buyers' market and property is a lot cheaper than it was a couple of years ago."

She came up with around six small farms and country houses that had been sold in the previous three months. The fifth one she showed him was Mountainside Farm. And the words of the intercepted phone message stood before him—"Be sure they can see the mountain."

None of the other names were as obvious as this, although Mack realized he had no clues whether the other five houses could see the darned mountain or not. But since none of them was any longer for sale, he could not really ask for the brochures. And if he did, he was certain he would not be given them. He just needed to remember them.

He asked Aimee if this was the specialist broker for his kind of search, and she assured him that Cutlers had been for a century the pre-eminent real estate brokerage in the area for all farms and upmarket homes. "We have a tie up with Sothebys," she added. "Although my grandfather thought they might be a little . . . well . . . razzle-dazzle for us."

"Yes, I can see that," said Mack, thoughtfully. "This office itself feels like a room in a stately country house." Aimee smiled, and he asked her if she had any local maps printed off for clients. She walked across the office to a small chest of drawers and produced two. One zoomed tightly in on Torrington only, the other was a much bigger scale and took in the entire area, north to the Massachusetts border, and west to New York State.

Mack asked if it would be okay to scribble in the amounts of money paid where the houses sold. "That way I can show my wife, and then we can take a drive around and get a feel for the area and its costs," he said.

"Good idea," Aimee, writing in $875,000 over the place on the map where Mountainside Farm stood. She filled in the others, and as she did so Mack logged in his notebook the other five names.

Ultimately, though he saw the error of his ways. He had the names. He had the prices. And he had the locations. But they were jumbled up both on the map and in his mind. He couldn't really tell whether Mountainside Farm was way over there next to Haystack Mountain, or at the end of Main Street, Torrington.

One thing he had not screwed up, however. He had left no trace of his interest in Mr. Faisal al-Assad. And he folded his maps, promised Aimee he and his wife would be back in the next couple of days. He left the name Charles O'Brien, and set off on his search for the country property that Faisal al-Assad may have already purchased.

The main trouble with the entire area, he decided, was it was full of goddamned mountains. Every house inside a forty-eight-million-mile radius could see the mountain. "Fuck it," said Mack, wryly.

BACK AT THE FARM, the newly bearded Ibrahim and his team were gathered around the big table studying a detailed map of the interiors of the main buildings at Canaan Academy. These plans are readily available at any town planning office, and even on the Internet. Indeed the school prospectus for parents contained a double-page spread detailing classrooms, the gymnasium, dormitories, and the Great Hall. A member of one of the Sleeper Cells, this one located in Hartford, had accessed this one.

But the principal problem being discussed was not the general layout of the location, but that they had no one on the inside, which was rare for an al-Qaeda operation in any country in the world. Indeed the Beslan program had been built around the insertion of "advance men," posing as workmen and taking jobs inside School Number One during the vacation, hiding explosives and mapping out the vulnerable points in the school.

The Canaan hit would have none of these luxuries because there had been so little time to organize it. Ibrahim, Yousaf, Ben, and Abu had been released rather suddenly, and in the opinion of the al-Qaeda executives, they had no other field operatives capable of such a high-level assault on the Great Satan.

That was why the United States had been free of attack for so long. Al-Qaeda's top commanders had died in Tora Bora, and they had never been replaced. But happily, they now had a new recruiting operation, located in the judicial rooms of the U.S. Court system, carried out by American judges anxious to act in absolute fairness and return these illegal combatants to the battlefield.

That was why Ibrahim Sharif was presiding over this remote group of terrorists, who were planning the most vicious and utterly outlandish assault on American school children in all of history. And their reasons were simple: *It worked in Russia. It'll work here. With the guidance of Allah, we may now make the strike that will drive the Infidel out of the Middle East for ever.*

It was, of course, a mindless and lunatic plan. Such an assault would do no such thing. It would merely infuriate the Americans, whose president would be compelled to hit back, hard. Ibrahim and every single one of his cohorts was a fanatic, both extreme and irrational.

But Ibrahim was not a fool "We do not have any worthwhile recce in place," he said, "and that is a major disadvantage to us, because it means we have to make a frontal attack. But we cannot just charge in and somehow blow the place apart, because that would probably mean blowing ourselves up at the same time.

"And while Allah approves that sacrifice, and awaits us all on the other side of the bridge, it would not be in His interest for that to happen. Because He would prefer we live to fight another day, and once again strike down the Infidel."

"Then how will we launch our attack?" asked Ben al-Turabi.

"Well," replied Ibrahim, "We need to get those boxes into the school. I think they should be marked in big letters with something innocuous, and then wheeled in through this door right here on the side. Not the main entrance."

Everyone peered over to see the plan. "Guess we'll have to take a couple of handcarts since three of them will weigh close to six hundred pounds," said Yousaf. "And what do we do when we get 'em in there. Light a fuse?"

"I'm coming to that," said Ibrahim. "But first we need to mark the boxes. So we need a can of paint, probably green—not red or black, because those colors can mean danger. And we need those stencils where you paint in the gaps to form the letters. That way they'll look official."

"And what goes on the boxes?" asked Ben.

"How about a couple with the words Athletic Equipment, for the gym. Maybe Weights or Barbells."

"What about the other ten?"

"We could have six going to the kitchen labeled Flour or Corn Oil. How about Sugar or Coffee? There's almost a thousand kids in this school. They must have big boxes coming in all the time."

"And the other four?" persisted Ben.

"Oh, Disinfectant, Soap, Detergent—perhaps one just marked Wholesale. It's not a problem. Boxes marked like that being brought in through a side door by a uniformed man, marked so anyone can see what they contain—not even suspicious."

"But who will bring them in?" asked Ben. "We can't go in there wearing hoods and masks?"

"Of course not. We'll have one of Mike's boys go shopping in Torrington. Buy us some smart workmen's overalls, paint, brushes, stencils, and the rest. We also need a large book of invoices, white, yellow, and blue. A man with invoices is official."

"Invoices," said Mike. "That's a nice touch."

But who's going to detonate it all?" asked Abu Hassan. "We cannot do it, unless we want to die. Who do you have in mind? A couple of short-order kebab cooks in the kitchen?"

"Jewish guys don't eat kebabs," volunteered Ben.

"Well, not pork kebabs," said Abu Hassan.

"Shut up," snapped Ibrahim. "I am setting the explosive to detonate on an electronic time-fuse inside each box. We drive to the side door and deliver the boxes to various pre-planned locations. We slide them off the hand carts and place them strategically around the ground floor of the school.

"They will all be electronically linked to a master switch, which works by radio link. I had considered a satellite but I don't think that's necessary. A simple, powerful impulse will make the connection. Each box will have an electronic sensor fitted into wood. It's important that the boxes face out—not facing the wall that is.

"The detonator can be activated from the bus as it leaves the school grounds, and all twelve bombs will explode simultaneously two minutes later. That's the timeline. In that time, the bus will be at least a mile away. We'll abandon it somewhere remote and switch to the regular vehicles, heading straight for Boston.

"I'm aiming for the Mass Turnpike within twenty-five minutes of the explosion because the Connecticut State Police will be in charge, and we want to be over the border in a different state as quickly as possible.

"Yousaf, Ben, Abu Hassan, and I will fly out of Logan that night, direct to Madrid. The rest of you will just go home and keep your heads down until further notice."

"That's a good plan," said Abu Hassan.

"Not mine, I'm afraid. I have just been chosen to carry it out. The entire strategy was mastered by Shakir Khan and his Saudi advisers. Faisal al-Assad was very important. And there will be great rejoicing at home when we carry it out. We will be heroes of the al-Qaeda movement."

"When do we carry it out?" asked Yousaf.

"The date is next Friday. So we need to be efficient. But not in a tearing rush. We move carefully, and we prepare thoroughly. That way we will make no mistakes. I have the greatest confidence in every one of you."

"Is the date firm?"

"Very firm. It's a special day at the school, with many, many more people than usual. According to my orders from Faisal, it's called Abraham's Day, and all the parents will be there from around 10 a.m. Shakir Khan is looking for a hit before noon. That gets us all out in time for the evening flight to Madrid, where our passports are in good order."

"There is just one thing," said Mike. "I'm concerned about the entrance to this property. I don't know if anyone will suspect something is going on, but I do think we should post a guard down there. Not some armed killer parading around with a Kalashnikov. Just someone out of sight in the woods."

"One of your guys?"

"Yes. I'll brief Ali. He'll do it. He's big and agile, spent a few months in the Pakistani Army."

"Speaking of Kalashnikovs," said Abu, "will we take weapons in with us, I mean when we enter the school building?"

"Oh, I think that would be essential," said Ibrahim, "because we might be apprehended by someone, or stopped, or questioned. And then someone would have to die. Our rifles should be in soft holders and placed on top of the boxes. If we have to fight our way out of the building, we'll be ready. But I don't think that will happen. We'll be too well organized."

"Wouldn't matter much if someone did have to die," said Abu Hassan. "If they're in that building, they're going to die anyway."

"Everyone's going to die, except us," said Ibrahim.

THREE HOURS LATER Mack Bedford was on his way down the main road to East and West Norfolk. He had checked out two of Aimee's sales, and now he was on his way to Mountainside Farm, which he believed represented his best chance. He did not of course have a name or an address, just the sum of $875,000 scribbled on a map. He would probably have to ask where the house was once he reached the approximate area.

By now Mack guessed he may be around Torrington for a couple of days, and, driving along, he suddenly spotted the Blackberry River Hotel, a red-brick building in its own grounds, set back from the road. He decided to check in for a couple of nights, just to give himself a reasonable base. He was like al-Qaeda in that way; he needed a solid platform from which to launch an attack.

He talked to the receptionist, reserved a second floor double room, and dumped his bag on a big comfortable chair. It was growing colder outside and he pulled on his soft, waterproof combat boots, the ones he'd worn at the bridge on the Euphrates. He wore a black turtle neck, his navy sweater, and a heavy-duty, dark-blue and red parka.

Back downstairs, he asked the receptionist if she'd heard of Mountainside Farm and she told him precisely where it was.

"Cross the river, and turn left down the road. The farm's about a mile down on the right, entrance through a copse of trees."

"Who lives there?" he asked.

"Don't know," said the girl. "It's been on the market for months. But I did hear it had been sold this week."

Mack thanked her and took a quick peak around the hotel. There was a nice downstairs lounge, and the restaurant looked charming. He said he'd be there for 8 p.m.

It was three o'clock when he finally set out and he found the house easily, then driving past and coming to a halt about a half-mile down the road. He pulled off onto the grass and stepped out of his vehicle, taking with him the binoculars he always kept in the Nissan. He slung them around his neck, zipped up his parka, and stepped back into the trees, moving slowly toward the blacktop drive he could see up ahead.

He left the track and walked through the undergrowth to the end of the treeline, standing some forty yards from the gatepost that marked the end of the wood and the beginning of the private drive. There was no sign for a private road, or a warning to trespassers. Nothing to betray this was Mountainside Farm.

From this vantage point, Mack still could not see the house or any of the farm buildings. The blacktop drive swung right, and there were more trees on its left side two hundred yards further on.

Mack moved further left, along the old broken post-and-rail fence, which had once been constructed to delineate the entrance wood from the pasture. Before the Manhattan botanist got a hold of the place, that is, and let it slide rapidly downhill.

He was now standing fifty yards to the left of the gate post on the left side of the track. There was a clump of bushes here, which had not only devoured the fence, but had wound themselves around the trunk of a scrub oak forming a prickly barricade. In Mack's judgment it would have made a perfect "hide" for a duck-shoot, if there'd been any ducks. Which there weren't.

"Friggin' suburbs," muttered Mack, who was, when it came right down to it, a raw-boned hunting/fishing Down Easter from the most rugged coastline in the United States. He smiled at his own sarcastic assessment of this mountainous wilderness, set two hundred fifty miles southwest and several light years away from the land he really loved.

He slipped into a prime spot in the "duck hide" and trained his binoculars on the farmhouse he could now see jutting out behind the far stand of maple trees. There were lights in the downstairs rooms, but no cars outside, and the big double doors to the barn were closed.

THE DARK-SKINNED, Punjab-born guard, who was observing Mack from a position almost a hundred yards away had made a colorful journey from his home village in Pakistan to West Norfolk, Connecticut. A devout Muslim, Ali had been recruited to the Taliban at a very young age, and then joined that section of the Pakistani Army that owed no loyalty to its comrades nor to the national government.

Ali had always been a freedom fighter, with sympathies only for the hard-line religious fanatics who had, before 9/11, ruled Afghanistan. In the ensuing years, having been almost destroyed by the U.S. forces, the Taliban had been making a rapid comeback, striking at the Pakistani Army over and over.

Ali, who had been an enormous favorite of the Taliban leader Baitullah Mahsud, had been dispatched to join the Pakistani National Army and work on the inside. And his successes had been formidable. He and Mahsud had staged constant attacks on the official forces, and even more constant raids, during which they stole automatic weapons, grenades, mines, and all the equipment required to make suicide vests.

With Ali's inside information, the Taliban pulled off some dreadful military-style coups, bombing and blasting their way into the headlines, and effectively running up a battle-scarred recruitment flag, which appealed to young Pakistani and Afghanis who were as fanatical and misguided as Ali himself.

But the Pakistani government started to hit back. Baitullah Mahsud was killed by an American Drone, and Ali's position as master spy, traitor, and confidante of the boss became too dangerous. He deserted, and headed back to the lawless tribal areas of South Waziristan, the FATA (Federally Administered Tribal Areas), which lie to the south of the Khyber Pass right on the Afghan border.

With the Swat Valley under constant watch by the official military, these vast FATA lands of no cities and few towns became the second most important training grounds in the world for al-Qaeda and the Taliban. Driven ever closer by the western and homeland forces ranged against them, the two organizations now combined.

They built joint camps where they instructed young men in manufactured combat zones. Deserters from the Army, like Ali, were appointed to positions of immense authority, training the new arrivals in weaponry, explosives, and unarmed combat.

Stolen arms were run in through the mountain passes on a daily basis. And by night they fought in the hillsides alongside local warlords who thought they could defeat the U.S. Army.

Ali and his rookies crept silently through those almost impenetrable mountains, seeking out and attacking American patrols. They tried to bomb and booby trap their own national Army. They selected any target that would thrust them into the Western media. They sent in suicide bombers to strike at cricket teams and innocent women and children in their own city market places.

But eventually, with a price on his head, and a manhunt being conducted to locate and arrest him, Ali was spirited out of the country on the usual student route to Bradford, England. From there, in possession of elaborate documents, obtained at great cost by al-Qaeda, he made it into the United States on a three-month course in Western Literature at a Boston-based college. From there he promptly disappeared, and hooked up at last with Mike's Sleeper Cell, which had been his ultimate objective ever since he vanished from the nuclear-armed forces of Pakistan.

As he stood silently in this Connecticut woodland with a German Luger tucked in his waistband, Ali, one of nature's everlasting combatants, was wondering who on earth was this character with the binoculars, staring across the field directly at the house in which was being planned the most secretive, classified operation that al-Qaeda had conducted for years.

He could, he supposed, have defied Ibrahim's orders and shot the guy dead, no questions asked. But Ali was a veteran, and he'd been on the run. He knew the consequences of indiscriminate killing in a place like the United States. Nothing but trouble. Lucky for Mack Bedford, who did not know he was there.

Ali understood the significance of the stranger's presence. And he knew the questions that needed to be answered: (1) Who was he?; (2) Was he working for the police or Intelligence services?; (3) Could he have been just a bird-watcher or some nature nut?; (4) Did this mean someone was on to them?; (5) Did this also mean they should all pull out of here right away?

Ali understood one other thing: The only person who could supply immediate answers to those questions was the guy with the binoculars. And since he was not permitted to shoot him, Ali needed to capture him, and either coax or punch those answers out of him.

The present and former Pakistani militant could feel the ground was wet beneath his trainers, soft and quiet. But parts of it were badly overgrown and difficult to walk over without stepping through vegetation. He was accustomed to a quiet approach toward his targets, but this ground would be a little noisy for a silent stalking.

Still, the guy with the binoculars was dressed in civilian clothes and would be unsuspecting. And Ali knew how to frighten the life out of a victim when making a surprise approach from behind. He'd been taught that all of his life by instructors and also by his father who had been a member of the 1980's Mujahideen—the modern masters of the art of slitting the throats of young Soviet officers in the Afghan mountains.

He began to move forward, slipping between the trees, making a line of sight that kept him hidden from the direct gaze of the interloper. He had advanced, zigzagging unobserved for sixty yards, keeping his eyes on the trees, and always keeping a substantial tree trunk between himself and the guy with the bins.

His next move was one of around ten yards, and this required him to move left, around eight feet, and then go forward in a straight line, directly at the next tree, behind Mack. He made the eight-foot walk silently, hesitated, and then took two short strides forward.

And that was where he stepped on a thin dead branch, fallen from a scrub oak. It snapped, creating a muffled sound, too heavy to be a small woodland creature, too light to be a grizzly, and too sharp to be just a small falling branch.

Mack Bedford heard it and froze. Years of patrolling the same mountains where Ali had fought had taught him that to regroup, swing around, or relay anxiety in any way would be a poor—if not fatal—idea. He had to remain still, projecting unawareness.

He raised the binoculars, and swiveled his left eye trying to work out whether his stalker was armed. He spotted Ali standing still as a statue next to a tree thirty yards away, or, in U.S. Navy parlance, "right on his six o'clock." Both of the man's hands were free and unencumbered at his sides.

Mack betrayed nothing, and decided to allow something he had never once permitted any instructor to do in SEAL Sniper School. He would let the man "walk up on him," and, if he so wished, grab him from behind.

Plainly, if the man had been some kind of a gamekeeper, he would already have shouted and announced his authority. It was more likely to Mack that the bastard was indeed a terrorist and might even have been the big fella, Ben al-Turabi. But he had not been able to see that clearly in his split-second of vision around the left lens of the binoculars.

He would not even have considered allowing a "walk up" if the man had been carrying either a knife or a gun, but that didn't seem the case. Mack understood military odds, and right now they were heavily in his own favor, with only a remote likelihood that he'd have to kill his attacker. Because that would mean he'd have to call Ramshawe and get the clean-up squad in, ahead of the Connecticut State Police, which could blow everything. No, Mack would not kill the man unless he truly had to.

Ali stayed frozen for a full minute and then began once more his advance, more careful now, tip-toeing across the ground, and then making a sudden and brutal lunge at Mack, ramming his right forearm around the former SEAL commander's neck and squeezing the windpipe with all of his strength.

Ali stood six-foot-four, a tad taller than Mack. He knew to raise Mack's left arm up into a harmless high position and then keep throttling the windpipe until he received a sign of submission. He was not, however, prepared for Mack's right elbow, which came around with the ramrod power one of the steel drive rods on a steam locomotive.

The back of that right elbow exploded on the side of Ali's head, almost cracking his skull. And a fraction of a second later the left elbow made the same arc and crashed into the Pakistani's left temple.

The speed and animal strength of his quarry had stunned Ali, but not taken him out of the fight. With his brains zinging, he somehow hung onto Mack's neck, and the big Navy SEAL moved into Phase Two of this classic U.S. Special Forces maneuver.

He leaned forward, and, through his own wide-apart ankles, he clamped an iron-grip on the back of Ali's lower right leg, hauling him off balance, straightening up and then crashing back, lying, as it were, in the Pakistani's lap.

Now both were on the ground. Ali had let go of Mack's neck as he tried to save his backward fall. But it was too late. Ali was down, on his back, and his straight right leg was jutting through, beneath Mack's crotch. And the SEAL had a hammer-lock on the back of Ali's ankle. He was, in effect, sitting astride Ali's right thigh.

Ali winced backward, and Mack leaned back and heaved, ripping the hip joint out of its socket. Like all SEALs, he'd practiced this with a fight partner a thousand times, and it never failed. The main difference between hard training and this was the defeated SEAL would tap twice on the victor's back, signifying that he was helpless. This present attacker would not walk unaided for a minimum of eight months.

Mack sprang to his feet, placed his right boot on Ali's neck, and said quietly, "Okay, pal. Now tell me, who the fuck are you?"

In a long and colorful career in combat, Ali had never been in such pain, nor so utterly amazed at any turn of events. He just lay there, drifting toward an agonized unconscious state, trying to focus on the face of this monster, who had, he knew, completely disabled him.

Mack reached down and yanked the pistol from Ali's belt. And the Pakistani militant was lucky he was not Ben al-Turabi, because if Mack had recognized him, he would have shot him straight between the eyes. One terrorist at a time, two at a time, or altogether, it would have made no difference to Lt. Commander Bedford.

As things were, he drew back and hurled the handgun into the middle of the wood, to a place where it probably would never be found. He stared into Ali's face, and recognized only that he was gazing at someone from the Middle East, perhaps an Arab, more likely a Persian or a Pashtun.

But just then two things happened. Both bad. Ali passed out with the pain from his wrecked leg, and heading down the blacktop drive was some kind of a ramshackle black pickup truck. Mack could see there were two people in the front seats, but there could have been more in the rear.

In reality, he was just witnessing a couple of Mike's team on their way to the shops in Torrington, to buy the green paint and overalls. But he didn't know that. So he turned away from the stricken Ali, and headed back into the woods since he wanted to avoid being fired at by terrorists with AK-47s.

It had, he decided, been a confusing incident. His brief was simple: to take out Ibrahim Sharif, Yousaf Mohammed, Ben al-Turabi, and Abu Hassan Akbar. Right now he had no idea whether they were in the house or anywhere near Mountainside Farm. He did not even know if this Faisal al-Assad was in the house, nor indeed whether Faisal even knew the four men he was after.

That would take more investigation. But not now. It was far too dangerous for him to remain on this property, unarmed, in broad daylight, having maimed one of their guards. There were probably too many of them, all heavily armed, and his orders were to work quietly, in complete secrecy.

Mack watched the truck race by. It turned right along the road toward Torrington, and would very soon pass his own parked black Nissan. Mack hoped they would not remember it, and, glancing back at the property, he exited the woods and turned in the same direction along the road as Mike's fertilizer truck.

He was unaware of the significance of the vehicle. But, out of habit, he watched it through the glasses as it disappeared, and he wrote down the registration number in his notebook, noting also that it was a *Dodge Ram, with Massachussetts registration, and that it was old, black, and muddy.*

Then he walked back along the deserted road to the Nissan and looked forward to a cup of tea in the Blackberry River Hotel, right there by the fire, as darkness descended across these cold mountains.

BY 4:30 P.M. Ali had not showed up at the farmhouse. Mike's boys had phoned in from Torrington and said they had not seen him guarding the wood when he they drove by. At 5 p.m., Ibrahim formed a search party to coincide with the arrival of the others.

He sent three of his team down to the front woods, where Ali was extremely easy to find since he was yelling his head off from a spot fifty yards along the post-and-rail fence, right by the duck hide. He'd been there for around ninety minutes with his leg now swollen to the size of a New Jersey pumpkin. He was freezing cold, in overwhelming agony, unable to move, and embarrassed beyond belief.

They drove the truck along the field and manhandled him onto the flatbed as carefully as possible. They drove him back to the house and listened while he explained what had happened. But his information was poor; he was not even certain he would recognize his attacker again.

Ibrahim conducted a brief conference with Yousaf and Ben and

Abu, during which they accepted that Ali could not be admitted to an American hospital. There would be questions, requests for his name and address. And when he could not answer, an inevitable call to the police. He could not leave here. But neither could he stay while he was in this kind of medical state, feverish, screaming, and unable to move on his own. At 5:40 p.m., Abu Hassan walked into the main room of the farmhouse and shot Ali dead with two shots to the back of the head.

"God speed unto Allah," intoned Ibrahim, and four of the group picked up the body, took it outside, and dumped it in an outhouse. It was an ignominious end to a brave but foolish young man.

AS ALL THIS WAS GOING DOWN at Mountainside Farm, Mack Bedford was pouring his second cup of tea. He had changed his shoes, removed his parka, and was reclining in a fireside chair. He was reading a magazine, half-heartedly looking at the ads for winter vacations, when he came upon one that brought back vivid memories.

It was a tour of the Holy Land, a place where he had once served, assisting with the training of the Israeli Defense Force. It listed the stops—the Sea of Galilee, the Dead Sea, parts of Jerusalem, and south to Bethlehem and Hebron, and then the other historic town in the Negev Desert, Be'er Sheba, with its layers of history. The town where Abu Hassan had committed mass murder at the 2004 bar mitzvah.

Mack and some of his colleagues had loved Hebron. Although it was in Israel, it had one of the most naturally Arabian centers anyone could imagine. Mack remembered the sight of farmers, coming into the market with their produce in great panniers strapped to the flanks of their camels. He remembered the sheep and goatherders, and the *casbah* with its pottery, sculpted olive-wood, and colorful glass.

He and his men had been taken by Arabs to see the town's huge Islamic school, home to almost two thousand students. He could recall immediately the warmth and generosity of the local people, their delight if any of the SEALs knew even a smattering of Arab words.

He remembered the fresh fruit, especially the pale, sweet Hebron-grown peaches, treasured throughout the Middle East. But most of all he remembered the gigantic edifice of the Tomb of the Patriarch, which dominated the city from its high and windy hill. Mack would remember until the day he died the feeling of pure humility he experienced when they told him that inside those mighty sandstone walls was the last resting place of Abraham, in the Land of Canaan, where he forged his Covenant with God.

He could, almost, remember the quotation from Genesis, which was engraved on a plaque: "And the Lord said unto Moses, 'I have heard the cry of my people in Egypt, for I know their sorrows, and I have come down to deliver them out of the hand of the Egyptians, to a land flowing with milk and honey. To the place of the Canaanites.'"

He smiled at the memory of the guys from Foxtrot Platoon, SEAL Team 10, who'd been with him in Hebron. Chief Petty Officer Frank Brooks, PO Billy-Ray Jackson, and Gunner Charlie O'Brien. They were all gone now, killed by an illegal missile fired by terrorists across the Euphrates River.

Mack put down the magazine and sipped his tea. He had some serious thinking to do, mostly involving what might happen when someone finds the guy with the broken leg. Right now he was amazed at how much he suspected, but how little he really knew. And he tried to distill his knowledge, and indeed his plan.

Who now owned Mountainside Farm? Could it now be occupied by the four men he was supposed to kill? And how could he find all this out without getting himself killed? There was also the question of what they were up to—and how it all might tie in to a potential hit on "Abe's Place," wherever that may be. He took another long look at the big-scale local map that Aimee Cutler had given him. There was the $875,000 farm with its clear view of Haystack Mountain. There was Torrington, and there was Route

44, which ran right past the hotel. He had spent little time checking out the land beyond his ops-area, especially the mountains between here and the New York State border.

The lettering that marked these mountains was printed sideways, running along the length of the peaks. Mack turned the map to read it and then sat, bolt upright, almost capsizing his Earl Grey tea, as he read the words before him: "Canaan Mountains."

Canaan! He'd just been thinking about that—the ancient town of Mamre in the desert, now known as Hebron, where the Jews first came to Israel. Now here was its twin, a small town in Connecticut, also called Canaan, right in the middle of the mountains.

Mack knew this was a Damascus moment, "kinda like that Greek son-ofabitch in his bathtub." The Greek word "Eureka!" entirely escaped him, for the moment at least. But Mack knew, he was, at last, on to something. He was closing in on Abe's Place. That meant he was closing in on the terrorist target. And, if he wasn't wildly mistaken, Ibrahim, Yousaf, Ben, and Abu Hassan were already in Mountainside Farm, or on their way.

He stood up from his chair and walked over to the receptionist, who was reading the paper. "Ma'am," he said, "can you tell me if there's an important school or college in the town of Canaan?"

"Well, there is one," she replied, "But it's nearer to here than the town. Canaan Academy. It's a very expensive boarding school, like Choate, or St. Paul's."

"Hmmm," said Mack. "I never heard of it."

"Well, it's a kind of specialist place, I believe," said the girl. "It's somehow attached to a Judaic Study Center. I think the students are mostly Jewish, and rich. It's really a boys' school, but I think there are some girls there."

"Is it big? I mean not just a place for a coupla dozen potential rabbis?"

The girl laughed. "Hell, no," she said. "It's huge. I think there are about a thousand students. We never see them here. I think they are allowed into Canaan about once a semester or something."

"Aside from that, they keep 'em locked up, right?" said Mack.

"Guess so. Keep those guys hammerin' away at the Old Testament."

Mack chuckled. "Where is it exactly?"

"Straight along the main road out here—that's Route 44 toward East Canaan. About two miles, on the right. Big entrance, stone pillars, with lions on 'em. Iron gates, long drive. Can't even see the school from the road."

Mack planned to visit the following morning. But right now he had a long night ahead of him. He retreated to his room for a hot shower and a glance at the television news channels. He guessed, correctly, that the usual menu of bombs, death, shootings, failed medical care, cancer, rape, misery, and remorse mostly delivered by reformed beauty queens who smiled in the wrong places, would depress the hell out of him.

The hotel was a warm and cheerful place, and Mack wore just an open shirt with his light blazer down to dinner. He ordered a beer at the bar and then settled down to a grilled swordfish steak, which he loved, along with French fries and spinach. He'd listened for years to health fanatics telling him there was a danger of too much mercury getting into the swordfish population. But he'd never heard a Maine fisherman agree with that, and they knew a lot more about deep-water fishing than anyone else.

And those swordfish were often caught in the turbulent tidal rips of the Grand Banks fishing grounds, eight hundred miles off the northeast coast of the United States. Mack never understood how there could possibly be mysterious drifts of chemical mercury out there as he dove with relish into his perfectly grilled white fish.

He had a fresh fruit salad for desert, with just a single scoop of vanilla ice cream. Then he sipped a large black coffee for a half-hour, and watched the end of the Yankees playoff game. As a loyal Red Sox fan, he hoped the Yanks would get beat, and was irritated when they won 9–1.

At 11 p.m. he returned to his room and changed back into his outdoor gear, adding a woolen navy scarf and gloves. Waiting for the upstairs corridor to be empty, he slipped out, down the stairs and out of the back door, not wishing to be seen looking like a renegade from a mountain rescue team. Not tonight.

Mack fired up the Nissan and set off to cross the Blackberry River. It was no distance, but he did not turn back toward the entrance to Mountainside Farm. Instead he went the other way, and found a narrow lane that he guessed ran up the north side of the property next to the long line of woods. He estimated the direct line across to the house and deliberately drove a half-mile further on. He found a secluded spot, pulled off the road, and parked the Titan out of sight in a copse.

Once more Mack slung the powerful binoculars around his neck, zipped up the parka over his scarf, and began walking back along the narrow lane, the way he had come. He slipped back into the woods on his right, and set off through the dark trees, walking somewhat noisily, but certain he was alone.

When he reached the end of the wood, he stood on the edge of a wide field and trained his binoculars on a cluster of lights he could see in the distance, some eight hundred yards away. When his eyes became accustomed to the darkness, he could see the farmhouse from a different angle from the one he had studied in the afternoon.

It was a bitterly cold night, and he could sense the frost forming on the grassland in front of him. There was a crunch to the ground as he moved toward a big tree and took up position leaning on the trunk, steadying his glasses.

There was no one in the yard. He could see no guard. And the barn doors were closed. But all the lights were on in the downstairs floor of the house, and there were lights in a couple of the bedrooms, one of which he now guessed contained the guy who'd tried to jump him. Poor bastard.

It was almost midnight now, and Mack decided this was as good a time as any to get a look into Mountainside Farm, check out whether any of his prime suspects were in residence. Plainly he could not charge in there with a machine gun blazing. At least not tonight, since he did not carry any firearm. Nonetheless he might consider taking them out one by one if they were taking turns going outside. The only weapon he carried, the sheath jammed down the back of his pants, was his SEAL combat knife, which had proved very useful on Ilkley Moor, in England.

The field in front of him was wide, flat, and devoid of trees. No cover for Mackenzie Bedford. So he just started walking, striding out beneath the stars and a bright moon. He knew he would be invisible from the house, because moonlight gives a false dawn. It's never as bright as you think. It's just a pale reflector, romantic but subdued, nothing like the sun. Mack knew a lot about moonlight.

He kept striding out, going for the back of those barns, aiming, as always, for the shadows. It was like patrolling Baghdad without the SEAL recon units. But a lot of it was exactly the same.

Mack's senses had gone up tenfold as he moved into the darkest places, using what SEALs call the "dead space," the areas the enemy cannot see. He stayed behind the biggest barn, and tried to get a clear view around the end wall, assessing the distance to the house. But he did not dare move too far in case there was a guard out here, standing silently. He picked up a sizeable rock and tossed it out into the empty yard, knowing this would bring someone running if there was a sentry on duty. But there was nothing.

Mack trained his binoculars on the farmhouse window, straining to see if there was anyone inside he might recognize. He could see the flickering blue light of an old television inside the room, and, through the glasses, the back of someone's head. He guessed they would all be facing the television, away from him. "Fuck," he muttered.

He waited for two or three minutes and then made a decision. He would cross the yard and make for the east wall where there was a wide window. It was dangerous, but if he made it without an uproar, would save a lot of time. Just in case, he unsheathed his combat knife and, crouching low, raced across the yard, his soft desert boots making no sound on the rough ground.

Mack crouched below the window, his heart pounding, as he

tried to decide whether to peer around from the left or right side of the glass. Which way would provide the best and fastest view of the men in that room? Because he was never going to stand straight up and perhaps be noticed immediately. There were no curtains, thanks to the cheapskate botanist.

And it was all very bright. There were outside lights on the porch, and outside lights on both barns, none of which were as bright as the light flooding out of the house. Mack, crouching in the tiny shadow below the window, was breaking about seven SEAL codes right here, ones that dealt with risk. Unnecessary risk. And he knew it. He was acting impatiently, a taboo in the Special Forces.

Then something truly terrible broke out. There was a sudden, distant roaring sound, and it was growing closer by the second. Sonofabitch sounded like a combine harvester or a fishing dragger revving into its jetty. This was a big powerful engine, and for a moment Mack thought it might be a helicopter.

And then it seemed to slow down, but revved forward again, with big headlights illuminating the woodland down by the entrance. Whatever it was, it was heading straight for the house. "Jesus Christ," murmured Mack, aware that the first thing those lights were going to illuminate was a Navy SEAL with a fucking dagger in his right hand, hiding under the living room window.

There was only one course of action. He had to get out of there and quickly, because that goddamned truck was coming up that blacktop real fast, and he had no idea how many people were in it.

Mack spun left and bolted around the far side of the house, away from the headlights. Big mistake. This was uncharted territory, and therefore a SEAL no-go. He reached the back door area and ran headlong into a guy carrying an armful of logs into the house. He knocked him flying, with logs everywhere.

The man was too surprised even to cry out, and he'd whacked his head hard on the concrete. Mack never even looked back, never saw the blank face of Abu Hassan, eyes shut, trying to regain his feet.

Mack knew only that the huge truck was roaring its way into the farmyard, perhaps with a delivery. And he did not want to be caught in its headlights. He raced across the yard, gratefully into the darkness behind the barns. Only when he was well concealed did he risk a look out, and even then it was difficult to see, because the truck's lights were head-on to Mack, and they were so bright everything behind them was blackness.

He could however see the frenzied activity among the residents of the house. One by one, they came running out, each man toting a Kalashnikov. Two of them were heading straight for the big barn. Two more were talking to the driver. Mack saw two more, both with rifles, emerge from the house, and again he felt that old familiar feeling of the one-man army against the world.

Basically he could not remain in this hornets' nest. He had no firearm, and if they caught him, or even saw him, he was as good as dead.

It was more or less at this point that he decided to skulk away across that field, and live to fight again another day. Swiftly he headed for that frosty grassland, running hard, crouched low, covering the ground in the sinister gait of the fighting SEAL, deceptively fast, and difficult to see from a distance. He went straight back to the woods, back to the lane that would lead him to the hotel.

Behind him he heard the truck rev up a few more times, and he heard the hiss of its air-breaks. When he reached the woods, he turned around to take one more look through the binoculars. But there was nothing. No people, and no truck. The outside lights were off and the barn was closed.

On the way back to the hotel, Mack found himself wondering precisely what was in that barn. And whether the big truck had left. He certainly could not see it, and he had not heard it depart. And still he could not identify one single resident of Mountainside Farm.

It had been a dangerous night, he decided. Big risk. No reward.

IBRAHIM SHARIF was in a quandary. He sat with his team around the botanist's ancient table and reflected that everything had gone more or less to plan. They had the explosive; the bomb conversions were going nicely. The school bus was in the barn, tucked away behind the bales, essentially disguised as a haystack. They had three more guys in place, the Hartford-based Sleepers who had bought the bus at the auction and then driven it across New York State to the farm. There had been little to stand in their way as they moved forward to conduct the greatest Islamic Day of Glory since Osama's men hit the Towers.

Ibrahim had been briefly concerned that whoever had broken Ali's right hip may have been working for some subversive U.S. security agency. But surely if that was the case, something would have happened by now. Someone official would have been in touch, probably with Faisal al-Assad himself. But that had not happened. If it had, Faisal would by now either have been in contact or arrived here in person. He was, after all the owner of the property, and he had no criminal record.

No, what was vexing Ibrahim was the sight of a groaning, moaning Abu Hassan Akbar, who swore to God he had been knocked flying by a huge running man, of superhuman strength, who could have walked through a brick wall. "He could have killed me," said Abu. "It was like being hit by King Kong."

"Who's King Kong?" asked Ibrahim.

"I seen a film," grunted Abu, unhelpfully.

Ibrahim was concerned. Each set of events on its own was feasible. Attacker number one, who crippled Ali, may just have been in the woods and fought back when Ali challenged him. The guy who flattened Abu may just have been taking a shortcut across the property and collided with Abu in the dark as he tried to avoid detection when the bus arrived.

But it was the coincidence that bothered the al-Qaeda leader. Were these men one and the same? Was there some unseen enemy out there trying to screw up their plans? In Ibrahim's judgment this was impossible, because such a person must have been official, and in that case, something would have happened by now—a search, a raid, even a bomb, or a visit from the police, the FBI, the CIA, the military, even the detested Mossad. But there was nothing except a dead Ali, and a bump on Abu's head.

Ibrahim had been uncertain of his ground when the conversation started, and he still was.

MACK AWAKENED early and tried to assemble his thoughts. Whatever his suspicions, whatever his knowledge, he could not "go official" on this mission. That was a major part of the operation. He couldn't go to the police and tell them that a bunch of maniacs holed up in a local farm with several tons of dynamite were about to blow up a local school. His orders were plain: He was to take out Ibrahim Sharif, Yousaf Mohammed, Ben al-Turabi, and Abu Hassan Akbar, and without letting anyone know that he and some of the most senior security chiefs in the United States had been involved.

Mack had a light breakfast and set off along Route 44 at nine the following morning. When he reached Canaan Academy, he was mildly surprised to find the big iron gates were open. There was no guard. Not even a gardener in sight. He swung into the entrance, driving between what he assumed were the mighty stone Lions of Judah on the gateposts.

The drive was almost a half-mile long, surrounded on both sides by vast lawns, which formed a parkland with tall oak trees set at a generous distance one from another. Up ahead was the enormous main building of the school, with a high clock tower, and ramparts along the south side of the roof.

Mack guessed this building housed the majority of students, and probably all the classrooms and principal halls of the school. Set around this gray-stone fortress were a half-dozen further buildings, same stone work, and almost certainly places for specialized study—laboratories, art rooms, or, perhaps, even the school library.

On second thought, Mack decided there would be no outside library. This was the kind of place where the library would be front and center, in the middle of the main building, a showpiece of knowledge and learning.

He parked the Nissan alongside a row of yellow school buses, and walked toward the main double doors of Canaan Academy. Mack turned the big brass handle and pushed open the high, left-hand wall of stained red oak. He entered a cavernous front hall with a wide staircase, a balustrade forming a gallery all around on the first floor, and corridors leading off in several directions.

Mack spotted a sign for the school office and headed in that direction. When he arrived, he saw that was no door, only a wide entrance. Inside was a large desk where a forty-ish woman with swept-back dark hair and glasses sat. She glanced up with the practiced air of one who is used to people strolling in and out of her domain anytime they felt like it.

"Good morning, sir," she said. "How can I help you? I'm Marie Calvert, the school secretary."

"Thank you, ma'am," replied Mack. "I'm sorry to intrude like this, but I'm trying to locate a cousin of mine, a mathematics teacher who I believe may be on your faculty."

"Oh? What's his name?"

"Frank Brooks," lied Mack.

"Brooks? I'm very sorry but we do not have any member of staff by that name. A few years ago we had a kitchen assistant named Doris Brooks. But I think she died."

"Hope it wasn't food poisoning," said Mack, boldly testing the sense of humor of the Canaan school secretary, who did not, incidentally, have one.

"Most certainly not," replied Marie Calvert. "It was a road accident."

Mack decided to change the subject. "The only thing I remember Frank told me was the headmaster was named Abraham," said Mack. "Tell the truth, I can't recall whether it was a first or second name."

"Well, that could not be us," said Ms. Calvert. "Our headmaster is Mark Jenson. I'm sorry I can't help much."

"Did you ever hear of a Connecticut headmaster named Abraham?" asked Mack, "Possibly another school. Frank definitely said it was a large boarding school with Judaic connections."

Ms. Calvert thought for a moment, and then replied, "There are not many establishments like this outside of New York City. But we do fraternize and I honestly cannot think of one place with anyone in authority called Abraham."

"How about Abe—or Abie?" persisted Mack.

"I don't think so," said Ms. Calvert, slightly haughtily. "Not for a headmaster, surely."

"Well, I guess not."

Mack was slightly disappointed. He accepted that "Abe's Place" could merely have meant Canaan Academy in veiled speech. But the great Arnold Morgan would not have liked that, on the grounds of vagueness, not enough bite, or likelihood of truth.

If the headmaster here had been called Abraham instead of Mark, he could have moved ahead and tackled the real problem. That signal the Brits had intercepted would finally have been clarified.

But all was still confusion. And still he did not know the whereabouts of the guys he was supposed to rub out. It could just as easily be a bunch of bank robbers in Mountainside Farm. This Canaan set-up may still be a terrorist target, but he needed that last elusive piece of evidence. And he was not going to get it here, sitting socializing with the austere Ms. Marie Calvert.

Just then there were footsteps in the corridor and a tall, dark-haired man of around fifty walked into the office. He immediately turned to Mack, probably on the grounds that this might be a prospective $30,000-a-year parent. According to the receptionist at the hotel, the place was full of the scions of Wall Street investment houses.

"Hello, I'm Mark Jenson," he said. "I hope Marie is helping."

Mack stood up and held out his right hand, "Charles O'Brien," he said. "I'm awfully sorry to bother such a busy place, but I'm try-ing to find a cousin, Frank Brooks, and I mistakenly thought he worked here. Math teacher."

"Not here," said Jenson. "Any other clues?"

"Well, I was just telling Ms. Calvert that Frank said his boss was called Abraham."

"Abraham—hmmmm, that's a very big name around here. But I don't know of a headmaster Abraham."

"In what way?"

"This Academy has one great celebratory day of the year aside from the regular Jewish festivals like Yom Kippur and Rosh Hashana. It's the annual day we open the school to parents and rel-atives with a choral festival and the school play, followed by a recital by the school orchestra and individual musicians. Matter of fact it's next Friday. It's named in honor of our spiritual founder. Abraham's Day."

10

MACK MADE A WORLD-CLASS effort at feigning nonchalance as he stood up, shook hands with Mark Jenson, nodded politely to Marie Calvert, thanked them both, and walked calmly back toward the entrance hall with a slow and rhythmic stride.

What he wanted to do was charge down the corridor, slam through the huge door like a cartoon character leaving a splintered silhouette, jump across the Blackberry River, and take Ibrahim and the Towelheads and throttle them *en masse*, before they could do any damage.

Steady, Mack. This needs real thought, because the success or failure of this mission depends on secrecy. That had always to be in Mack's mind, and he knew it. He simply could not phone Mark Jenson back and tell him to double and treble school security on Abraham's Day. Neither could he phone the police. Because that would lead directly to questions, identification, reports, records, and probably the release of Ibrahim and the rest on the grounds they had, as yet, done nothing provably wrong.

Mack had to face it, as he walked across the wide front courtyard of Canaan Academy. He had always been, and would always be, that same "Shadow Warrior" of his old command, always working in secret. And the only people on earth from whom he could seek assistance were other men of the shadows—Johnny Strauss and Benny Shalit.

Mack now knew he had found the terrorist target—Canaan Academy on Abraham's Day. He'd read all the communiqués worked out by the Intelligence agencies, and he was left with one chilling thought: that the al-Qaeda attack on the Russian school in 2004 was conducted by the same enemy he himself now faced, and that enemy considered the Russian school an enormous triumph.

Al-Qaeda had not just carried out their murderous attack on any old day, they had gone for the most special day in the semester—the opening day of the Russian school year, September 1, the traditional Day of Knowledge. The most festive day in the Russian academic calendar, when parents and relatives were invited to attend all the celebratory events.

Now here was Mack at the Canaan Academy, with Abraham's Day, an identical celebration of learning and achievement, just eight days away. He knew when and where al-Qaeda would attack again, and it was entirely up to him to stop them.

Mack now had all the pieces in place except for one: He wanted to know who really owned Mountainside Farm—who had received that convoluted veiled telephone call from the Middle East, and then bolted to northwest Connecticut to purchase, in cash, a base for a terrorist operation.

In Mack's mind, there was no doubt that this was Faisal al-Assad, but he wanted proof. Because if Faisal had indeed been the lynchpin in this operation, Mack, along with Johnny and Benny, was going to need some important answers.

Mack climbed into the Nissan, pulled out his cell phone, and dialed Banda Fine Arts in New York. Johnny Strauss answered, and Mack spoke to him in the manner of a kind of telegram: "Please check computerized Connecticut property tax records for Mountainside Farm, West Norfolk, Connecticut 06058. New owner important. Query: Faisal al-Assad, 300 East Sixty-Ninth Street. I'll call back in an hour."

Strauss moved immediately, calling a member of the Sayanim, a Connecticut State Senator, who was back on the line in thirty minutes. "This property was purchased several days ago by a New Yorker named Faisal al-Assad in cash. It's registered as a working farm, but it's only thirty acres, and there are no tax records for income on either produce or livestock."

"You're a hero, Jake," said Strauss. "This is everything I wanted."

Mack called back early, and just said, "Is it him?"

"Affirmative," said Strauss. "What now?"

"I want to get after him," replied Mack. "I'm calling Benny. If al-Assad bought that farm for Ibrahim, he's as guilty as the rest. But Benny will come up with some background, and I think we need to know it."

BEN SHALIT moved quickly after speaking with Mack. He ran every possible check on Faisal al-Assad, both through the Mossad operation in the Washington embassy and the head office in Tel Aviv. There was little on him, except that the Saudi corporation, for which he worked, was owned by those titans of the Arabian construction industry, the bin Ladens.

This did not automatically make him guilty of anything, since the family had unloaded Osama as a total embarrassment several years ago. Nonetheless, there were still some relatively suspicious incidents.

Al-Assad had twice been photographed by the Mossad in company with Shakir Khan, once at a government reception in Islamabad, and once, much more significantly, at a hotel in Madrid, three weeks before al-Qaeda bombed the four trains heading into the huge downtown Atocha station.

No one ever pinned anything on either Khan or al-Assad, but London's Scotland Yard was always profoundly suspicious of both men. After the massacre on the Spanish railway, both British and Spanish police delved deeply into al-Qaeda's continued presence in the Spanish capital. And they turned up some immensely pertinent details.

One involved the founder of the Spanish al-Qaeda cell, the Syrian Imad Yarkas, who established a strong association with the known jihadist Amer el Azizi, and with the Jordanian killer Abu Musab al-Zarqawi. It was they who dispatched an al-Qaeda field operative to videotape New York, including the Twin Towers, before 9/11.

Also in 2001, Spanish police swooped down on the Spanish terrorist cell and arrested Yarkas and sixty-two others. They ransacked their headquarters and found Faisal al-Assad's phone number among the computerized records and on cell phones.

They never located him and made no attempt to contact him when he reappeared three or four years later in New York as a very senior international executive for the bin Laden construction empire. And this was extremely awkward for the Americans, because the Saudi firm now contained some of the richest men in Arabia, personal friends of the king and many of the princes.

Bin Laden's family firm had built several palaces and restored ancient holy buildings for the royal rulers, and it was plainly not politically correct to start arresting their top executives and business ambassadors in New York City, whatever they may have done in previous years.

But now things were looking very different, and there was no longer any doubt as to the guilt of the man who had bought the farm as headquarters for the operation. Faisal al-Assad would need to do some fast talking. Because Johnny and Benny were not investigators or arresting officers. They were executioners, and they operated on behalf of their embattled nation, under the hidden flag of the Mossad.

Then came another sudden and totally unexpected development. Jarvis Goldman, the banking Sayanim from Gotham National, called Strauss to inform him a $2 million wire transfer to Faisal al-Assad's account had just come in, but not from Saudi Arabia as usual.

"It came in from the Anglo-Saudi Investment Bank on Lombard Street, London," said Jarvis. "Account of a law firm named Howard, Marks, and Cuthbert. I thought you may want to know that."

The name meant nothing to either Strauss or Shalit. But they checked with the Mossad basement in Washington, and almost received a round of applause.

The London attorneys, rehoused in new offices, had been the victims of the early morning blast on the night of the Guantanamo verdicts, the legal decision that had freed Ibrahim and his team. Their offices had been obliterated by the Mossad bomb, but no one had died, and no one had ever discovered who blew up the building. But it was understood that Howard, Marks, and Cuthbert was a critical link in the legal chain that was working on freeing the Guantanamo inmates. Now it looked as if they might be in deeper than that.

But now the noose was really tightening around the neck of Faisal al-Assad. Metaphorically, that is. Benny Shalit almost always used a garrote. The two Mossad men called Mack Bedford back and said he needed to come down to New York. They were going to visit the man who had helped organize the mass murder and wounding of two thousand people in Madrid, and who had now arranged the financing for the coming operation against the Jewish students. Johnny and Ben might need extra muscle, because Faisal might by now have extra bodyguards.

Running against the commuter traffic, Mack hit FDR Drive at 5 p.m. and ran south to the East Fifty-Third Street exit. He took a turn south on Second Avenue, crossed to Park, and came up right on the doorman's whistle at the Waldorf Astoria, facing north.

"Checking in, sir?"

"Hell, no," replied Mack, leaving the engine running. "I live here."

He collected his room key and headed upstairs, glad to have a world headquarters in the city, even if it was costing, someone, around five hundred dollars a day. Directly inside the door was a small envelope on the carpet. Inside was a single sheet of message paper that read, "7:30 p.m. southwest corner Sixty-Ninth and Lexington. I'll be there, Benny."

Mack made a quick check of the wardrobe and the message service. His clothes were all in place, his laundry was back. There were no messages.

Devoid of any meaningful exercise since he had snapped Ali's right hip in half, he decided to complete the SEALs normal training routine: four hundred push-ups, divided with four thirty-second breaks. Then he ordered room service and ran a bath while he ate.

He tipped about a half-pint of bath oil into the hot water and realized too late he'd grabbed the ladies bottle; he emerged from the water a half-hour later smelling like a Japanese brothel.

Night was closing in on the northeast coast, and he'd noticed an early chill in the air when he arrived. It was about ten degrees warmer than in the Connecticut mountains, but it was still cool, and getting cooler.

Mack wore a dark tan turtleneck under a suede jacket in the same color. He debated wearing regular shoes, but decided on his soft combat boots, just in case he needed a fast foothold on a shiny wood floor. "Fucking empires have been won and lost on decisions like that," he muttered.

He shoved his slim black leather gloves into his jacket pocket along with his wraparound black sunglasses, placed the "Do Not Disturb" sign on his door handle, and left.

A swift walk through the hotel to the rear entrance, near the famous old Bull & Bear Restaurant, brought him out on Lexington, where he turned north and headed up the west side of the street. It was close to a mile up to Sixty-Ninth, and Mack strode out in the cool autumn evening, crossing the wide two-way thoroughfare of East Fifty-Seventh Street, and up past Bloomingdale's.

When he reached Sixty-Ninth Street he headed to the northwest corner, where he concealed himself in a doorway and watched the corner across the street. *What if the note on his carpet had not been written by Benny? What if Johnny's organization had been compromised? What if al-Assad's cutthroats were somehow expecting him?*

There were a lot of ways to die in the line of duty, but Mack elected to eliminate one of them, by not waiting like a sitting duck, idling in the gun sights of the most ruthless and dangerous men in the world. He decided to stay well hidden till Benny showed. And Benny was late.

He was just beginning to wonder what happened to Benny when he pulled up in a cab ten minutes later, looking around for Mack.

Mack crossed the street to join Benny, and together they walked up to Second Avenue to meet Johnny, who was already inside the locked building.

"Neat," said Benny.

"Thank you," said Strauss.

"You got an apartment number?" asked Mack.

"Sure," said Johnny. "It's on the buzzer list outside the front door. Faisal al-Assad, plain as day. Twenty-one D."

"Do we have a plan?" asked Mack. "I mean, do you want to question him? Ask him precisely who's in Mountainside Farm?"

"Yes. But it might be tricky if he's got bodyguards in there with him," replied Benny. "This guy's a friend of the friggin' King of Saudi Arabia, right? My guys know all about him."

"That's why the police have not picked him up," said Johnny. "These days no one wants the king to be pissed off."

"Well, what do you plan to do? Walk in, then kill him and the bodyguards?" said Mack with deliberate oversimplification.

"We'll play it by ear," said Johnny. "But this Faisal guy is involved in mass murder, and we're not leaving him alive. I don't want to kill bodyguards. But we may have to keep them quiet."

"Guess we better get up there and find out what's what," said Mack. "I'm here to help, but I'm not going to take out Assad. Those are not my orders."

"No need. I'll do it," said Benny, the man from the Mossad.

They walked to the empty elevator and were slightly disoriented when a young woman in a dark business suit appeared to come out of nowhere and joined them, pressing the button for the twenty-seventh floor. Johnny reached over and pressed eighteen, twenty, and twenty-four. No one spoke and they disembarked, each on one of the wrong floors.

Five minutes later, they met up at the stairs on the twenty-first floor. Standard undercover procedure.

Now they walked down the corridor to number 21D. Mack stood back and Benny rang the bell. No reply. Benny rang again. Silence.

"Fuck," said Johnny. He tried to open the door, but it was locked. He tried to open it with a credit card, sliding the card between the door and the doorpost, level with the handle, and to everyone's amazement, the door opened.

Benny stepped softly into the foyer and checked behind the door. "Two other locks, none of them active," he said.

"He's gotta be here," said Strauss. "No one goes out without locking in Manhattan. Maybe he's asleep."

They walked quietly into the main room, which was beautifully furnished. Three striking marine paintings and a couple expensive-looking prints signed by Andrew Wyeth hung on the walls. But the place was quiet. The kitchen was tidy, but empty, with no sign of anyone having taken nourishment or even had a drink, even coffee.

They walked down a short corridor to the master bedroom. Empty. They opened the closets. Almost empty. They opened the bedroom drawers. Bereft. Checked the hall closet for coats. None. Mack picked up the phone. Dead. Switched on the cable television. No signal.

"Fuck me," said Benny. "He's gone."

"Mountainside Farm?" asked Johnny.

"Yeah, right," replied Mack. "How about Guantanamo Bay? I don't think so. This tricky little sonofabitch is on his way home to Riyadh."

The three of them wandered disconsolately around the apartment, checking drawers, opening closets. But there was nothing much to be found. Faisal had packed his stuff and cleared out.

Except for a somewhat esoteric clue in the waste basket next to a large antique desk.

"What is it?" asked Benny.

"It's not much," said Mack. "But I think we might have solved the Penn Station bomb mystery. Those four little bastards crossed from one side of this country to the other by train, and they stayed here." He showed them the Amtrak rail ticket stubs he'd found in the trash. The date was correct, and they were stamped in light blue, big letters: *CARDINAL*. "I just found their tickets."

MACK MOVED HIS STUFF from the Waldorf Astoria to the Blackberry River Hotel the following morning. The drive took him almost three hours, and he was glad for the time alone. He needed to think.

Because his prime task was one of surveillance, he not only had to make positive identification that the four ex-Guantanamo prisoners were in residence at Mountainside Farm, he had to establish precisely how they intended to hit the academy. Only then could he make his decisive move to end their attack and their lives. But first he needed to know their plan.

Mack had no doubt his top-secret mission was achievable, although he suspected it might involve of lot of night-work. Freezing cold night-work. Goddamned dangerous night-work.

He pulled into the parking lot of the Blackberry River Hotel at around 2 p.m. and headed directly to his room, which appeared to be just as he had left it the previous evening. He was tired after the long drive and crashed out on the bed for a couple of hours. He read the local newspaper, the *Register Citizen,* and went downstairs for a beer and a steak at around 7 p.m., adopting a similar procedure to his previous evening. After dinner, he made a quick change into his combat gear: his navy sweater and scarf, heavy parka, boots, binoculars, gloves, and knife sheathed and tucked into his waistband.

Again Mack made his exit through the rear door when the coast was clear, and drove back across the Blackberry River, concealing the Nissan in the trees and walking through the woods on the farm's northern border. He took up his old position, staring through his binoculars across the frosty field, straight at the farmyard and house. This time the outside lights were all on and the barn doors were open. Mack could see only piles of straw through the open door, and there was no guard on duty outside. He thought he could hear the distant hum of a running engine, but he could see no vehicle.

He waited for another fifteen minutes, back in the dark shadow of the woods, but he could see no discernible activity. And at a few minutes before 9:30 he began his walk across the dark and freezing field, aiming for the shadow of the barn.

Fifty yards from the shelter of that rear wall, he began to realize he had misjudged the situation. There was clear and obvious noise coming from somewhere. In fact it sounded like an active workshop in a Navy shipyard.

He could hear the periodic whine of an electric drill, the intermittent thump of a nail gun, and the rattling revs of a big running engine. But he could see nothing around that corner into the well-lit farmyard. Whatever was happening was happening inside that barn.

He moved back along the wall, to the far end, and tried to get a better angle on the open door. But that was no better. The only spot with a front and center view of the goddamned haystack was from the front door of the house in which were residing around ten armed cutthroats.

Mack assessed that this was not a good spot for him and considered requesting that Coronado fly in a box of hand grenades, which he could activate and hurl in through the window. But upon reflection he decided this would not help his strict secrecy policy.

EX-NAVY SEAL SHOT DEAD
AFTER BOMB BLAST AT WEST NORFOLK FARM

Mack's imagination was apt to run riot at times like this, and every instinct told him he could not possibly attack a group this large, especially since all appeared to have loaded Kalashnikovs at their disposal.

No, he would have to wait it out, until the barn workers elected to turn it in for the night. But who knew when that would be. From across the yard, using the binoculars, he could see at least six other men sitting inside watching television, their backs to the window.

The night shift pressed on until just before midnight and then the noise stopped. The engine was switched off, the drill went silent, and there was only the murmur of voices as the lights went off and a group of five men came out of the barn. Mack watched four of them walk over to the front door. The fifth stayed to fasten a big padlock to a chain on the double doors. "Fuck," said Mack, still waiting in the shadows.

Just then the downstairs lights in the house went out, which robbed Mack of a shot at getting to the window and trying to make some identification. His chance of getting into the barn, without breaking in and making one hell of a noise forty feet from the nearest bedroom, had also passed.

With immense reluctance, he turned and headed back across the field. Again he had taken a big risk, and again no reward. "Towelhead pricks," he grumbled, knowing that the following night might mean an even greater risk.

IT WAS ALMOST 1 A.M. on a brand new Tuesday morning when Mack finally arrived back at the sleeping hotel. He walked through the reception area and stood by the dying embers of the log fire in the residents' lounge. He'd been this cold before, but not in living memory.

He finally hit the sack just before 1:30 and slept the deep sleep of the just. The following morning he stayed in bed until 8:30. He had a light breakfast—coffee and a couple of croissants with apricot preserves—and immediately left the hotel.

He fired up the Nissan and headed straight down the road to Torrington. As he passed the front entrance to Mountainside Farm, he noticed there was a figure in a heavy black jacket standing alone in the woods, about twenty yards to the left of the track that led to the blacktop.

"I don't think he's been there all night," muttered Mack. "But you never know. Poor bastard."

He covered the eighteen-mile journey in a half-hour, parked in a lot at least a half-mile from Cutlers (not wishing to run into Aimee), and walked down to the hardware store he'd noticed on Main Street. He wandered through the aisles and picked up a hefty-looking padlock and key, as well as a slim flashlight. Lastly, he moved over to the heavy-duty area and found a bolt-cutter, with thirty-inch handles, just in case.

He gassed up the car and drove straight back to the Blackberry River Hotel, where he spent the day either sitting by the fire, locked in his room, reading, sleeping, or going through a SEAL exercise routine, which would certainly have put a civilian in his grave.

Mack skipped lunch, just drinking a couple of cups of coffee, but headed downstairs for an early dinner at 5:30 p.m. He ate grilled New England scrod, with spinach, salad, and fizzy water. No starter, no potato, no bread, and no dessert. Maybe later. Mack Bedford never went to war on a full stomach.

At 10 p.m. he said goodnight to the receptionist, who manned the front desk until eleven, and slipped quietly up to his room to change. Remembering he'd been what he poetically described as *colder 'n a well-digger's ass*, all night over at Mountainside, he wore a T-shirt, then two dark turtlenecks, his heavy navy sweater and scarf, parka, gloves, and combat boots.

He moved softly down the back stairs and out the rear door. Moments later he was on the road, aiming the Nissan at Norfolk central, and over the bridge toward Mountainside. There was hardly another vehicle on the road, and while he wondered whether there was in fact an all-night guard at the entrance, he did not drive back toward it.

Instead, with his headlights lowered, he drove through the darkness up to his usual copse of trees and parked out of sight from the road. He shoved the big padlock and key into his pocket, and picked up the heavy bolt-cutters. It was pitch black when he crossed the road and entered the wood that guarded the north side of the farm.

Mack knew the way by now, and navigated his way through the trees in zero visibility. He arrived at his usual spot and trained his binoculars on the farmyard across the wide field. Again he could see there was activity, with lights on in the farmyard, barn doors open, more lights inside, and, just faintly, probably because he guessed it was there, the faint hum of a running engine.

There was just one difference. Mack could see one man standing outside the barn, about forty feet across from the front door. He could see no one else, but the supreme magnifying power of his Special Forces binoculars pulled up an image that Mack, quite frankly, could have done without. The guy was holding an AK-47, unmissable to a Navy SEAL.

In itself, this was not a problem. Mack could have crept up on the guy and killed him any one of a dozen ways. But dead bodies he did not need. Because right then these lunatics might abandon the mission. And this did not fit in with Mack's plans. Obviously, he intended to end it for them. On his terms. In his time. And in a way that would cause al-Qaeda and everyone involved with them the most shattering damage. In Mack's view, dead bodies were a major pain in the ass.

He picked up the bolt-cutters and set off once more across the crunchy acres of the freezing field.

As he drew nearer, he once more made for the shadows, crouching low and half-running, the classic mobile stance of the Navy SEAL coming in for the fast attack.

He reached the night-black cover of the barn wall, and kept stock-still for three minutes. Discerning no movement, he just stood and listened to the industrial din emanating from the barn. He edged along the wall, and peered around the corner, a course of action that offered him two separate pieces of bad news.

First, there was the armed guard, leaning on one of the barn doors, his rifle slung across the lower part of his chest. *Like fucking Che Guevara, stupid prick, Mack thought. He makes one wrong move, I'll shove that Kalashnikov straight up his ass.*

There are only a few people in this world who could make such a statement and mean every word of it. Most of them are United States Navy SEALs.

The second piece of bad news had to do with the padlock. It was in place on the near door, but from what Mack could see, it was locked and there was no key jutting out. That meant someone had the friggin' key, and that someone probably intended to lock up when the barn workforce quit for the night.

Mack considered that he had an eighty percent chance of fooling that someone, and he just decided to wait it out. But somehow, sometime on this night, he, Lt. Commander Bedford, was going to find out what the hell was going on in that barn. And if he didn't like it, it was not going to happen.

Twenty minutes later, Che Guevara took a coffee break. He called into the barn and asked if anyone else wanted any. A voice called back, "Four, please, all with sugar." And Mack watched the guard walk over to the house.

The door opened. The light flooded out onto the farmyard, and was gone when the door closed again. Mack came out of the traps like a greyhound. Luckily the right-hand door was pushed back beyond the ninety-degree line to the barn, which put the padlock slightly out of sight to the yard, but closer for Mack.

He reached the lock and softly jolted it, pulling down hard. As he feared, it was securely locked. Wielding the bolt-cutters he snapped the blades onto the padlock's cast-steel curved bar and cleaved it in half. He twisted it off, shoved it in his pocket and re-placed it with his own padlock. He snapped it shut, just as the first one had been, but Mack left the new key jutting out of the hole.

He picked up the cutters, checked the spare key was in his pocket, and bounded back into the shadows. Elapsed time: less than one minute.

He watched the guard return ten minutes later, bringing with him a tray of five cups of coffee. He walked into the barn, presumably to distribute the hot drinks, and emerged holding just one cup. Temporarily the noise from inside subsided, but it started again in five minutes—the drilling, the dull thump of the nail gun, and the running engine. Mack could only wait.

Finally, at around 12:30 on the new Wednesday morning, the motors died. The lights went out in the barn, and five guys trooped out. In the false light of the yard Mack could have sworn one of the men there was Ibrahim Sharif, the terrorist he always thought he recognized.

He'd studied the photographs long and hard, but still he could not be sure. One of the five was a very big guy, and Mac thought it could easily have been Ben al-Turabi, but again he could not be certain, because they were mostly facing away from him.

Precisely as last night, no one lingered long in the living room of the house. The television light went off, and so did all of the downstairs lights, except for the one in the kitchen. There was no longer a guard in the yard but the outside lights were all on.

Mack watched someone emerge from the front door and walk across to the barn. He pulled first one door shut, and then walked three strides back for the other. He closed them together, and without hesitation, twisted the key in Mack's padlock. He opened the lock bar and threaded it through two of the big chain links. Then he pushed down on the bar to shut it, twisted the key once more to double-lock, then pulled it out and dropped it in his pocket. Mack smiled the smile of the profoundly cunning.

The man walked back to the house, entered through the front door, and shut it behind him. Mack watched the outside lights go out and then he slipped from out of the shadows.

Softly he walked to the center of the wide barn doors, and opened his own padlock with the spare key. The chains fell slack, and, putting the padlock in his pocket, Mack eased open the big door and slipped through the narrow gap. He pulled the doors shut behind him, and turned his new flashlight onto the wall of straw that towered over him. Right now he could see nothing remotely industrial.

He moved to the side and shone his flashlight the length of the straw wall. Then he noticed the wide front "wall" was not joined to the side "wall." There was a space between the big square bales that formed the entire structure. Mack could see they were all held together by lengths of dark red twine.

He edged through the space and found himself inside a large shoebox-like structure, all made of straw, with no ceiling. Mack found this incredible. But more incredible was the single content of the box: one large, full-sized yellow school bus, good for about thirty passengers. From out of its doors came a succession of cables. The entrance to the bus was wide open, and Mack stepped inside and shone his light.

The entire rear end of the transporter was stacked with wooden cases, some nailed down hard, some half open, others completely open. On the floor were a couple of drills, a nail gun, several screwdrivers, a couple of hammers, and two small hand carts. The bus felt warm as if the heating system had recently been running.

Mack walked back outside and checked the space around the "shoe box," inside and out. On the left, the area inside the barn's end wall, was a pile of transparent plastic sacks that contained a white powdery substance, like cement or sugar. All around were plastic cans of fuel oil, maybe even diesel. And in the air was the deeply unpleasant whiff of ammonia.

Mack would have known that smell anywhere. It was the one that lingered after a blast from an IED. It was the aftermath of an explosion from an ammonium nitrate fertilizer bomb. And it had also been in the caches of explosive that Foxtrot Platoon had ransacked out of the Afghan mountains last time they were on duty together.

Mack walked around to the front of the bus, and on the front destination-display above the driver's seat was one word: CANAAN.

"Mother of God," breathed Mack. "They're going to drive this fucker into the school and blow it to high heaven, right in the middle of Abraham's Day. And they got enough explosive in there to knock down Wall Street."

He re-boarded the bus and walked back to the rear seats. He re-examined the bags of white powder, noting that they each contained over fifty pounds of ammonium nitrate fertilizer. He also found sacks of nitromethane, two bags of powdered ammonia, and five tied nine-inch high bundles of dynamite, all agents to increase the intensity and speed of the explosion.

"Holy shit," whispered Mack. "These bastards are not joking."

He switched off his flashlight and moved to the door, easing it open and squeezing through the narrowest possible gap. There were no lights on, and he grabbed and re-locked his padlock. At which point two people each received the greatest shock of their lives—Mack Bedford and the guard he referred to as Che Guevara, who suddenly walked around the side of the barn.

The guard froze and Mack instantly shone the flashlight directly into the man's eyes, blinding him. He temporarily grappled for his rifle, but then lost consciousness when Mack landed a thunderous right hook on the side of his chin, fracturing his jaw in two places.

Mack wheeled away to his right and ran past the corner of the barn, where he grabbed the bolt-cutters and headed out to the field like an Olympic sprinter, pounding over the frozen ground, his heart beating furiously, his ears straining for sounds of an uproar back in the farmyard.

He never broke stride. And, racing in the cold glow of a pale moon, he reached the treeline and crashed into the welcoming shadows. For a few moments he stopped and trained the binoculars on the farm. Nothing. No lights. No movement. No sound.

Swiftly he ran through the trees and across the road. There was not a car in sight, and in the dead silence of the night, the Nissan, when it started, sounded to him like the re-launch of the space shuttle.

He drove quietly into the parking lot of the hotel just before 2 a.m. Then he crept through the darkened rear section of the downstairs area and headed to his room, where he immediately picked up a message from Benny, asking him to call him when he got in, no matter the time.

Mack called Benny from his cell phone. "I didn't know you'd be up this late," Benny joked. "I got some news, probably not operational but extremely interesting."

"Shoot," said Mack.

"The man from 21D landed in Riyadh via Paris two days ago, and we tracked him to one of the royal palaces, where he met with several imams and Saudi princes. Yesterday he left on a royal flight, one of the king's Boeing 747-300s. It landed in Peshawar, and a government registered car took him into the city. He's staying at the home of a very senior minister, Shakir Khan."

"Guess that figures," replied Mack. "They were in Madrid together, right? Just before the trains were bombed."

"Correct. And our guys think Shakir's the instigator of that phone intercept the Brits handed us."

"Well, it looks like this thing's gonna blow on Friday. I need you and Johnny to head up here today, and I have a whole list of things for you to bring."

"You're sure about this?"

"One hundred percent. Now grab a pen."

Mack asked for tape, det-cord, and electronic detonators with a 300-yard range control box. He also requested a Satnav GPS system with full radar fitted into a laptop, a couple of hammers, screws, screwdrivers, metal brackets, batteries, a battery-powered drill, flashlights, electric wires and cutters, and black cammy cream, the SEAL's special device to take the shine away from faces in the moonlight.

Finally, he asked for C-4 plastic high-explosive or Semtex, the favorite of both the Navy SEALs and the Mossad. It's neat, clean, and easily transportable—it's not too heavy and it comes in small off-white blocks that are easily lashed together with duct tape. Also it blows like a sonofabitch. Terrorists used it to blast a hole in the portside hull of USS *Cole* in October 2000, and to knock down the U.S. military housing complex Khobar Towers in Saudi Arabia.

"What the hell are you planning to blow up?" asked Benny. "A fucking mountain!"

"No, but I can't afford a mistake. See you later, buddy."

MIKE, THE HEAD of the Boston Sleeper Cell, inactive since 2001, didn't know what hit him. He had walked quietly out into the deserted night garden of Mountainside Farm and had somehow found himself in a war zone.

He was unconscious for forty-two minutes and woke up with a fractured jaw, lying on the freezing ground, and rapidly descending into shock and dehydration. He dragged himself to his feet and staggered into the house. Ibrahim was appalled at what he saw. His colleague's jaw was swollen like a football on one side of his face, his head was bleeding where it had hit the ground, and he looked as if he might die here and now.

"I think someone hit me," Mike grated through teeth clamped together to relieve the pain. "I need to get to a hospital."

Ibrahim did not especially want to order yet another of his team to be shot dead. And he assessed that may not be necessary since Mike was walking wounded, not flat on his back unable to move. Nonetheless, he understood that Mike was no longer a part of the operation and that he could not go to a hospital around here, certainly not the one in Torrington.

He asked Mike if he could whistle up a couple of replacements in Boston. The broken terrorist was optimistic, and Ibrahim ordered one of the newer arrivals to fire up the muddy truck outside, and drive Mike to Boston, where two replacements would be ready to make the journey back.

"You mean you just drop me at home?" gritted Mike, "And let me make my own way to a hospital?"

"I have no choice. Give Ben the numbers of the new recruits and get moving. Allah will look kindly upon you for your sacrifice."

Right now, the murderous pain in Mike's face was all-consuming, and he wanted to tell the boss that he couldn't give a damn about Allah's kindly looks. He cared only for a doctor. He knew the jaw was broken, and he knew it needed resetting and probably wiring together. He also knew that whoever, or whatever, had hit him resembled nothing less than a sledgehammer.

They wrapped Mike in a blanket and helped him into the passenger seat of the jeep, and Ibrahim called a meeting to discuss the exasperating series of "accidents" that had taken place in the past few days. None of them understood what had happened because aside from this unknown assailant, no one was bothering them.

The Americans seemed completely unaware of their activities. Except for this raving lunatic running around in the dark flattening people.

There was no measurable danger, no set of rules, except to stay out of the farmyard after dark. Mike had offered no more clues than the other two, apart from saying there was a bright light shining directly into his eyes before he got hit, like he'd been hit by a car or a truck, and caught in the headlights.

But there were no cars or trucks on the farm. Someone had punched Mike to the ground. Either that or hit him with a club, or a baseball bat. But who? Who the hell waits around in the dark to whack people? Thieves? Robbers? It beat the hell out of Ibrahim.

What Ibrahim did know was that half the Muslim world was awaiting news of the forthcoming attack on the Great Satan. Everything was already in place: the time, the dates, the entry, the explosive, the staff, the communications. The project was long past the point of no return. It could not fail. This was the most momentous glory to Allah since 9/11, and he was the head of it, chosen by the Great Ones to take both Islamic and personal revenge on the Satan. For him, there must be rewards of an unfathomable nature, rewards that would one day be bestowed upon him by Allah Himself.

For he would ultimately cross the bridge, and the three trumpets would sound for him as he entered Paradise. The pleasures of the virgins would await him, and surely the Prophet himself would be there to welcome him home. Ibrahim had never been a seeker of personal glory, but now he stood on the threshold of either earthly glory or undying martyrdom.

Quite frankly, he preferred earthly glory, but martyrdom in the personal service of Allah was a rarified and exalted thing, and if he should be called upon to make that final and most glorious sacrifice, then he would walk willingly forward to serve his God. Meanwhile he intended to remain light on his feet, as it were, utilizing to the fullest his extremely sophisticated command of the English language perfected in the cafés around Harvard Square.

MACK BEDFORD'S REQUEST for high explosive was channeled through a convoluted chain of command. Benny Shalit passed it on to Johnny Strauss, who then passed it to his principal contact in the CIA, who alerted Captain Ramshawe, who put in the formal request to Admiral Mark Bradfield, the ex-Carrier Battle Group Commander, who now occupied the Chief of Naval Operation's chair in the Pentagon.

The CNO instantly flashed an encrypted signal to Rear Admiral Andy Carlow, Commander, SPECWARCOM, Coronado. He had it relayed on to the SEAL base at Virginia Beach, which sits on the Atlantic, east of the gigantic Norfolk Naval Base, with its four miles of waterfront on the Hampton Roads Peninsula.

Every one of those signals was marked FYEO. Every one of them was seen only by those of the highest possible rank. Even the president did not count; he stayed on the bench, out of the secret loop decreed by America's Security Chiefs.

The Norfolk base is home to seventeen U.S. Navy Strike-Fighter Squadrons, F/A-18 Hornets and Super Hornets, and is the sole East Coast Master Jet Base, having, in its time housed such tyrants of the U.S. air space as the fabled VF-101 Grim Reapers.

The base is on permanent standby for World War III, and Johnny Strauss's boxes suggested that might have already broken out, so urgent and intense was the packing and loading operation. When the two twenty-four-inch boxes were finally sealed, they were placed in the back of a jeep and driven instantly to the Norfolk Station airport, where a Naval aircraft was fired up and ready for takeoff.

The pilots were given the destination only after the boxes were loaded, and the flight took off to the southwest, banked hard to port, and headed north up the Atlantic, staying four or five miles offshore as they headed to the unobtrusive and relatively calm Westchester County Airport, thirty-three miles north of midtown Manhattan.

This second-line airfield, with its modest 6,500-foot runway, was originally built for the frontline air defense of New York City shortly after Herr Hitler declared on December 11, 1941, that the Reichstag was in a state of war with the United States of America. Since then, the U.S. armed services have always kept one foot in the Westchester operation, but not since Adolph became so openly disagreeable had such a state of pure military priority been announced both to the control tower and ground staff.

The Naval aircraft came in over the tall trees at the end of the Westchester runway and landed with the kind of practiced gentleness you need when you have a sizeable box of C-4 plastic explosive on board.

Four naval guards who had traveled with the cargo unloaded it and placed the boxes with great care in the rear section of Johnny Strauss's dark blue SUV, which was parked on the concrete apron, right behind the wing. It was 11:30 a.m., and Johnny Strauss and Benny Shalit still had more than a hundred miles in front of them.

Beyond the airport, they looped around two miles to pick up Route 684, and headed straight to the Connecticut border.

They pulled into the hotel parking lot at almost 2 p.m. Both men were starved; they hadn't stopped since their journey began at nine that morning.

Mack met them in the lobby and checked them in. He'd already ordered three steaks for lunch, but before they went to the dining room he helped them manhandle the three boxes out of the car and up to his room, since he did not want them unattended in a vehicle parked outside a hotel.

It was 3:30 before they checked the boxes for content. Everything was there, and some of it may not be necessary, but Mack had ordered an explosive package for all seasons. He'd thought of everything, and the three men sat in Mack's room and conducted a detailed briefing that lasted the rest of the afternoon.

The former SEAL had an unusual working knowledge of underwater demolition, and he knew how to set and detonate explosive charges of just about every possible description. All SEALs were demolition experts, but it was not such a refined course as that taught to members of the Mossad.

The fact was, the Israeli Secret Service regarded a stick of dynamite as their weapon of choice, and believed that all of Israel's major problems could be solved simply with high explosive. As the years had gone by, and Palestinian terrorists had become more and more daring and malevolent, the Mossad had fallen back on the fastest, most brutal and reliable form of attack.

Which was why Benny Shalit was about to become a cogwheel component of this Black Operation. His specialty was electronic detonation, a subject Mack Bedford had most certainly mastered but was not a world-class operator. Benny was just such a man.

He was a disciple of Meir Dagan, the small, taciturn former general who now headed up the Mossad. Dagan was a former Paratroop Brigade Commander, a veteran of all the conflicts, the Six-Day War, the Yom Kippur War, and the more recent battles with the trigger-happy rocket battalions of Hezbollah in the Lebanon. He'd fought in the desert, across the burning sands of the Sinai; he'd fought in the hills, on the Golan Heights.

He'd been awarded the Medal of Courage for his services two years *before* the Yom Kippur War had even started. And in that heartbreaking conflict, he'd fought with unbridled courage, shoulder to shoulder with his great friend Arik Sharon. Meir Dagan had spent almost a half-century defending the Jewish State, and Arik put him in charge of the Mossad.

One of his first recruitments was Colonel Benny Shalit. Within months they'd blasted four known terrorists to hell and back with violent bombings. They'd foiled three major Islamic attacks on the Israeli State. And in Damascus, they'd blown the top Hamas military strategist to smithereens with a car bomb. Unrepentant, Meir Dagan's Mossad blithely admitted what they'd done.

Somehow or other, the former general had given the most fearsome Secret Service in the world an even sharper killer edge. Young Colonel Shalit worshipped the ground upon which General Dagan walked. He placed him in the first rank of all-time Israeli commanders, as indeed did Arik Sharon. And he shared with him one shining philosophy: a skillfully rigged bomb is superior to all other weapons of limited destruction.

Such was the man who now moved into position as Mack Bedford's right hand. "Bomber Benny," as he would now be known, was no stranger to combat against Hezbollah and Hamas, but on an excitement scale of one to ten, this one had Benny running at around twelve.

He selected the C-4 explosives and held the nine-inch-long oblong-shaped cakes in his hand, weighing them without thinking, checking the brackets that would hold them, handling the brackets, examining the screws.

Benny spent even longer on the electronics, spreading the parts out on Mack's bed, stripping out the wires for length, testing the battery connections. "Better get this stuff in line," he said. "Don't want to be doing it tomorrow under pressure."

At the end of the afternoon they divided their tools and explosive into sections, packed everything away, and headed downstairs. They checked out the television evening news, and at 7:30 had dinner, during which Mack ate only an omelet.

At 10 p.m. they put on their parkas and took out the laptop in to the parking lot, where Benny loaded the software and tuned it to the wavelength of a small electronic device, which he had installed on the rear seat of Mack's Nissan. All three of them could see the green pattern of the screen's background and the steady sweep of the radar beam making its endless circular clockwise motion.

"Okay, we're hooked up to the satellites," said Benny. "Mack, why don't you take the vehicle about a mile away somewhere out toward the farm. And then call in on the cell."

Mack climbed in and set off, crossed the bridge and turned left, ran right past the farm entrance and pulled up a half-mile down the road. He called Benny's cell and was told, "Might as well go another couple of miles, then turn around and come back."

Mack did as he was told and headed right back to the hotel

parking lot, where he found Benny and Johnny right where he'd left them, staring at the screen.

"We're golden," said Benny. "Tracked you all the way out and all the way back. Wherever we put that little bug, it'll tune right in and show us where it is."

"Outstanding," said Mack. "Now I could use some sleep. Gotta be sharp tomorrow. You been up for almost twenty-four hours. Breakfast at ten?"

"Good call," said Benny. "See you then."

THURSDAY MORNING dawned brightly in northwest Connecticut, with a cloudless blue sky and the dazzling pale sunlight of mid-October. All seemed especially well in the world as the three secret vigilantes prepared to go to work—Mack Bedford to try to protect his country from further assault; Johnny Strauss to nail the killers who had already raised their swords against Israel; Benny Shalit to carry out the bidding of the vengeful Meir Dagan.

Their aims were diverse yet noble. Jointly noble. But unless these three separate men worked in perfect unison, the following day might live in history as a day of notoriety, when hundreds of innocent people would die.

All was most certainly not well with the world, and the bright sunshine of the day heralded a false dawn. A front was closing in from the southeast, directly off the Atlantic, and the forecast for tonight was, quite frankly, lousy.

All the men had seen the forecast for rain. They all had waterproof parkas and their boots would be fine, but they had only woolen hats, which would rapidly begin to feel like dead black sheep on their heads.

"We got two choices," said Mack. "We either get soaked crossing that field or we get some headgear. Maybe black sou'westers."

"Jesus we'd have to go to the coast, maybe Bridgeport or New Haven," said Strauss. "They're both darn near a hundred miles away."

"That's out of the question," replied Mack. "We can't split that

far apart from the op-area within ten or twelve hours of H-hour."
(*Military*: "H" for Hit.)

"No," said Benny, "but how about some of that sleek waterproof
stuff bikers wear? Black racers' hoods. There's gotta be a sports
shop in Torrington."

"That's the big idea of the day," said Mack.

"True genius has many outlets," confirmed Benny, modestly.

They decided to stick together because the plan called for such a
total level of cooperation, one missing person would put the entire
operation in danger. They drove swiftly into Torrington, where
they found a sports shop that specialized in mountainclimbing,
mountain biking, mountain hiking, and mountain camping.

They stocked enough black waterproof racing tops with hoods
to outfit the massed riders of the Tour de France for ten years. And
Benny bought himself a new pair of black calfskin gloves, so thin
and perfectly fitted they would have suited a brain surgeon. The
expedition took them only twenty minutes.

Mack wanted to make one more trip, across the street to the
hardware store. There he purchased four thick leather box handles
and steel brackets, along with three more flashlights and extra batteries, in case of a malfunction. He then had two more copies cut
of the keys to each of their vehicles.

It was after noon by the time they arrived back at the hotel.
They had another pot of coffee by the fire in the lounge, and went
into the dining room for lunch at 1:30 p.m. The waiter talked them
into fresh flounder, which he said had been landed in the small
hours of that morning in Stonington, the old Connecticut whaling
port up on the Rhode Island border.

"Three flounders, spinach, and fries," said Mack. "You got us."

All three of them laughed, a rare occurrence in these final
hours before the mission. Nerves were tightening, and all of them
knew it. Instinctively, each was just a tad more careful in what he
said to the others now. Jokes were welcome, but not at anyone else's
expense. Irony was fine, but it had to be humorous. Sarcasm was
not fine, and was more or less outlawed.

These unspoken sensitivities form the silent heart of all military black-operations, missions where men are going to the brink,
like tonight's, where all three could go down in a hail of machine
gunfire, out there in that frozen field north of Mountainside Farm.

The flounder was supreme, fresh as the waiter had promised,
and they returned to the fireside, each with a notebook in which his
personal tasks would be listed—the ones that could bring down the
mission if accomplished late, badly or, worse yet, forgotten. Mack
insisted each man also copy the others' duties, just in case they lost
someone. He then distributed the spare keys so that each had instant access to either of the vehicles, in case the regular driver was
shot or killed. That, of course, included himself.

As the hours went by, the tensions grew, and everyone pretended things were fine. Mack was worried about the weight of the
boxes on the long walk across the field, but to fix on the handles he
would have to drill noisily, and he could scarcely do that in the residents' lounge of the Blackberry River Hotel. Neither could he do it
in his room without someone thinking he was committing murder. But he didn't want to use up any battery power. He needed a
wall outlet to drill eight holes in the sides of the boxes—all this for
a couple of minutes' work. Damn.

In the end he decided on the bedroom, with a major diversion
outside in the corridor. Just before 5 p.m., he went to the maid's
station at the top of the stairs on the second floor and hauled out
the cart that contained jugs of ice water, bed linens and waste baskets. He pushed it toward No. 28, and then capsized the entire
thing with a crash of broken jugs, ice water, and God knows what
else.

The drill started instantly. Mack shot into his room and picked
up the phone, telling the receptionist something shocking had happened in the corridor right outside his room. She'd better send staff
and maybe come herself. He was uncertain what had happened.

Within moments there was chaos in the corridor. All twelve
members of staff on duty for the evening—maids, waiters, cooks,

kitchen hands, and the doorman—were up there, shouting, righting the cart, and clearing up the mess.

Benny Shalit's screaming electric drill went unnoticed as eight neat holes were bored into the boxes. And while the general panic in the corridor continued, Mack and his men screwed two leather handles onto each one. And they did not leave the room until peace was restored on the second floor of the Blackberry River Hotel.

On a normal night, all three of them would have found rich humor in the uproar Mack had caused. But not tonight. They each ate a light dinner, and hardly a word was spoken.

At 10:30 they emerged from their rooms, hoods down behind their shoulders, faces blackened with SEAL cammy cream, gloved hands carrying the boxes, the two fully loaded M4 light machineguns tucked into the wide leather belts, concealed under the parkas worn by Benny and Mack.

Just in case.

11

THEY CREPT THROUGH the upstairs corridors of the hotel like three cat-burglars, walking on tip-toe, peering around corners, making their stealthy way toward the rear door, carrying the boxes.

"What the hell do we do if someone comes out of one of these rooms?" asked Johnny.

"Blow his brains out," whispered Mack. "What else? I'm joking. We can tell 'em we're going to a costume ball dressed as urban spacemen."

"Urban what?" whispered Strauss.

"Shut up," said Mack, chuckling. "We're nearly there."

They made the parking lot without being seen by anyone. Mack insisted they all check their lists and their ignition keys for both vehicles. They loaded the boxes into the rear of Mack's Nissan, climbed in, and set off for the woods on the north side of the farm.

It was raining now, not hard, but sufficient enough to need the wipers. That was the bad news. The good news was there was no moon lighting up the black cloudy skies and the freezing wide field that lay before them.

The wind was just getting up from the squally weather front that had swept in off Long Island Sound, and Mack assessed it would drive straight into their faces as they traversed the field. He could feel the hard sou'wester faintly rocking the car as they drove across the river.

It was pitch dark as they edged into the copse on the far side of the road. With the headlights off, no one could see a thing, but there could be no flashlight used. They pulled up their hoods, hauled the boxes out of the rear door, and set off across the road.

On the plus side, the leather handles had made carrying the boxes much easier than Mack had imagined. He took the center spot, holding one handle in either hand. Benny was on the right, Johnny on the left as they walked line-abreast into the woods on the far side of the narrow road.

Right there they switched position, with Benny taking the center spot and Mack leading the way through the trees, which now loomed dimly in the dark like old friends marking his route to the field. When they reached the edge Mack ordered the boxes opened and most of the nails removed.

"We don't need to make a sound over there," he said. "Just leave the lids lightly tapped down so they come open without squeaking."

He stood up and trained his binoculars on the farmyard. He could see more activity than he had seen on previous nights. There were probably a dozen people moving around. All the outside lights were switched on, and so were the ones inside the wide-open barn.

"We better wait till that crowd thins out a little," Mack muttered. "They are all armed. And we don't know if they have night-glasses. If someone spotted us, it'd be like walking into the jaws of death."

"Screw that," said Johnny, mildly.

And so they waited. Eleven o'clock came and went. Twenty minutes later, they watched seven men leave the yard and return to the farmhouse. However, many of the ones who had been working in the barn were still there, and there was one guard standing outside the big wide doors.

It did occur to Mack that the right hook he'd landed on the guard's jaw the other night may have put them off the entire idea of a having night watchman. Unknowingly, he was right. None of Ibrahim's men had the slightest intention of sitting outside the front door of Mountainside Farm, in the dark, waiting for some crazed cage-fighter to show up probably baring his steel teeth, before putting yet another of them in intensive care. Fuck that.

They were brave, and they were prepared to lay down their lives for Allah and Islam. But not that brave. When the downstairs lights went out, and the senior staff retreated to bed, the night watchman would be back inside the front door. Fast.

Mack watched it happen. And from all the way across the field, he sensed the fear as the front door slammed shut suspiciously quickly, and the lights stayed out.

Now Mack and his troops picked up the boxes and set off across the cold, flat, windswept acres. Three of them abreast, cursing the rain—especially Mack, who had both hands full, and could not even wipe the water out of his eyes.

The field was growing muddy now, and their boots squelched on the soft slippery surface. To Mack they sounded like a trio of arctic sea lions splashing through the shallows. He hoped the guys in the barn stayed there.

They crept over the last hundred yards very slowly, crouched down, one hesitant step at a time. It seemed to take double the time he had spent crossing that field on his own over the hard crisp frost. Finally they made the shelter of the barn's rear wall, gratefully dropping their heavy load, getting their new bearings and taking a breath.

Mack looked around the corner into the yard and was surprised to see the outside lights were now off. In fact, the only lights he could see in the whole place were inside the barn. The bus motor was shut off, and the only sounds were metallic, perhaps tools being stored away. At five minutes before midnight, three men walked out of the barn and turned off the lights. One of them pulled shut the big doors, hooked the padlock into the chain, snapped it closed, and locked it with the key. Mack saw him take the key out and drop it into his pocket. So did Benny, who muttered, "Christ!" under his breath, "How do we get in?"

Mack did not answer as they watched the barn workmen cross the yard in the phosphorescence of the rain and disappear through the front door. No more lights went on.

They waited five more minutes, and then Mack edged around the wall, took out his personal key, and unlocked the doors, holding them a couple of feet apart and letting his team in. He also seized the chain and padlock, and took them both with him. There were three reasons for this: he could throttle someone with the chain, fracture someone's skull with the heavy padlock, and if he had the locking mechanism, no one could imprison them in the barn.

Once inside they went to work, carrying the boxes into the straw enclosure and placing them at the far side of the bus. Mack ripped off the lids and shone his flashlight in, while Benny pulled out the cakes of C-4 explosive, which he had already taped together into eight sets of four. Plus two bundles of dynamite.

Benny rolled under the bus with the tape and the brackets. Mack positioned two flashlights to shine with maximum illumination for Benny. As needed, he passed him the big screws, the screwdriver, and the electric drill.

Johnny Strauss, his machine gun drawn, climbed into the bus and counted the boxes containing what he knew were packed bags of high-explosive, the ammonium nitrate Mack had smelled so clearly last time he was here.

He exited the bus, leaned down, and told Benny the entire bomb cargo was stacked in the rear half. He heard the Mossad hero scuffle back a couple of feet on the stone floor beneath the bus, and he heard the crackle of the duck tape as the Israeli ripped it off, cutting sections with a knife, lashing his own private bomb into a shape of maximum upward-blasting efficiency.

At this point Johnny took up his station inside the enclosure, standing watch over the narrow entrance between the front straw bales.

"Someone comes in here, blow him away," whispered Mack. "We might have to abort the mission, but you miss the guy, and we're all dead. There's too many of 'em."

"Mack, old buddy, I'm a former infantry officer in the Israeli Defense Force. I'm a Mossad assassin. We don't miss, okay? I've never missed. That's why I'm still breathing."

Mack laughed quietly. And Benny called back from under the bus. "Okay, guys, start handing me the electronics. It's gonna take the biggest part of an hour. Lemme have the box and the brackets first, and I need help. Mack, get under here yourself, will you?"

It was pitch dark in the barn, and the rain beat down upon the corrugated tin roof. The only light in the entire place was from the flashlights aimed under the bus, and they sent a ghostly refracted glow out along the straw bales. Beyond that, in the rest of the area, there was only darkness.

Mack rolled underneath, taking the two flashlights with him to direct the light better onto the precise section Benny was working. Benny was aiming the drill and when he hit the start button, it screamed to life. It then screamed even louder when he drove a bore-hole into a steel strut beneath the fuselage of the bus.

"Fuck me!" breathed Mack. *"They could hear that sonofabitch in Torrington."*

The drill stopped and all three men stopped breathing, afraid that the front door of the house would somehow catapult open and ten crazed terrorists would come rushing to the barn.

"Wasn't too bad out here," hissed Johnny from beyond the

bales. "The straw really muffled it. From outside the barn walls it would be even softer, and inside the house, I bet you could hardly hear anything."

"Darned near deafened me," said Mack.

"Don't worry about it," replied Benny, "I'm only going to do it three more times—for the moment."

"Jesus Christ," said Mack.

Benny hit the start button, and under the bus Mack nearly had a heart attack. The drill shrieked, bored into the metal, leaving a neat, clean, round hole.

"Beautiful," whispered Benny.

The actual drilling had taken only fifteen seconds each time, and Johnny again confirmed the straw had deadened the sound brilliantly. What none of them knew, however, was that Mountainside Farm was not quite as sleepy as it appeared.

IN IBRAHIM'S LARGE BEDROOM, on the south side of the house, there was a major strategy meeting in progress. The boss had just asked for a copy of the Canaan Academy floor plan, and Ben al-Turabi couldn't find it.

"Damn," he said, "I must have left it in the darned bus."

"What the hell was it doing in the bus?" Ibrahim wanted to know.

"I took it over this evening, while I was on guard duty," replied the tall Palestinian terrorist. "In case anyone's forgotten, I'm hauling the first two bomb cases into the school and they're both marked 'Coffee.' I just wanted to check the layout one more time, from my entrance door on the side, to the kitchen area."

"Well you'd better go out and get it, since you're the only one who knows where it is."

"Okay, boss," replied al-Turabi. "Be right back."

Ben was annoyed with the way Ibriham had spoken to him and he decided he'd take his own sweet time going back out into the freezing night. So he made two stops on the way to the front door. The first was at the bathroom; the second at the kitchen, where he filled the big kettle and put in on the stove. Then somewhere a phone rang, but Ben couldn't find it before grabbing the door handle and heading out to get the map.

UNDER THE BUS, Benny Shalit had just connected the batteries, and a tiny red light was blinking intermittently on the detonator. The Mossad man pushed it aside for a few moments while he stripped some electric cable ends and wound them onto the power pack terminals. Right at this moment, Ben al-Turabi slammed the front door, wind-assisted.

The pounding rain was drowning out some sound, but Johnny Strauss almost had a stroke when he heard footsteps approaching. With supreme presence of mind Johnny pulled the door tight shut, wheeled back through the straw gap, and hissed, "Mack, Mack! someone's coming, heading straight for the barn."

The ex-SEAL team leader never hesitated with his commands. "Benny, clear the decks—get the tools and equipment under the bus. Johnny, grab a box and get on station at the back-end, behind the luggage trunk. Stay concealed and don't take him out unless you have to. Knife, not gun."

Mack himself switched off the two flashlights, stood up, and hauled the second box back to the wall, out of sight. Now he could hear someone trying to open the barn door, which would not have provided much of a challenge since the padlock and chain were in Mack's pocket.

Whoever was coming in had a flashlight and did not bother to turn on the two bulbs that lit the barn, poorly, from the center of the ceiling. Mack rolled silently under the yellow school bus. The intruder stepped through the door, leaving it swinging open in the rain.

Mack just hoped to God the new arrival was not the man who

had finally locked that door when the shift was over. Because, if so, *he would surely notice the fucking chain and padlock were no longer there.*

There'd been few breaks on this night. But right now they had one. The big ex-Guantanamo Bay goalkeeper had left early, and had not the slightest idea whether the barn had been secured by padlock or not.

He didn't notice and didn't care. He just wanted to find the stupid architectural floor plan, shove it under his coat, and get the hell out of this freezing farm building, back to the house for a cup of coffee, and a couple of the sweet Iranian pastries Faisal al-Assad had given them.

All three of the saboteurs heard Ben al-Turabi slouch across the stone floor to the straw entrance. Behind the bus Johnny could see him, flashlight in his right hand, machine gun slung over his back, a position that would render him at least seven seconds late with his first shot, if Johnny had to kill him.

Then, to his horror, he noticed that the tiny flickering light on Benny's equipment was casting a red glow on the floor about five feet back from the main automatic doors. He dared not shout a command, nor even an alert. Mack and Benny could see al-Turabi's feet, and one of his leather shoes was actually reflecting the red glow every time it flickered. Benny could not reach it, and neither could Mack, but Mack had managed to lunge sideways to block the menacing glow with a couple of fingers.

Al-Turabi had noticed nothing as he climbed into the bus and clumped around inside, shining his light around until he found the floor plan on the wide armrest next to the driver's seat. He folded it a couple of times, pushed it under his jacket, and left, carefully closing the door behind him, leaving the barn precisely as he had found it.

For three minutes no one moved or spoke. Mack kept his fingers over the flickering lightbulb and the only sound was the rain pelting down on the cold tin roof.

Benny was back into action first, fixing the electronics to the underside of the central area of the fuselage. Every now and then he would issue a curt instruction to Mack. *Gimme six more feet of that wire, the thin black one. Strip the ends for me, will you? Small screwdriver, Mack. Duct tape, cut me four feet. Okay, large battery. That should do it.*

It was now twelve minutes after 1 a.m. on Friday morning—Abraham's Day at Canaan Academy—and Benny Shalit was done. Except he had one worry. "Mack," he said, "I'm concerned about the strength of that steel floor above our bomb, because it stands between us and the massive amount of explosive stacked inside the bus. I've done everything I can to 'shape' the charge, making it blast upward, but I'm still afraid that floor might provide too much of a shield."

"Christ, Benny, I don't want to take any chances like that," replied Mack. "Any thoughts?"

"I was thinking of drilling up through the floor again, and connecting their bomb cases directly to our dynamite, which will explode instantly."

"Det-cord?" said Mack.

"Precisely. We got a good-sized roll of it in that box back there, and it just gives us that one edge that makes us foolproof. When those bundles of dynamite blow, they will fire the det-cord, which I'm gonna feed right into four of their boxes."

"Okay, buddy. Let's go. How long?"

"I'd say twenty minutes."

"Where d'you want me?"

"Right next to the bus, holding the cord, the knife, and the duct tape. Just keep handing the stuff to me. I'm gonna drill through the floor and then through the wooden base of the packing cases."

"Jesus, don't drill right into the sacks of ammonium nitrate," said Mack. "Heat sets 'em off."

"Right now, Lt. Commander, you are telling God how to open the Pearly Gates."

Mack laughed as the Israeli slid back underneath the bus, and Mack and Johnny held their breath every time he unleashed the drill, boring straight through the floor of the bus, and up into the wood cases. Four times he drilled, and four times the steel tip drove into the cases above.

Then Benny made one of his most dangerous requests. "Get in the bus, Mack," he said. "When I feed the det-cord through make sure it goes into the small hole, bottom of the crate. I'll finish down here, then I'll come up and help."

His last request was four fifteen-foot lengths of the military's favorite explosive, the stuff that burns along at two miles every three seconds. And while Johnny and Mack began to clear up, Benny attached the det-cord to the chassis, and threaded it up through the tiny holes he had made, right into the bus.

By the time he emerged from the underside of the bus, the place was almost ship-shape. The boxes were neatly stowed with the residue of the saboteur's gear, and they were much lighter. But they still had to be carried away.

Benny and Mack climbed into the bus and Mack heaved the bottom cases upward, while his buddy shoved the det-cord right into the base, through the holes he had bored, to rest about a hundredth of an inch from the high explosive, inside the box.

They gathered at the door, and the little electronic power-indicator flickered cheerfully beneath the school bus, casting a soft, triumphant glow on their skill and daring. Mack hoped to hell that big fella with the goddamned flashlight would not show up again during the night.

Holding the remains of their work in the boxes, they slipped out into the rain, hoods up. Mack refitted the chain on the barn door, and turned the key in the padlock. And they set off across the field, walking through the mud, each of them content with their efforts.

Mack had just one last question. "Benny," he said, "what would happen if that guy did go back to the bus. If he did see the active red light, found it our little gift, and their expert tried to dismantle it?"

"That wouldn't be good," said Benny the Bomber. "Not for them."

"What d'you mean?"

"I booby-trapped it good," replied Meir Dagan's right-hand man. "Anyone lays a finger on that device, the whole lot will go up like Nagasaki—bus, barn, and farmhouse. No survivors. Probably better for everyone."

"Perhaps," said Mack, "But not really. Because if that happened, the police would be out looking for a culprit. If our plan works they will not do that. Because the terrorists will plainly have suffered a malfunction in the course of their evil actions. Blew themselves up by mistake, eh? It's happened before."

IBRAHIM SPREAD OUT the school floor plan and, as an afterthought, called Ben al-Turabi over and checked he had locked the barn. He knew the Palestinian was a very focused killer, but matters he considered trivial were inclined to go by the board.

"You lock up after you left the barn?"

"Wasn't locked, boss. I left it like I found it."

"What do you mean, not locked? I did it myself when we left. With the key."

"I didn't see the lock," said Ben.

Ibrahim thought al-Turabi was a kind of a whacko much of the time. And he just said, "Asif, go and check the barn's locked up, will you?"

And three minutes later, the former bin Laden hit-man, now living in the United States, was back.

"Barn's locked, chief," he said. "Regular chain and padlock, like always. Couldn't open it. No problem."

Ibrahim glanced around for Ben al-Turabi, couldn't see him, and rolled his eyes heavenward. "And stay out of the pastry tin," he called out. "You're getting heavy."

Back at the Nissan, Benny fired up the computer, shoving the special plug into the Titan's electric socket. The radar screen came on, and two small lights flashed to confirm the satellite connection. Three miles away, and Benny could "see" the bus as if it were right in front of him.

"You beautiful little thing," he muttered, as the radar sweep began. Mack backed out of the woods and onto the dark, deserted lane. They crept back into the hotel about ten minutes later, transporting their gear in the boxes.

There wasn't a sound in the sleepy hotel as Mack opened the back door and they crept along the upstairs corridor into their rooms. They would shower and change, but there would be little sleep for anyone this night. They needed to keep track of that atom bomb of a school bus every minute. While Mack did not expect it to move much before 10 a.m., this was a chance he could not afford to take. They would work two-hour shifts, with two on duty while the other one slept. All the while they would keep an eye on the radar and on the GPS locater.

Mack and Johnny took the first shift, watching the screen until 4 a.m. They observed no movement on the farm. The radar scarcely varied except for the occasional automobile on the road. When Benny took over for Johnny, there wasn't much to see either. At 6 a.m., Mack finally rested for a couple of hours, until breakfast was ordered and delivered to the room.

All the while they watched the screen, and the bus never moved.

BY NINE THE NEXT MORNING, all ten of Ibrahim's soldiers were ready. Most were armed with automatic pistols, which had arrived with the ammonium nitrate. But every one of them was armed with an AK-47 slung across his shoulder like a Mexican bandit. Ibrahim lined them up in the barn, in military formation, two rows of five. Each man wore regular civilian clothes, shirts with a collar and a tie. But each man wore a long, dark blue work-coat, with a name stitched on to the left chest pocket in white letters. An American name, like Skip, Fred, Charlie, Frank, Ray, or Richie.

The assault team leader, now with a full black beard and full authority, spoke to them formally, and he told them their plan had been prepared and strategically perfected very brilliantly. So far there had been no major problems, and it was the will of Allah that they would go in with their courage high, and carry out the attack, which may very well drive the Great Satan out of the Middle East forever.

"To you alone will there be glory on this great day," he said. "You alone will be remembered in all of our history. School children in Saudi Arabia, Pakistan, Afghanistan, Iran and Iraq, Syria and Lebanon, will learn of your triumph for decades to come.

"You will be remembered as the Holy Warriors who followed in the teaching and footsteps of the Great Osama. You will touch Allah with immortality. For there is but one God. And that God is Allah . . ."

And all ten responded, "Allah is Great. And He alone will lead us to the light."

"Gentlemen," said Ibrahim, "many of us have spent long years in captivity. Many of us have been tortured and humiliated. Our religion has been kicked aside, our beliefs scorned, our faith challenged. We have borne witness to the insults made against the Prophet, and to the Koran, which contains his sacred words.

"But today is the Day of our Revenge. Allah has decreed this shall be our Day. American blood will be spilled, as ours has been spilled. Allah has sworn that revenge shall be ours: that our enemies shall lie dead at our feet. Allah has given us *THIS DAY!*"

And Ibrahim's voice rose as he bellowed: "DEATH TO THE INFIDEL! DEATH TO THE INFIDEL!"

And the Holy Warriors raised their AK-47s above their heads, and they chorused together: "DEATH TO THE INFIDEL! ALLAH IS GREAT!"

Ibrahim paced in front of them and began to speak more calmly. "My brothers," he said, "when this mission was planned, we had hoped it could be modeled on the great triumph of the departed Islamic commander Shamil Basayev, he of the immortal brotherhood of the Riyadus-Salikhin Reconnaissance.

"Never forget their mission was financed and trained by al-Qaeda, and they held the great Russian Army at bay for three days in their own town of Beslan. They stormed and then dominated the school, and then the town. No military operation since 2001 ever brought such endless glory upon our jihadist revolution. Or such world attention."

Ibrahim allowed the words to sink in. And then he said, "We had thought it a dress rehearsal, that we might one day copy the plan. But increased U.S. security has made that impossible. Today we must fight as a smaller, yet equally well-armed force. We could not place a reconnaissance team in the school, and neither can we storm it.

"But much has been learned and perfected. It was the high explosive that conquered Beslan. And the high explosive will bring down Canaan.

"The objective, as before, is the total destruction of the school and everyone in it. Students, teaching staff, and parents. All of them will be Americans, many of them sons of the great Wall Street financial families. As an added bonus, most of them will be Zionists."

Ibrahim pointed out that the mission was a little more than an hour from start time. And he added, "As before we have selected the day when the school will be most crowded. In Beslan it was the first day of the autumn semester.

"At Canaan Academy, it will be Abraham's Day, when the Zionists honor the founding father of Israel. You have all studied the operational plan, and you all know the two entry doors we will use. The school bus will not look in any way suspicious, and we will pull up on the edge of the circle with the bus facing down that north side of the school."

At this point, for emphasis, Ibrahim flourished the school architectural plan and pointed to the wide concrete area that led to a double swing door at the side of the school.

"This one is always open," he said. "But the second door, about fifty feet further along may be shut. Not locked, but closed in cold weather. Like now. Our first handcart, with two crates on board, will go straight to that door, pushed by Fred and Charlie.

"The second handcart, pushed by Joe and Skip, will have three boxes on board. They will go directly in through the first door, and turn right down that corridor. At the end they will find the dining room, walk straight across it to the serving area on the left, and unload their three boxes. They will place one box under the back stairs, and the other two, labeled 'Flour' and 'Sugar,' outside the kitchen door."

Someone asked if there was any possibility they may be challenged?

"Absolutely not," said Ibrahim. "You look like delivery men, and you will be acting like delivery men. And anyway, the entire faculty at this time will be in the assembly hall for the start of the morning choral concert."

"But what if someone asked where the hell we thought we were going? What if some parent gets suspicious and calls security?"

"That, my dear Ben," said Ibrahim, "is the beauty of this operation. Like most American schools, there is no security. That is why the Great Ones chose this place.

"However, each of you will have your rifle tucked into your belt beneath your left arm, barrel pointed downward. Should you be challenged, you will draw it, and shoot down the person instantly. Remember they will all die anyway."

Abu Hassan Akbar, aka "Joe," liked that part. He raised his Kalashnikov and confirmed their creed, "DEATH TO THE INFIDEL!"

Ibrahim, despite his calm and calculating demeanor, wanted to tell the ridiculous little killer to shut up, but at this stage that might have seemed sacrilegious. He nodded only an affirmation of Abu's natural aggression.

"You will have noticed," he continued, "that we differ from Beslan in one very special way. Shamil Besayev felt the need to storm the school and capture it. That got them world headlines. But it was the destruction of the school, the enormous death toll, which earned them immortality.

"Changing circumstances in America's *national* security have forced us to refine our plan. But the Great Ones may have reached those conclusions alone. Thus our mission is sharp-pointed, focused. And our aim is clear—the total destruction of the school.

"We have dispensed with the more colorful aspects of Beslan, the recce team in School Number One all summer, the spectacular forced entry, the glory of watching the Russians squirm before us, the standoff where our Muslim brothers held all the cards.

"No, my brothers. We do not require any of that. Just the elimination of more than a thousand United States citizens. That will bring us all the glory we need."

Ibrahim called for questions. And there was only one, from Yousaf Mohammed. "I accept that the first two handcarts will go into the school without causing attention," he said. "But will it not seem strange to see seven more cases being unloaded from the school bus, right outside the building, by a group of men all dressed the same?"

"It might," replied Ibrahim. "But there will be no one outside on that north wall. Any late arrivals will be hurrying in through the front door. We will have four men on the carts, four more will enter the school to help with our unloading and box placement. Our final two men, 'Joe' and 'Fred' will be pulling the crates out of the bus."

"And should anyone stray down that north side?" asked Yousaf.

"Shoot them, on sight."

THE BUS HAD NOT MOVED one inch by nine o'clock, and Johnny Strauss was about ready to leave. It had long been agreed that the two Special Forces men, Mack and Benny, would operate the business end of the operation, and that Johnny Strauss, New

York terrorist hunter, would make a photographic dossier of everyone involved. At the end of the mission, Johnny wanted to know precisely who was dead and who was alive. He wanted pictures of suspects. He wanted clear prints of everyone who came to Mountainside that morning, and everyone who left. Not to mention those who came back.

His weapon of choice was a thirty-year-old Canon given him by a newspaper photographer friend. It had a fabulous Long-Tom zoom lens, not too big and easily focused. Johnny's buddy swore to God he shot the *Jerusalem Post*'s front-page spread of the assassination attempt on Pope John Paul II in St. Peter's Square in 1981 on that very camera.

Right now the Canon, loaded with new black-and-white film, was in its leather bag in Johnny's SUV. He would develop the pictures himself in the basement of Banda Fine Arts.

They shook hands before he left and wished each other luck, and then Johnny was gone, directly to the wooded entrance of Mountainside Farm, where he would conceal himself in the dense trees across the narrow road. The other two had another cup of coffee and kept on watching the screen. The bus still had not moved.

Mack and Benny were ready, organized to the smallest degree. The Nissan was waiting in the parking lot, and the portable detonator was on a hair-trigger once it was switched on. Just so long as that little red light on the other detonator kept flashing under the yellow school bus.

INSIDE THE ACADEMY there was a kind of controlled chaos. Everyone understood where they should be, where they wanted to be, and where their offspring wanted them to be. Sometimes these three separate objectives came together as one. But mostly not, and the school corridors seethed with activity as parents and students made for the assembly hall and the school staff did what they could to guide their gigantic flock.

The school secretary, Ms. Marie Calvert, had already been in touch with the Torrington Police Department, to check the arrival of the cruiser that customarily parked at the main gate. This was mostly to prevent traffic queues, but also to check out arrivals, and to direct obvious commercial traffic to the school's east gate, across the playing fields.

Officer Tony Marinello was already ensconced at the entrance with a checklist in his hand, informing him that all attending parents would have little green stickers featuring the Star of David on their windshields. All three of the school's yellow buses would be arriving, two of them with visiting choirs, and one of them from the Yale Choral Society, which was shortly coming in from New Haven.

There was no foot traffic, and Tony was directing newcomers straight up the school drive, where the playing fields on the left near the main building were being used as runoff parking lots.

All school festival days attract heavy traffic, but a big country boarding school where so few of the students have parents anywhere near the place brings another dimension to the word travel. Hundreds of people were arriving from miles and miles away, tired, irritable, just wanting to park, get out, and find a cup of coffee. Some arrived early, before 8:30 a.m. Others thought they were running late and that events would start without them. And in the middle of all this, Officer Marinello had his work cut out to keep a semblance of order.

Two of the school buses were in before 9:15, and the Eli's showed up ten minutes later. Tony Marinello waved them through, acknowledging two of the drivers he saw quite often locally. Right now he was sending a big white laundry van around to the east gate. Along the road there was a line of cars building, waiting for him to remove the single red traffic cone he was using for flow control. Tony took his duties very seriously, no matter how small, or insignificant, they may have seemed.

At the age of twenty-eight, he was one of the most ambitious police officers in the entire state, and his diligence had already been no-

ticed by his local commanding officers. He read the newspapers as-
siduously, and, unlike many of his colleagues, he understood the true
significance of Canaan Academy. Tony understood, because he had
made it his business to find out. He had that kind of mind, the kind
all police officers should have, the kind that would surely take him
right to the top of his chosen profession.

What he had seen when first he had passed this way was a
grandiose entrance, the black iron gates, the stone lions, the manicured lawns, and beyond, a building that looked, from here, like a
summer residence for King Henry VIII and all his wives. Tony,
who was, at the time, in the process of certification from the Connecticut Police Academy in Meriden, swiftly worked out that
somewhere, somehow, millions and millions of dollars were required to run this place. And he researched the life out of Canaan
Academy, in the end understanding that this was the nursery for
great Wall Street minds.

Future heads of legendary Wall Street investment banks were in
attendance here. Sons and grandsons of men who had run fabled
banks like Goldman Sachs, Lehman Brothers, Lazards, JP Morgan,
and the New York Stock Exchange, were studying at the end of that
long, tree-lined drive.

By the time he was through, Tony Marinello appreciated precisely the meaning of educational establishments like Canaan.
And his further general knowledge of the international situation
was also impressive. He understood the threats and hatreds that
were often directed at the Israeli nation. He'd read the words of
that maniac who somehow ran the Islamic Republic of Iran. And
he knew there were many Arab countries that wished Israel would
cease to exist.

To Tony that meant a lot of extra vigilance whenever he was
dealing with anything with Jewish connotations. He believed there
were dangers lurking everywhere. And he was a police officer in
the United States, serving in the Great State of Connecticut, the
Constitution State. It was his duty to be alert.

To many of his colleagues, this early morning task in the middle of nowhere would have been regarded as nothing more than a pain in the ass. To Tony it was an honor. Here he was, in command of the main gate to the academy, trusted by the school and by his superiors to guard the students and protect their interests. Tony Marinello took it all extremely seriously. He moved the traffic cone and he waved the automobiles through, and he watched the windshields for the stickers.

IT WAS AFTER 9:30 and as of yet, no vehicle had left Mountainside Farm. Johnny Strauss was stationed in deep thicket, camouflaged by an autumn-red bush, surrounded by undergrowth and trees. It would have taken two men with three tracker dogs to find him.

The trusty and historic Canon with its zoom-lens was protected in its soft-leather case, and Johnny was scanning that wide, wooded area on the opposite side of the road all around the rough entrance to the farm, watching for vehicles making their exit. But he was also sweeping the area, checking for human presence in the trees. He was already on his guard, but he needed to know if he had an enemy right across the street. So far he had seen nothing.

He took a couple of shots of the woodland, and put in a call on his cell to Mack to find out if anything had shaken loose. But there was nothing yet. The electronics under the bus were all still active, but nothing had moved. And Strauss told Mack he had not seen anyone, either on foot or in a vehicle. There was not much to do except wait.

AT 9:45 IBRAHIM ordered his team to start moving the straw bales that formed the front wall of the "shoebox." Most put down their rifles to begin the heavy lifting. In teams of two they hauled the bales down and dropped them on the floor, where four more guys stacked them on a cart and dragged them to the end of the barn, eight at a time.

It was hard to accept how heavy straw bales could be. Every time Ben al-Turabi hoisted one up onto the stack, he swore to God someone had filled it with cement. It took fifteen minutes to remove the wall.

Ibrahim now spoke for the first time this morning about the getaway plan. "All of our explosive will be detonated simultaneously, by me," he said. "Each box has a timed detonator, which has been adapted to receive an electronic impulse. The device was made by one of our Boston Sleeper Cells.

"The detonators have been extensively tested, and a sensor on each box is individually programmed to receive the signal. I will not detonate until every last one of you is out of the building. When the last box is in place inside the academy, you are to make a very fast exit. Do not draw your weapons unless you have to."

Ibrahim's instructions were to use the first door, because he would be outside in the pickup truck they'd been using all week. "By now the bus will have moved, up to the East gate, and you will pile into the rear of the truck.

"We will all drive together to the east gate. Abu will take the wheel, and I will detonate the bombs as soon as we are a hundred and fifty yards beyond the school walls. By then we will be traveling at sixty miles per hour, or thirty yards per second. Take into account the five-second delay on the remote control and that puts us three hundred yards clear when the bombs explode. We reach the bus thirty seconds later; everyone boards it and hits the deck."

"How long before the police arrive at the school in force?"

"Probably fifteen minutes. They have to come from Torrington."

"Where will we be at that point?"

"Probably approaching a little town called Sheffield to our north, over the border in Massachusetts. It's the only town around there with a fast stretch of highway, about five miles long. Get us some distance. And get us out of Connecticut."

"Who'll be driving?"

"I will," replied Ibrahim.

The men now began to move toward the bus, and Ibrahim

spoke to them one last time. "You are all highly trained. Most of you have attended the camps in Pakistan, masterminded by the Glorious Osama. So make him proud of you, my brothers. And remember, your destiny is controlled by Allah alone. And Allah is great."

Abu Hassan Akbar put on his bus driver's cap and climbed into the driver's seat. The rest followed in single file, sitting mostly on the floor. Ben al-Turabi sat on a seat next to Abu, who now started the engine and drove through the barn doors and into the farmyard. He hit the button to close the doors and revved the engine.

MACK SAW THE TRACKER dot move for the first time on the screen. It was only about an eighth of an inch, but Mack was watching. He leapt to his feet, and exclaimed, "That's it, Benny. That bus just left the barn."

They unhooked the computer, closed the lid, and headed out to the parking lot. Everything they needed was in the Nissan, and they were on their way within seconds, Mack at the wheel.

Benny sat in the back seat with the open computer, and before they reached the car-park exit, he said, "The bus is moving, down the drive toward the road. They're about three miles behind us right now. Hit it, Mack."

The Nissan swerved right at the road, and Mack drove along toward the school. But a half-mile before he got there, he turned hard right, and then took a long left sweep through the woods, and came out on the northeast side of the school fields. They were looking straight across flat, mown grass, about two hundred yards to the main building.

JOHNNY STRAUSS HEARD the school bus rumbling down the drive long before he saw it. Thirty yards before it reached the road, he started shooting, and in the bright morning light, he caught a set of brilliant photo portraits of both Abu Hassan Akbar and Ben al-Turabi.

They turned left at the gateposts, and Johnny shot them again, now from quite close range. There was no doubt in his mind who was in charge of that bus—they were the two serial killers of the Netanya Hotel and the Be'er Sheba bar mitzvah.

Right behind the bus came another vehicle, a kind of ramshackle farm truck, covered in mud with a lot of dents. He was almost certain it was the same one Mack had noted a few days previously. But he shot a good one of its registration, just to check.

He also shot excellent pictures of both men in the front seats, front- and side-on. The driver was Ibrahim Sharif and the passenger Yousaf Mohammed, although neither man was known to him personally. But again, Johnny had been looking at that set of prison prints from Guantanamo for so long, he felt like he knew them. This time, however, there was a problem. The driver was fully bearded, and despite sensing it was the once clean-shaven Ibrahim from the photographs, Johnny could not be a hundred percent certain it was him.

Still, he believed these were the guys Mack Bedford was after—Ibrahim and Yousaf. And he called the former SEAL commander right away, just to let him know the line-up; to let him know the two men he wanted most were not on the bus. And that one of them had grown a full beard since the Guantanamo pictures.

Mack was not pleased. And Johnny Strauss, the King Terrorist Hunter, felt obliged to remind him, "In my game, you just gotta tell it like it is."

"Bullshit," replied Mack ungraciously. "When you're talking to me, tell it like I want to hear it!"

And they both laughed, despite everything.

MEANWHILE, Benny had the radar positioned on a low tree branch, hooked up to a power-pack, and sweeping the grounds of Canaan Academy like a beached Navy destroyer. Traffic had virtually ceased since the first concert was about to begin, and the school orchestra was tuning up.

There was no one else on the road, which meant there were no "paints" whatsoever on the screen, just that familiar "ping" as the arm swept around. Mack and Benny were laying low, literally hunkered down against the tree, waiting for the action to begin.

Across the field, Mack could see the three yellow school buses he'd spotted on his visit with the headmaster. As he stared at them through his binoculars, he wondered if they had been out this morning.

Benny was holding onto the remote control as if it contained his own heart. Like Johnny, he wanted Ben al-Turabi and Abu Hassan Akbar a lot more than he wanted the other two ex-prisoners. And he knew his prime targets, the scum who had massacred Israeli women and children, were on that school bus. Which, in his opinion, could not survive the next ten minutes.

ABU CHANGED GEAR and aimed the bus over the Blackberry River. Four minutes later he came roaring past the hotel, headed for the front gates of the academy, where Officer Tony Marinello was still on duty.

Inside the bus, everyone except Abu was crouched down on the floor as low as possible, under the seats if necessary. Anywhere to stay out of the sight of any guards or police officers who might be at the gates to the school.

Abu Hassan was giving a running commentary of their position. "Okay, we are about one mile from the main gates now. There is hardly any traffic, but I'm going to slow down at the school road signs and make our approach at twenty miles an hour."

Moments went by before Abu spoke again: "I can see a police cruiser ahead at the gates. But I don't see a policeman. I intend to drive straight in, so you'll feel a lurch as we swing right when we get there. If the officer signals me to stop, I will pretend not to see him, and carry on, straight up the drive.

"Like Ibrahim says, this bus has a Canaan sign above my seat, and it looks very official. I'm trying to look as if I'm just going home. And you will be the same, just regular delivery men going about your ordinary work."

NOW SITTING in his cruiser just outside the entrance of the school, Tony Marinello could see a fourth school bus of the day driving toward him along Route 44. He didn't pay it much mind, though, until he noticed its turn signal flashing. Seconds before the bus made a right turn onto the school grounds, the driver raised his right hand in a brief wave of recognition. Tony nodded and raised his left, returning the gesture.

But something wasn't quite right here. He reached up to his checklist that he'd jammed into the visor above the steering wheel. Three buses, not four.

Tony thought maybe there was a screw-up—that Ms. Calvert had written three but meant four. He decided to call it in.

Captain "Buzzy" Hannon came on the line. "Hi, Tony. What's up?"

"Sir, I got a slight discrepancy here. I'm at the gates of the academy, and my list shows three school buses scheduled to enter the premises. A fourth just drove in, and I just want to check that's a list inaccuracy."

"Hang on. Let me check mine," he said, and there was a short pause. Then he spoke again. "Looks like I'm also showing only three school buses. Why don't you go check it out. Take a drive up to the school office."

"What if I find something? What if it's an illegal bus? Can I demand to search it?"

"It won't be, kid. But, if it is, and you have suspicions, call in for backup. I just don't want any heroics in the environment of a school, hear me?"

"Don't worry, sir. I won't frighten the kids."

Officer Marinello slipped off the handbrake and headed through the gates and up the long drive to the main buildings.

THERE WAS A five-miles-an-hour speed limit on the school drive and Abu Hassan did not plan to break it, nor commit any other faux pas, which might draw attention to his bus. Nor did he think much of the police car about a hundred yards behind him.

This was the first time the hit men had been alone. Ibrahim and Yousaf had swung the old Dodge truck off to the right. They planned to take the scenic route and enter through the east gate, rendezvousing with the bus somewhere along the north wall of the main building later.

Abu Hassan Akbar checked his watch and tried to gauge time and distance to the target parking spot. He was on the straight part of the drive now and he guessed it was around six hundred yards to the main door. He called out a new bulletin to the nine men cramped down on the floor.

"We're about four minutes out," the veteran Palestinian merchant of death estimated. "Start preparing to get out. Fred and Charlie first. Joe and Skip next. Handcarts in the trunk."

And then he took a piece of paper from his pocket and began to read the words Ibrahim had said *must* be the last words they heard before going into action: "This is from our leader," he told them, keeping one eye on the road ahead as he read. "We are only moments from staging the World Trade Center all over again," he began. "That was the greatest of all missions, and it is the one we have waited so many years to repeat. Because that was the mission that terrified the Great Satan.

"And now the fate of Islam lies in your hands, and I know you will not let anyone down. You have the courage. You have the skills. And you fight under the banner of Allah. You will leave no survivors. Let the will of Allah be done."

The bus continued its stately progress along the drive, tracked by Officer Marinello, and now watched by Mack Bedford and Benny Shalit from the other side of the north playing fields.

Meanwhile the Dodge truck was hurtling along the country lanes that led to the east gate. Yousaf was in command of their remote-control detonator, which would ultimately blow the bomb boxes. He asked Ibrahim to slow down a little while he made one final adjustment to the electronics.

Abu Hassan still thought nothing of the police cruiser that seemed to be following him, and he stared ahead at the clock tower high above the school. It was one minute before 10:30 a.m. Inside the packed assembly hall, the orchestra and the massed singers of three choirs prepared to launch the proceedings.

The hall held thirteen hundred spectators, in addition to the forty-five musicians, now quiet in the orchestra pit, and the one hundred fifty singers, now assembled on the stage.

Mark Jenson, resplendent in his Harvard gown and wide blue academic sash, called the auditorium to silence and welcomed everyone to Abraham's Day, for the one moment in the year when everyone reflected on the founder of the Israeli nation.

Canaan Academy, he reminded the audience, was "twinned" with the Hebrew School in the small town of Kiryat Arba, the biblical name for Hebron, which stands below the hill on which the Jewish settlement is built. "And today," he said, "I would like us to reflect for one silent minute, on the Tomb of the Patriarch, the wondrous building that dominates Hebron, and the last resting place of Abraham in the land where he forged his Covenant with God."

A giant photograph of the tomb was then illuminated behind the choirs, and two long notes were blown on the Ram's Horn, the traditional musical instrument of Judaism, the only musical instrument in the world that has not changed in five thousand years.

The auditorium fell silent as the audience reflected on their own roots and the beginnings of their nation. Those who had been to Hebron closed their eyes in prayer, and saw in their mind's eye the massive structure of the tomb, where the remains of Abraham and his wife Sarah, lie alongside those of his sons and their wives, Jacob and Leah, Isaac and Rebecca.

When the minute's silence was concluded, Mark Jenson stood up and spoke to the audience once more. "With our thoughts now in the Holy Land, we should offer personal prayers for peace to return to our distant land, and pray that it will continue to be, for us, the land of milk and honey promised to Moses by God."

The Ram's Horn sounded twice more, and the school orchestra struck up the overture to the hymn, which begins with the most sacred word in Judaism:

> *Jerusalem, Jerusalem,*
> *Lift up your voice and sing,*
> *Hosanna in the highest,*
> *Hosanna to the King.*

The words, sung with aching beauty, by the high trebles, in harmony with the newly formed tenors and baritones of the senior class, rose in an uplifting swell that drifted out from the high windows and across the lawns and woodlands of Connecticut.

Mack Bedford and Benny Shalit heard it clearly as they watched the bus moving slowly up the drive, and the man from the Mossad was visibly moved. He stood up, as if for a national anthem, and he held his detonator out in front of him, watching the indicator light flickering on and off, he hoped, synchronized with its twin under the fuselage of the bus.

Right now they knew only one thing. The tracker device was definitely still working. They stood quietly watching the bus draw nearer, as the voices of the Canaan Academy choirs wafted out over the golden oak trees that lined the drive.

> *Jerusalem, Jerusalem,*
> *Thou city ever blest,*
> *Within thy portals first I find,*
> *My safety, peace, and rest.*

Mack Bedford had his mark mentally on the drive. Two giant oak trees planted quite closely were his halfway point, when he assessed the bus would come within range. The next hundred yards would be the last it ever traveled.

Staring through his binoculars, he said quietly, "Halfway, Benny. Stand by."

And Benny's right hand moved imperceptibly to the black button on the top of the box, the red light still flickering.

"We're in range. I got two hundred fifty yards . . ."

"When you're ready, buddy."

"Okay Benny, NOW!"

"Contact."

And the choir still sang the heavenly words of Jerusalem:

> *Where tears and weeping are no more,*
> *Nor death, nor pain, nor night;*
> *For former things are passed away,*
> *And darkness turned to light.*

At which point, Benny's red light went out. His green light suddenly glowed. And beneath Ibrahim's yellow school bus the detonator did its work. The eight sets of plastic C-4 high explosive blew upward with a muffled blast, smashing asunder the floor of the bus.

In the same split-second, the two bundles of dynamite exploded with a dull *WHOOOOMPH,* and the fizzing det-chord ripped up into the boxes, unleashing the brutal demolition power that is packed into a ton of ammonium nitrate high-explosive—a homemade carpet bomb that would have obliterated Canaan Academy.

It made short work of the bus. And it caused a blast nothing short of sensational. Flames shot three hundred feet into the air as the bus disintegrated upward, rising fifty feet off the ground in a blazing yellow kaleidoscope, hurling off huge hunks of white-hot metal like the Rings of Saturn gone berserk. It was Nagasaki 1945 in northwest Connecticut.

Officer Tony Marinello's cruiser took the full brunt of the outward blast. It catapulted over backwards onto its roof, bounced and made another clean half-somersault and landed on its four wheels. Tony, saved by his seat belt, went into shock, watching the burning, twisted wings, doors, seats, and whole swathes of the roof raining down. Three massive oak trees, four hundred years old, with trunks thirty-five feet around, were lying flat on the ground, two of them on fire.

The fertilizer bomb had been built to make sure fifteen hundred people died inside the school. Now the ten riders on the bus, Abu and Ben among them, were halfway across the Bridge to Paradise as the incinerated automatic doors of the school bus, glowing red, finally fell to earth.

"Nice job, Benny," said Mack Bedford.

"Not too bad yourself, buddy," replied the Mossad's chief New York agent.

> Thy goal is fixed, one thing I ask,
> Whate'er the cost may be,
> Jerusalem, Jerusalem,
> Soon to arrive with thee.

And the music died in the hall, while the great stone building shuddered to its foundations. No one inside the concert room saw anything. In fact the only living witness to the explosion, aside from Mack and Benny and the police officer, was Ms. Calvert, who had been watching from the window before it cracked from end to end, and now stood in terror of what she had seen.

She somehow sleepwalked to the telephone, dialed 911, and was switched through to the Torrington Police Department, where Buzzy had Tony Marinello on the other line, reporting that a Canaan Academy school bus had just been hit by a bomb. "Whoever had been in that bus could not have survived. Nossir. It's like fucking Baghdad here," he confirmed. "Terrorists, sir. They gotta be terrorists. I never saw anything like this."

The station chief could tell his man was in shock, and he told both Tony and Ms. Calvert he'd have reinforcements out there momentarily, plus the fire department and ambulances.

"I'll take the reinforcements and the fire trucks," said Tony, "but don't need the ambulances. Anyone who was in that bus just got cremated. I'm real certain of that. The metal just melted. You can't get within a hundred yards of the wreckage, it's that hot."

Ibrahim and Yousaf had just turned into the east gate and were making fast time down the north end of the drive when the bus blew. They couldn't see anything because the academy itself stood between them and Abu's big yellow time-bomb.

But they heard the blast. If they'd been ten miles away, they'd have heard that. The building was still standing, although on the other side, way beyond the south portico, there were flames and black smoke rising up as if from the fires of hell.

Ibrahim somehow knew the bus had gone up on the grounds that if you have a lovely wide parkland, an historic stone-built castle, and an old school bus crammed with fucking dynamite, and there's a sudden mighty explosion, it's probably not the parkland or the castle.

He knew it was over and that they had failed. And he knew he and Yousaf had to get the hell out of Dodge, as it were. He also knew there were not that many places to hide. He jammed his foot on the brake, spun the wheel, tearing up the lawn, and headed right back the way he just came.

Two miles away, hurtling down a woodland path, Mack and Benny were headed straight for the Blackberry River Inn, and almost collided with Johnny Strauss and his SUV when they arrived.

"I guess that wraps it up for Benny and me."

"What about the other two?" asked Mack.

"Mack, both Johnny and I are financed by the Mossad. And this Ibrahim and Yousaf have committed no known crime against the nation of Israel," said Benny. "And that's our brief. It would be like asking the immortal Wiesenthal to go after the Tamil Tigers."

"Not his business, right?" said Mack. "What about a cup of tea? For my ungrateful teammates."

And the three of them laughed as they walked. And, for a change, they used the front door of the hotel. No one noticed Benny was still gripping the remote-controlled detonator, gripping it as if he would never let it go.

12

BRAHIM'S GETAWAY STRATEGY, if his school-bus bomb had worked according to plan, had been to make for the hills, and cross the border into the State of Massachusetts. Right now, he had no idea what to do, and he was very scared.

His little army had plainly been wiped out. And the failure of the mission had knocked the bounce right out of him. He was not, however, as scared as Yousaf, who was trembling uncontrollably in the passenger seat, and saying over and over, "They'll send us back to Guantanamo. I know that's what they'll do."

Ibrahim had to remind him quite forcibly they had not been captured by anyone yet. And Yousaf was to shut up forthwith and allow his long-time friend and leader to think.

Yousaf, however, was unable to shut up, and he kept blurting out his innermost fears, finally admitting he was frightened to death they'd send that bastard Staff Sergeant Ransom to catch them and take them back to their cell block in Camp 5.

"Yousaf," said Ibrahim, "I want to tell you three things. First we are not yet captured, second we are not yet being hunted, third we have just one objective and that's to get the hell out of the United States and stay there."

"But, we can't do that," moaned Yousaf. "They'll close the airports, search people, put up road blocks, blockade ships."

"Look, Yousaf," said Ibrahim, "It is important we don't panic. I know we had to shoot and kill to get into this place, but it's always easier to get out. We have our traveling bags, we have our legal documents, and we have money. We also have friends. So stay calm. And have faith in Allah. He will guide us home."

"I have been thinking one thing," said Yousaf. "If we had blown up the school, we'd be even more wanted by the authorities. We only blew up a bus, and that's not nearly so bad. Maybe we got a better chance now than if we'd been successful."

"Maybe we have," replied Ibrahim. "Maybe we have."

They were in the Connecticut town of Canaan, now, and so far there were no road blocks. It was only five minutes since the explosion. And Ibrahim registered his only success of the day so far, when he turned hard right off the downtown area and headed up Interstate 7, less than a mile from the border.

Thoughts cascaded through his mind, all of them about the historic city of Boston. For him, the place represented a refuge, a network of al-Qaeda Sleeper Cells, of safe apartments, several owned by Osama himself, others owned by bin Laden family members. Not all of them were friendly, but neither were they hostile.

There were Islamic contacts there. There was the Mosque for the Praising of Allah in Commonwealth Avenue, the Masjid Al-Quran, Mohammed's Mosque. Ibrahim had friends who had flown from Pakistan to study at the Islamic Society of Boston.

And yet, for all of its undercurrents of friendship, Boston was embarrassed up to its Brahmin ears by the events of 9/11. Both flights, which hit the North and South Towers of the World Trade Center, American 11 and United 175, had taken off from Boston, and the city had been branded the terrorist launch pad.

The airport staff had been cleared of any wrongdoing, but the police department, right there on New Sudbury Street, was full of hard-eyed Boston-Irish officers who were apt to stare very beadily at anyone who looked like a native of Arabia or anywhere in the Middle East.

On reflection, Ibrahim Sharif, with his black beard, swarthy looks, and horrendous background, photographed and printed in Guantanamo Bay, of all places, was inclined to give the City of Boston the widest possible berth.

Which left him with a series of questions, all of them unanswered, and probably unanswerable. Where do we go? Who can help? How do we get out of the USA? Do the Connecticut police have any idea what happened? What we planned? Are they already after us? Does that mean a local manhunt or a national one?

Right now the old Dodge truck was hurtling down the freeway near Sheffield, and Ibrahim planned to go straight for another eleven miles before swinging right, up Route 23, and then heading directly for the Massachusetts Turnpike.

He just wished he knew the scale of the trouble he was in. And he needed a companion with whom to talk it over. But Ben al-Turabi and Abu Hassan had crossed the bridge, and Yousaf had dissolved into fear. Ibrahim was, for the moment, on his own.

JOHNNY AND BENNY headed back to New York, while Mack collected himself before briefing the heavyweight U.S. security chiefs on the events so far. He was not much looking forward to it, because a bang the size of the one at Canaan Academy should have been quite sufficient to end his mission, and it hadn't. Only half of it.

The good news, however, was that he had not brought himself any attention to himself. No one knew of his involvement, which was precisely how it was supposed to be.

Mack returned to the Waldorf Astoria at around 2 p.m., to a message that Johnny would be there at three o'clock. Benny had quietly disappeared back to the Israeli Consulate on Third Avenue.

Mack immersed himself in a hot bath where he always considered he did his best thinking. And he reflected on the slightly obscure truth that if he'd blown up Mountainside Farm, or the bus while it was still there, or the bus while it was driving along a public highway, there would have been a complete uproar, investigations, arrests, and huge publicity. And he might not have nailed all four of them, and thus would have no idea who was dead and who was still alive. Also innocent civilians might have been killed or wounded.

No, his master stroke was to have allowed the terrorists to kill themselves, to blow themselves up on private land, wiping out only the bus—and a couple of oak trees. This way, somehow, the police were absolved of any responsibility. They did not even know about the terrorist plot, and they could spend all the time in the world trying to find out. So far as the great State of Connecticut was concerned, there had been no casualties.

"It was like the friggin' bus was driving itself," concluded Mack. "The driver and its occupants were not even officially in the country. We got a couple of Peshawar bus drivers strayed seven thousand miles into East Norfolk, and set fire to a school bus with no kids in it. I like that. I really like that."

He just about had time to dress before Strauss arrived with the photographs he'd shot at the entrance to the farm. There were good shots of the bus and of Abu Hassan and Ben al-Turabi. "Unmistakable," said Mack, admiringly.

The photographs of Ibrahim and Yousaf were of equally good quality. Yousaf was just about identical to the Guantanamo prints, but Ibrahim's beard changed him drastically, and Mack stared at it very hard.

"You know, Johnny," he said, "I've always thought there was something familiar about this guy. But when he was clean shaven, I never got a handle on it. But that beard changes things. You got great shots of him from different angles, and he had the driver's side window open."

He stared again at the black-and-white prints of the terrorist leader, and he said, very quietly, "I know this guy. I arrested him in some shitty little village up in the Afghan mountains a few years ago. And before I did it, I damn near drowned him trying to get him to talk."

"Drowned him!" said Johnny.

"Yup," said Mack cheerfully. "I grabbed him by his beard and held him underwater in the rain barrel. I was trying to get a grip of the village supply of TNT at the time. This little bastard had just blown up a truckload of Marines plus a couple of SEALs. All buddies. He was darned lucky I didn't break his fucking neck."

"You sure he was guilty?" asked Johnny.

"That's one thing you can put your life savings on," said Mack. "Our guys in military INTEL up in those mountains don't make mistakes. If they're not certain, they don't speak. And if they don't speak, we don't move."

"You ever seen the other guy before?" said Johnny.

"Not sure," replied Mack. "There were two of them up in that village. And the guy in the passenger seat of the Dodge could easily have been the other one. But he was heavily bearded up there. Mostly what I remember of him was he wouldn't stop spouting the Koran at me while we were searching for the dynamite. So I kicked him straight in the ass."

"Did you find the dynamite?"

"Hell, yes. We always found it."

It was time for Mack and Johnny to go their separate ways. Johnny would retreat to Banda Fine Arts and transmit the photographs to the CIA in Langley. He had contacts in there as good as Mack's were. And Mack would deliver a full report of the events to Bob Birmingham in East Norfolk.

To the CIA boss he would reveal all, because the CIA was not in any way interested in getting to the bottom of whatever crime had been committed. They were interested in the pure and simple elimination of Ibrahim, Yousaf, Ben, and Abu. And while they were gratified to know that Ben and Abu had left, they wanted only to know when and where the other two were scheduled also to die.

Mack revealed everything he knew to the CIA about Mountainside Farm and the school bus that had been converted into a traveling bomb. And, as he had suspected, Bob Birmingham just wanted broad brush strokes on the current whereabouts of the two men he wanted dead.

Mack provided the registration number, and a good description of the old, mud-caked Dodge truck he suspected Ibrahim and Yousaf had fled the scene in, and told Bob he could expect very good photographs in the next hour.

"Good," said Birmingham. "Keep at it."

IN THE MEANTIME, the Torrington police chief was trying to work out what, if anything, he should investigate. All of the human remains had been blasted widely all over the parkland as well as incinerated. Microscopic DNA testing might yield something but none of the forensic guys was holding his breath.

No one had been reported missing. The CIA had said little about the farm. And, aside from a few cracked window panes on the south side of the school, there was no damage, not a single scratch on any of the students, and no harm to either teachers or parents. As major bomb blasts go, this one had somehow been absorbed. And yet, there was something so utterly shocking about such an explosion so terrifyingly close to a large private school packed with the sons of extremely important people . . .

The CIA divulged there was some terrorist suspicion, but plainly all of the terrorists were dead, blown up by their own hand. Except for two. In the opinion of the CIA's criminal investigation department, two of the ringleaders had not been in the bus, but rather had been on standby to get everyone away after the deed was done. But also in their opinion was that there was no point in alarming the population with a story that suggested U.S. authorities had uncovered and prevented a massive terrorist hit on a U.S. school, and that there was now a nationwide search going on for two of the ringleaders. Because the secondary effect of that would be to put the said ringleaders instantly on their guard.

So with a minimum of public announcement, the agency requested the Torrington police be on the lookout for a black, old and dented Dodge Ram truck, probably muddy, with a Massachusetts registration number, which they supplied. They advised that the truck was likely still in the Torrington area, within a two-mile radius of East Canaan.

They also advised the Torrington police that in the truck were two known terrorists, Ibrahim Sharif and Yousaf Mohammed, both originally from the Afghan/Pakistani mountains, both former inmates of Guantanamo Bay, and that both were likely armed and extremely dangerous.

The station chief put Captain "Buzzy" Hannon in charge of the case, with the swiftly recovered Officer Tony Marinello as his assistant. If he'd searched the entire country, he could not have found two more zealous policemen, nor two less likely to allow it all to be kept under wraps.

Within one hour, they had ransacked Mountainside Farm, and found very little except a lot of spilled ammonium nitrate in the barn. There was no sign of personal possessions because everything had been burned the night before or was in the bus when it blew.

They questioned people at the school, but no one had seen anything. Mark Jenson especially could not help, now paralyzed with fear about what this near attack could mean for the school—for current students and new enrollment—with Canaan's new reputation as number-one al-Qaeda target.

It was soon clear to Hannon and Marinello that there was little to be gained from continued questioning of people who were not even witnesses. And the only person who had seen anything,

Ms. Calvert, had had an emotional breakdown over the events and tendered her resignation.

Mark Jenson called a staff meeting in the Common Room for 6 p.m. to discuss the future of the academy. He was keenly aware that if they decided to go ahead, as normal, and another bomb was to hit the school and kill several hundred students, he would be held accountable.

Tony Marinello did his level best to convince the headmaster that the chances of the killers returning were extremely remote, simply because people here would be ever on their guard. "Sir," said Tony, "you probably have the safest school in the country. They never come back."

"You may very nearly be right," Jenson replied. "But they hit the World Trade Center back in the mid-nineties. And, as we all know, came back for a more successful second try in 2001."

"Different, sir. Very different. The Twin Towers were a world symbol of U.S. power, unmatched anywhere. There was nothing comparable. This is just a school. There are hundreds like it. And any one of them will do just fine for a terrorist group trying to frighten the populace."

"Well, we do like to think we have unique qualities here at Canaan . . ."

But Officer Marinello was already out of the door, with his case, in his own opinion, proven beyond reasonable doubt.

THERE WAS A GENERAL ALERT out for the scruffy Dodge Ram throughout New York, Connecticut, Massachusetts, Rhode Island, Vermont, and New Hampshire. But this general alert did not instantly develop into a manhunt, because the evidence that there had been a suicide bomb was too strong. Thus state troopers in the half-dozen states that surround Connecticut were not fired up and lasering their way down the highway, searching for the old Dodge banger to the exclusion of all else.

Ibrahim was on the Turnpike heading for Boston within forty

minutes of the explosion. He felt more relaxed in Massachusetts, but the truth was, he had no idea where he was going. But by a process of elimination he'd arrived at one single word. North.

South led back to the Mexican border, which gave him the shudders, even though it had been Hassan who had shot dead the two border guards. New York also gave him goose bumps, both because of the bomb in the men's room and his sneaking suspicion that Faisal al-Assad had flown the coop.

Ibrahim had no idea how intense the police dragnet was right now. Indeed, he had no idea whether they even had a description of the truck he was driving. Nor if they even knew he existed. But his suspicions were those of an international terrorist, of a professional killer who was being groomed to become one of bin Laden's right-hand men.

He needed to get centered. To develop a plan. To him, there was nowhere south where he could reasonably seek refuge. Or escape. Airports were out of the question. So were major seaports. Which ruled out almost everywhere. The only border he'd ever heard was possible to cross illegally was Canada, mostly because it was nearly four thousand miles long. No one could patrol all of it.

Ibrahim needed to make contact with someone from the organization. He got off the highway at the next exit, and headed to a rest stop near the town of Blandford, a ski resort located in the Berkshire Hills. It was high, spectacular country, and he considered it likely that reception would be excellent on his cell.

Ibrahim dialed the number of Faisal al-Assad on Sixty-Ninth Street, the apartment that had been his home for several days. The phone had plainly been disconnected, but Ibrahim's call was a big mistake. The New York police were wire-tapping that apartment, given Assad's connection to the farm. Ibrahim's call went straight through to the police, who could actually answer. When one of them asked who was speaking, Ibrahim did not respond, just stated that he wished to speak to Mr. Assad. Again they asked for identity, trying to keep him on the line, but Ibrahim sensed an intervention, and clicked off his phone.

The NYPD raced through the procedures to trace a call, but it took too long, and they came up only with a wide stretch of country in the Berkshire Hills, probably off Interstate 90. They logged the beacon but nothing else.

But they did not need anything else, because that beacon was precisely twenty-three miles from Canaan Academy, where there had been a bombing less than a hour ago. The coincidence was undeniable. Ten minutes later, in the collective minds of the both the Connecticut and Massachusetts state police, there was no doubt that the two known terrorists, photographed getting out of Mountainside Farm, were heading for Boston.

Ibrahim, too, experienced a sudden heightening of the senses. That phone call, he guessed, had betrayed him, to an extent. He had no idea how the U.S. police could possibly know his identity, or his role in the blast that blew the bus. But these were Americans, and they were not like other people. They knew everything.

Ibrahim was growing more scared by the minute. Yousaf had gone into a total decline, and he sat staring at the Berkshire Hills as they rushed past the old Dodge truck. But Yousaf did not see the golden autumn slopes before the snows. All he could he see was the hot, dry wasteland of eastern Cuba, and the brown, neglected grassland and vegetation around the Guantanamo Bay prison.

He wasn't saying anything, but he was trying to think of ways to help Ibrahim. However, the sudden appearance of two state police cruisers coming the other way at high speed, blue lights flashing, sirens blaring, jolted them both into the reality of their situation.

Yousaf sat upright, and muttered, "They're not looking for us, are they?"

Ibrahim replied, "I don't think so. Not yet. But I'm getting off this highway right now."

He swung off the turnpike at Exit 3, before Springfield, and headed north, driving through the Berkshires on minor roads where his truck looked more at home than on a major highway. He kept heading north and east, aiming for the coast, way above Boston.

He was uncertain about this particular compulsion, but during his two semesters at Harvard he'd often traveled with other students up to coastal Maine for long weekends, sometimes fishing, sometimes hiking.

And like so many generations of Boston students, he'd loved that wild country, its loneliness and its permanent atmosphere of a lost time, of living in a bygone age. Maine was a throwback of a state, and in the opinion of many, it was a throwback to better and more kindly times. So Ibrahim was headed for Maine, where he could not only think, but there was also that 490-mile border that Maine shares with Canada, where only a couple of roads actually cross from one side to the other.

Ibrahim was clueless about the loneliness of that horseshoe-shaped frontier line, the paucity of highways or even roads, the hostile weather, and the impossibility of traveling across those mountains and into Canada. Also he was not sure why he thought Canada would be a much easier proposition for a wanted man than the United States. For the moment, he was concentrating on finding the correct roads to take him north of Boston, and he continually left the principal north- and east-running throughways, ducking and diving onto country lanes, adding many hours to his journey.

As darkness began to settle over New England, he pulled up at a rest stop and told Yousaf to fill up the truck with gas, paying for it with cash. He then walked over to a quiet area outside the restaurant and made a phone call to his old master, Sheikh Abdullah Bazir, in Muslim Bradford.

It was 11 p.m. in England. The Sheikh had left the mosque and was back in his basement office. Ibrahim quickly explained that his U.S. mission had failed, and that almost everyone involved had been killed in the blast.

Sheikh Abdullah himself was a highly skilled bombmaker, and

he actually winced when he was told the size of the device, and the volume of enhanced ammonium nitrate Ibrahim had used. "They must never have had a chance," he said of the men on the bus. He expressed deep regret about the deaths of Ben al-Turabi and Abu Hassan, and assured Ibrahim that tonight he would pray for them. To beg Allah to accept them as Martyrs to his cause, and to welcome them now into Paradise.

And then he told Ibrahim what he needed to hear most: That he would get both Ibrahim and Yousaf out of the United States. He would immediately alert Shakir Khan in Islamabad, who would contact the Sleeper Cells in the American Northeast. If more funds were necessary, they would be arranged through the holy men in Riyadh and through a labyrinth of law firms in London and the United States.

Now Sheikh Abdullah ordered Ibrahim to drive on into lonely country, to stay out of cities and off highways. He advised him it was safer to travel in the dark, but to stay well clear of the U.S. police. He was to call in whenever possible on this land line at this time, 11 p.m. Bradford. Then he asked for Ibrahim's cell-phone number, which would only be used in an emergency. Meanwhile he would endeavor to plan a route for them, out of the United States.

Ibrahim felt better now. He went inside the restaurant and purchased a box of cheeseburgers and fries, which he and Yousaf consumed in the parking lot. Once again they headed north, crossing the New Hampshire border south of Nashua, and heading up to the White Mountains.

They stopped at a small motel and checked in for the night, again paying in cash. They rose early and made their way back toward the Atlantic coast, crossing mountainous country as they drove along Route 2, up toward the city of Bangor.

They reached the downtown area without incident, and headed for a parking lot. They took their bags, left the Kalashnikovs clipped under the fuselage, and headed into a big supermarket, with an attached restaurant. Yousaf walked to the counter and purchased coffee and sweet pastries; Ibrahim went to the magazine area and bought a road atlas, which provided a complete state-by-state tourist guide to the United States, Canada, and Mexico.

Ibrahim almost choked on his coffee when he saw how impossible it looked to cross into Canada via Maine. He already knew that one of the roads in was I-95, which had customs officials, Canadian immigration, and major police security at the border. Too many terrorists had tried. Too many had been caught.

Ibrahim poured over the map. There was a ferry to Nova Scotia from Portland, Maine, but they were already a hundred miles north of Maine's largest city, and neither of them wanted to head back south. Ibrahim finally deduced that their only chance was the fast ferry to Yarmouth, Nova Scotia, which left from Bar Harbor every morning.

Ibrahim was relieved. He helped himself to a second pastry and asked Yousaf to fetch another two cups of coffee. Half an hour later they decided to make the final leg of their long journey to the coast of Maine. They picked up their bags and were about to leave the supermarket when Ibrahim froze. Out in the parking lot, precisely where the Dodge was stationed, were two state police cruisers, blue lights flashing. Standing at the rear of their parked truck were two troopers, both with notebooks, both writing.

Ibrahim dragged Yousaf back inside, grabbed a cart, and placed both leather traveling bags at the bottom. He then began filling the cart with cabbage, lettuce, bags of potatoes, and mixed salad, piling it all on top of the bags.

He then headed to one of the checkout lanes and began bagging up the vegetables. It took ten minutes before they were ready to push the loaded cart outside; when they reached the door, the two troopers were still there, the only difference being that one of them was speaking on his cell phone. Now one thing was very clear to Ibrahim: he and Yousaf were the very definite targets of a police manhunt.

There were probably two or three hundred other vehicles in

this supermarket parking lot and the troopers were interested in only one, the one driven by two known terrorists, ex-Guantanamo, and plainly now wanted by Connecticut state police in connection with a bomb and the attempted murder of fifteen hundred U.S. citizens.

The vehicle's registration number had obviously been circulated and any minute the police were going to find two AK-47s clipped under the fuselage.

"Walk," said Ibrahim. "Walk slowly with the cart, like everyone else. Head in the opposite direction of the truck and those two cops. Act like you're going directly to your own car."

Yousaf looked doubtful, but he did as he was told. They reached the far end of the lot, and were now as geographically far away from the cruisers as they could be without leaving the parking lot.

At this point there were a lot of options, all of them flawed. Grab the bags and get a taxi. Hopeless. Grab the bags and find a bus station. Worse. Find the road to the coast and try to hitch-hike. Ridiculous. Grab the bags and find a car-hire. Lunacy. Steal a car. Better. But only with the driver. The difference might be hours of safe driving before he was missed; the other method, just to take a car and vanish, might have the police on their tail within ten minutes.

"Keep pushing," said Ibrahim. He now walked beside the cart, which allowed him to plunge into his own leather bag to search for the pistol he'd been given by Mike and the Sleeper Cell guys when they arrived with the fertilizer. Because it was farthest away from the main doors, this area of the parking lot was the least busy. There was a line of eight parking spaces and only two of them were occupied. A four-foot high concrete wall separated the lot from the busy downtown street running past.

Ibrahim slipped the pistol into his jacket and helped push the cart toward one of the parked vehicles. And there they waited, never even glancing way across the lines of cars to the spot where the cops were still standing by the old Dodge.

After five minutes a new cruiser pulled in and joined the other two. The troopers had decided to seal off the supermarket and question everyone still shopping. *No need to bother with people out in the lot. If this Ibrahim and his buddy Yousaf had come out already, they'd have headed for their truck. And if they'd tried to make a break, we'd have seen them.*

Ibrahim was on the verge of becoming desperate when Mr. Jed Ridley, a sixty-eight-year-old local bank manager and lifelong resident of Bangor, came walking slowly toward them. He stopped at one of the two parked cars, unlocked the doors, and packed his shopping bags into the trunk.

Ibrahim watched him settle himself behind the wheel of his dark red Chevrolet. He started the car and tapped on the driver's side window.

"Sir," he said, "I think your back tire . . ."

Mr. Ridley opened the window and Ibrahim shot him dead, straight between the eyes. "Pull him out of the seat, and we'll load him into the back," he said. "Come on Yousaf, pull and lift."

Yousaf was stunned. He was surprised the shot had made so little noise, and amazed at the cold-blooded daring of his leader. He was also thrilled there were no other shoppers anywhere near.

They hauled the late Mr. Ridley to his feet, as if he were merely feeling faint, and walked him the two steps to the rear door. They shoved the body into the back seat, rolled it forward on to the floor, and began to pile the contents of the trunk on top of it.

Mr. Ridley thus disappeared, under the salad and off the map. Ibrahim got behind the wheel and headed for the nearest exit. Mr. Ridley's Chevrolet headed out toward Main Street and then south down the road to the coast. It was, by now, afternoon, and soon it would grow dark. The Chevy needed gas and the roads, off season, up here in sparsely populated Maine were lonely.

BACK IN THE SUPERMARKET, the police had the area sealed off. No one could come in. More importantly, no one could get out. There was a duty officer at each of the rear doors and the automatic main doors were all locked. The police spent the first half hour separating the women and children and releasing them right away, since none of them fitted the descriptions of Ibrahim and Yousaf.

There were then obviously innocent men, guys the police knew by name or even by sight. They were released immediately. The officers then proceeded to march each person individually to his vehicle, watch him unlock it, and then drive away.

But at the end of it all, the muddy old Dodge was still out in the parking lot, alone, and basically without an owner.

It was already seven o'clock, and Mrs. Barbara Ridley was among several dozen people who had called the police department wondering after their family members and friends. She, like the others, was told there had been a major police delay at the supermarket, and no one should be overly concerned. It was all a little time-consuming, but routine.

By 9 p.m., however, eight hours after Ibrahim had shot Mr. Ridley, there was no doubt the man was missing. He was not even on the police list of people who had been checked out at their vehicles. Two officers drove around to his house and found his wife distraught.

At 10 p.m. they launched a statewide hunt for the Chevy, which had, by this time, been dumped in a dense pinewood, way out of sight of the road, at the northeast end of Mount Desert Island, three miles from Bar Harbor, and forty-four miles from Bangor. The car would not be found for two days.

Ibrahim and Yousaf had decided to walk into the dark town and find the ferry port. Luckily for them, the weather this year on the northeast coast had been a real Indian summer, so much so that the ferry company that runs the world-class supership "the CAT" had decided to operate until the end of October. This was a lifesaver for Ibrahim and Yousaf, who otherwise would have been stranded in North America.

But the ferry didn't leave until morning, and they had nowhere to sleep. And Indian summer or no, it was still damned cold at night on the coast. Still, it wasn't snowing and it wasn't blowing, which was excellent news since neither terrorist had anything warmer than a leather jacket.

They walked down the hill of Main Street and reached the waterfront, where they found the ferry terminal. As far as Ibrahim could tell, their best chance for a place to sleep would be a moored boat they could try and get inside.

All he could find was a thirty-eight-foot lobster boat, up on blocks outside a small boat workshop. That would do, if its cabin door was open, but it would be a real pain to climb up and find it was all locked, and colder than it was at ground level.

. Also, they'd have to be out at 7 a.m. in case the workshop guys started early. A light but very cold wind was gusting in from the east, and Ibrahim decided they would take their chances, climb up into the lobster boat, and hope to find shelter.

Luck was still with them. The door to the cabin was open, and inside it was surprisingly less cold than standing on the jetty. There were two comfortable seats and the two men from the Middle East crashed out immediately on Bar Harbor's dry dock.

And in a deep and absolutely unknown irony, Mack Bedford was also sleeping in a chair on the Maine coast. He had reached home eighty-nine miles to the south that afternoon and had now fallen asleep on the sofa, in front of the fire, watching the Red Sox. He'd played baseball with Tommy for almost an hour before dinner, and he was just as tired as Ibrahim and Yousaf. But Mack was warmer than the terrorists. Definitely warmer.

Anne had gone to bed, leaving her husband snoring gently. For now, Mack was at peace, for there was nothing else he could do except to wait for the two hit-men from the Hindu Kush make another mistake.

Ibrahim and Yousaf were up and out of the lobster boat before 7 a.m. and made their way to breakfast at a nearby diner right on the jetties ten minutes later. Afterward, Ibrahim purchased tickets, taking their passports and student visas with him. No one asked to see Yousaf separately, and no one recognized that the passports had been the work of skillful forgers.

They filed in with the substantial morning crowd, boarded the huge dark blue CAT, and took their seats on the ship, which in high summer coped with 775 passengers plus 250 cars. Today it was not full to capacity, but it still had plenty of people among whom Ibrahim and Yousaf could get thoroughly lost.

The local police had been requested to keep a close eye on the ferry terminal during the day in case the two missing drivers of the Dodge truck showed up. But because this still was not yet considered a murder hunt, the state police sent only one already-busy officer to check out the ferry terminal fifteen minutes before the 9 a.m. departure. Except Ibrahim and Yousaf had left at eight.

They had boarded separately. On the way to Nova Scotia, they tried not to be too startled by headlines such as those in the local coastal Maine newspaper that read:

NEW ENGLAND MANHUNT
FOR TERRORIST SUSPECTS

Or, on an inside page,

BOMB BLAST IN SCHOOL GROUNDS—
CONNECTICUT POLICE BAFFLED

And then: **BANGOR BANK BOSS GOES MISSING**, followed by three paragraphs about the missing Mr. Ridley.

SEA CONDITIONS on the Gulf of Maine were choppy but not rough as they ploughed across the long swells, which form out here where the Atlantic washes up into the wide, 120-mile-long Bay of Fundy, which divides Nova Scotia from the eastern coast of New Brunswick.

Yarmouth, their ultimate destination on the southwest headland, stands adjacent to Dennis Point, the largest commercial fishing wharf in Atlantic Canada. Over a thousand fishermen and women make their living there, fishing for a variety of ground fish and shell fish, most notably lobster. It is also home to a fine trawler fleet.

Other large sport recreation boats cater for the tourist industry. And heavy tonnage foreign vessels are often brought here for servicing and repairs. Because out beyond the safe harbors of Nova Scotia, in the great waters of the North Atlantic, conditions can be very rugged, even for the best-built commercial boats.

Halfway to Nova Scotia, Yousaf finally appreciated that he hadn't been much help so far, but he now ventured to ask Ibrahim if he had a plan. He was unsurprised by his colleague's irritation. "I do not have a precise strategy," Ibrahim said, rather grandly, "except to get off this ferry, and get through Canadian customs and immigration.

"Ports like this are used to dealing with a large number of cars and passengers, and they are not very strict, simply because so many people are going back to the USA tonight. That's why I bought us return tickets on the five o'clock ferry, to show them, if they ask."

Yousaf was forced to agree that had been a bit of a master stroke. "And you remember, Yousaf," Ibrahim said, "our passports are perfectly in order. They both have legal stamps showing where and when we entered the United States. Also when we must leave. Our student visas are also valid. They both specify our Western degrees, mine from Harvard, yours from London University. Now you should go and sit somewhere else."

Yousaf wandered off, and for a while stood at the rail, gazing into the distance off the south-facing starboard beam. He had to admit it. Ibrahim had been a very fine leader, although he had no idea how he could have been so careless as to allow the bomb to go off three hundred yards before the school bus reached its destination. And the more Yousaf thought about it, the more troubled he became. Ibrahim had said the bombs would explode when he himself detonated them. *It was not just one bomb it was many, to be laid by our men all over the school. How come they all went off at once? I know Ibrahim did not explode them, because I was sitting next to him. I also know there were no timed charges because I helped to make every one of them. And I know they do not go off on impact. Even if the bus had crashed, the bombs would not have detonated.*

Yousaf was puzzled. Something had set them off. He understood that. But it surely was not a member of his team. Because there was nothing to set them off, except for Ibrahim's remote control, and he himself had been holding that from the time they left the farm. *So what was it?* Yousaf did not know.

The problem exercised him so greatly, he waited another half-hour, and with the Nova Scotia coastline well in sight, he went back and sat next to Ibrahim and asked him quietly, "Do you know what it was that set off our bombs so long before we intended them to detonate?"

"I have thought of little else since it happened," replied the terrorist leader. "And all I know is, there's nothing we constructed or fitted to the bomb-boxes that could possibly have set them off. Nothing. They were made to explode when my remote controller sent in the electronic pulse for which they were built. If you'd dropped a building on that bus, the bombs would not have gone off."

"Well, what could it have been?" asked Yousaf, vacantly.

"They must have been exploded by another device."

"You mean someone else exploded our bomb?"

"I do, because there cannot be any other explanation if we didn't do it."

"You mean someone must have dropped a bomb on our bus?"

"No. That would be impossible, because it would have required a low-flying fighter plane, and we'd have seen it."

"Then someone fired a guided missile across the academy park, and it went straight through the side of the bus and blew the boxes of ammonium nitrate?"

"No. That's almost, but not quite, impossible. Although the American authorities could have achieved that very easily. They only needed to call in their all-powerful military. But they would not have done that. They'd have dealt with the whole problem at the farm, charged in with a hundred troops, blown the bus, and the barn, and the house, and then shot all of us."

"Bastards," muttered Yousaf, "Damn bastards."

The huge CAT superboat, with its aerodynamic swept front end, continued racing across the water, and she ran smoothly, even with the short chop to the surface as there was today. Yousaf returned to his own seat and sat down thoughtfully, understanding there was one more barrier to cross, Canadian immigration, and they were home free, out of the United States.

By now he could see the coastline, and the headland of Yarmouth, jutting out, hiding the port from the ships making entry from the west. The CAT ferry with its shallow draft came roaring up to the jutting point of land and swerved hard to port for the ten-minute run up to the harbor in calm waters.

When it docked, there were long lines of passengers disembarking and a long line of automobiles trying to crawl out from the bowels of the ship. Because there was so much congestion, those holding U.S. or Canadian passports were usually waved through swiftly, especially those who were obviously returning that evening.

Ibrahim was among the first in line, and handed over his Pakistani passport and his student visa.

"Returning today?" asked the immigration officer.

"Yes, sir," replied Ibrahim, offering his ticket.

The officer stamped the passport, and waved him through. It was the same with Yousaf eight minutes later. "Have a nice visit," said the official. With that, the two terrorists had officially left the United States of America.

Ibrahim knew their destination was ultimately the fishing docks at Dennis Point, where he hoped to buy a couple of passages to Greenland or Iceland or somewhere else halfway across the north Atlantic. He still had a few thousand dollars tucked in the bottom of his leather bag and decided to board a very crowded bus headed that way. Yousaf only just managed to get on.

The docks were busy, with trawlers coming and going. Two large freighters were moored in the harbor, and Ibrahim learned they were in for repairs but couldn't pay the bill; everyone was awaiting money from the shipping company's Moscow headquarters.

The ship with most activity was moored alongside: *Odessa*, a two-hundred-foot Russian trawler from the Murmansk Fleet, characteristically rusty, in need of paint. Ibrahim went to see the captain, a heavyset, lifelong trawlerman named Igor Destinov. He spoke chronically broken English, but understood this Arabian-looking character was trying to hitch a ride to somewhere. To him it sounded like anywhere, and such men were dangerous. Igor, however, was not concerned about that. He was concerned only about the price.

He explained as best he could, that he was on a 1,500-mile journey up to the Greenland port of Nuuk on the west coast, 160 miles south of the Arctic Circle. There he was transferring fifty tons of refrigerated Atlantic cod to another Murmansk vessel, the *Gorky*. After that he was going around Cape Farewell, and across the southern waters of the Denmark Strait to Iceland. He expected to be in Nuuk in five days, and in Iceland six days later.

Also he was not in the habit of taking on passengers who may be wanted by the Coast Guard or the police in the United States or Canada. "You don't care where we're going!" he bellowed. "That means you and your friend been very bad boys, and that's not good for Igor. *HA! HA! HA!*"

Ibrahim cooly asked, "Is there a price you would accept for such a risk?"

"Depends how bad you are!" laughed the Russian seaman. "You commit minor crime like rape or drunk, I'd probably take you for five hundred. You do something fucking terrible like murder a police I make that five thousand."

Ibrahim could not help himself laughing. "We just got mixed up in some terrorist attack that didn't even happen," he joked. "No one got hurt or anything."

"But how do I know you're not telling the truth. Say I take you, and you blow up my fucking ship, what then?"

"Unlikely," said Ibrahim. "Neither of us can swim."

This almost reduced Igor to rubble, he was laughing so hard. But then he said, "Tell you what, I don't know you, and I wouldn't take you for a thousand dollars because you might cause me big trouble."

"How about three thousand for both of us, all the way to Iceland?"

"That sounds like a nice deal for Igor," he said. "You pay before we leave. I not trust terrorist. My aunt got killed by Chechen maniacs."

"I pay now. Cash," said Ibrahim. "And I'd like to move into a cabin right away."

"You give Igor nice bundle of U.S. greenback worth three thousand, you can have mine," said the master of the *Odessa*. "Fuck me, yes. Go fetch your friend."

Ibrahim and Igor shook hands, and the Russian accepted the thirty hundred dollar bills, which Ibrahim handed over. Then he left the ship to walk down the jetty and collect Yousaf from the dockside diner. They were ensconced in the ship by 3 p.m., and Ibrahim had no intention of going ashore again until they were on the cold shores of Iceland. Also he had no idea where Iceland was.

MACK BEDFORD stayed in close touch with Captain Ramshawe and Bob Birmingham, and they were all agreed that the former SEAL commander may as well remain at home, near a telephone, for the moment when Ibrahim and Yousaf broke cover, as they surely would. At that point they would decide a proper course of action.

Meanwhile both the NSA and the CIA were extremely grateful to him for almost single-handedly deciphering the intercept of the signal from Pakistan, foiling the terrorist plot against Canaan Academy, and taking out two of the four most wanted men from Guantanamo. All in secret, without leaving a trace.

The first moment they had a fix on Ibrahim Sharif and Yousaf Mohammed, the entire security force of the United States would be at Mack's disposal. They had just been witness to both the capabilities and intentions of these lunatics, which had confirmed the wisdom of their decision to have them killed.

Also, there was no one in the United States legal system who believed there was any military or government involvement whatsoever in the deaths of Abu Hassan Akbar and Ben al-Turabi. They had, after all, blown themselves up; no third party was even suspected, never mind named.

Mack Bedford's performance had been superlative. He and Anne had dinner together that second evening he was home, while Tommy stayed overnight with friends in Bath.

It was a long way from summer, but Mack always grilled outside until the first snow appeared, usually in the first week of November. Tonight he fixed one of his Down East masterworks: Lightly grilled swordfish steaks he'd been given by a lifelong friend, Brad Andre, skipper of a local dragger. He'd landed it only that morning on a long-line in deep water out beyond the Seguin Light. Brad had sold the huge fish to a restaurant agent for a fortune, but before he let it go, he cut two prime steaks, one for his own family, one for Mack's. He'd dropped it off on the way home—just walked in and placed it in the fridge, with a note scrawled on the white wrapping paper: *"First one of these I've caught for three years! Four hundred pounder. Took 45 minutes to land him. Sonofabitch! Brad."*

Mack marinated the fish in herbs and olive oil, and grilled it over charcoal. One turn only to brown both sides, and served with melted butter and parsley. He and Anne shared the steak and a bottle of California Chablis and retired early to bed.

YOUSAF AND IBRAHIM were given the choice of having dinner with the twelve-strong crew or by themselves at the end of the galley. They chose the latter because practically anything they had to say was sufficiently private to put them both in the slammer for many years, if overheard by the wrong people.

And it set a precedent. They always ate by themselves and did not fraternize with anyone, not even Igor, who reasoned their three thousand bucks had bought them as much privacy as they wanted.

During the meal, Yousaf once more broached the prickly subject of the bomb. "Any more ideas?" he asked.

And Ibrahim replied, "Just a few." For a few minutes there was silence, and then the terrorist leader spoke again, "I don't think anyone bombed the bus from the air, or hit it with a Stinger missile. If we start by considering that was the biggest thing by far that went wrong, we should then go back and examine everything that went wrong. Try and get a pattern. Now, what was the first thing? Come on, Yousaf. Think."

"Well, I can't see it has anything to do with the bomb. But I suppose it was when Ali got in a fight with some local guy in the woods."

"Correct. Except he may not have been some local guy. We don't know who he was. We only know he arrived more or less the same time as Ali, who was on his first-ever watch, and ended up snapping his hip socket almost in half. That wasn't a local guy, Yousaf. That was an expert in unarmed combat. Like we're supposed to be."

"Okay," said Yousaf. "Then what?"

"Next night, late, in comes Abu Hassan saying some huge guy, bigger and stronger than King Kong, flattened him in the farm yard and then vanished."

"Okay. Next."

"Mike, who's supposed to be on guard, comes in with a broken jaw, and says some guy hit him on the chin with a sledgehammer. Was it the same guy who broke Ali's hip, and flattened Abu? I think probably. And why did I not put these three incidents together? Because I must be very, very stupid. But I take full blame."

"None of us put them together," said Yousaf. "They all seemed so separate, unconnected. Like accidents."

"Which bring us to the most serious item. Do you remember the night Ben went back to the bus for the school floorplan?"

"Of course."

"Well he came back and said quite definitely the barn door was not locked. No chain. No padlock. He didn't say maybe. He said for sure. So I asked Asif to go out and check, and when he came back, he said the barn was locked like always with the padlock and chain."

"And who was right?"

"They were both right. There was no chain and padlock on the door when Ben said there wasn't. He might have been a bit flakey. But he wasn't that flakey. When Asif headed out there about ten minutes later, there was now a chain and padlock on the door."

"Huh?"

"You know what I think? Someone cut our padlock off during the previous three days while we were working and replaced it with one of his own, almost identical. He left it there unlocked, with the key in. When our last man locked up in the pitch dark, he was locking a different padlock. And the intruder outside had a spare key, which allowed him to enter our barn anytime he wished, all through the night when we were asleep.

"Except for once. That's when Mike walked around the barn and this character smashed him to the ground, broke his jaw, perhaps with a sledgehammer, and then vanished."

"I'm trying to fit all this together," said Yousaf.

"That's very simple," said Ibrahim. "On one of those nights, probably the last one, he enters the barn, maybe with a helper, and they rig a bomb up under our school bus, with a remote control just like ours.

"And then they waited, hidden in the trees on the school grounds. When we arrived, they detonated their own bomb, which blew our ammonium nitrate, killed all of our people, and wrecked our attack on Canaan Academy."

"You can't be serious?"

"Can't I? You can trust me on this. I have considered the problem from every angle. There can be no other explanation. It was that English bastard with the pipe who said, 'When you have eliminated the impossible, only the truth remains.'"

"Okay. You have solved the practical action of the problem. But now I ask you the real question: How did anyone know what we were going to do, where we were, and what our target was?"

"And that's the one no one can answer," said Ibrahim. "Because that could only have been discovered by someone who tapped into our most secret conversations. And I don't know how that could have happened, or who could have done it."

"I suppose we could have had someone on our tail in Bradford," said Yousaf, "or even Mexico. There were messages passed from Peshawar and Islamabad. We don't know how secure Faisal al-Assad was. And we definitely don't know if anyone mentioned Canaan Academy."

"Whoever it was must have been connected with the U.S. Government," said Ibrahim. "Because only governments, or very big organizations, can operate like that. But this group did not behave like a government. They behaved like gangsters. There is no end to my hatred of the Great Satan."

"Or mine," said Yousaf. "I did not think it was possible to hate anyone as I hate them."

THE FOLLOWING MORNING, as the sun rose out of the Atlantic, the two terrorists slept soundly in their bunks on board the *Odessa*. It was 6:30 on the U.S. mainland, and two young girls riding their ponies in the pine woods just north of Bar Harbor discovered the Chevy that had belonged to the Bangor bank manager, Jed Ridley.

Fortunately, they did not discover the bank manager himself, who was resting in peace under the salad in the back. But the vehicle was in such an outrageous place, driven into heavy undergrowth almost out of sight, the girls decided to tell someone. The Chevy was empty and apparently abandoned.

They took their time, and told their parents at around 8 a.m. after they returned from the stables. By the time the police had responded it was nine o'clock, and they finally hauled the vehicle out at 9:45. That was when they discovered the missing Mr. Ridley lying dead on the floor in the back.

A police ambulance took the body back to Bangor, and the announcement hit all the news channels by noon. No one was especially excited that Mr. Ridley was dead, or that he had been found in his car just outside elegant Bar Harbor, summer playground of the rich. It was that he'd been shot dead with one bullet—and that he had disappeared from the same supermarket parking lot where an old Dodge truck, which had been used by two known terrorists, had been abandoned.

To the detectives in charge of the case it looked suspiciously as if those two terrorists, identified by the CIA as Ibrahim Sharif and Yousaf Mohammed, both of either Afghani or Pakistani descent and both ex-Guantanamo Bay, had used the bank manager's Chevy as a getaway car.

And there was only one reason for them to drive down to off-season Bar Harbor, and that was the ferry to Nova Scotia, the one way they could cross a national border without too much trouble.

The Maine State Police Department was on the line to the Canadian authorities immediately. And at exactly 2:30 p.m. two Royal Canadian Mounted Police cruisers came howling into the Yarmouth ferry port, sirens blaring, lights flashing.

They weren't looking for a couple of questionable foreign bombers, who may have committed a crime far away from here. They were looking for two murderers, trying to escape justice. Two murderers who had shot and killed a well-respected United States citizen and dumped the body into woodland over at Bar Harbor. They immediately sealed off the ferry port, warning everyone that there would be extensive questioning, and that the 5 p.m. ferry would be subject to delays.

It was the beginning of an elaborate and thorough investigation. But by this time, the *Odessa* had already cleared Dennis Point and was headed out to the open sea. Much like their erstwhile colleague, Faisal al-Assad, Ibrahim and Yousaf had already flown the coop.

13

THE AL-QAEDA DISASTER in the hills of Northwest Connecticut resonated all the way to Peshawar, where the local
bazaars simmered in stifling ninety-degree heat, sheltered as
they were from the cooling breezes that wafted down from the
Khyber Pass.

Pakistan is a talkative country, and in Peshawar, rumor, innu-
endo, and the occasional fact, rip around those marketplaces
with reckless uncertainty.

Everyone seemed to know that something had gone shockingly
wrong in North America. Al-Qaeda men had died. There had been
a stupendous accidental explosion. The expedition had been sabo-
taged. Osama bin Laden had called a Council of War right here on
the western hills of the Swat Valley, even though no one had seen
him for nine years.

Not one of Peshawar's three million citizens knew precisely

what had happened in West Norfolk. Not even Shakir Khan, whose government car had just deposited him in the dark alley-way leading to the *Andar Shehr,* right outside the side gate to his grandiose walled residence.

The assembly of the North West Frontier Province had risen for the day, and Mr. Khan was accompanied by his assistant, thirty-year-old Kaiser Rashid, whose two brothers were both decorated Taliban commanders.

Like everyone else in Peshawar, they had but one subject to discuss, and almost as little to go on as the chatty merchants of the Old City, who were confidently informing their clients about the premature bomb blast seven thousand miles away in Connecticut, as if they had helped to fit the detonators.

Shakir Khan himself had heard an outline of the catastrophe via a cell-phone call from a village high in the Hindu Kush. The caller's informant was in Riyadh and had seen coverage on the al-Jazeera television channel. His details were sketchy, but it seemed there had been an enormous explosion on a school bus packed with dynamite. No one except the driver and passengers had been hurt, and none of the victims were known to the school authorities. The school was Canaan Academy.

Shakir Khan was appalled. Not so much at the death of some of al-Qaeda's most daring warriors, but at the obvious leak there must have been, to allow an outsider to ruin the operation.

They entered the courtyard of the house and walked to the fountain where they each filled a stone cup with water and tried to cool off. The water was cold and tasted delicious, fresh from the racing mountain streams that provide for the city. But they were both overwhelmed by disappointment at the wreckage of their well-laid plans, so long in formation, so careful in execution, so expensive to organize, and now in ruins.

Khan paced the courtyard. He knew the Americans were clever, damned clever. And he knew they had sent three professional assassins up here to Peshawar presumably to eliminate the four freed prisoners. However he was unable to suggest even one place where a leak on this scale might have originated.

He accepted the British police might be tapping the telephone of Sheikh Abdullah Bazir in Bradford. And he'd heard of the three al-Qaeda hit-men who vanished out on Ilkley Moor. There could have been a leak in Spain. Or in the Muslim center in Mexico City. But Faisal al-Assad was rock-solid in New York. And if someone had traced and tracked him into Connecticut, that someone must have had some deep prior knowledge.

Unless Faisal himself had become a traitor. And that, he decided, was impossible.

At that point Kaiser Rashid's cell phone vibrated and the political assistant retreated to a shaded corner of the courtyard and spoke quietly. He returned two minutes later to relay the message to his boss. "Sir, I have some news, some very good, some very horrible."

Shakir Khan did not reply. He simply turned his head a fraction sideways, and raised his right eyebrow, a gesture that had saved him a lot of talking in his lifetime.

"Ibrahim Sharif and Yousaf Mohammed are both alive," said Kaiser. "That much is definite. They were not on the bus."

"And? . . ." replied Khan, bracing himself for the "very horrible."

"Sir, they are both wanted by the Americans for murder. There is a manhunt for them, going on in two countries, the USA and Canada."

"Who did they murder?"

"The manager of a bank in Bangor, in Maine, up near the Canadian border."

"Were Ibrahim and Yousaf robbing his bank?"

"No one said that, sir."

"Well, where are they?" asked Khan, fairly stupidly.

"If the Americans knew that, I suspect they would have arrested them," said Kaiser. "The man's body was found in a place called Bar Harbor, which is a ferry port on the Gulf of Maine."

"Does that mean they escaped on the ferry?"

"I think they might have, sir. That's what the Americans think, and there is a big police search going on for them in Nova Scotia. That's where the ferry goes."

"But our people have heard nothing from them?"

"Not so far. But the Canadian police believe they are hiding out somewhere in Nova Scotia."

"This is very terrible," said Khan. "Very terrible indeed. But if they do make contact, my orders are that everything in our power must be done to rescue them and bring them home."

AT EIGHT O'CLOCK that same morning, the *Odessa* was shouldering her way through big seas and a stiffening nor'easter up the coast of Nova Scotia. Like all Murmansk fishing boats, she was built for rough weather and, if necessary, pack-ice. Her bow was heavily reinforced with steel, and her powerful Russian diesels drove her twin screws with warship efficiency.

Charts for that three-hundred-mile long eastern coast of Nova Scotia read like those for the UK. Once she'd made her hard left turn past Cape Sable the previous afternoon, *Odessa* had steamed past local seaports like Liverpool, Bridgewater, Halifax, and Dartmouth.

Ibrahim and Yousaf did not see much of these, however. Captain Destinov had run ten miles offshore all through the night, all the way up to Cape Breton Island. The two passengers did not see much of anything in this weather since neither of them had dared to go outside.

Ibrahim and Yousaf had never seen the ocean, except out of an aircraft window. They were both mountain men, and their main overseas ops areas had been in Baghdad and Kabul, both miles inland. Neither Ibrahim nor Yousaf had ever been on a ship, and now they were suffering an ocean-going baptism, on this rolling Russian dragger, where everyone felt every pitch and yaw.

By Igor's rough water standards, this had not been at all bad.

There had been no green water over the bow, yet. And because the Nova Scotia Coast Guard was always so touchy about foreign nationals fishing their waters, he had no nets out. So *Odessa* had run hard, packed with fish, and low in the water, making 12 knots, which would put her in the famously choppy seas on the Atlantic side of Cape Breton Island around four o'clock this afternoon.

Ibrahim and Yousaf, meanwhile, felt seasick to the point of suicide, which can happen to those who have spent a lifetime on land. The day was profoundly unhappy for both, but the evening was truly awful. It was almost 5 p.m. when they ran past the wide estuary bay of the Strait of Canso, the narrow throughway that cuts Nova Scotia in two. They then set off on their 180-mile journey around the east and north coastlines of Cape Breton Island.

They left the land to port, but still ran several miles offshore. For much of the way the rough waves were right on *Odessa*'s starboard beam, but then they turned into a surging, quartering sea, which was constantly trying to slew her stern around and drive her out into ever more dangerous waters.

Ibrahim and Yousaf were too ill to sleep, too sick to eat, and too frightened to move from their cabin. Ibrahim reasoned that Captain Igor plainly knew what he was doing, and he obviously intended to bring this ship home safely. Yousaf, on the other hand, believed Igor Destinov was a suicidal maniac who was taking them all to the brink of hell. He retreated to his bunk and covered his head, unable to comprehend how this tin-can wreck of a ship, which smelled like a half-ton of dead fish, could possibly get anywhere, without sinking to the bottom of the ocean. In silence, except for releasing the occasional anguished burp, Yousaf waited for his God to relieve him of his misery, and deposit him, dead, on the floor of the Atlantic.

They ran all night, up past Point Michaud and Cape Gabarus, finally turning northeast in the small hours, and steaming past Glace Bay and Sydney Mines. It was dawn the following morning when they turned into the wide, calmer waters of the Cabot Strait, which runs between Nova Scotia and Newfoundland.

By now Captain Igor had headed out even further offshore, and he had the helm himself when they adjusted their course six degrees to three-six-zero. This took them through the middle of the Strait and into the world's largest estuary, the Gulf of Saint Lawrence, which drains the mighty river of the same name, and, of course the Great Lakes.

The last point of land in Nova Scotia, Cape North, stands seventy-five miles from the southern tip of Newfoundland, Cape Ray. Out some eighteen miles from Cape North stands St. Paul's Island, known among Canadian mariners as the "Graveyard of the St. Lawrence," owing to centuries of ships, both steam and sail, that had been wrecked there due to big seas, powerful tides, gale force winds, and gigantic rock ledges. Captain Igor gave St. Paul's a very wide berth, running due north and leaving the island five miles off his port beam.

Ibrahim had begun to feel much better, and in the middle of the morning, he took his cell phone out on deck and tried to make contact with his masters. There was still no connection to Faisal al-Assad in New York, and he tried Sheikh Abdullah in England. Somewhat to his amazement the Yorkshire-based imam answered his phone.

He was genuinely thrilled to hear from Ibrahim, because he knew things had gone wrong in Connecticut, and he didn't know until now that they were safe.

Both men understood the danger of lingering too long on the telephone, and the business part of the conversation was conducted with slick efficiency. Sheikh Abdullah had Ibrahim's cell number for any emergency, and he understood the two terrorists were on a Russian trawler, out of Murmansk, and currently crossing the Gulf of Saint Lawrence.

Ibrahim explained they would land in three or four days time, in Nuuk, the capital city of Greenland and the biggest fishing port in the country. Their captain had business to conduct there.

Ibrahim said that he trusted Captain Destinov, and already had accepted there would be a twenty-four-hour stopover before they proceeded on a fourteen-hundred-mile voyage to Iceland. This would take them across the ten-thousand-foot deep Irminger Basin, that freezing northern corner of the Atlantic where the pack-ice comes rumbling and groaning out from the Greenland Coast, sealing off the entire eastern part of the country for the winter.

Sheikh Abdullah did not much like the sound of all that, but he took careful notes, and agreed to have money wired to the main office of the Bank of Iceland, which would be awaiting them upon their arrival in Reykjavik.

They would leave the ship in the big southern Iceland fishing port of Vestmannaey, and from there take a short local flight up to the international airport. There were many foreign flights in and out of Iceland these days, and Ibrahim said he would leave it to his commanders to book him and Yousaf to somewhere in Europe, probably Amsterdam, and then on to Peshawar or Riyadh, wherever was most convenient.

He and Sheikh Abdullah agreed to speak again when the *Odessa* docked in Vestmannaey.

MACK BEDFORD was pacing so much, he was wearing out the carpet in the living room as the first snows of winter blew against the house. He'd just gotten off the phone with Captain Ramshawe, who had briefed him on the latest police Intelligence regarding the ex-Guantanamo fugitives.

Both the Canadians and the Maine State Troopers believed Ibrahim and Yousaf were still hiding somewhere in Nova Scotia. There was a reasonably efficient photographic security system in the ferry port in Yarmouth. They had spent hours comparing the disembarking passengers with the prison pictures and those taken by Johnny Strauss, and they had plainly identified the two Middle Eastern terrorists who had landed on Canadian soil.

The Mounties issued a full statement about the dragnet they had placed around the ferry terminal, and the diligence with which they had searched for the men. A detective inspector expressed his sincere appreciation of the work that had gone "beyond the call of duty." He was also confident the fugitives could not be far away, and that the Royal Canadian Mounted Police would get their men in the end, they always did.

Mack had an atlas fully opened on the sofa, and he was referring to it every few minutes. He had now arrived at an irrevocable conclusion, which he expressed to himself in rich Navy SEAL parlance: *There is no way those two Towelheads are still friggin' around in Nova fucking Scotia.*

He had it all reasoned out, and he stood in the center of the room and issued an impassioned soliloquy to anyone who cared to listen, which was no one. Anne and Tommy were not due home for another hour.

IBRAHIM SHARIF and Yousaf Mohammed, he stated. Both highly educated, Harvard and London. These are two guys who are able to deal with imperatives. They knew to clear the datum immediately when their bus blew. They knew to get out of Connecticut. Somehow, when Johnny's pictures were circulated and the hunt for their number plate was on, all along the East Coast, they knew before anyone else they'd been rumbled.

They knew to abandon the Dodge truck, and that they could forget about public transport. They knew they needed an anonymous new car, and it took 'em about five minutes to get one. They knew not to just *take* one and risk getting caught when the driver reported the theft. They waited for him, and they knew that to shoot him stone dead would buy them time. Already fucking nearly two days.

They knew not to drive back across Maine, running the gauntlet of the state troopers. They knew to head for a lonely country road, and they picked the one that led to the only ferry port in that part of the country.

And where's that ferry going? It's going to Dead End City. Nova Scotia, where there's only one highway out, over the Fucking Nowhere Bridge, or whatever it's called, back to mainland New Brunswick.

Except you could seal all of their little airports, plus the highway, with about four guys. Not the best place for a terrorist leader to run. "I think I'll charge into a fucking rat-trap and wait till they find me!"

But no. That's not what they did. Because Nova Scotia has boats and ships. Freighters and fishermen. And about a zillion miles of coastline, jetties, seaports, and harbors.

And those al-Qaeda guys have plenty of money. Any goddamned halfwit could hitch a ride on a big freighter or a trawler if he had several thousand U.S. dollars. And these two characters are not halfwits.

They went to Nova Scotia alright, but not to hide out. They went to get out. By sea. You want to find them? Start checking out all ships that left Nova Scotia ports in the thirty-six hours after Mr. Ridley was murdered. Because Mr. Sharif and Mr. Mohammed are in one of them right now.

MACK CALLED Jimmy Ramshawe to share his conclusions. He suggested that the CIA speak to the Canadians about charting every vessel that sailed out of Nova Scotia from the moment the first ferry available to Ibrahim landed in Yarmouth, through the next forty-eight hours.

"Christ!" said Jimmy. "That might be five hundred ships."

"You want to find those guys, that's what you have to do."

"Can't we eliminate some right away?"

"Yes. Those two would not want to be in any boat that's going out into deep water, and then coming home to Nova Scotia. They'd want an international ship, fishing or freight, that's sailing away and not coming back."

"That should narrow it down," said Jimmy.

"But it won't make it any easier. Right now they could be on a ship that's still in Canadian waters, but it's much more likely they're out in the open ocean, in international waters, with a captain they've paid well."

"Well, not even the bloody Mounties can stop and search that, right?" said Jimmy. "We don't have any rights out there. And if we wanted to arrest them when they make land, we'd have to apply for warrants and extradition and Christ knows what else—when we don't even know if the bastards are on board."

"Even if we did, we'd need the Royal Canadian Navy to deploy their entire Atlantic Fleet—that's about half a dozen frigates and a couple of very old destroyers."

"Mack, old buddy," concluded Jimmy, "There is no way this is going to happen. Maybe they'd have helped if Ibrahim and his mates had been successful. But they're not about to rearrange their entire naval defense policy to catch a couple of blokes who might have shot the bloody bank manager."

"Then we're just going to wait it out, right?" said Mack. "And I don't mean wait for the Mounties to catch 'em. I mean for someone to make a mistake, and get rumbled on the systems. Like they did before."

"Guess so," said Jimmy.

"But, you can assume they're on a ship," said Mack. "Maybe even holding the captain at gunpoint. And there is one action we can take. We should alert our surveillance guys everywhere east of Nova Scotia. I mean all the SOSUS stations. Just give 'em the buzzwords, tell 'em who we're after, coupla guys on a freighter."

"I'll get it done, Mack. But something better shake loose soon, otherwise we'll miss them. And they'll make it to the back end of the Hindu Kush, protected by a bloody army of Taliban and al-Qaeda warriors. What happens then?"

"I'll go in after them," said Mack. "And when I find them, I'll take them out."

SHEIKH ABDULLAH BAZIR put an e-mail through to Shakir Khan immediately: *Our children expected to arrive Reykjavik in about a week. Excellent fishing but they need cash. Will you arrange tickets Reykjavik–home. All love from me and the family. Abby Bazir.*

The wily old Bradford mullah was better at this than Shakir Khan. It was a message of the utmost simplicity. Plainly family. Plainly not worth intercepting. Completely effective. Completely secret.

Shakir Khan was full of both admiration and gratitude, and he asked Kaiser to go inside and switch on the government wall computer, so they could begin to follow the long journey home of Ibrahim and Yousaf. Kaiser would fix the money and the tickets tomorrow.

They agreed on the Bank of Iceland and Icelandic Airways to Amsterdam. Both the bank wire and the air tickets would be issued in names coinciding with the passports Ibrahim and Yousaf first used to enter England many weeks previously.

THE *ODESSA* STILL ran strongly through the Gulf of Saint Lawrence with that hard nor'easter right on her starboard bow. A lighter vessel would have been riding up on the crests, heeling left, fighting the ocean every step of the way. But the *Odessa* was a heavyweight in these bleak near-Arctic waters, and she had a zillion tons of solid steel in her bow.

If necessary she would act as her own ice-breaker, riding up on the ice shelf and allowing her front-end weight to smash down on the frozen section. Most people believe that an ice-breaker somehow cleaves her way forward, cutting the ice and shoving it aside, but that's not the case. The ship actually rides up and crashes down.

Big trawlers, out of one of Russia's most northern ports on the southern shores of the winter-frozen Barents Sea, are built to withstand the most unimaginable conditions. Despite Yousaf still feeling more dead than alive, the ship and its crew were ultimately in safe hands.

They pressed on along their three-six-zero bearing, all the way up the west coast of Newfoundland, heading to the Straits of Belle Isle, that narrow northern exit from the Gulf, where the fierce tidal waters fed by a thousand swift-flowing rivers wash out into the Labrador Sea.

Captain Igor glanced at the flashing light on his port side and checked his chart. From Yarmouth, they'd just put seven hundred nautical miles under the keel and were approaching the halfway point of their voyage to Greenland. The hefty Russian seaman felt the ocean swell raise the ship as they pushed out to Belle Isle itself, which stands in the mouth of the twelve-mile wide Strait.

He left that to starboard and headed out into the open waters and chilly silence of the Labrador Sea. The ocean he would cross was about two miles deep in the middle; a fact he understood the ailing Yousaf was not anxious to contemplate.

Out there, *Odessa* would be in very lonely international waters, although the first couple of hundred miles comes under the jurisdiction of Canada. But Igor Destinov had no intention of fishing. Greenland was his objective, and he intended to keep his nets dry until he reached the Vestmannaey off the coast of Iceland.

Besides, he had made a deal with Ibrahim and his sick friend, and while he would keep his end of the bargain, he wanted them out of his life as quickly as possible.

And so they kept going, passing over great shoals of cod and halibut, for three days and three nights, until they reached the great port of Nuuk, which is set at the head of three enormous Greenland fjords, 150 miles south of the Arctic Circle.

There was no one there to greet them, which to Ibrahim meant the Americans did not know where they were. Captain Igor moored at a loading dock and transferred his fifty tons of frozen Atlantic cod to the hold of the *Gorky*. They immediately took on fuel, and cleared the harbor by nightfall, heading south to Kap

Farvel on the southernmost tip of Greenland, a distance of two-hundred-fifty miles.

It was a twelve-hundred-mile run from Farvel to Iceland, and for Ibrahim it was lightened by the slow but definite improvement in the condition of Yousaf. "Sometimes very good to be that sick," said Captain Igor. "Sometimes you never get sick again."

"Not good to get that sick," replied Yousaf. "Not sometimes. Not ever."

"Ungrateful bastard," bellowed Igor, shaking with laughter. "I'm trying to encourage you."

"No need," said Yousaf. "This is my last-ever voyage. I'd rather live in a cave."

"Hey!" roared the Captain. "That's my personal cabin you're insulting. I throw you overboard, ungrateful bastard!" This final flourish of wit was entirely too much for Igor, who had to let go of the wheel so he could wipe his eyes with his big seaman's gloves.

"This is our last night," he added. "You drink some vodka with me. Make you feel better. I tell the cook to grill steaks for us. Fed up with fish."

Ibrahim had been trying to read a Russian magazine during this highly intellectual exchange, but he heard that last piece of information very clearly. This would be an excellent time for him to call Sheikh Bazir, because from here it was only a two-hour time difference—5:30 p.m. in Bradford and the mullah would be in his office before evening prayers.

Outside on deck the sun was shining, although the weather was very cold. But the skies were clear, and Ibrahim guessed there would be first-class reception from his phone to the mullah's in Yorkshire's high country. The deck was deserted. The ship was running fast, due east, and Ibrahim dialed the number. Sheikh Abdullah was again delighted to hear from him and addressed him as "My son," which was a good sign.

He told the mullah, "This Russian trawler docks in Iceland tomorrow afternoon. Yousaf and I will leave right away by air from the airport near Reykjavik. When we get on that flight to Europe it will be the first time I have smiled since before the bus blew at Canaan."

Sheikh Abdullah was cautionary. "Be careful with your words, my son. There are many ears in the North Atlantic."

"Not here on this ship," said Ibrahim. "The deck is deserted. I'm all alone."

"Good-bye," said the Sheikh. "And may Allah bring you home."

Ibrahim was right about one thing. The satellite reception was very good. Too good. And the entire phone call was picked up and recorded at the United States Navy listening station at Husavik, on the cold north shore of Iceland.

This is one of the most sophisticated surveillance operations on earth, situated as it is in the middle of the GIUK Gap—the Greenland-Iceland-UK throughway for Russian submarines in the narrowest part of the Atlantic.

Every Russian underwater boat heading out into the real world from their northern bases passed through here every week of the Cold War. The American and Royal Navy technicians logged every one of them, from the relatively small diesel-electric Kilo Class hunter-killer inshore boats, to the thunderous ICBM-carrying Typhoon Class nuclear giants.

Neither the Americans nor the Brits have ever dropped their guard. They still say if a whale farts up here in the GIUK, half a dozen U.S. surveillance operators in Iceland have about four hemorrhages apiece.

This is also the most sensitive area for SOSUS—the U.S. Navy's ultra-secret SOund SUrveillance System—the long-range sonar network of electronic wires laid in "squares" across the sea bed, waiting to sound a very loud alarm when any ship, submarine, ocean liner, fishing boat, or warship crosses one of those lines.

The system does not give an accurate GPS location, but it puts the ship in a "square," probably ten miles by ten miles. Once the ship comes out of that square, an alarm goes off like a klaxon in about six different places.

Like several ships in the area, Captain Igor's *Odessa* had already been located making a beeline for Iceland. But there had not been any heavy electronic communications around Iceland for most of the day. There were no warships, only fishing boats, and the Husavik operators were used to their chit-chat about the weather, and more or less ignored it.

But Ibrahim's phone call to Bradford was not fisherman's chit-chat. And those GIUK operators were fantastically alert for anything out of the ordinary. And when a young technician suddenly picked up a half-crazed Arab terrorist checking in with his masters, the Husavik system went into overdrive, recording, interpreting, decoding, checking for encryption.

And Ibrahim sounded like Buzzword International, thanks to the alert issued by Captain Ramshawe. "Yousaf," one of the names, fitted. "Russia trawler" was perfect. Destination: obviously Reykjavik, Iceland. Onward flight to Europe. And then, of course, the jackpot phrase: "the bus blew at Canaan."

The only facts they did not know were the name of the ship, where it had come from, and to which particular Icelandic fishing port it was headed. Iceland is a big place with a lot of ports, and it is not American, so there would need to be diplomatic assistance to breach the quite close cooperation between the fishermen of Russia and the Iceland fleet.

Husavik's short report was instantly relayed to Naval Intelligence in Washington. Captain Ramshawe called Mack Bedford in Maine.

"I'm going to the Middle East, right away," Mack said. "We've got a good chance of missing these guys in Iceland since we don't know where they're landing. They could even have a private jet waiting for them. And it's always impossible for our guys to move fast in a reluctant foreign country.

"They're going home. And they're moving fast. You can try Iceland, but I wouldn't count on it. Just keep your eye on the ball. You don't want them publicly dragged into an American court and then tried for murder. Because then you're back where you started. Two dangerous terrorists in the slammer with a hundred lawyers trying to get 'em out. You don't want them in the slammer. You want them dead."

"Whatever you say, Commander. Whatever you say."

MACK PACKED HIS big leather grip and waited for the Navy helicopter to pick him up for the short flight to the Brunswick base. There, as before, he would board a Royal Navy aircraft flying between Washington and RAF Lyneham in England. He was actually across the Atlantic before the *Odessa* arrived in Vestmannaey.

When the *Odessa* did arrive, shortly after noon, both Ibrahim and Yousaf were surprised at the remoteness of the location. Vestmannaey is a large island off the south coast of Iceland, and its seaport is often the busiest fishing harbor in the country. A quarter of a million tons of fish are caught there every year.

But the rest of the island is nearly deserted, with a truly spectacular coastline, high cliffs, vast green fields, and empty seas. There is a small airport behind the harbor, and Igor arranged a ride for them, a flight up to Keflavik International Airport.

"You take my friends to airplane," he told the taxi driver. "And don't worry, they got heavy U.S. dollars. Rich mysterious men."

Ibrahim could have done without that, and sensed he paid through the nose for his ride. But it was quick, and a small local airline agreed to fly them immediately the twenty-five miles to Keflavik for two hundred dollars each.

By this time there was a single American CIA agent from the U.S. Embassy on duty in the airport, but his task was unenviable. The airport was busy, and he had no idea which airline he was looking for, nor indeed where his targets were heading.

As it happened, Sheikh Abdullah Bazir had been very smart in masterminding the tickets. When he found out the ETA of the *Odessa*, he dovetailed it with the Iceland Express nonstop flight FI503 to Amsterdam out of Keflavik International, departing at 3:30 p.m. He booked them first class, and counted on Ibrahim to get them there a few minutes before 3 p.m. That way, he knew, there would be no waiting around.

Ibrahim and Yousaf disembarked their private local flight and walked into the airport. They made one stop at the Bank of Iceland desk and picked up a package of cash they knew would be there, subject to identification with their forged passports.

They both then walked to the Icelandic Express desk, where they were treated with immense courtesy and handed their boarding passes.

"You can go straight to the departure gate," said the pale blonde check-in girl. "The flight will leave on time."

The CIA agent never had a chance. FI503 roared into the cold empty skies at 3:35 p.m. and set a southeastern course, straight across the Norwegian Sea, twelve hundred miles to the Netherlands.

When they arrived in Amsterdam, Ibrahim and Yousaf went straight to the transfer desk, where their tickets were waiting—first class on KLM's 12:30 a.m. flight to Dubai, arriving at 5:35 in the morning. There was a two-hour wait in the desert kingdom before the connecting 9 a.m. flight to Lahore.

They used this time to find some breakfast, especially Yousaf who had eaten nothing for about week and had lost about fourteen pounds.

Fed, watered, but thoroughly exhausted, they arrived in Lahore at 11:10 a.m. (local), having lost four hours across the time zones. Awaiting them was Kaiser Rashid, with a small private passenger jet, provided by Shakir Khan, mainly because Lahore is situated way southeast on the Indian border, 240 miles from Peshawar.

Mack's journey had been relatively simpler. He'd been provided with yet another military flight, this time from RAF Lyneham to the U.S. Air Force Base at Landstuhl, up near Germany's western border with France, about fifty-five miles southwest of Frankfurt.

From there he'd been flown nonstop in a huge military Boeing, the C-141, directly to the massive sprawl of the five-thousand-acre

U.S. base in Bagram, Afghanistan, a place where thousands of troops were stationed in lines and lines of bee-huts, with the one long runway running right down the side of the whole complex.

This had been home to Mack Bedford twice before, and, as the Boeing made its long approach, he could see there were already white peaks on the towering Hindu Kush mountains. Below them he could see almost sheer escarpments, which looked impossible to climb, but he and his SEALs had fought their way up them and across them, in search of the sullen, silent warriors, who were trying to reinstate the Taliban.

To Mack it seemed his personality changed as soon as he saw this place. It had been a war zone for so long, it had an effect on even the most hardened SEAL commanders. It was a place where no one dared to drop their guard, and there was only one reason to come here: combat.

This wasn't training. This was real. Sometime in the not-too-distant future he, Mackenzie Bedford, was going to face armed tribesmen, mountain men who would not be fussy whether they slit his throat or shot him dead.

He could see squadrons of parked aircraft, and Chinook helicopters, and he could see the main executive block, where INTEL, Planning, and Surveillance had private areas. He would, he knew, be given private quarters in there, like some visiting general, instead of a veteran combat commander with a thousand friends on base.

But Mack knew the rules. He was to remain out of sight. The fewer people who knew he was there, the better his masters would like it. But unlike everyone else, he was moving in on a pure hunch: that Ibrahim Sharif and Yousaf Mohammed would return home, the way Pashtuns always did, answering the ancient summons of their tribal ancestors, obeying the call of their own souls, to walk once more in those verdant green mountain passes, and to rejoin two-thousand-year-old Pashtun communities in far-lost villages, where their friends and loved ones still lived.

There was so much of the American Indian in these people.

They were all expert trackers and livestock men, supremely skilled with any kind of weapon, and capable of moving through those mountains in almost complete silence.

Mack had prided himself in his capacity to remain absolutely motionless, in any position, during his time earning Honor Man in SEAL Sniper School. But to these people his soft, wary tread probably sounded like an express train coming through. He and his men were quiet, but not as quiet as the native mountain men. And if he wanted to carry on breathing, that was an important fact to bear in mind.

The Boeing touched down at Bagram eight hours after leaving Landstuhl. A Navy staff car met him at the bottom of the aircraft steps, and he was driven immediately to the block where he would be housed. There he was greeted by the base commanding officer, whom he knew on equal terms from his previous life as a SEAL, and taken to his new quarters.

"Mack," said the CO, "you can dine with me and my staff any time you wish. But if you want to be alone, that's fine too. I have not been briefed on your mission, but I do know it's highly classified. I have, however, been told that you are to be given every possible assistance in weaponry, combat clothing, INTEL, comms, and transportation. You can count on all of that."

Mack shook his hand. "Thanks, Eric," he said. "I appreciate it."

"By the way," said the CO, grinning, "I have of course guessed why you are here. And I understand you have done a fantastic job so far on whatever mission it is. But I'm still not sure why you think you're on the right track up here in these godforsaken mountains."

"Just counting on a couple of little sonsabitch murderers coming home to Mommy," replied Mack, inelegantly.

IBRAHIM AND YOUSAF bought a two-day-old copy of *USA Today* in the airport at Lahore, and there, on page seven, they found a short news item under the headline:

MOUNTIES CONFUSED OVER VANISHING MAINE MURDER SUSPECTS

Halifax. Thursday. The Royal Canadian Mounted Police have called off their manhunt in Nova Scotia for two men wanted for the murder of Bangor bank manager, Jed Ridley, more than a week ago.

The two suspects, both believed to be from the Middle East, apparently took the ferry from Bar Harbor, where Mr. Ridley's body was found, hidden in his own car, which had been driven into deep woodland.

For several days, Canadian investigators were certain the two men were somewhere in Nova Scotia, while they attempted to gain passage on a ship leaving the country. A spokesman said last night they now consider the men had left the peninsula even before the search began. Associated Press.

Ibrahim found something immensely satisfying in that news item. He had pitted his wits twice against the Great Satan. The first time he had lost, but the second time he had won. There was something exhilarating about that, and he happily regaled Kaiser Rashid with the story of their adventure all the way up to Peshawar in the government private jet.

Kaiser himself was deeply impressed by the care and efficiency with which Ibrahim had prepared the mission. And he did not believe the leak, which had obviously alerted the Americans to the forthcoming attack, was anything to do with the operational team that Ibrahim had led.

Shakir Khan's assistant was another al-Qaeda disciple being groomed for the highest rank. His first-class law degree from King's College, London, set him apart from most other members of this fanatical underground brotherhood. Kaiser's intellect made him invaluable to Khan. But the fire of the revolutionary zealot burned within him, and Kaiser's instincts were trusted by men in the highest places.

Right now his instincts were telling him someone had hacked into their carefully planned communications; twice, so far as he could tell. Once between Peshawar and Sheikh Abdullah in Bradford, England. And again between Pakistan and New York.

His reasons were cold and legal: three of our men on Ilkley Moor died because someone knew they were coming, and someone knew why they were there. The New York intercept was the same. Someone knew about Mountainside Farm, otherwise they could not possibly have blown our bus before we could blow the school. We never communicated directly with Connecticut, only New York.

What concerned Kaiser was the possibility of a straight leak, a spy, or a mole. "It's one thing to be intercepted by a national military surveillance," he told Ibrahim. "That's just bad luck. But it's another to have a spy operating among us. That's far too dangerous."

He had nothing but admiration for Ibrahim, his intelligence, his courage, and his daring, and deep down Kaiser felt that somehow the organization had let Ibrahim down. He was sympathetic when both of these al-Qaeda field operators told him that they wanted to go home to their families, up in the mountains. They'd both been away for many years. And such had been the intensity of the training in the camps up in the Swat Valley, there had been no time to go home, not even for a day.

Al-Qaeda was determined to recover from the Canaan setback and move fast on another mission that would rival 9/11 in U.S. devastation. In Kaiser's view, the experience of Ibrahim and Yousaf was priceless, and he would insist they were a part of it.

However, if they were not allowed home, their hearts may not be in it. It was critical to any future mission that Ibrahim and Yousaf be contented warriors. They needed to be taken home for a couple of weeks' recuperation.

Kaiser reasoned they had both been through hell, and Allah

had smiled upon them both by bringing them safely home against near-impossible odds. Reuniting them with their families was, in Kaiser's opinion, the will of Allah.

As soon as their aircraft landed, all three men—Kaiser, Ibrahim, and Yousaf—attended a formal debriefing in the big house behind the *Andar Shehr* in Peshawar. Aside from Khan and Kaiser, there were three other al-Qaeda men in attendance, all of whom would accompany Ibrahim and Yousaf home.

There were the two brothers, Ahmed and Gholam Azzan, Pakistanis by birth, forward commanders and assault instructors in al-Qaeda. Ahmed was thirty-eight years old, the senior by two years. He had served bin Laden faithfully through all the years of jihad, and intended to continue doing so, whether or not The Sheikh had died in the U.S. onslaught in Tora Bora.

The Azzans had both been born in the Swat Valley in the river town of Madyan, as had Shakir Khan himself. The third man in attendance was Captain Musa Amin, a one-time commander of the most successful small Taliban army in the Hindu Kush. Two hundred strong, they had harassed and killed any U.S. military personnel with whom they came in striking range.

The Americans, however, had, in the end, very nearly wiped out this entire force in a lethal ambush, and Amin at the age of forty, had been forced to flee. Badly wounded, he had reached one of the al-Qaeda training camps and slowly risen back to his former prestigious position, chief instructor and forward commander.

There was no finer mountain warrior than Captain Musa Amin, no more skilled tracker, no better gunner. And he was desperately protective of his nephew, Ibrahim Sharif.

Shakir Khan took it upon himself to bring al-Qaeda's new favorite sons home. Their objective was a tiny village called Kushram. It was situated below one of the high plateaux, around seven miles from the village of Sabray, which was built on similar lines, set into the steep mountain. Indeed, Sabray shared the same village elder, a hickory-tough old gentleman of seventy-eight summers, upon whose word rough Taliban terrorists trembled.

With only two ovens in the entire village, Kushram might not have been everyone's ideal. But it was home to Ibrahim, and in a way, to Captain Amin, the brother of Ibrahim's mom. It was also home to Yousaf, whose own parents had died, and who had no other roots except the immediate family of his oldest friend.

Shakir Khan listened very gravely to Kaiser Rashid's suspicions about the leaks, and he declared he would launch a private investigation. However, he understood the most pressing issue was to get Ibrahim and Yousaf home, and he outlined his plans.

There would be five of them altogether, including the Azzan brothers and Captain Amin. They would travel by road from Peshawar, 140 miles up the winding, mountainous Highway 45 to Chitral airport. From there, Khan would organize a Pakistani Air Force helicopter to take the five men seventy-five miles into the Hindu Kush, landing them on the high plateau above the village of Kushram. From there they could walk the mile down to the houses.

The incredibly blurred line between official government troops and armed al-Qaeda loyalists was never more vividly illustrated. The sheer number of disloyal regular officers and men in Pakistan's armed forces was bringing the nation to the brink of civil war.

The officers were devoutly loyal to the Taliban and to al-Qaeda, and they wanted the government overthrown and the Islamic extremists in power. And they were happy to organize brutal and murderous attacks on their own commanding officers and colleagues in order to achieve their aims.

When a man like Shakir Khan gave an order, it was carried out, because Khan was a known and celebrated Muslim extremist, and he knew to whom he should issue that order. Nonetheless, he still worked for the ruling government. Could there ever have been a more treacherous set of circumstances prevailing in any nation on earth? Especially in a country with a nuclear capability, as Pakistan had. The truth was, particularly up here on the North Western Frontier, no one knew whose side sections of the Army were on.

However, it was all pretty good for the homecoming kings.

They would leave at first light, and, of course, on such a journey in this part of the country, they would all need to be well armed. When the black government limousine arrived for the drive to Chitral, it would be loaded with five AK-47s and ammunition belts, plus a box of four hand grenades. The connecting Air Force helicopter, a Russian-built Mi-17 transporter, with its distinctive portside tail rotor, would bring them, in addition, four rocket-propelled grenades.

Neither the roads nor the airways were any place to travel in Pakistan these days; not without being armed to the teeth. And the ever-present danger, even for Air Force helicopters flying very high over the Hindu Kush, was the possibility of being hit with a missile fired by the Taliban.

Shakir Khan wished them all well before retiring to bed; he was not yet awake when they left for Chitral at six o'clock the following morning. Neither for that matter, was Kaiser Rashid.

It took them four hours to make the small airfield at Chitral, and the helicopter was waiting. They gathered up their weapons and ammunition and climbed aboard. There was a three-man crew, including the navigator, and his job was critical, for there are no roads or railways to guide a pilot up here; just deep valleys and towering peaks, up to twenty thousand feet. As a point of contrast, these peaks were more than ten times the height of Haystack Mountain.

The GPS numbers were vital because it was difficult to take a mark on the steep escarpments down below. It was essential to have a fast, armor-plated Kevlar aircraft to fly across this border, which is why Shakir Khan had chosen this Russian warhorse.

They lifted off the runway with the sun at their backs, silhouetting them to any enemy operating out to the west of them. But the pilot was highly trained, and he immediately climbed ten thousand feet, then fifteen thousand. They could still get hit, but the height and speed of the aircraft made it increasingly difficult. The Taliban rocket men could be somewhat efficient at low level, but they were not *that* good.

The journey took only a half hour, flying at 140 knots all the way, up near its service ceiling of twenty thousand feet. The pilot came down on GPS numbers, although Ibrahim and Yousaf could see the village clinging to the mountainside below the plateau.

They were asked to disembark as quickly as possible, carrying their weapons and bags. All five of them stood in the high pastures, a couple of hundred yards from a sizeable herd of goats, and they watched the helicopter take off straight up into the cloudless sky, before clattering away, back east to Pakistan.

The al-Qaeda men slung their ammunition belts diagonally across their chests, pulled their rifles onto their shoulders, and they headed down the steep grass slopes, straight toward Kushram's main street, straight toward the home of Ibrahim's parents, third house on the left.

BACK AT THE BAGRAM BASE, Mack Bedford was preparing. He had made a rough estimation of the ETA of the terrorist's flight from Europe, and another guesstimate of the time it would take them to reach Peshawar, where the first intercepted phone call had been made.

By now he was sure, that if he were correct, and they were indeed coming home, they would be there by now. In strictest confidence he had asked an old buddy, now working right here in INTEL, to stay alert for a new cell phone, probably belonging to the guy who had tried to blow the Connecticut school.

This was all routine for these INTEL guys. They had spies and moles everywhere, which was how the SEALs had long been so brilliantly successful at locating the worst terrorists and getting them sent to Guantanamo Bay. He checked every couple of hours for some indication that Ibrahim and Yousaf had arrived at last in Kushram.

Right here, Mack was dealing with déjà vu *all over again*, to quote the immortal Yogi. Six years ago, he'd gone through this very process, checking it out over and over, trying to get the go-ahead to take his SEAL Team 10 guys and nail these mountain bastards who'd killed fifteen Marines and two of his SEAL brothers on the outskirts of Kabul.

And they'd achieved their objectives. And here he was again. Same mountains, same bastards, same mission. Except that this time he would be alone, and the unspoken fear that dwelt within him was that this Ibrahim fuckhead would recognize him.

Six years ago, they had stared into each other's eyes. There had been pure hatred between them. Ibrahim had spat at him. In turn Mack had grabbed him by the balls and half-drowned him in the rain barrel.

If he screwed this up to even the slightest degree, he would be shown no mercy. He would be tortured, and then they would empty their rifles into his face so that no one would ever recognize him, even in death.

For a normal human being, such a possibility would be frightening beyond endurance. But for Mack Bedford it produced only a rising of what he called the "Hours of the Wolf," a phrase he had borrowed from the Swedish film director, Ingemar Whatsisname. It was a phrase that, for him, described a personal feeling of such surging fury, such a blinding red mist of anger, there was no going back.

He had not felt it once since that day at the bridge on the Euphrates when he'd shot down the twelve Iraqi terrorists who'd just wiped out half of his platoon.

But he felt it now, just at the memory of that day in Kushram when Ibrahim had spat in his face. He remembered, too, the pure hatred on the face of the Afghani, as SEAL Team 10 had arrested him. And he remembered also the intentions of these people toward the innocents of Canaan Academy.

The Hours of the Wolf were welling up inside him, but he fought down that old feeling of uncontrolled anger. Because that rising fury always signaled the moment when Mack felt he was indestructible, with the strength of ten men.

And that could lead to recklessness in the face of the enemy.

And the former SEAL commander had a lot of reasons to avoid that, at all times.

THE FIVE HEAVILY ARMED al-Qaeda field commanders walked down the hill in a kind of military formation—Ibrahim and Yousaf together in the lead, the Azzan brothers and Captain Amin right behind them in a line of three.

All five wore Afghan tribal dress, the *shalwar kameez*, the traditional tunic and baggy white trousers, the long *dupatta* scarf, and the small *pakol* hat. Between them the Azzans carried the box of RPGs.

By now the villagers had spotted them and had swarmed to the top of the one narrow through-street, which snaked down their mountain. Ibrahim and Yousaf led the homecoming. Everyone began to clap, and the children jumped up and down and yelled, "Welcome Home!" as they had been instructed.

Ibrahim's father ran forward to greet the son he had believed he would never see again. Because news of the catastrophe in Connecticut had by now traveled far, all the way to the high peaks from the seething bazaars of Peshawar's old city.

There was no resident of the Hindu Kush tribal lands who was unaware that ten al-Qaeda martyrs had perished in a distant land serving the cause of Allah. Everyone in Kushram had thought Ibrahim and Yousaf had died with the others.

Ibrahim's father, his arms around both his son and Yousaf, wept with joy. The other three al-Qaeda warriors were swept up by the throng and half-carried into the main street, where the village arrived with green tea and the once-a-month luxury of sweet pastries, baked today, especially for this occasion. Everyone, it seemed, knew they were coming, despite the total absence of telephones, television, radio, or even electricity.

It took two hours for the excitement to die down and for the women to return to the two ovens in the village to begin preparations for the evening feast, which the elders had sanctioned. It took a tribal caucus for permission to slaughter three goats, because it was the milk from these farm herds that kept everyone alive throughout the year.

The feast would begin in the afternoon because when darkness fell up here, the mountain went pitch black, and everyone was compelled to retire to bed.

Meanwhile there was astonishing activity at Ibrahim's home, where he had not set foot for six years, not since Mack Bedford had manhandled him across the threshold, kicking Yousaf hard in the ass for good measure.

No member of the family had ever forgotten the humiliation of that day. Ibrahim's defiance and bravery, the terrible insult to Yousaf, the lady next door inconsolable after a SEAL had broken her son's jaw for spitting at him. It was said that Ibrahim's father had never spoken a word while his son was a prisoner of the Americans.

Today was a day not just of joy, but of remembrance for the lost heroes on the Connecticut school bus. Of celebration for the return of the village sons. The accompanying senior al-Qaeda commanders represented a confirmation of the high regard in which Ibrahim and Yousaf were held, probably even by bin Laden himself.

Way up here, ten thousand feet above sea level, and yet another ten thousand feet below the mountain peak, there was much for which to be thankful as the warriors mingled with the elders and the goatherders, selecting sites for the armed sentries tonight.

Wherever al-Qaeda and their Taliban comrades were gathered together, it became an automatic military garrison. The mountains were silent, but that did not lessen the dangers to these renegade illegal combatants, implacably waging war against the Pakistani Army, the Afghan Government's Army, and the United States. They could never drop their guard.

EVERY DAY AT BAGRAM, busloads of Afghan workers poured into the American base. In addition to all the electronic surveillance being conducted here, it was from these gangs of laborers, carpenters, builders, painters, and concrete mixers that critical information was often gathered.

The entire Afghani workforce was seeded with U.S. INTEL, listening for the whispered word, the off-guard moment, the accidental betrayal. Waiting for the Afghani who had something to sell.

Unsurprisingly, it took about ten minutes that morning for rumor to sweep through Bagram that two known al-Qaeda terrorists had arrived back in their village from the United States.

Mackenzie Bedford was ready to act. He went immediately to the CO and announced he was going in tonight. He needed to get kitted out, and required a ride in a helo for the insert. He wanted to land around four miles north of his target zone, and then walk in through the pitch dark of the mountain, with his map, compass, GPS, and night glasses.

He understood that on no account could he take with him a bodyguard, since the American military still had no business pursuing Ibrahim and Yousaf. The State Police of Maine could make a case, but not the Pentagon, where the generals and admirals could never be seen riding roughshod over the rule of law in the United States of America. Ibrahim and Yousaf were free men until some terrorist act could be *proven* against them.

Mack's activities in Northwest Connecticut would remain forever a secret. Now two of his former colleagues brought his gear over to his quarters. He needed his battle harness with extra magazines, and two hand grenades. He would take a trusted M-4 light automatic rifle, a SIG-Sauer 9mm pistol, and a combat knife. He took a couple of MREs—Meals Ready to Eat—consisting of beef jerky, energy bars, and peanuts.

At 2130 a young SEAL from Team 10 arrived to tell him a Black Hawk UH-6O was running about a hundred yards away on the runway. Around his head Mack was now wearing a camouflage bandana, what SEALs call their "drive-on rags," and his face was blacked out with cammy cream.

He wore combat boots with his rugged woodland pants and top. Thick leather gloves were jammed in his pockets in case the helo could not land and he needed to fast-rope to the ground.

Bagram never sleeps, but it was quiet outside the block where Mack was staying. The young SEAL messenger led the way, and the former commander shouldered his machine gun, and stepped out, in full combat gear, face unrecognizable in the dark. All SEAL teams look like this when they're "going in." The difference here was that Mackenzie Bedford was unseen by either his colleagues or his commanders. He was all alone.

He strode across the blacktop and boarded the Black Hawk, the U.S. Army's frontline utility helicopter, with its sixteen laser-guided hellfire missiles, ready at all times. Especially here.

The doors slammed shut and they took off, the rotors screaming as they climbed quickly to five thousand feet, then clattered away to the northeast. Forty minutes later the landing controller called back, "Sir, we're in the drop zone. But it's heavy woodland on this side of the mountain, and we can't land."

"Fix the rope," said Mack, "and take it with you."

The ramp went down. The rope snaked down. The pilot hovered about thirty feet above the ground. Mack pulled on the gloves and grabbed the line, testing it for weight.

"Okay, sir. *LET'S GO!*"

Grasping the rope, Mack swung out and slid down as fast as he could go, as there is nowhere quite as vulnerable as halfway down a drop-rope, perhaps already in the sights of a Taliban marksman.

He hit the ground, just a tad harder than normal, and crawled silently into the undergrowth, listening as the helo's engines increased and watching as it rapidly gained height, before rocketing away over the trees.

Mack didn't move or make a sound for fifteen very long, accurately timed minutes; standard SEAL procedure after a drop behind enemy lines.

He kept his back hard to a tree trunk, not wishing to emulate even one of those dozens of young Russian conscripts whose throats had been cut by the Mujahadeen twenty years ago, right here in these same lawless mountains.

Eventually he stood and shoved the gloves in his pocket. He checked his GPS and compass. He had a long walk ahead of him, a good hour down a straight blacktop road, but probably five hours from here, in uncharted woodland, in which he needed to check his every step. His gear weighed thirty pounds and the terrain was rough, hilly, and sometimes slippery on gravel or mud. He was an armed packhorse, trying to walk as delicately as a ballet dancer, through a black forest.

He set the compass to 180 degrees and began walking due south. The terrain was overgrown, and he eased back on each forward step to avoid breaking a twig or crushing a small bush. The mountain men have ears like sonar beams, and the slightest sound would betray his position.

At one point he slipped into a dry ditch, and he heard the shale crunch under his boots. For a second his heart stood still, and again he stayed motionless for two minutes, listening. But again there was no sound or movement in this petrified night forest.

Once more he picked his way forward, stepping softly, holding his hands in front of him and feeling for a branch to grip, trying not to break it. At times the escarpment was almost too steep to retain his footing, but he'd done this many times before. It took all the patience he could muster as he pressed forward, slipping, sliding, and stumbling below a rising moon, toward the sleeping village of Kushram.

He was almost a mile above the houses at 5:30 a.m. when he arrived on the plateau. And he was amused to find that his assumption from the satellite pictures of a flat green pasture turned out to be a field of opium, Kushram's main crop and source of income.

He knew the way down, and his night glasses would guide him. He also knew that if Ibrahim and Yousaf were in residence there would be guards. But more than anything, he knew the battle creed of the Navy SEALs in such circumstances: speed and surprise, plus, if possible, intimidation. Because that's how you achieve your objective.

Mack moved forward, staying off the regular track, and watching for a crop of boulders above the houses. He'd used that for cover a half-dozen years ago.

But when he focused the glasses on the rocks, Mack froze. Sitting right there, with an obvious AK-47 in his hands, was a tribesman, obviously a sentry on the last watch of the night. He seemed to be facing the village and talking, gesticulating, to another person. At which point, Mack had the second guy in focus. He was looking through big Russian binoculars, and he too was pointing, up the hill to where Mack was hunkered down in tall grass.

"Fuck," breathed Mack. "They've seen me." And his mind raced. Right now it was two against one, but if these two raised the alarm, it could be ten against him.

Things seemed to move in slow motion as he studied the two tribesmen, watched them move apart, and then begin walking up the hill toward him, coming in from two wide angles, working as a team. In western terms, this was a regular pincer movement. Zulu warriors used to call it "the horns of the buffalo." There was nothing new about it, and the antidote was universal—one of these guys had to go, and fast. Mack understood this would mean betraying his position, but he liked the odds better.

He could still see the first one, the sentry Ahmed Azzan, but the other one was moving flat along the ground. It was still dark, but Mack had night sights, and he slammed a bullet straight between Ahmed's eyes, killing him instantly.

Now, where the hell's this other bastard? Ahmed fell without a sound, and Mack guessed the sniper on the ground did not know what had happened. For two minutes, which seemed like an hour, Mack lay there, not moving but scanning the terrain as best he could.

And suddenly Gholan Azzan launched his attack. He had

worked his way around silently, coming up on higher ground behind the former SEAL, right on his six o'clock. He was unaware whether Mack was alone, or part of a team, and he wielded a curved, razor-sharp herdsman's knife.

Down the hill he came, racing over the ground, baggy clothes flapping. His soft sandals made no sound on the grass. The dagger jutted from his right hand. There was murder in his heart.

Ten yards out, Mack still had neither seen nor heard him. But there was a thump on the ground as the Pathan tribesman launched himself through the air, his right arm raised. Mack caught the blur of the attack in the corner of his eye, and he rolled left with all of his strength, holding both hands in front of him in the classic SEAL unarmed combat defensive position.

Gholan Azzan tried to twist in the air, to zoom in on his quarry, and he slashed downward with his dagger, trying to stab Mack in the throat. But he was a few inches wide, and the blade just nicked Mack's upper left arm.

Now Mack had a two-handed grip on his assailant, and he clamped his fist on the man's beard, holding the head still while he whipped back the right arm, snapping it at the shoulder.

Azzan screamed. Mack could not stop him. But he sprang to his feet and launched a steam-hammer kick, which landed right below Azzan's open mouth. The force rammed back his head and broke his neck. It was like being hit by a freight train.

The body was still twitching in its death throes when Mack elected to press home his attack. Gathering up his rifle he ran out to his left and on down toward the houses. He came in across rough ground, sliding and scrambling down the mountain to the base of the village and the main street.

There were a lot of people asleep right here. But he'd never have a better chance. He could hide, and select his position here, and attack when the time was right. Also, he knew where Ibrahim lived, and in the soft dawn light, he stared across the street to the house where he had once forced the terrorist to show him the cache of TNT.

He tried to get his bearings, to remember precisely where he'd been before. It seemed familiar, but unfamiliar. For a start, he could not see the rain-butt. Neither did he see the crooked smile of Captain Musa Amin, stationed on the flat roof of the house with a Vladimirov KPV-14.5 heavy machine gun, hijacked years ago by the Mujahadeen from an abandoned Russian tank.

Captain Amin had the American in his sights. And he had one disintegrating steel belt of ammunition. Somehow he knew his comrades up the hill had been hurt in a battle with this monster American, and without hesitation the captain opened fire. He had the minor problem, however, of never having used one of these hard-kicking ex-Soviet tank-busters before.

He thought he'd taken aim, but it ripped at his grip and he let go too fast. The gun lurched left and then right, and the huge bullets blew out in every direction, tearing a pattern in the wall ten feet from where Mack was standing. He had no time to run because this lunatic with the HMG was about to knock down the fucking town the way he was going.

Every door Mack could see was shut. But there was a big window right behind him and he shoulder-charged the glass, diving up and through it, rifle first, more reflex than design. He crashed into an empty room smothered in thick glass, and followed by a hail of machine-gun fire that spit, smacked, and cracked into the walls, cushions, and furniture.

By some miracle he was not hit, and he was safe on the floor, out of the downward angle with which Captain Amin was wrestling. *But if he gets control of that fucking thing, I'm history,* was Mack's only thought. *He could hold back a goddamned Platoon with that thing.*

The captain had seen Mack's entry into the house and decided to finish him right there and then, without spraying another two hundred rounds all over the village. He hauled up an RPG, a weapon with which he was an expert, shoved it into a firing tube, and fired it straight at Mack's window. Missed. By three inches. It hit the wall and knocked down half the front of the house in a massive cloud of sand and brown dust.

Mack saw it coming, the tell-tale white plume of smoke, and he dived though the back door, out onto an almost sheer escarpment, down which he fell with all his gear for almost forty feet. "Fuck me," said Mack. "I'd better kill this bastard before he kills both of us."

With the street now immersed in an enormous cloud of brown dust, Mack made his way back up the cliff, and used the dust-cover to reach the far side of the street unseen by the populace. He made it to another hillside at the back of Ibrahim's house, where he could still see the back of Captain Amin on the roof, adjusting the angle of the HMG.

For the moment, Mack was done with bullets. He hooked the pin out of his first grenade and hurled it straight onto the roof, where it detonated with a stupendous blast, killing Amin, blasting him into the street, caving in half the roof, and obliterating the KPV-14.5 and its wheeled base.

At this point the still clean-shaven Yousaf, terrified, came running out of the back door, waving his Kalashnikov, but choking with dust, unable to see. He'd never see again either. Mack recognized him instantly, and gunned him down with a short, deadly accurate burst from the M-4. *Speed and surprise, baby. Never fails.*

That left only one. But Mack Bedford was not about to hang around waiting for the village to recover its composure, and its courage, and come after him. Nor was he waiting for Ibrahim. He guessed the al-Qaeda fanatic was badly disoriented, maybe even injured in the rubble where the roof had caved in.

Mack had no idea what awaited him through that back door, what eyes were watching him. But if he delayed his attack, there was a good chance he'd die. There were probably fifty Afghan men in Kushram, all armed, and every one an enemy.

If he went now, the odds were with him. And the former Lt. Commander of SEAL Team 10, husband of Anne, father of Tommy, stepped through the back door of Ibrahim Sharif's house.

He found himself in the main room, face to face with Sharif Senior, who was covered in dust, watching him, with his dagger drawn. Ibrahim was dragging himself out from under the debris, holding his rifle.

His father raised his dagger and came straight for Mack's face, but the former SEAL swiveled and landed a crashing upward blow under his chin with the butt of his rifle. As his father flew across the room, Ibrahim by now was on his feet, but dazed, concussed, and uncoordinated. He stared at the American's face, ignoring the M-4, and there was a leer on his face as he said slowly, "So, it's you again, Satan. This time you die."

He raised his AK-47, just a little, before Mack studded four bullets in a dead straight line right across his forehead. And Ibrahim Sharif, terrorist, murderer, fanatic, and Islamist, fell dead at his feet.

Mack Bedford turned on his heel and walked out, into the dustbowl of the street, which was still quiet, its populace still cowering in their dwellings, away from the machine-gun, hand-grenade, and rocket battle that had taken place over the past fifteen minutes. Two houses had been essentially destroyed, and no one was moving.

Mack jogged onto the mountainside and made his way to the high ground. And even as he did so, he heard that familiar *bom-bom-bom-bom* of the Black Hawk's fifty-four-foot main rotor clattering over the high peak above the village, coming in to get him, to haul him out of the opium field and to take him back to rejoin the U.S. Navy SEALs, Team 10, Foxtrot Platoon.

Epilogue

MACK BEDFORD ARRIVED home in Maine to find a short, impersonal, life-changing holy grail of a letter awaiting him:

Dear Commander Bedford,

It gives me great pleasure to confirm your promotion, and your new command of SEAL Team 10, active upon your arrival in Coronado. In my congratulations to you, Admiral Mark Bradfield has asked to be included.

It was signed Rear Admiral Andrew M. Carlow, Commander SPECWARCOM.

The letter was expected, and yet somehow out of the blue. Anne and Tommy both knew they were going back to California and would follow Mack west as soon as the school term ended.

For now it was business as usual in the Bedford household, preparing Dad for a long tour of duty. It took about three days and was made infinitely easier when the local shipyard chairman, Harry Remson, said he would rent their house indefinitely, using it for his visiting children and their families.

What also made it easier was the complete lack of paperwork required from Mack's previous mission. No debriefing, no reports, no lessons learned, no recommendations. Nothing. Not even a phone call.

The highest-ranking security chiefs in the United States, both military and civilian, wanted to know only that the four most dangerous killers freed from Guantanamo Bay were dead, and would trouble them no more.

And they definitely knew that. Because the news came through, encrypted, about twenty-five minutes after Mack had almost blown off the head of Ibrahim Mohammed.

For a few brief, glorious moments, peace reigned at the National Security Agency, the Pentagon, and the CIA. And no one wanted more. Jimmy Ramshawe, Andy Carlow, Bob Birmingham, and Mark Bradfield all wore the secret smiles of unknown, unseen warriors.

Mack flew out of Brunswick, touching down six hours later on the southwest runway, U.S. Naval Air Station, North Island, Coronado, mid-afternoon. He stepped out of the aircraft wearing his Trident for the first time since they'd cruelly hit him with the friggin' GOMOR (General Officer Memorandum of Reprimand), the one that had ended his career. Almost.

His former combat driver, Gunner's Mate 2nd Class, Jack Thomas, out of Nashville, Tennessee, wore a grin as wide as San Diego Bay, as he stood on the runway and greeted his old boss. Then Jack drove him back from the same airport where he'd said good-bye a year previously, after the court martial.

"Everyone's just real pleased y'all comin' back," he said. "We missed you, sir."

"Thanks, Jack," replied the new commander. "I missed all you guys, too. Wasn't one day I didn't think of every last one of you."

"Even me, sir?"

"'Specially you, kid. How many times did you save my life in the old armored vehicle?"

"Twice, sir. Both times in Baghdad."

"And here we go again. Any word where 10's going next?"

"We hear Afghanistan. Nothing definite. But you're a bit of an expert on that place, right, sir?"

"Yeah, I've been there."

Prologue

The most revered square of blacktop in all the United States military
somehow looked even blacker beneath a pale, quartering moon, which
was presently fighting a losing battle with heavy Pacific cloud banks.

Its name, "the grinder," could give a man the creeps. It was a place
where men had, for generations, been crushed, their spirits broken, their
will to succeed cast asunder. It was a place where dreams were ended,
where limitations were faced. It was a place where tough, resolute military men threw in the towel, publicly, and then slipped quietly away.

It was also a place that represented the Holy Grail of the U.S. Navy
SEALs, the place where their battle had begun and ended with the awe-
inspiring moment when the fabled golden Trident was pinned on the
upper left side of their dress uniform.

No member of the U.S. Navy SEALs has ever forgotten that moment.
And for all their lives, the holders of the Trident strive to live up to its
symbolic demands. Everyone who receives it expects to earn that honor
every day throughout the entire tenure of their service.

Such a man now stood alone on the north side of the square. Commander Mackenzie Bedford was back where he belonged, right here on
the grinder, the place where he had once stood as his entire class voted
him Honor Man, the young officer most likely to attain high command
in the world's toughest, most elite fighting force.

There were only twelve of them—the survivors of a six-month or-
deal, which had seen 156 applicants crash and burn, most of them DOR,
or Dropped On Request. They were good guys who just couldn't make

it—couldn't take the murderous training, the endless pounding along the beach, the cold Pacific, the swimming, the rowing, the sleep deprivation, the log-lifting, the elephant runs. Not to mention the stark SEAL command, *Push 'em out*—shorthand for a set of up to eighty eye-popping, muscle-burning, brutal nonstop push-ups. For most of them it was just too much.

But the SEAL instructors do not want most of them. They want only the elite, the young iron-men with the indomitable will to excel, the guys with the strength, speed, and agility, who would rather die than quit.

Not to mention the brains. There are no stupid SEALs. Seventy-five percent of them have college degrees, and they fight and struggle their way through outrageously demanding courses: weaponry, marksmanship, Sniper School, navigation, map-reading, unarmed combat, mountaineering, parachute jumping, even medical courses, in preparation for battlefield duty.

SPECWARCOM commanders have one everlasting comment about the dreaded BUDs course that bars entry to their establishment: *It's harder to get in here than to Harvard Law School. Different, but harder.*

Commander Bedford, dressed in dark blue for the first time in more than a year, walked quietly across the grinder, relishing every step. He'd dreamed of this moment since his court-martial on a charge of mowing down innocent, unarmed Iraqi civilians on the banks of the Euphrates River.

The officers who presided over the legal proceedings did not believe the Iraqis were innocent, unarmed, or even civilians. And the SEAL commander was found not guilty. However they had issued an "officers' reprimand," which finished him in the United States Navy.

There was not one member of the SPECWARCOM community who believed this could possibly be fair. But it took a year to reinstate him under the most extraordinary circumstances. Last night, he dined with Rear Admiral Andy Carlow, the newly-promoted commander-in-chief special operations command, and had agreed he should begin the second half of his career as a senior instructor.

And now he was on his way to a meeting in the office alongside the grinder with six of the instructors, including the chief, a Southerner named Captain Bobby Murphy, a veteran of the Gulf, and a man who would always held a special place in Mack's heart.

The instructor had stepped forward to shake his hand when Mack received his Trident. He'd said simply, *I'm proud of you, kid. Real proud.*

Since then, they had become friends, trained together, and served together on the front line in Baghdad. And now he was going to see him, to take up his new appointment, a six-month stint as a senior BUDs instructor.

It was slightly unusual for a newly promoted SEAL battlefield commander to work as an instructor. But Mack had requested the position to test his fitness and to bring his vast combat knowledge to a new generation of SEALs who might one day serve under his command in another theater of war.

Bobby Murphy was awaiting him in the brightly lit office across the veranda, where the DOR guys leave their helmets and ring the bell before leaving Coronado. The grinder, the veranda, the hanging brass bell, the line of helmets. This was a place of SEAL folklore. Just the sight of it caused Mack's heart to miss a beat.

He entered the office and was taken aback when all six of the instructors stood up and applauded. Each one of them shook his hand and welcomed him home.

Captain Murphy had already formulated a game plan. "Mack, old buddy," he said, "I think you should start as proctor to the next BUDs class when they begin INDOC. It'll be useful for them to start their training with a decorated combat veteran. Let 'em hear some real words of wisdom."

"Fine with me," said Mack. "But right after that I'd like to take a different set of guys through Phase Three, if there's no objection."

"Mack, there's no one I'd rather appoint, if you're certain about your own fitness." Bobby Murphy was very serious considering, of course, that Phase Three BUDs—Demolition and Tactics, Land Warfare—was the most demanding ten weeks in the program. And the instructors were revered as the toughest, fittest men on the base.

"I'm good for it," he said modestly.

"You're good for anything," grinned Murphy. "Matter of fact, I very much like the idea of you coming in to finish them in Phase Three. Especially if you stay with them 'til Sniper School at the end. If I recall you were pretty good at it yourself."

"Yup, not too bad," replied Mack, both of them knowing full well he had been voted Sniper Class Honor Man unanimously and to this day was reckoned to be one of the greatest SEAL stealth marksmen there had ever been.

"Anything else?" asked Captain Murphy. "Like how do you want the students to address you?"

"I think *Instructor Mack* would be fine," he said. "I'm a SEAL, and I'm well known around here. I prefer first names among the brotherhood."

"I agree," said Bobby Murphy. "I'll make it known that from now on, you're *Instructor Mack*."

* * *

And so, three days later, at 0500, Commander Mack Bedford jogged down to the grinder where Captain Murphy introduced the new class going into INDOCTRINATION—prior to the start of BUDs proper. He told them that Commander Bedford was a decorated SEAL combat commander in Iraq and Afghanistan and, as their proctor, would guide them through the first weeks of their training.

He then formally handed over the students to the care of his old friend, the teak-tough officer from Maine. "One hundred and seventy two assigned," said Captain Murphy.

"*HOO-YAH, INSTRUCTOR MACK!*" roared the class, with one echoing voice.

The words split the dawn air, and the sound reverberated through Mack Bedford's soul, because they were words he thought for so long that he would never hear.

He stood before them like Alexander the Great inspecting his legions. And then he stepped forward and said quietly, "*Push 'em out.*"